SA

By

C. J. Boyle

ISBN: 9781080637560
ASIN: B07VP5SBGD

C. J. Boyle

~ SPECIAL THANKS ~

I'm nothing without the people who support me and my work. There are so many people I'd like to thank, too many to list here, for encouraging me to continue writing.

Judy Arsenault – you've always been in my corner cheering me on. I'm so glad to have you as a friend. Your encouragement means a lot to me.

Dana Ritz – You always manage to find the errors I can't see. Thanks for being my editor and my friend. You're awesome!

Jack Byrne – You write the best reviews! When you pen your book, I'll be the first to read it!

You all mean a lot to me!

Chapter One

Sara stood at the podium sweating profusely and staring out into space. Her blue eyes glistened and stung with tears that threatened to grow larger and flow freely from her eyes. She swallowed hard and pushed her blonde hair off her shoulder. She was dressed for a warm day but all she could think about was how cold her toes were. She tried to scan the crowd for a friendly face. It felt like she had been standing up there for ages when in reality, it had only been about a minute. She was only able to get out her first sentence before it hit her that she couldn't say anything good about Sarisart and mean it. Everyone was there. All the poor souls that she tricked into colonizing another planet instead of the moon. Everyone that stood before her trusted her implicitly. They all thought they knew her and her heart. None of them suspected she was a liar.

The colony was only two years old but it felt like they had been there for two decades. That was probably because the last two years had been terrible and they had taken a toll on her, not to mention, the entire colony. Sara spent much of her time in a deep depression that was hard to rise out of. Every problem they faced, every hardship they had to endure, and every death... she took personal responsibility for. Soon after they arrived, she began to realize that she had made a horrible mistake. She never should have brought the Moon's Eye to Sara's Heart. Andrin could have easily given her so much more information. He may have looked like a very tall, very pale alien from another planet but he claimed to be her direct descendant. He had all kinds of proof to substantiate his claims and she fell for it hook, line, and sinker.

That was twelve years ago. Her first visit to Sarisart included being kidnapped by mercenaries, a ride in an airplane, and a wormhole. A recipe that should never be combined. She had designed a rocket that could unfold into a self-contained colony. It was made in such a way that more could be sent up and connected to the existing structure. It was brilliant, if you were to ask her. Back then she was so proud and full of herself. Andrin had convinced her that when she got back to Earth, all her dreams about building her moon colony would come true. Except for one major change. After they blasted off, they would be sucked into a wormhole and planted on Sarisart two thousand years into the past. He convinced her that she was singlehandedly responsible for his entire civilization. Maybe it was her inflated ego, maybe it was the fact that the scenario included a hunky husband named Andrew, but she agreed to go through with it. After all, it was fate, right? And you can't change fate, right?

Her people spent most of their days working in the fields either harvesting food or planting more. It wasn't a coincidence that they brought an abundance of seeds. They also brought over two hundred fertilized chicken eggs to incubate and hatch. Even so, eating a chicken was rare. They were still cultivating the flock and trying to ensure its survival for generations to come. But they were very thankful for the eggs they produced.

Cultivating the flock and trying to ensure its survival.

She crunched the numbers several times. There was simply no way that one hundred and twenty people could populate an entire species. Make that one hundred and eleven because nine people had already died. It didn't matter how they died, she blamed herself. It was her fault. All the scientists in the colony got together and decided that in order to propagate the species, each colonist had to agree to procreate with other people. Other people other than their spouses. Of course, the parents weren't to be chosen at random. They would be chosen according to DNA. Sara knew that more than likely; the children would be matched before they reached childbearing years. Scientists were assholes. They were blunt and point of fact. It didn't matter that some people didn't want children. What mattered was that it had to be done for the good of the people. They argued that children could be created with invitro and surrogacy. Technically, the 'parents' didn't have to raise the child. But someone had to. And everyone agreed to do it. Everyone... including her. But that was before.

Her eyes connected to Martinez. His dark curly hair was long and unruly but it looked good on him. His gold badge reflected in the sunlight as he silently tried to encourage her to continue by smiling and nodding at her. It made her flashback to the time when they first met. He was one of the aforementioned mercenaries that helped abduct her. Perhaps *abduct* was a harsh word. Back then, the story as she understood it, was that her father wanted her to come home. Her father was a General in the United States Air Force and when he wanted something, he got it. He enlisted the help of a special ops team called The Boy Scouts and the rest was history. Literally. But the story, as she understood it now, was that Andrin had somehow convinced the General that his daughter was in danger. It was one of the now obvious ways Andrin manipulated events so that he could ensure his peoples future.

She hated Andrin with every fiber of her being. She should have refused. She should have said no. Screw the fucking paradox. In all likelihood, she would have met and fell in love with Andrew in an alternate timeline and they'd still have a son named after him. Drew was the light of her life and the only reason she was still hanging on. She caught a glimpse of a woman holding a newborn baby approaching the stage. The stage was nothing more than the back balcony of the recreation center that was completed just in time for the colony's two-year anniversary. She cleared her throat and looked down at her hands for a moment. When she looked back up, she put on her best 'I'm okay' face and continued her speech.

"I may be the Captain of the Moon's Eye and the Chancellor of Sarisart but I am not the sole leader and as I'm sure you're aware… I haven't been as present as I should be. But I vow to myself and all of you that I will try and change that. We've obviously had our ups and downs since we landed here two years ago. We've lost people that we care about but we continue to survive and thrive. Today, we celebrate that fact with a new addition to our colony." Sara held her arm out to the side where the woman with her baby stood. "Everyone, please welcome Bella Warren Sweetwater. She's our third birth since we landed and our first girl!" She held her hand out and motioned to a couple in the audience. "I'd like to congratulate both the Warren's and the Sweetwater's who contributed to little Bella's creation and," she smiled broadly, "remember, it takes a village to raise a child."

It takes a village to raise a child. It's a good thing. Otherwise, poor Drew would have starved to death a long time ago. Since everyone seemed to be distracted by the baby, she slowly made her way off to the side and as soon as she was clear, she made a run for it. She had to get away and be alone for a few minutes. All she wanted to do was disappear so that she could be alone for a while. She ran off the pathway around one of the mighty pseudo trees to her target destination. It was a place she went frequently since it happened. She sat down on a large tree root that had become her bench over the last year. Some of the trees on Sarisart were very special. Just like the ones on her first visit to the planet, the trees were very tall with massive trunks and all of them pulled moisture from the atmosphere… or anything wet that happened to touch them. They didn't learn the true nature of the trees until they landed on Sarisart permanently. They were almost entirely hollow and the trunks were actually a type of air root. The deep blue and purple leaves were still one of the best parts of a sunset. She stared at the ground as tears began to stream from her eyes. She pulled a little tin pillbox from the inside of her jacket pocket and looked at it.

"I thought I'd find you here." She flinched and put the pillbox away as she looked up. Martinez was standing there looking down at her. He smiled softly. "You okay?"

Sara rubbed her eyes and sniffed. "Just out of curiosity, what are you going to do if I say no?"

His dark eyes looked out into the woods for a moment as he breathed in some air and then exhaled. "It's a warm day for a change."

He sat down next to her, put his arm around her, and then rubbed her opposite shoulder softly. He smelled a little bit like aftershave even though it was clear he hadn't shaved in days. She concluded that it must be his underarm deodorant. It struck her as a weird thought considering the circumstances. She privately wondered what men would smell like after they ran out of their supply. There was no shortage of flowering plants around the colony, but some of them smelled like sewage.

"Today was our anniversary." She frowned as she tried in vain to stop her tears.

He smiled and almost laughed. "I know. I was Zeeman's best man, remember?"

"Everyone says that it's been over a year and that I should move on." She motioned to the ground in front of her. "As if I can just change how I feel." The guilt she felt played across her face. "I only have myself to blame."

Martinez focused on the spot that she pointed to. "You can't blame yourself for what happened to him."

"Yes, I can, Martinez. You have no idea. This, everything, it's all my fault." She rubbed her eyes again and shook her head. "None of this ever should have happened."

"What are you talking about?" He rubbed her arm again. "Hmmm?"

"Nothing." Sara suddenly remembered herself. "Forget it." She scooted away from him. "I want to be alone."

Martinez rubbed his forehead and thought for a moment. She fully expected him to get up and leave but he didn't. Instead, he grabbed her hand and held it. He looked her in the eye. "I'm going to tell you a story about Zee that I'm sure you've never heard, okay?"

It had been a while since she heard anyone refer to her husband as Zee. Zeeman was his last name so everyone in his troop called him Zee. He told her he hated the name so she always called him Andrew. She looked down at the sheriff's hand on top of hers and had two simultaneous and equal impulses. The first was to pull her hand away from him in anger and the second was to place her other hand on top of his and caress it. She did neither. It took every fiber of her being but she rejected her impulses and held his gaze. She nodded at him.

His eyes seemed to darken as the shadows around them moved with the breeze. He suddenly looked away as if he was reconsidering. He cleared this throat. "You know that I don't do relationships, right?" He took a deep breath. "They always end badly. I should have stuck to my guns and stayed single." He looked away. "This is hard to admit but, the truth is, I had a gun in my mouth when Zeeman knocked on my door three years ago."

Sara's mouth dropped open. It was clear she wanted to say something but he held his hand up to stop her. "Please, let me finish."

She closed her mouth and went into listening mode. Martinez never talked about feelings or his past and even though she considered him a good friend of hers, she knew very little about him.

He rubbed his face again and appeared anxious. "Like I said, I was in a bad way. I had a freshly broken heart and I just didn't want to live anymore."

It was a complete surprise to her for a few reasons. She couldn't imagine a scenario where Martinez would want to end his own life nor could she see him with someone romantically. After all, when they first met, he claimed that he could never be interested in her because he was only interested in himself. She always believed that he preferred it that way. An autosexual man. Her heart was swelling with emotion for a multitude of reasons but mostly she felt special because he was confiding in her. A fleeting thought about how rough his hand felt floated away as she scrutinized his face carefully. She wanted to ask a million and a half questions about who it was that broke his heart and what they could have possibly done that was so bad that he wanted to kill himself but she was scared to ask. She didn't want him to suddenly clam up and run away.

"There I was, with my gun in my mouth, and I was about to pull the trigger when there was a knock at my door." He squeezed her hand. "It might sound a little strange but I suddenly became concerned that someone might hear me shoot myself and come in just in time to save my life." He shrugged. "And I didn't want that to happen. I yelled at whoever it was to go away. And Zee yelled back at me to open the door."

Sara smiled. "That's when he recruited you for the mission."

"Yeah, if he had been just a few minutes later, I'd be dead." He turned toward her a little bit more so that he could look at her. "But that's not what this is about. Sara, I'm sorry it's taken me this long to tell you this but… he told me we'd be coming back here. He told me everything."

She was genuinely shocked. Part of her was angry that her husband kept something so major from her and part of her was angry at Martinez. "You've known all this time?"

He had a look of profound guilt on his face as he nodded his head so slightly it was almost imperceptible.

"Why are you telling me now?"

"It occurs to me that you might need a partner in crime." He let her hand go and placed his on her shoulder. "I'm sorry. I didn't know if I should say something or not."

Sara suddenly launched herself at him, wrapping her arms around his neck, and hugging him tight. She must have caught him off guard because she didn't feel him return her hug at first. After a few seconds, he hugged her back. She was glad that he knew the truth because he was right. She needed someone to talk to and confide in.

"Excuse me, Chancellor Zeeman?"

Both Sara and Martinez looked up with a start. A young woman named Melody was standing there with a slightly amused look on her face. At first glance, one might not know if Melody was a woman or perhaps a teenaged boy. She was very petite with short curly hair that could almost be classified as an afro. It was light brown, short on the sides, and fluffy on top. Sara had always thought the woman needed someone to believe in her so she tried to be that for her but she found it very hard sometimes.

Her look of amusement turned into a bonified smile. "I'm sorry to interrupt whatever this is, but the celebration dinner is about to begin. Everyone is expecting you."

Martinez stood up and then helped Sara to her feet. She shot Martinez a look. She couldn't help wondering how long the woman had been standing there. "Of course, Mel, lead the way."

The celebration dinner wasn't as bad as she thought it would be. Just knowing she had a confidant made her feel so much better. She and Martinez sat with a group of people on the balcony of the recreation center so that she could keep half an eye on her son, Drew. The building was made with the hands of every able-bodied person who lived in the colony. It was 'log cabin' style but made with incredible workmanship. Once they landed on Sarisart they had to locate iron deposits so they could use it in their 3D printers. Sometimes, when she looked at something the colonists made, she was thankful they were all hand selected for their skill. She leaned forward a little to see Drew as he ran around in the grass below. He was playing with Travis O'Malley Jr, or just Junior for short. Even for a woefully depressed widower, Drew was and always would be the greatest love of her life. He was the cutest little six-year-old you ever saw. The boy was as sweet as he was evil but those big blue eyes of his could get him out of any jam. She watched him as he played catch with his 'brother' Junior. The boy couldn't catch a football if it gently floated to him like a balloon. But he sure tried. She smiled as Junior pushed his shoulder-length blonde hair behind his ears just like his father always did. He gave Drew some words of encouragement that she couldn't hear and then threw the ball to him again. Drew leaned in while simultaneously clapping both hands toward the ball. The end result was the ball hitting him square in the chest and then falling to the ground. For a moment, Sara was concerned that he might start crying but he didn't. Instead, he rubbed his chest where the ball hit him and started laughing. Sara laughed too. She was glad he was happy.

When she looked around the table, Sara suddenly found herself in a situation that had become all too familiar lately. Everyone at the table was staring at her. She should have been listening and participating instead of being in her own little world. Mel was sitting next to the good Dr. Bowman. He was in his early thirties with sandy blonde hair and blue eyes with very toned arms. Right next to him was his wife Zola. Sara didn't like the woman because she was always rude but her behavior paled in comparison to that of Mel's. There were no bounds to her genius but unfortunately, she was also a sociopath. The woman looked at Sara as if she was waiting for her to say something. She finally turned to look at Martinez who was rubbing one of his eyebrows. He was clearly uncomfortable. He winced at her and shook his head.

Sara looked Mel in the eyes. "Did I miss something?"

"No," Mel laughed. "I was just telling everyone that I found you and Martinez necking in the woods."

Sara's mouth dropped open. "We weren't necking!" She looked at Martinez who couldn't help smiling. That only made things worse. She felt her face get hot with embarrassment. "We're just friends!"

Mel beamed a smile at Sara. The woman always made her slightly uncomfortable. She turned her attention to Martinez. "You're a real good-looking man, Sheriff. Why is it that I've never seen you with anyone?"

"Yeah, Marty," Zola joined in, "why is that?"

Sara was horrified on his behalf but she knew he would never answer the question. He was a very private person and it was rare for him to reveal anything about himself. Case in point, no one knew his first name. Which was why people started calling him Marty. He rubbed his forehead right above his right eye again. It was as if there was an itch he always had to scratch but only when he was uncomfortable or, perhaps, just trying to think.

He cleared his throat. "Once I realized that my next relationship would probably end in murder-suicide, I decided to quit women altogether."

Sara eyed Martinez. She wanted to grab his hand and hold it. It was the second time that night that the man had mentioned suicide and it concerned her greatly.

Mel suddenly laughed and grinned at Sara. "Which one of you is Murder and which one of you is Suicide?"

~ * ~

The next morning, when she opened her eyes, she became aware of one thing. She couldn't move. She was pinned in place and held closely by someone with far more body heat than should be possible. It took her a minute to realize that she was in her tiny living room and that she and the good sheriff must have fallen asleep on her couch. She tried to move again but he didn't budge. She was comfortable and warm and felt... safe. If it wasn't for the fact that she had to go to the bathroom, she might have stayed exactly where she was. She closed her eyes and momentarily drifted off to sleep until her bladder woke her up again, this time with more urgency than before. She inched her way forward and downward so that she could effectively slide out of his arms and onto the floor. She sat on her heels for a moment and looked at him. She gently moved the hair out of his face and stared at him. He looked so peaceful. It was funny that she never noticed the shape of his lips before. She leaned in and touched his scruffy cheek and smoothed her thumb across his growing beard. He sat with her all night long listening to her theorize about the paradox and the future. Talking to him was somewhat cathartic. She needed to air out her dirty laundry and he was with her the whole time. He didn't judge her or place blame, he just listened.

She got up and went to into the bathroom as her need to pee intensified. It had been almost thirteen months since Andrew was killed and she was still finding it very hard to live life without him. Every time she was happy, she felt guilty. If she went too long without thinking about him, she felt guilty. And if she thought about moving on… she felt guilty. Andrew deserved better. She leaned in the doorway and watched Martinez sleep. It was utterly remarkable but if her calculations were correct, she actually got five hours of uninterrupted sleep. She shook her head and frowned. She decided to leave him where he was and go start her day. After all, the colony didn't run itself… and she had promised to do better.

Chapter Two

"Uncle Marty!"

Martinez blinked open his blurry eyes only to see an excited child bouncing up and down in front of him yelling his name. Even though he had no clue what time it was... he knew it was way too early to deal with that. The child climbed on top of him and proceeded to nudge his shoulder until he sat up. Even as he was being assaulted by the tiny, yet adorable child, he couldn't help noticing that he could still smell Sara's perfume.

"Okay, Drew! Okay!" He laughed.

He grabbed Drew and tickled him as he screamed with delight. Martinez had become his stand-in father over the past few months and enjoyed spending time with him. But he never had the pleasure, or misfortune, of waking up in the same house as him. The boy jumped off the couch and grabbed Martinez by the arm and tried with all his formidable might to pull him to his feet. He resisted at first but when it was evident Drew wasn't going to give in, he let the little pipsqueak pull him off the couch. He led him into the kitchen where Junior was preparing breakfast. The kitchen was barely the size of a small walk-in closet. It had a small stove, a refrigerator, and a countertop table with two stools. Junior may have looked like a man in his mid-twenties but he was only twelve years old. When they traveled to Sarisart the first time, it was by way of an airplane and a wormhole. It was during that brief time that a biomechanical bug attached itself to O'Malley. It soon became evident that its function was to clone the host and Junior was the result. But he was no normal child. He grew very quickly and was incredibly smart. He was ninety percent of the reason they were able to finish the Moon's

Eye in the first place. Without the propulsion technology that he developed there wouldn't even be a Sarisart.

Martinez picked Drew up and set him down on the stool. "Where'd your mom go?"

Drew reached across the table and grabbed a piece of fruit out of a bowl. "I dunno."

Junior slid a bowl of oats across the table to Drew but spoke to Martinez. "She went to see Dr. Bowman." He took a sip of water out of a plastic cup.

"Why don't you call her?" Drew zoomed a spoon full of oats into his own mouth.

Each time Junior swallowed, he made a loud gulping sound that annoyed Martinez profoundly. "Why?"

"Why are you here?" Junior set his cup down on the counter a little harder than necessary. "I don't approve, by the way."

Martinez was by no means a stupid man. He surmised what Junior meant by his statement and he found it insulting. "I've known Sara since before you were nothing but a growth on your father's stomach. I don't need your approval for anything."

Drew's eyes shot open. "You were a growf on your dad's stomach?"

Junior pointed at Drew but whispered at Martinez. "See what you did? That stuff is supposed to be kept secret."

It *was* supposed to be kept secret and he knew it. He never should have let the little bastard piss him off. To the rest of

17

the people in the colony, Junior was a twenty-four-year-old genius who developed new and exciting things. To Martinez, he was a creepy little kid that looked exactly like his namesake, O'Malley. His father loved him more than life itself but after his 'child' aged only five years but appeared to be ten, and was infinitely smarter than he was... he relied on Sara to raise him. O'Malley had all but abandoned him because he didn't understand him.

Martinez bent over and smiled at Drew. "No, he wasn't a growTH on his dad's stomach!" He ruffled his hair and then hugged his head to his chest. "I was just teasing." He pulled his jacket on as he headed to the door. "Tell your mom that I'll talk to her later."

As he walked outside into the courtyard, he chastised himself for his slip of the tongue. He rationalized it by telling himself that even if he had said it in front of an adult, it would have been regarded as a weird joke. He watched his shadow creep across the dead grass in front of him as he listened to his footsteps crunch it flat. Since the days were much longer than they were on Earth, the sun wouldn't be up for another four hours. The weather on Sarisart was volatile and unpredictable. One moment it would be a pleasant warm day and the next, everyone is running for cover because ice shards were falling from the sky. A jacket was almost mandatory attire. If you didn't have one on, you better have one with you. A solar year was also very different and consisted of only one hundred and sixty days. That was a fact that was easily determined while in orbit around the planet before they landed. He looked up and saw the very formidable, very large, and seemingly too close red giant planet in the sky. The Unan referred to as Tavis and it was only visible for about thirty days out of the year. Even though it was clear they were never going to get back to Earth, they all agreed that they would keep two calendars.

18

They would celebrate birthdays and holidays as they normally would following the Earth calendar and they would keep track of Sarisart's seasons with a special calendar that reflected the days of the solar year.

During his first visit to Sarisart it was determined that the days were thirty-four hours long but the solar system was different then. It had two suns. A fact that confused the shit out of him. He wasn't a scientist but he knew that a solar system had to have balance in order for life to exist on any planet within it. After the new sun appeared, that balance had to be dramatically disrupted. But he wouldn't have to worry about that because he would be long dead when it happened. Since they currently only had one sun, the days were only four hours longer but it was enough to screw up everyone's natural clocks. Most people required six to eight hours sleep after being awake for sixteen hours. But on Sarisart, if you went to bed two hours after the sun went down, you would always wake up several hours before sunrise. It wasn't hard to get used to four additional hours but even after two years of it, he still found it weird.

Martinez decided he needed to go check on the status of his ammo so he headed past the mess hall to the blacksmith's shop. The colony was already abuzz with morning chores. He could smell the wonderful aroma of bacon coming from the mess hall and it made his stomach growl. If they were to spend the rest of their lives on a different planet, at least they'd have bacon. Or at least a close, reasonable facsimile. Because, of course, it wasn't bacon because it wasn't from a pig. No, it was from a very large rodent that just tasted like pig. The sausage from the animal didn't quite taste like sausage but it wasn't bad. When his stomach growled again, he knew he had to go get breakfast or regret it later. The mess hall wasn't big enough to allow everyone to eat at the same time so most people either staggered the times that they ate, or they simply took their food 'to go' and returned the plates and eating utensils later. Of course, building the rec center next to it wasn't a coincidence either. People wanted to be able to eat together and enjoy each other's company on a larger scale.

The mess hall was one of the first inflatables that they had to set up. When they left Earth, colonizing one of the other planets in the solar system consisted of buildings that could be set up quickly. They had to be durable, practical, and last several years. But who could have imagined that would translate into inflatable habitats? Eventually, all the equipment in the inflatables would be disassembled and moved to more permanent buildings but the colony was still in the baby stages so some projects would have to wait. The door was left open wide so when he stepped through it, he made sure to close it behind him. He was immediately greeted by the warm smile of the cook. She was actually the only person over fifty that was allowed to board the Moon's Eye. Everyone else in the colony was under forty-five years old at the time of launch. The only reason she was allowed to join the mission was because she had a special skill. Not only did Agatha know how to make clothing using a loom, but she also knew how to make one. Moreover, she knew how to spin the cotton into yarn and make thread. Of course, when the woman applied for the mission, it was to be the head cook not the sew master. No one knew it, but every aspect of everyone who applied was scrutinized in far greater detail than anyone could have imagined. When they first set out for the moon, the woman's hair was obviously died black and looked somewhat unnatural. But now, it was dark gray with white highlights. She had deep laugh lines around her eyes and a mole square in the middle of her dark eyebrows.

Martinez smiled. "Good morning, Aggie."

She scooped some grits into a bowl and handed them to the person in front of him before turning her attention to him. "Good morning, handsome."

He chuckled. "Agatha, please."

She handed him a plate full of food and then pointed at him. "We've talked about this, hot stuff. It ain't sexual harassment if you like it." She winked at him.

Martinez smiled and shook his head. By her definition, if it was only sexual harassment if the subject didn't like it, then he was being sexually harassed. But Agatha's comments were always fairly innocent so he ignored them most of the time. He turned around and headed for the tiny two-person table in the corner where he usually sat but Mel stepped in front of him effectively blocking his path.

"Hey, Murder." She looked him over from head to toe. "Aren't those the same clothes you were wearing yesterday?"

He immediately side-stepped her and put his plate on the table. "Go to hell, Mel."

"Do you know why I like you, Sheriff?" Mel tipped her head to the side and rocked back and forth slightly.

Martinez sat down at the table and picked up a piece of bacon and took a bite of it. It was cooked perfectly and just the way he liked it. The only thing he didn't like, was a rude and obnoxious bitch ruining his food nirvana moment. "I don't really care. If you don't mind, I'd like to eat my breakfast in peace."

She didn't budge. "Nobody will say what is really on their mind because I'm the mentally disabled weirdo. But not you."

Martinez looked up at her. She obviously wasn't going to leave until she was satisfied. "They're not being polite because you're mentally disabled. They're being polite because they think you'll snap and go on a murdering spree. And since you're a sociopath, you won't even feel guilty afterward."

"I know the difference between right and wrong."

He sighed and rolled his eyes. "And yet you still called me a name designed to piss me off."

He made sure he made eye contact with her. She stood silent for a few moments as she thought about his words. She suddenly smiled and walked away. "Whatever."

Martinez watched her leave. The woman brought new levels to the word annoying. He was relatively confident that the first murder on Sarisart would involve her and if he were a betting man... he'd bet she would be the victim. He never liked the decision to let her come along but it wasn't his, it was Sara's. She felt that the knowledge that Mel carried in that beautiful mind of hers was worth the risk. If anyone had bothered to ask his opinion, he would have been glad to give them an earful as to why it was a bad idea. After he finished eating, he went straight to the blacksmith's shop. David Bayer was one of the largest men that he had ever seen and most likely the strongest one too. Every time he stood next to him it made him feel small. He walked through the door expecting to see David 3D printing his bullets but instead he was pouring molten metal into some molds. Martinez stood still and tried not to make a sound because he didn't want to startle him while he was doing something so delicate.

"I'll have your bullets for you by the end of the day, Sheriff." David poured the last mold and then put down the ladle. He took a deep breath and looked at Martinez as he took his work gloves off. "Do you have it on you?"

Martinez furrowed his brow. "Of course not. It's back at my cabin hidden where no one can find it." He lied. His gun was where it was most of the time. It was on him.

"How do I test the bullets if I don't have the weapon?" David's voice was so low it sometimes rumbled.

Martinez had to tip his head up to look him in the eyes. He knew everyone in the colony better than they knew themselves. A mercenary had to study his targets. He had to know what made them tick. He applied those skills to do his current job. He knew which colonists he'd never have a problem with and which ones were one argument away from a domestic disturbance. David was a giant pussycat. He was also ex-military with top security clearance. Martinez took a huge risk telling him about the gun he smuggled aboard the ship but the blacksmith seemed to understand why he did it. A lawman had to keep the peace and in order to do that, he had to instill fear. Which is what he told David. The true reason he smuggled the weapon was obvious. The only real weapons they had when they blasted off were tasers and guns that shot bean bags. It was a good thing that crossbows were easy to make. They also had several 3D printed shotguns with ammo but the sheriff's weapon was special. It was a Glock nine-millimeter. He reached into his pocket and pulled out a thumb drive. He placed it on the counter and then used his index finger to slide it across the table to David. He picked it up and looked at it.

Martinez rubbed his chin. "Remember our agreement."

"Where'd you get it?"

Martinez raised an eyebrow. "Does it matter?"

It was porn. Lots and lots of porn. But it wasn't his, it was seized from one of the teenagers who must have smuggled it aboard the Moon's Eye. But at least it was 'normal' porn and nothing he considered immoral or illegal. The fact that he himself and a teenager were able to smuggle things aboard the ship made him wonder what else he might find in the future but that didn't concern him at the moment.

David put the thumb drive in his pocket and then looked at the door. "My students will be here soon."

He didn't have to tell him twice. Martinez nodded. "I'll be back later."

It was time for his rounds anyway. He needed to walk the perimeter of the colony to make sure everything was okeydokey. It was something he did every morning. And every morning everything was fine. But he knew that the one morning he didn't do it would be the one morning something was wrong. As he walked into the woods, he could hear voices so he gravitated toward them. It was Mel teaching a class full of children that ranged in ages. Per the requirements of the colonists, Mel could teach children but there had to be another adult present. He walked past a few of them looking for an additional adult until he found one. It was Sara. She was standing just off to the side while the resident sociopath taught her students. She smiled at him when they made eye contact which caused him to reflexively smile back. He carefully made his way past two kids without stepping on them and then took up residence beside her.

He bent his head down slightly and whispered. "Good morning."

Her focus was on Mel and her lesson. Without turning her head, her eyes rolled toward him briefly before shushing him. They stood shoulder to shoulder while they watched Mel address her class. She stood in front of one of the faux trees with her hands clasped behind her back. She was wearing a khaki vest with lots of patches on it which made him think she was a Girl Scout at some point in her life.

"As you know, the tree you see behind me isn't a tree at all, it's a group of plants, much like orchids, that have grown together in a symbiotic community." She touched the trunk of the tree and then smoothed her hand downward. "It may look like an ordinary trunk but it is the roots of thousands of plants that have grown together over thousands of years." She looked at Martinez and Sara standing together and her eyes lit up. He locked eyes with her and silently told her not to do whatever it was that she was thinking. She smiled and turned her attention to a child that was standing in front of her. "But we're not here to talk about the pseudo trees. We're here to talk about what lives on them and in them."

She kneeled down next to a flowering plant that glowed brightly in the dark. It was about three feet high with a large cup-like flower on the top with a strange bulb that glowed in the center. From where Martinez stood, it looked like the plant had a type of fuzzy netting that seemed to grow out of the top of it and up the side of the tree like a mold but he knew better.

"If you come real close, you'll notice that a clever spider has chosen to craft his web near the light that this luminous plant gives off." Mel pulled her hand forward as if doing so would draw her students to her.

Martinez didn't have to be looking at it to know what they were seeing because he had seen it before. He smiled as he imagined what the kids might be thinking when one suddenly put a voice to it.

"Ew, look! It looks like it's made of glass!"

Sara laughed causing him to look at her. She was smiling ear to ear as she watched the children and he couldn't help smiling too. He knew that the child was talking about the spider and not the web. It was largely translucent which made it reflect the light from the flower. Mel started talking again.

"Now, see the insect that just landed on the web right there? Watch the spider as it feeds off its prey." She stood up and took a step back so that the kids could get closer. "Remember the rules, kids. We have to use universal precautions here. Remind me again what that means?"

Several children spoke at once. "Treat everything as if it's dangerous until proven otherwise."

"Yes! Very good! Now this particular arachnid isn't dangerous but it definitely can bite so be careful."

Mel made her way over to Sara and Martinez and stood next to them. "Murder," she nodded at Martinez. "Suicide," she nodded at Sara. "Fancy meeting you two here."

Her words infuriated Martinez so much that he immediately turned to her to yell at her but Sara stepped in front of him. She tipped her head toward the kids and then shook her head. He knew she was right. Causing a scene in front of the children wasn't wise or necessary. She put her hand on his chest and pressed softly before rubbing it back and forth. "I got this, Martinez. Why don't you go finish your rounds, okay?"

One of his eyebrows went up. He didn't like being dismissed but he did as he was told. "Okay. I'll see you later." As he walked past Mel, he lowered his voice considerably. "Dick."

He heard her laugh as he walked away. He let her get to him again. He had broken one of his golden rules. Don't share. When you share, you give people knowledge that they can later use against you. He didn't even know why he opened up about how he felt about relationships but he blamed it on the home-brewed beer and the fact that Sara was sitting next to him. He felt comfortable around her and he forgot himself. He promised himself that it wouldn't happen again.

27

Chapter Three

Sara sat on Dr. Bowman's exam table fully clothed and swinging her feet back and forth. The doctor's suite was one of the largest in the colony for obvious reasons. His quarters were attached so that he'd always be close to his patients and his clinic. Of course, Dr. Bowman wasn't the only doctor on Sarisart, he was just the most senior. One of the reasons he was chosen for the mission was his work genetically altering marijuana plants and extracting the oils to treat various medical conditions. Sara couldn't seem to sit still and kept transferring between sitting Indian style on the table or letting her legs dangle off the side. She reached into her interior jacket pocket and pulled out the little pillbox and looked at it. She sighed. The doctor had given her some specially grown orange. They were tiny, orange, BB-sized berries that grew on bushes pretty much everywhere on Sarisart. The berries weren't addictive but once the teenagers figured out why they were told to stay away from them, it was all over. One berry was enough to make an adult male laugh his ass off for an hour while feeling no pain so several of them could potentially kill someone. Unfortunately, with repeated use, the effects of the orange were felt less and less so if a user wanted to get high, they would have to take more and more.

Most of the people of Sarisart followed the established laws, but where there are laws, there are lawbreakers. She was so fixated on the pillbox that she didn't even notice when Dr. Bowman came in and sat on the stool in front of her. He sat in silence waiting for her to notice him but when she failed to, he cleared his throat. She quickly straightened up and looked at him so he smiled broadly.

He took a deep breath and let it out. "So? How are we doing?"

"We want something that works." She gave him a half smile and handed him the pillbox.

He looked inside and raised an eyebrow before glancing at her. "It's empty."

He had originally given the altered berries to her to treat anxiety and help her sleep, but she found herself popping them like tic-tacs. She stared at the doctor's knee and considered telling him and even thought about ordering him not to give her more, but she couldn't bring herself to do it. She not only wanted more, but she wanted a stronger dose.

'At least I'm not out in the woods picking my own,' she reasoned to herself.

The doctor pulled his keys out of his pocket and stepped over to his medicine cabinet. He asked her more questions while he refilled her tin. "Have you been experiencing any hallucinations?"

"No."

He glanced at her. "Dizziness? Loss of consciousness?"

"No."

He closed his cabinet. "How are you sleeping?"

Sara looked down and shrugged. There was no way in hell she was going to reveal the fact that she actually slept five hours straight the previous night because it wasn't likely to happen again. She rubbed her sweaty hands on her jeans and looked up at him. "I don't. Not really."

29

He held out the pillbox to her by holding it between his index and middle fingers. She took it from him and immediately opened it up to see how many he gave her. She was hoping it would be full but instead it only had twelve inside. She pushed the berries one by one as she recounted them and tears started to sting her eyes. She looked back up at him and he gave her a stern look.

"No more than four per day. I'm not refilling them early anymore. Not even for you." The doctor sat back down on his stool and took a deep breath and let it out slowly.

Sara may have been self-centered but she still had the capacity to recognize when someone had something on their mind. She put the pillbox back inside her jacket pocket and tried to blink her eyes dry. She knew whatever was on his mind, she wasn't going to like it. "What?"

"You're going to have to stop taking them sooner or later. Especially if you're going to have another baby."

"Not this again." Sara jumped down from the exam table.

The doctor stepped in front of her. "Sara, everyone agreed. Even Zeeman."

She sidestepped him and continued towards the door. "I don't care, Chad. I told you, I'm not having…" She stopped and turned around. "Wait. Why did you say it that way?"

His eyes shot open and he blinked a few times. "Sara, it's not what you think."

If that was true, why did he look so goddamned guilty? She knew what was happening and she didn't like it. She ran out of the clinic at full speed with her heart racing and tears streaming down her face. She knew it to be true. She knew it. Some bitch in the colony was pregnant with her dead husband's baby and she was supposed to be okay with it? Well, she wasn't and she never would be. She ran out into the courtyard and wiped her eyes dry with her sleeves before fishing around in her pocket for the pillbox. She carefully pinched one with her finger and thumb and quickly placed it under her tongue. Sara closed her eyes and shook her head. She had spent the last year trying to pull herself out of depression and the worst pain she had ever felt and just when she thought things were getting better, the proverbial rug was pulled out from beneath her. The truth was, she wasn't the type of person that could wrap her entire identity into someone else. She loved Andrew more than words could say and losing him crushed her but there was more to it than that. She blamed herself for his death and everyone else's.

One of the good things about the orange was that it was fast acting. She could feel her heart rate begin to slow down and it got a little easier to breathe. She suddenly wished she had waited until she was alone and at home when she took the pill so that she could lie down and relax. All she wanted to do was sleep for a week. That's all she ever wanted. Sleep.

Her attention was suddenly drawn to a man and a woman chasing a teenaged girl out of the mess hall. She knew what was happening before being told. The teenage girl was Izzy Morgan. Both of her parents died the same day Andrew did, in the exact same way. Izzy was only fifteen at the time and she didn't take the loss very well. She had been acting out almost daily ever since. But the girl was on thin ice with everyone.

The woman yelling at her was the cook, Agatha. She was in her fifties and had dark gray hair. She was in mid-sentence when Sara walked up. "If you want something to eat, you have to contribute! You don't do anything to help anyone! All you care about is yourself!"

Izzy screamed back. "I don't have to listen to you!"

Sara identified with Izzy because they both lost people they loved but she had the same discussion over and over with the girl. She called to her. "Izzy! Come here!"

"What!" The girl spun around and stared hatred at her.

She tried to remain calm but she was already upset and the girl's disrespect for her and everyone else was pissing her off. She waved at Agatha and the man and they both went back into the mess hall. "Izzy, who do you think you're talking to?"

"Why won't you just leave me alone?!"

Sara took a deep breath. "Izzy, your parents died over a year ago. You can't keep using them as an excuse to act out." She tried to put a hand on her shoulder but the girl dodged her.

"Don't touch me!"

"Everyone needs to contribute, Izzy. Everyone." She lowered her voice. "You need to find a way to move on."

"Like the way you moved on with the Sheriff?" She looked past Sara at someone so she turned around. Martinez was watching them.

"We're not talking about Martinez right now but if we were, I'd say that he's a good man that I'm very lucky to have as a friend." Sara was losing her patience with the girl.

"Oh please! Everyone knows you're fucking each other!"

Sara slapped her so hard across the face that it literally echoed through the colony. The girl's whole head whipped to the side as a hand covered her cheek and she sucked in air sharply. Sara stuck her finger in her face. "I will not be spoken to that way," she growled. "This is the fourth time we've had this talk. If I don't do something this time it'll make me look like an asshole. Do you understand that?"

"I don't care." She crossed her arms and cocked her head to the side. By now, a crowd was gathered around them, listening.

Sara shook her head. She didn't like that she had to do this in public because if she made a ruling, she'd have to follow through with it. "Izzy, everyone must contribute. If you're not in the fields today, you don't eat tomorrow."

The girls mouth dropped open and several people in the crowd gasped.

"If you're not in the fields tomorrow, I'll give your home to the Foster's. And if you're not in the fields the next day, I'll give you a crossbow and a backpack and you can get the hell out of here because we don't need you, Izzy. You need us." She held her gaze for what seemed like a few minutes. "Is that clear?"

Izzy didn't respond.

"Is… that… clear?"

"Yes, okay? Yes!"

Sara turned to leave and then reconsidered. "And you'll do grief counseling three times a week with Gloria."

"Fine."

Sara stared at the ground while she walked away as fast as she could but made brief eye contact with Martinez as she passed. She never understood how rumors were able to spread throughout the colony so quickly. Everyone always seemed to know everything about everyone. Leave it to a bratty teenager to draw attention to something that she had trouble dealing with in the first place. It was hard for her to admit that she might be having feelings for someone else and now every move she made would be watched closely by everyone. If she had to guess, everyone probably knew that she couldn't get through the day without taking orange. She needed to be alone so she decided to go sit with Andrew for a while. Logically speaking she understood that her husband's spirit wasn't grounded to the spot where he died so going there didn't bring her closer to him but somehow, it made her feel that way. She sat under the pseudo-tree staring at the spot where he died thinking about ways that she could have possibly prevented it.

The damn things looked like huge black insects with pincher claws large enough to snap a man in half... which was why the children called them bisectors. When something as terrifying as that walks out of the woods, you weapon up and run away. You don't stand around and wait for the monsters to make the first move. That was back when they believed that they were at the top of the food chain. For eleven months everything was peaceful, quiet, normal, and mundane. The sudden attack by creatures was akin to an active shooter in a movie theater. Not only was it completely unexpected but no one was prepared for a battle. No one, except Andrew and Martinez. They shot at least a dozen of them as casualties fell on both sides. But the only casualty she cared about was Andrew. His death effectively crippled her. Nothing made sense anymore and she hated everyone and everything.

She was suddenly disgusted with herself so she stood up and brushed off her pants. She was tired of feeling sorry for herself. She knew the only thing that would distract her from her thoughts was work. The geothermal power plant they built ran off of steam and it needed a new turbine. She went back home and grabbed her toolbox when her comm chirped.

"Dr. Bowman to Chancellor Zeeman."

Sara rolled her eyes and then pressed the button on the comm clipped to her jacket. "Is this an emergency?"

"We need to finish our conversation."

She walked down the path into the sunlight. "Go to hell."

In order to get to the powerplant, Sara had to walk past Martinez' house. It was a small one-story log cabin with a covered porch where some wood was neatly piled. He was outside chopping wood with no shirt on. His shoulder length hair dripped with sweat and his pecks and abs glistened in the sun. It was a sight to see. At least the four teenage girls gathered not ten feet from him thought so. They were giggling and admiring him when she walked up.

"Alright, ladies! That man is more than twice your age! Get on, now!" Sara pointed to the colony behind her. They gave her some dirty looks and rolled their eyes at her but they did as they were told.

Martinez turned around when he heard her voice. He looked in the direction of the departing girls and then grinned at her before shaking his head. He brought the ax down hard in order to sink the head into the top of a piece of wood and then he let go of it. He walked over to the railing on his porch where his shirt was hanging in the sun and picked it up. He brought it up to his face and patted it dry before moving the shirt downward onto his chest. She stopped in front of him watching him dry his abs. He could tell that she was ogling him so he pretended to be shy and held his shirt against his chest to cover himself.

He tried his best to act demure. "What are you looking at?"

Sara pointed at him. "I think your pecks might be bigger than my boobs." She laughed.

Martinez frowned and peeled back his shirt far enough to examine his chest. "Not quite." He chuckled. "Do you need me?"

It was definitely an interesting choice of words. She knew what he meant. He was the sheriff, after all. Her relationship with Martinez started over ten years ago and two thousand years into the future. It started out an honest one and it hadn't changed. She was never afraid to say anything to him. She never had that type of relationship with anyone. Not even Andrew. She watched him wipe his hands off with his shirt and then looked him in the face.

"I don't know, Martinez. I'm starting to see you as the sexy beast that you are and it's making me have... thoughts." She managed to surprise even herself with her words and instantly turned red.

Martinez laughed pretty hard until he realized he was the only one laughing. He narrowed his eyes at her. "You're not laughing."

She raised her eyebrows at him and eventually smiled. She pointed past his cabin. "I'm going to shut down unit three and change the turbine to a slightly larger one."

Martinez glanced over his shoulder toward the powerplant. "By yourself?"

"Why, you don't think I can?"

He looked uncomfortable for a moment. "No, I know you can." He looked over his shoulder at the powerplant again. It was roughly two hundred yards away. "Keep your comm on you. I'll check on you later."

He managed to make her feel all warm and fuzzy inside for wanting to protect her while simultaneously pissing her off for ordering her to keep her comm on her. She continued past his cottage and to the powerplant. Just looking at the small building made her feel bad about herself. Everything they accomplished in the colony was preplanned years before they arrived. There was definitely no need for geothermal energy on the moon. Nor would there be a reason to put a satellite into geosynchronous orbit directly above the colony. But there was on Sarisart. It was literally the only reason the comm devices worked. Aside from her husband, poor Junior was her only confidant when they were secretly planning to set up life on another planet. Andrew listened to her rantings and ravings about all the things that were going wrong, and Junior helped her figure out the science behind the things they needed to do. She was very smart but she couldn't hold a candle to Junior's level of intelligence. It was the nanobots that ran around inside of him. She often wondered if they ceased to function if he would suddenly be a normal twenty-four-year-old kid.

The building was made out of four different family units. They were sturdy and waterproof and would last at least seven decades. She liked working with her hands. It calmed her down and allowed her to think. She picked up her automatic drill and pressed in the cross-tip attachment and then removed the cover over the circuit box. Of course, since she's forever unlucky, as she removed the metal cover, the corner cut her finger.

"Ouch! Son-of-a-bitch!"

She watched the blood bead into a ball on her index finger before sticking in her mouth and licking it clean. She looked at her finger again and watched it bleed again. It was a little cut but the blood flowed freely. She went back to her toolbox and opened the bottom drawer. She was a mother and as such, she always carried bandages. She smiled as she placed the band-aid on her finger. Every time she got hurt, she would often say or cry out, "Son-of-a-bitch!" And every time she said it, it reminded her of her friend Crosby. He was as black as a man could be and so muscular, he could put the fear of God into anyone. But he was also a giant teddy bear. He was the first of her abductors to befriend her and offer his protection.

Hours had passed before she realized that night had fallen. She was almost done and she never liked to leave things unfinished. She liked to complete everything she started and if she could do it in the same day, all the better. It wasn't because it gave her a feeling of accomplishment. It was because if something happened to her, the job was complete. No one had to worry about it. After another hour passed by, she was watching her success spin so fast it was making her hair lift off her shoulders. She walked over to her jacket and found her pillbox. She wasn't feeling anxious or sad but she knew if she didn't take one, she wouldn't sleep. She stuck one of the berries under her tongue and started to gather her things.

"Sara?"

She jumped about a foot into the air and spun around quickly to find Dr. Bowman standing there. She put her hand over her heart. "You scared the hell out of me!"

The doctor tipped his head to the side and laughed. "I'm sorry. I didn't mean to."

Her heart was still racing. "How'd you find me?"

"Your comm." His blue shirt matched his eyes perfectly. "We need to talk."

She walked over to her toolbox and grabbed a ratchet. "I came here to get away from you."

Sara tried her best to ignore him and went on with her work. The doctor was a good caring man but she didn't want to listen to him tell her who was pregnant with Andrew's child. Her eyes pleaded with him. "I don't want to hear anything you have to say. Please, just leave me alone."

"Look, Sara. I get that you're not ready to deal with this but…"

She quickly walked out of the building and away from him but he caught her arm. "Chad, just don't!" She pulled her arm from him.

He put up his hands. "Fine. I just came to tell you that you can't... banish Izzy from the colony. And I don't want her working in the fields either. Doctor's orders."

Sara's eyebrows shot up and her mouth dropped open. "Dr. Bowman, Izzy is only a teenager! Please don't tell me that she's the one carrying Andrew's child!" Her heart thumped against her ribcage so hard it concerned her.

The doctor looked at the side of the building as if the words he needed to say would be written on it and he only needed to read them. "Izzy volunteered to be a surrogate. I guess she thought it would be easy or something." He nervously shifted his weight. "It's not Andrew's child."

Sara put her hand against her chest over her heart. "Then whose it is?"

He took a deep breath and let it out. "Do you really want to know right now?"

She looked at the ground and thought about it for a moment. She was incredibly relieved but the doctor obviously had more to say. She cleared her throat. "No." She pulled her jacket on and then zipped it up. Her eyes teared up as she whispered. "Please don't use Andrew. I don't know if I could handle it."

He looked her in the eyes. "I couldn't even if I wanted to." He took a deep breath again. When night had fallen so did the temperature. His breath seemed to take form and float away from him. "I'm risking my life by telling you this but... Martinez came to the clinic a few months after your husband died and forced me to destroy his samples." He considered for a moment and then pointed at her. "And when I say forced..."

"I get it," she interrupted.

"I'm just saying that maybe you shouldn't tell him or anyone else that I told you." He turned to walk away. "We will need to finish our conversation sometime soon though."

As the doctor was walking away from her, she closed her eyes for a moment. "How could you do this to me?"

He spun around quickly and pointed his finger at the ground. "Again, everyone agreed! Everyone! Even you!" He angrily waved his hand to the side. "You gave me your eggs for Christ's sake!"

Sara stared at him. She had trouble coming to grips with the situation. "You didn't even give me a heads up."

He took a step forward and looked her in the eyes. He was obviously angry but spoke low. "What part of this do you not understand? I already had permission. I didn't need to ask for it." His demeanor changed when he realized she was crying. He jammed his hands in his pockets and then tipped his head to the side. "You could have come to me. You could have said something sooner." He shrugged. "Look, just because it's yours doesn't mean you have to raise it."

"Of course, it does!" Her eyes shot open. "How would that look?"

The doctor shook his head. "Is that all your worried about? How it would look?" He turned around to leave again.

Sara called after him. "Who's the father?"

He didn't even bother to turn around. "I can't tell you until I've told him first."

41

He waved his hand to the side. "I'll get back to you."

She was stuck in place, watching him walk away from her until he disappeared into the darkness. She had a son made by love, a godchild made by a paradox, and a child on the way made by science and an asshole of a doctor named Chad.

Chapter Four

Junior was working in his shop trying to fix a broken drone. If he wanted to explore the planet without actually leaving the colony, he needed it to be working. He pressed the soldering iron to the circuit board while he thought about his first flight with it. Unfortunately, it was also his last. The planet had frequent ion storms caused by solar flares which fried the circuitry. Saying that he should have known better is a huge understatement. Protecting the electronics by hardening them was something you did as a rule. Especially if you were talking about space travel or exploring unknown worlds. Something behind him made a constant low tone so he put down the solder and turned around. His shop was small but it served him well. It was full from top to bottom of bits and pieces of electronics. Some he harvested from now unused equipment; some he was crafting from scratch. The tone was coming from his tablet. He stared at the it as his face turned pale.

"That's impossible." He whispered.

He pressed the comm that hung off his collar. "Junior to Chancellor Zeeman." He waited a few moments for a response. "Junior to Sara, are you there?" He shook his head and whispered to himself. "Of course, you're not. You never are." He knew his only alternative was to call only other person that knew the secret. "Junior to Sheriff Martinez."

His comm sparked to life. "This is Martinez, what's up Junior?"

He pressed his comm again. "Meet me in the command center as soon as possible. It's important."

43

"I'll be there in five."

The command center was the bridge of the Moon's Eye but now it served as a communications hub between it and the satellite in orbit. They also used it to monitor some of the operations within the colony. Junior sat down at one of the stations and signed in to one of the computers. What he saw on his tablet was an utter impossibility. The alarm bell that was going off was alerting Junior to the fact that there was a rather large spaceship in orbit around Sarisart. He frantically typed on the keyboard and called up the video on the monitor in front of him. It was massive. It was at least the size of a United States naval aircraft carrier and looked just as threatening. He found himself pestered by a growing urge to contact his godmother again. He was excited about this sudden turn of events because it meant his life would no longer be as boring. Day in and day out it was always the same. Nothing new ever seemed to happen. He tinkered with his toys and designed new ones but he never really experienced true joy anymore.

He heard the familiar sound of someone's boots hitting the metal steps as they jogged up the stairs ending in one final slam. Junior didn't need to look up to know it was Martinez. The man was the only person in the colony that he didn't particularly like. He was also the only other person on the planet that knew Junior's origin and he was a giant dick. He always treated Junior like he was an annoyance because he believed that his relationship with Sara was unnatural. Logically, it was. He was a boy who aged two times as fast as normal children and was infinitely smarter. His 'father' and his namesake loved him but after a certain point he no longer knew what to do with him. Imagine being the equivalent of a ten-year-old boy who never had a mother suddenly getting round the clock attention from a woman. A woman that he idolized and revered. She gave him the much-needed attention he craved and he fell in love with her in some very confusing ways.

Andrew treated him like a son and was a very understanding man. He knew how Junior felt about his wife and even had a few conversations with him about it. He said it was natural and nothing to be ashamed of but that nothing would ever come of it. Even though he loved the man's wife, he also loved and respected Papa Zee. He looked at Martinez as he walked up to him. Ever since his godfather died, he and Martinez had been co-parenting Drew when Sara was missing in action. And she was missing in action a lot. That's when Junior realized that Martinez hated him and why. It wasn't just because of his love for Sara. It was because he was jealous of his special relationship with her.

Junior's nose was suddenly attacked by the smell of men's cologne and laundry detergent. The sheriff had obviously spent some time primping in the mirror that day because he was also clean shaven and his hair looked like it had actually been combed. Junior wasn't an idiot. He knew that the change in his personal hygiene had to be a direct result of his impromptu sleepover with Sara the night before. He tried to push down the anger that it made him feel and be understanding but he found it difficult. Martinez was the rugged good-looking type that could have anyone in the colony he wanted so why, pray tell, did he want his best friend's wife?

"Where's ma?" Junior asked. "I tried to call her but she didn't answer."

Martinez grimaced. It was something the man unconsciously did every time Junior referred to her that way. Once he realized that it bothered him, he did it as much as he could.

"Last I knew, she was fixing a turbine."

Junior looked back at his monitor and then pointed at it. He watched Martinez' face as he looked too. It shifted from partially annoyed to utter shock. The presence of a ship in space changed everything and flooded Junior's mind with a million questions. Were they human? Were they alien? What did they want? Were they there for the people of Sarisart or was their visit just a coincidence? Have they already detected Sarisart? Those were just a few of the questions that he peppered Martinez with but the man didn't have any of the answers. But the sheriff managed to surprise him with one question.

"Can you contact them?" Martinez regarded him with interest. "Send them a message?"

Junior's mind started working on all the ways he might make that happen. The satellite wasn't rigged for first contact, there wasn't a need. The most he could do was use some of the exterior lights to send a message using Morse code. Of course, they wouldn't understand the message unless they were from Earth.

"Maybe. But I need ma," Junior said as he started punching at his keyboard.

Martinez grimaced again but nodded. "It's late. She's probably sleeping."

Junior laughed. "You do know who you're talking about, right?"

"I'll go find her." He turned to leave.

Junior turned back to his computer and started feverishly typing away. He suddenly thought about something. "If she's actually sleeping, don't wake her up."

He stopped before descending the stairs. He glanced back at Junior briefly. "I won't."

Martinez grabbed the rails and practically slid down the stairs. It was late but he knew that Sara wouldn't be sleeping. He hoped that she would still be at the powerplant but even if she wasn't, the colony wasn't that big, she had to be somewhere close. The night air was crisp and cold so he zipped his jacket shut. The damn weather did whatever it wanted. One day it felt like summer the next it felt like winter. He missed the seasons of Earth. He wanted it to be winter or summer but not both at the same time. The colony was dimly lit by solar lights but he knew it so well that he could navigate it in pitch darkness if he had to. There were clotheslines pulled between two of the inflatable living quarters with clothes on them. He always thought it was a strange thing. Hanging clothes to dry in frigid weather seemed counterproductive.

He decided to start his search at the powerplant and work from there. He quickened his pace a little bit and headed toward his cabin. It had been a long day and he was tired. He was usually in bed by that time but there was a domestic disturbance he had to deal with. The Decker family was definitely trying his patience lately. Mrs. Decker was a very passionate woman who liked to hit her husband when she was upset. A fact that would have kept them both off of the Moon's Eye if he had been known beforehand. Martinez helped Zeeman do background checks on everyone who applied for the mission. If any of them were dangerous in any way shape or form, they wouldn't have been approved.

47

He stopped dead in his tracks when he realized that his search was over before it even started. Sara was sitting on the steps of his cabin. He was looking for her, and he wanted to see her, but he still found it weird that she was sitting on his doorstep in the middle of the night. And it didn't take a detective to figure out that she must be waiting for him. He had to assume that she was having some issue that she believed he could solve. He watched her for a few moments. He couldn't see her face through the shadows but her body language suggested that she was upset.

Martinez didn't like it when she cried but it was a common occurrence these days. He walked up slowly and cleared his throat softly hoping not to startle her. It didn't work because she flinched before looking up at him. He smiled softly at her. "You know, it's unlocked. You could have gone in; it's freezing out here."

She sniffed loudly and looked away.

He tipped his head to the side and tried to see her face. "I've been looking all over for you. Why'd you turn off your comm?"

She rubbed the end of her nose with her bare hand. "Because the doctor used it to find me when I wanted to be alone."

He wanted to tell her about the spaceship because it was eating a hole in his head and wanted to get free but he knew it probably wasn't the right time. "And what'd he want?"

Her face turned angry. "To tell me that I'm going to be a mother."

Martinez' eyebrows shot upward and half of a nervous laugh managed to escape his lips. "I... I didn't even know you were…" He motioned to her. "Active. Uh, congratulations?"

Sara rolled her eyes up to him and stared at him as if he were stupid. "Izzy is pregnant with my child."

"Whoa." He sat down next to her. "That's wrong on so many levels." He considered for a moment. "Who's the father?"

She shrugged and shook her head. The silence of the night was as loud as the awkward pause was painful. Martinez wanted to say something but he was never good at the touchy-feely stuff. "People will be getting up soon. You need to go home and get some sleep."

She almost laughed. "I never really sleep."

He put his hands in his jacket pockets because his fingers started to sting from the cold. His dark eyes twinkled in the light as he grinned. "You seemed to sleep pretty good the other night."

She chuckled softly and looked him in the eye briefly. "That's probably because I had a big strong man to cuddle with."

He nodded. "Come on. Let's go." He stood up.

Sara didn't budge. She just looked at him with her sad, blood-shot, red eyes and waited him to clarify things for her. Martinez wasn't an exceptionally smart man but he knew people. The night before, when Sara unloaded her dirty laundry about Sarisart it relieved some of her stress which made her fall asleep. It probably had very little to do with his big strong arms but he was willing to give it the benefit of the doubt. In that moment, he convinced himself if cuddling with someone helped her sleep, it was probably because she was pretending that Zeeman was holding her.

Martinez held out his hand to her. "Come on. Let's go cuddle."

She looked at his hand for a few moments and then finally took it. He released it as soon as she was on her feet and then he pointed at his door before ascending the three stairs. It suddenly hit him that it was the first time he had company. He stepped to the side and let her pass as he scanned his living room for laundry or half-eaten food that he needed to either hide or put away before she saw it.

It was very sparsely decorated. He'd would blame it on the fact that they were on a different planet with very little to go around but the truth was… his apartment back on Earth looked much the same way. There was a handmade couch and a couple of end tables in the middle of the living room and the kitchen appeared to be nothing but a counter with a wood burning stove. It had a flat top with a pan sitting on top of it. He looked at Sara and wondered what she might be thinking.

Her eyes seemed to twinkle a little bit in the low light. She took a few more steps into the room as he closed the door. "Do you want some water?"

She ignored his question entirely and rubbed her eyes. "Looks bigger on the inside than it does on the outside."

"If I had a say in it, this room would be it." He pointed to the back of the cabin. "They said we needed to think of the future and who might live here after I die."

"Well that's morbid."

He smiled broadly. "Well, it's better than their original argument."

She raised an eyebrow at him and tipped her head.

He chuckled. "They were trying to convince me I'd need it when I got married and had children."

Sara yawned and then tapped him on the shoulder with her hand. "It could happen."

He motioned to one of the rooms and she exhaled loudly. She pulled her jacket off her shoulders and just let it fall to the floor before walking ahead of him into the bedroom. He watched her curiously as she kicked off each of her shoes on her way through the door. He suddenly found himself pestered by the fact that just invited his best friend's wife into his bedroom. He and Zeeman had been friends since they were in their early teens. They were literally wards of the United States Army and raised to be killers. Children can be impressionable and when you take a bunch of them who are desperate for attention and hand them guns, you got yourself murderers who want to keep daddy happy. Or the colonel, to be exact. But Zeeman was as good as they come. He was loyal and his moral compass kept the Boy Scouts from misdeeds that could potentially send them to hell for all of eternity.

Martinez took off his jacket and placed it on a hook on the wall. He looked at his small single size bed and began thinking of the logistics of two people sleeping in it. He pulled his shirt out of his pants and pulled it off revealing a white undershirt. He didn't intend to take off any more clothing except his shoes when he suddenly realized that she was taking off her pants. Seeing her unfasten her pants and pull them down past her rear scared him as much as it excited him but he couldn't look away. It was then that he saw the black leggings that she wore underneath and he was relieved. He pulled back the covers just enough for him to climb in and lay on his side. He had no ulterior motives for wanting to help her but he was nervous nonetheless.

Sara didn't seem fazed by the situation at all. She sat down on the edge of the bed before jamming her legs under the covers and then laying down next to him. She rested her head on his arm near his shoulder and made herself comfortable. Martinez watched her close her eyes and take a deep breath as if she was finally able to relax. He pulled the covers up and tucked them around them both and then put his other arm around her. He held her close as he closed his eyes and tried to sleep. This time it wasn't as natural as it was the first. At least not for him. The first time, she was so exhausted that she passed out leaning against him. She needed the sleep and he didn't want to wake her so he simply stayed put. Now he found himself nervous and unable to sleep. He laid there, holding her and smelling her perfume, as he chastised himself for his newest form of self-torture.

He must have eventually fallen asleep because the next morning when he woke up, he was on his back and she was holding him. One of her legs was laying over one of his and her arm over his chest.

He put his hand on her forearm and rubbed it gently. "Sara."

She hummed softly and then slowly turned over. A move that would make her fall off the bed if he didn't save her. He moved quickly and pulled her back on the bed while turning toward her. She cried out in surprise and then laughed when she realized what was happening. Seeing her laugh instantly put a smile on his face. They looked into each other's eyes as the smiles slowly dissolved into mutual wonderment.

She placed her hand on his cheek. "You shaved your face."

The combination of feeling her body underneath his and the warmth of her hand on his face was too much for him to resist. Their faces were so close, he could feel her magnetic pull. He wanted to kiss her. He wanted to, but he didn't.

She kissed him.

The kiss made his heart quicken and his body ready for the proverbial roll in the hay but his mind was racing, predicting the ultimate end. He couldn't allow it to happen. He broke free of their passionate kiss and looked her in the eyes. He could see that she wanted him just as much as he wanted her.

He backed away from her. "We can't," he whispered.

She grabbed both sides of his face and gently stopped his retreat. "Please," she kissed him gently on the lips and then whispered. "I need you."

He found himself kissing her again. She was making him high and drunk at the same time. She said she needed him. Those three words were all most men would need to hear. It was like a free pass. But he wasn't most men. He broke free of her kiss and pulled her arms away from his neck. "You need to leave."

The next few moments were probably the most awkward ones in history. He watched her as she angrily put her jacket on and jammed her feet into her shoes while she tried to hold back her tears. He didn't mean to hurt her. The way he saw it, he was preventing a terrible tragedy. His relationships always ended badly. Always. And he refused to do that to her. She stomped through his living room to the front door. He suddenly felt like a giant heel. He got up and hurried after her.

"Sara, I'm sorry." He tried to catch her before she grabbed the doorknob. He grabbed her arm.

She held her hand up at him. "No, Martinez, you're right. This was a mistake."

She opened the door and stepped outside into the cold air and slammed it shut behind her. She paused for a moment to wipe the tears that were streaming down her face away. She was embarrassed and confused and just wanted to disappear. The sun was beginning to rise as she bolted off his porch and ran toward the rec center and into the forest beyond it. Her heart was pounding in her chest as she rounded the faux pseudo tree to the spot where Andrew died. She paced back and forth as she tried to catch her breath. She stared at the patch of grass that used to be stained with her husband's blood while a new flood of tears streamed down her face.

"I really screwed up this time, Andrew." She fell to her knees and let the tears fall. "I really screwed up."

A large shadow fell over her from behind her which scared her. She was afraid that someone had happened upon her most recent breakdown but it was much much worse. She turned around just in time to see the biggest bisector she'd ever seen but this one was different. This one, had wings.

Chapter Five

Junior was pissed. Martinez went out to find Sara and never checked back in with him. Finding her should have been an easy thing because everyone had a tracking device inside their comms. Unfortunately, the only people who had access to the serial numbers was Dr. Bowman and Martinez himself. He knew that a ship in orbit around the planet would be just the thing to snap his mother out of her funk. She didn't come home at all or check in on Drew which wasn't like her. If Sara was consistent about anything, it was her son, Drew. Sure, he knew that his godmother loved him too, but he wasn't stupid. He was always going to be her priority. But Junior was never jealous or mad, it was the opposite. The fact was, Drew needed her more. Especially after papa Zee died. Not only did he had to deal with the death of his father but he also had to deal with the fact that part of his mother died that day too. That's a lot for a six-year-old to handle. That's when he and Martinez started to co-parent Drew like a dysfunctional gay couple who no longer loved each other. If Sara didn't have Drew then Junior did. If Junior or Sara didn't have Drew, then Martinez did. Needless to say, Drew spent most of his time with Junior.

Most of the day had gone by and there was still no sign of her. Throughout the day he must have asked everyone if they had seen her and the fact that no one had scared him. Some of the men were working in one of the hollow pseudo trees behind the colony. The trees were perfect for constructing multilevel living quarters without harming it. The trunks were actually roots that drew moisture from both the air and the ground but they were incredibly sturdy. They would have to be in order to hold up such a massive plant. That's where he found Martinez. He was attached to the outside of the tree by some rope. Upon closer inspection, there was a hole in the trunk for a window. He was obviously trying to level out the window by tapping a cutting tool along the edge with a hammer. Junior didn't know how he felt about the choice to use the trees in such a manner. Mel was the head botanist in the colony and she claimed that the trees wouldn't be bothered by such an invasion but he had his doubts. On Earth, humans did many things that they claimed wouldn't do any harm, only to find out years later that it actually did.

"Hey, Sheriff!" Junior yelled at him. "Ya ever think you might be forgetting something?"

Martinez stopped what he was doing and turned himself to look at Junior. "And what would that be?"

Martinez' answer angered Junior. There was no possible way that the sheriff would forget about that goddamned spaceship but he couldn't very well point that out in public. "Where the hell is ma?"

Martinez shrugged and then shook his head. "I just assumed she was with you."

Junior waited while the sheriff propelled down the side of the tree to the ground and then took off his harness. Say what you want about the man, he was definitely useful. Junior kept his voice low and looked him in the eye. "When you went out looking for her, did you find her?"

Martinez only nodded but the look on his face said volumes. He looked guilty. Junior pushed away the urge to make accusations and decided to be direct. "When was the last time you saw her?"

He never really got a straight answer to his question. Instead, he found himself in the command center staring at the spaceship on the monitor and waiting for Martinez to bring him the serial number to his mother's comm. With every minute that went by, he got more and more worried. At least he knew Drew was having fun. There were two other children in the colony that were his age and one was having a birthday party. He stared at the screen again and wondered what the ship might mean for their future. Andrin's notes never mentioned anything about alien spaceships. He knew about the paradox and studied it from every angle. Andrin said that Sara was the key to his civilization and that her altered DNA was part of all that. All that really meant was that she was now expendable. Drew was alive and on Sarisart and Dr. Bowman undoubtedly had her eggs on ice in his clinic. He, himself, did his part in the paradox. He got the Moon's Eye to Sarisart. If he died that day, on the spot, it wouldn't matter. The paradox would still be intact.

Of course, he didn't believe in time travel or paradoxes. If Spiderman comics taught him anything, it was that multiverses were a thing. That, and the fact that radioactive spiders could give you superpowers. The existences of multiple and similar universes in which the same people might live was far more believable than time travel. Every time Sara Newman left one universe, one of her counterparts did too. And when they returned home, unless it was obvious, who was to say it wasn't their original universe? Certainly, no one could.

He cued up the tracker program as soon as he heard a pair of boots hit the metal steps. Martinez placed a small piece of notepaper next to him with the serial number written on it in pencil. Junior quickly typed it in, hit enter, and then watched the map on the screen. He expected a dot appear near their quarters or perhaps in the rec center but certainly not where it seemed to appear. His mouth dropped open as he looked up at Martinez.

"How in the hell did she get fifty-six miles away?" Martinez stared at the screen in disbelief.

Junior was the genius that could think outside the box when most people couldn't. "Maybe she isn't fifty-six miles away. Maybe it's just her comm that is."

They both looked at each other out of the corner of their eyes and they just knew. "She's fifty-six miles away." They both said it together.

Martinez rubbed his face and then folded his arms across his chest. Junior eyed the sheriff carefully. He could plainly see that he was upset but he refused to make his mother's disappearance a bonding experience with a man he didn't like. Junior knew that the sheriff must be doing the same thing he was, thinking about the steps he needed to take in order to track down Sara.

Martinez cleared his throat and then hit the comm on his collar. "Martinez to Sara, come in." He eyed Junior for a moment. Junior suspected that the man wanted to say something to her but not in front of him. "Sara, please answer. Everyone's worried about you."

"Don't you think I've tried that?" Junior met his stare.

"Do you think it has anything to do with our new friends? This can't be a coincidence." Martinez gestured to the monitor. "She's the Chancellor. Maybe they wanted the leader."

"I don't know."

The sheriff reached into his pocket and held out a thumb drive. "Well, before we do anything, we have to determine if anyone else is missing."

Junior took the thumb drive and inserted it into his computer. The map in front of him suddenly populated with dozens of red dots that overlapped each other. The comms could be tracked even if they were turned off but not if they didn't have power. He tapped the bottom corner. "Ninety-eight colonists with active comms. These eight purple dots are the brats with ankle bracelets."

Martinez nodded. "Then I have a few people to check on before we leave." He stuck his hand in his pocket again and pulled out a handheld device that looked like a cellphone. "Send the names to my unit."

The sheriff left the command center in the same manner that he always did. By practically sliding down the handrails. He headed straight for Dr. Bowman's quarters. The doctor always had his comm turned on but for some reason his wife's wasn't working. The way he felt about himself was taking a serious hit because at first, he thought that Sara ran off on in order to purposely worry him and make him feel guilty for what he had done to her. Sure, it was true that she often took timeouts to be alone but it was never to punish anyone except maybe herself. The thought of never seeing her again was giving him a sense of urgency and desperation that he had never felt before. On the way to see the doctor he was able to check off three people on his list. He made it a point to stop them and order them to find their units and charge them up. Everyone knew the rules and they were made for a reason. One of them didn't even have it on her. Tran was a young Vietnamese woman who specialized in small engines and machinery. She was taller than most Asian women with a thin muscular frame with blue highlights in her hair.

"I don't see what the big deal is, Sheriff. No one ever calls me." Tran seemed slightly irritated because Martinez stopped her on the way to get dinner.

Martinez had to stop himself from yelling. He took a deep breath and exhaled slowly. "The big deal is Sara is missing."

Tran's eyes immediately went wide. She walked with Martinez to the doctor's clinic while she briefed him on the status of her work. The only vehicle the colony had was a jeep that was designed to work on a planet with no atmosphere. It had to be altered for the new environment. Making the alterations weren't that difficult but it worked on solar power and was completely electric. A vehicle such as that was okay for short distances but you definitely didn't want to take it exploring across the planet. Especially without her.

"I also have two motorcycles that I made myself," she said proudly. "So, when do we leave?"

Martinez didn't know Tran that well but the fact that she just volunteered for a search and rescue mission without knowing all the facts spoke volumes about her. "It's almost dark and we can't travel at night." He paused when it suddenly hit him that Sara would be spending the night, God knows where, in freezing temperatures. "Tomorrow morning at first light."

Tran took off to parts unknown, presumably to prepare for the next day's journey, while Martinez continued his trek to the doctor's quarters. He knew that the jeep could carry four people and some supplies but the more you packed it with the quicker it would run out of power each day. Considering the fact that Sara would need a place to ride home, the search party could only consist of five people. He knew Junior and the doctor would insist on coming which meant, counting himself and Tran, he needed one more person. Unfortunately, that one person was the one he often fantasized about killing.

The doctor was in his clinic working at his desk. Aside from the emergency at hand, there was a question in the back of his mind that he wanted an answer to but he was afraid to ask it. Dr. Bowman was so engrossed with what he was doing that he didn't even notice when Martinez walked in. He suddenly noticed that the door didn't fully close behind him so he grabbed it and pulled it hard against the door frame. It made a loud clapping sound that caused the doctor to flinch so hard he knocked his cup of coffee off the table and onto the floor. He looked up at Martinez briefly as he grabbed a towel and dabbed at the coffee on his desk and floor.

"Sorry, doc." Martinez stepped into the clinic. "I didn't mean to scare you... that much."

"What can I do for you, Sheriff?"

Martinez walked across the clinic and pointed at the door that led into the doctor's quarters. "I'm doing a headcount and your wife doesn't have her comm turned on. Where is she?"

Dr. Bowman sat back up and set his cup back on the table. "She and Linda went down to the lake with the kids." His eyes narrowed at Martinez. "Why are you doing a headcount?"

He told the doctor about Sara and the spaceship and swore the doctor to secrecy because he didn't want the colonists to panic. "There's no proof the two are related."

Checking off the other people wasn't very hard because they were all in the rec center. Everyone except Sara was present and accounted for and he wasn't sure if he was upset or relieved about that fact. If someone had disappeared with her, at least they would have been able to rely on each other. He needed to go talk to the person that would complete the rescue team but he wasn't looking forward to it. He walked toward the lake as the light from the sun began to fade. He knew that she liked to work as far away from the colony as possible which meant the she was working in the shop behind the barn. The shop had the strong scent of berries. It wasn't unpleasant, per se, but it was overpowering. She was obviously working on some kind of perfume or something. When he found her, she was standing over a large pot that was boiling the concoction inside as steam puffed above it like the smoke from a volcano. Martinez briefly placed a finger under his nose and wished he had a mask.

"Jesus, Mel. What the hell is that?" He stood beside her and watched as she poured some of the cooled potion into plastic jars.

She didn't even turn to look at him. "Well hey, Murder. How ya doin'?" She twisted the lid on the bottle and wrote something on the side of it with a magic marker. "It's shampoo."

Martinez knew that Sara had managed to choose uniquely talented people for the mission but he always had to wonder how they knew what information to bring with them. There would be no way of accessing Earth's satellites for entertainment or information so they had to have the foresight to know what they might need. It was a good thing that digital information didn't take up that much room.

"Just out of curiosity, did you know how to make shampoo before we left Earth?" Martinez watched her set up a new bottle with a funnel in it.

Mel's eyes rolled to look at him for a moment. "If that's your way of asking me if I knew we weren't going to the moon, the answer is; yes."

"Then Sara told you?"

She laughed as she poured the goop into the bottle. "Nope." She grabbed another bottle. "I can read lips."

Mel was more than happy to tell him the story. It was two years ago and just days prior to the launch. All of the chosen colonists were required to stay near the Moon's Eye because they were not going to postpone the launch for anyone. She was actually very excited and committed to the mission because it meant that she would be needed. She knew that her status as a sociopath would most likely prevent her from joining the mission but Captain Zeeman had signed off on her and she wanted to thank her for it. She looked all over mission control for her and almost gave up when she spotted her with her husband and Junior. They were alone in a conference room that was surrounded by glass on two sides. Mel had no qualms about interrupting. She walked toward the room prepared to talk to Sara when her lip-reading skills kicked in automatically. She stopped dead in her tracks and watched them, effectively eavesdropping on their conversation.

Sara grabbed her husband's hand and held it. "I just don't know if I can do this. We're basically lying to everyone."

Sheriff Zeeman shook his head. "We've had this discussion before, Sara. If we don't go, Junior and Drew cease to exist."

"Not necessarily." Junior gestured with his hand. "I've studied the paradox and technically all that needs to go is her DNA. All we need is a doctor to harvest some of her eggs."

Mel went over to her pot and stirred it before walking up to Martinez and standing so close to him that he was uncomfortable. She looked him right in the eyes and smirked slightly. "They noticed me watching them right after that but it was enough for me to draw some conclusions." She ran her hand over his bicep and then up to his shoulder. When he realized she intended to touch his face, he took a big step backward. She tipped her head to the side and smiled at him. "It was simple, really."

Martinez moved further away from her. The woman was a botanist and a chemist. He wouldn't put it past her to drug him and have her way with him. "Does she know that you know?"

She took a step toward him and held his glare. "Nope. Now you and I have a secret."

Martinez looked away for a moment. "Sara's missing."

Mel looked worried for a moment and then laughed. "What's the matter? Is Murder missing his Suicide?" She turned back to her work. "That's so cute!"

It was hard for him to be in the same room with her without fantasizing about drowning her in the boiling pot of shampoo. He knew that even on his worst day he would never do such a thing but the woman knew how to push his buttons. The main reason he wanted her on the search party was because of her knowledge of the area. He calmly told her everything he knew about the situation but purposely withheld the part about the mysterious spaceship orbiting the planet.

He clasped his hands together. "I'd like you to join us on the search and rescue mission."

She stopped working for a moment and stared at her table top. She nodded. "She's my friend."

"Fine. Be ready at first light."

Martinez knew if he was going to be of any use, he needed to get some sleep but he decided to check in with Junior first. He was in his shop tinkering with the drone. He watched him for a few moments as he tested it. It slowly floated upward and then hovered above the table top. Junior was definitely pleased. He gave Martinez a thumbs up as he walked in. His mind kept drifting to Sara and hoped beyond hope that his last moments with her weren't going to be his last moments with her. He had to apologize to her. He had to fix things. Somehow. The temperatures were going to fall into the thirties that night. Sara knew how to survive in the wilderness of Sarisart. They all did. It was part of daily training for the first several months after they landed. He hoped that she was safe but given the fact that her comm was on her and she hasn't used it, things didn't look good. As he walked to his cabin, he looked up in the night sky. If you looked carefully, you could see the satellite that was in orbit above the colony. He decided to try one more time. He pressed the button on his comm.

"Martinez to Sara." He listened for a few moments but no response came. "Sara, I don't know if you can hear this but… hang in there. Wherever you are, I'm going to find you and bring you home. I promise."

Chapter Six

Captain Britt Mason walked down the corridor of his ship with a single purpose in mind. A group of his men had taken a shuttle to the planet below to gather some supplies and no one had heard from them since. He was a handsome man who looked no older than forty with a finely trimmed beard and a full head of thick amber red hair. His mane was wavy, shoulder length, and just above his right eye was a streak of white that made him look more distinguished than he actually was. He was wearing a dark grey jacket with the words USS Newman embroidered above his heart. It was standard aboard the ship but he hated it. Mostly because it was no longer a military ship and he changed the name of it long ago. He had been the captain of the Swagger for the better part of three decades and he was no closer to bringing his people home than he was at the beginning. The missing men, while valuable, weren't as important as his shuttle. It was the only one they had, which meant they couldn't visit other planets without landing the Swagger. Unfortunately, landing the Swagger meant a permanent stay wherever they were forced to land.

He needed to get the shuttle and his men back and the only way he was going to do it was if he did it himself. He held his ring finger against the scanner that would open the door to his escape pod and waited. After a few seconds the door slid open and he heard her familiar voice.

"Hello, Captain Mason. Going for another stroll?" A female voice came through the speakers above.

"Well hey there, Lucy." He walked through the doorway as it shut behind him and he heard the familiar hiss of the airlock. "No, this time we're going down to the planet."

"Captain, I must warn you against such an endeavor. This escape pod does not have enough power to break through the gravitational pull of the planet when you wish to return."

Lucy was an artificially intelligent companion who was always with him. He relied heavily on her because all he had to do was ask for something and she gave it to him. She was once offline for three days and he almost went insane. Every time he thought of life without her it upset him profoundly. He wasn't in love with her or anything. That would be weird. He just needed her.

There was a seat angled in front of him that was meant to be accessible from a standing position. He turned around and leaned against it before strapping himself in. "I'm aware of that, Lucy dear. I'll attach the pod to the shuttle when I find it."

His seat began to move back until he was completely reclined and a glass dome slid in place above him. He couldn't help but smile because his escape pod looked exactly like a tiny, one man, flying saucer. It was actually a massive advancement in engineering back in the day. The escape pod could either be flown around in space or landed on a planet. But, like the Swagger, once you land there is no going back. He would be able to use the pod to get around on the planet but not to leave it. He had already stocked it with everything he might need for a few days. He hoped that he would find his men and his shuttle by then because he didn't intend to stay.

"Disengaging in T-10, 9, 8…"

Lucy counted it down for him as he prepared himself. Going from artificial gravity to none at all, even when strapped down, always made him a little queasy. He watched as the

Swagger got further and further away. He frowned when he got the sensation that something was crawling around on his head. He knew it was just his hair floating freely but it still managed to creep him out enough that he had to run his fingers through his hair, just to be sure. He turned around to reach behind the seat and grabbed his cowboy hat. He smiled in appreciation while he used one hand to smooth back his hair and the other to put the hat in place.

"Okay, Lucy bae, let's go check out that satellite."

He put his hands on the soft pads on the armrests and placed enough pressure on his palms to activate the thrusters causing his ship to zoom away from the Swagger at an impressive speed. The satellite was an unexpected oddity. They tried to communicate with it from the Swagger but the only information they could acquire was that it was made by humans. His right-hand man, or rather woman, Commander Hayes insisted that it was simply an accident of nature. She believed that the satellite was sucked through the wormhole just like they were, and that somehow, it managed to settle in orbit around the only habitable planet in the solar system. But Britt didn't believe in coincidences or accidents of nature. Which was why he wanted a closer look at it. He pulled up alongside of it and let Lucy take hi-resolution photos of it. He eyed the monitor closely.

"Well, lookie here."

He touched the monitor and zoomed in closer. The words Moon's Eye 2028 were etched on the side along with the handwritten signatures of at least twelve people. Britt didn't count himself amongst the smartest people on the crew but even he could figure out that most satellites were placed in a geosynchronous orbit. But they had already ran numerous scans of the planet below and couldn't find any signs of human civilization. That was most likely due to multiple solar flares that were disrupting the magnetic fields inside the atmosphere. He didn't need to look up the referenced Moon's Eye or any of the names inscribed on it because he already knew the story, and he knew it well. If the satellite was from the doomed moon colony project then the people were probably long since dead. But his people were alive. At least they were two days prior.

He looked at the planet below with excitement in his eyes. It had been far too long since he had set foot on any planet and he aimed to enjoy every minute of it. He rolled his pod once before increasing his speed. A ship as small as his would have to travel at a certain speed to break through the atmosphere of the planet without burning up upon entry. He angled his descent so that he would have ample time to slow down without slamming into the ground. The pod began to violently vibrate which made him laugh hysterically. He was definitely enjoying himself way too much for a man that may be taking a one-way trip. Once he finally broke through and leveled out, he found himself completely stunned by the planet's beauty. It was lush and green with rolling hillsides and massive purplish-blue trees that seemed to touch the sky. He reckoned that he could probably land his ship on one of them if he wanted to.

"Lucy, scan the area for the shuttle, will ya?"

Lucy's voice was decidedly sexier. "Yes, master."

Captain Britt laughed. "Lucy, we talked about this. That's inappropriate."

The shuttle's signature was undetectable. His only hope was that it would be somewhere near its last known coordinates. They were looking for uranium deposits that they could bring back to the ship. Thermal nuclear engines were a questionable improvement on a cleaner version designed by one of the geniuses who disappeared shortly after its maiden voyage. Using a nuclear engine in space meant that the radioactive waste it would produce would be disposed of where there was no life. It seems like a no harm, no foul situation until you factor in accidental exposure and the fact that eventually, you run out of uranium. Of course, there was also a little side project that he was working on that would eventually fix everything.

He had to admit, as much as he wanted to find the shuttle, he couldn't wait to land and take his first few breaths of fresh air. As they got closer to the coordinates, he slowed the ship and flew it lower so he could zigzag through the trees. It gave him the chance to really look around and appreciate the scenery. He was trying to memorize the awesome view of a small waterfall when his ship suddenly slowed on its own. He whipped his head forward in just enough time to see a giant black wasp-like creature fly in front of him. He watched it as it flew away and then squinted.

"Lucy, I'm pretty sure I saw boots!" He yelled as he changed directions and followed the bug. "Was that one of my men?"

The bug, whatever it was, flew significantly slower than his ship. He glided behind it and tried to focus on the person it was carrying.

"Based entirely on the size of the human, it is unlikely."

He watched as the thing flew lower and headed toward a giant clay hill with no plant life on it. His heart started to race as he noted the many dark ominous openings that led

71

inside. There were several reasons why a person wouldn't want to go in there but his need to figure out the mystery was too great. He parked his pod at the bottom of the hill as he watched it fly into one of the openings. The captain opened the top of the ship as it tilted forward and his seat helped him to a standing position. The air was crisp and cold which made him marvel at the steam from his own breath as it rolled away from him. He was momentarily stuck in place and too scared to move. His legs were filled with a sense of urgency that translated into widespread pain. They wanted to move and didn't like being held in place. He stood there in his cowboy hat wondering what in the hell he was thinking. He was very close to changing his mind when he heard a shriek of pure terror that made the hairs on the back of his neck stand on end.

Britt suddenly leaned into his ship and grabbed two things. His flashlight and his gun. Captain Mason knew that going after the woman wasn't the best idea in the universe. Now that his feet were firmly on the ground, he began to realize that something was off. Not with him but with the entire planet. He had to focus harder as he jogged because he felt like he was bobbing too high and moving too fast. The Swagger's artificial gravity was based entirely off of Earth's, so it was difficult for him to make the sudden adjustment. He tried to keep his eye on the exact opening that the creature when through, but it was high on the hill and it was hard for him to climb. He made a snap decision hoping that all the openings eventually led to the same place. He could hear her voice echo through the dark tunnel as he held his flashlight out in front of him while trying to do the same with his gun. He had seen it done many times in the movies but when it came down to doing it… it was much harder than it looked. Especially since his heart was beating as fast as it could and all his senses were on high alert.

The walls of the cave were smooth and gray but covered in a clear sticky substance that he tried to avoid leaning against. Every time he picked his foot up it made a sound that reminded him of walking around a movie theater. It gave him the impression that if he stayed in place too long, he'd get stuck. When he rounded a corner the powerful stench of ammonia hit his nose making him cover it briefly with his gun hand. All things considered, he figured that trying to save a woman was a good way to die. Of course, that was until he started to think about all the people he would be letting down. He stopped in place for a few moments and thought about it. The bastard that represented the evil and devious part of him almost convinced him to leave when he heard her again.

"No! Please!" She screamed in terror.

He couldn't do it. He couldn't leave. Not when he could possibly help. He pushed forward down the corridor where the path divided in two. He stood between the two doorways that promised to take him deeper into hell and listened. He thought he could hear her crying. He stepped to the left and listened carefully to see if the soft sobs were louder or softer and then he repeated with the right. He wasn't sure. His life was ruled largely by his gut instinct, why should that moment be any different? He looked up and made a silent prayer and then headed down the tunnel to the right. That's when he got the fright of his life. He bumped right into one of those creatures but this one was different. He was face to face with it, frozen in his mounting fear, certain in the fact that he was about to be eviscerated. The creatures dark head was thin and elongated with black horns that stuck out on both sides. Its eyes were dark and shiny and reminded him of the gross fish eggs his sister once tried to make him eat.

Its body was skeleton thin and had at least two sets of arms, one set with humanlike hands and the second set with huge lobster-like pinchers. Britt stared at it until he finally remembered that he had a gun in his hand. He quickly lifted it and pointed it at the creature but it didn't respond or move at all. He waved the gun back and forth in front of its face but it still didn't move. He looked to the monster's side and wondered if he could slide himself between it and the side of the cave. He pressed himself against the sticky wall and scooted slowly past the creature until he was clear of it and then quickly figured out his rescue mission was going to require a bit of climbing. Getting up to the next level was easier than he thought it would be. He put the flashlight in his mouth and tucked his gun into his pants before using his hands and feet on the sticky surface to climb his way to the top.

His heart was beating in his ears which made it difficult to concentrate on her voice. He carefully crept past three more of those bastards as he moved closer to the sound of her voice. She was pleading with the creature to stop... whatever it was doing to her. His fear and his need to leave were escalating by the minute. The captain held his flashlight out in front of him but couldn't seem to hold it still no matter how hard he tried. He slowly rounded a corner and got an incredibly up close and personal look at what the creature was doing to her and it was more horrifying than anything he could have imagined on his own. The thing was holding the woman up at eye level by her collar. She was obviously in terrible pain and he could plainly see why. A tendril or appendage of some kind was sticking out of her neck where her jugular vein would be. His eyes followed it from her neck all the way to the monster's neck. Britt's face twisted in disgust as he watched the appendage pulsate. He had to assume that it was feeding off of her and he had to stop it. The second he took a step forward the woman looked at him. Her eyes were sad and exhaustion showed all over her face. It was almost imperceptible but he could swear that she shook her head at him. He watched as the light seemed to fade from her eyes and the life drained away from her face as she lost consciousness. The creature disengaged the tendril from her and unceremoniously dropped her on the ground. That's when things got really interesting.

"Martinez to Sara, come in." There was a slight pause. "Sara, please answer. Everyone's worried about you."

A male's voice crackled from a device that must have been on the woman. It managed to startle the creature enough to make it move back and away from her. A move that revealed an intruder.

"Shit." Britt ducked when the creature swung at him.

He quickly crawled along the floor and grabbed the woman. He wasn't a particularly strong man but deadlifting her from the ground seemed incredibly easy. It made him feel like he had superpowers but he knew it was due to the gravitational difference. He ran forward and out of the corridor as all the dormant bugs became animated and pursued him. He knew it wasn't going to end well. He knew it was going to be his last day of life. But he also knew he wasn't going to just give in.

He could hear clicking sounds and a constant high-pitched noise that was hurting his ears as he ran. With each footfall he hoped he was getting closer and closer to freedom. Somehow, even during his heroic and stupid act, in the back of his mind, he was bothered by the familiarity he felt with the woman. He knew her from somewhere but that was utterly impossible. The bugs were literally at his heels and his arms began to burn even though initially she felt lighter than air. He could see light and smell fresh air ahead of him so he pushed harder. It's amazing how time seems to slow down when you're in mortal danger. It's the minds way of helping to ensure the survival of the host by allowing a person to notice opportunities and make sudden changes. All it seemed to do for him was give him more time to regret the things that he had done in the past and the things that he promised to do in the future.

When he got to the opening that would take him outside, he didn't stop to consider how high up in the hill they might be, he just jumped. He held onto the woman as tightly as he could as they slid down the smooth side. He glanced down at her face briefly and couldn't help praying that she was still alive. He hated thinking that he risked his life for nothing but it wasn't just that. He knew that she was important. He just knew it.

"Lucy! Come get us!"

There was no way they'd make it without her, the bugs were just too fast. The second his feet hit the ground, he hoisted the woman's body over his shoulder and started running. The pod sped out in front of him with the glass dome in the process of opening. He quickly turned around as he held the woman in front of him. The seat began to recline and the dome closed just as one of the bugs crashed into the ship.

"Lucy, get us out of here!"

"I cannot do that, Captain Britt." Her voice was level but soft.

A bead of sweat rolled down his forehead to the side of his face. "Yes, you can, Lucy."

"The added weight will overload my systems and cause catastrophic failure."

He was feverishly trying to adjust the seat straps to fit both of them to no avail. "If you don't, we'll die, Lucy. I'll die."

He clipped himself in and then put arms around the woman and held her tight as the ship rocked back and forth. The bugs were slamming themselves against the ship so hard it was causing them harm. A thick yellow substance was smeared on the glass in several places. It disgusted him so bad he closed his eyes and swallowed hard.

"Lucy, please. I don't want to die."

She was an A.I. with no capability of real love or friendship but he hoped his plea would work. The ship suddenly lurched forward and gained speed until he could feel weight of the woman's body pressing into him so hard that he had trouble breathing. Lucy was right. The added weight caused the ship's core to overheat. He heard a small explosion and knew that a crash was imminent. He lifted his legs and pressed them against the interior of the pod to brace himself as he grabbed the pockets of the woman's jacket in his opposite hands and gripped as tight as he could and closed his eyes.

The impact shifted her body hard to the right, slamming his knee against the control panel. When the pod came to a violent halt on the ground, he opened his eyes. "Lucy, are you still there?" There was no answer. "Shit."

Chapter Seven

Sara sat on the couch in her living room with Drew sleeping next to her. He was only eleven months old but he was already walking and running his poor mommy silly. His little head was on her lap as she worked on some plans for the Moon's Eye on her tablet. She was wearing one of Andrew's favorite Superman shirts and a pair of yoga pants. She had spent the entire day playing with Drew and looking at schematics so comfort was mandatory. She and Junior had been working on a new propulsion engine for the last year and it was almost complete. It was hard for her to believe but Sarisart was now within her reach. Almost every second of her free time for the last seven years was spent making sure her future would happen as it should. Living life within a paradox was stressful. It made her question nearly every move she made because she didn't want to change what was already written.

After their visit to Sarisart, the Unan brought her and the remaining members of the Boy Scouts, plus one infant, home. Her father helped the men get new identities, or proper papers for the ones they already had, and most of them went their separate ways. Sara and Andrew were a brand-new couple. They certainly weren't ready for marriage but when Andrew proposed, Sara said yes and they were married less than two months later. Of course, it didn't hurt that she knew it was going to happen regardless of when. She also knew she'd have a son one day. It made her giddy back then and that feeling never changed. She was happy. She looked down at her favorite little rug rat and smiled. His cheeks were fat and rosy and his hair was as white as fresh snow. She didn't think it was possible to love someone as much as she loved that kid. She'd do anything for him. Including move to another planet to complete a paradox that would ensure that she met his father.

Sara told Andrew the whole unbelievable story before they got married. At first, he didn't believe her and just accepted her as she was… a crazy person that he loved very much. But as things started to fall in place, he could no longer deny the truth. They never bought a house or put roots down in any one place for obvious reasons. Planning for the paradox might have been a little stressful but knowing that they were destined for life on another planet was freeing. Instead of saving money for the future, they spent it. If they wanted to do something, they did it. The hurdles she had to complete on the Moon's Eye colony may have been complicated but she knew what the outcome would be so she never let it bother her too much.

She suddenly heard the door open behind her so she looked up. Andrew walked into the living room through the little kitchen. He was in the midst of taking his leather bomber jacket off when he noticed her sitting on the couch with Drew. His hair had darkened a little over the last few years and had a hint of gray but it only made him handsomer. He dropped his jacket on the easy chair next to him and then held his finger to his lips as he crept forward. He bent down and gently scooped Drew up into his arms and then disappeared down the hall. She smiled as she watched him take their son into his room and her heart skipped a few beats. He was such a thoughtful man. He came back out a few moments later and walked toward her with a huge smile on his face. She knew that look well. She tried to make a straight face and looked back down at her tablet as if she was going to continue her work. She was barely able to save it before he gently took the tablet out of her hand and set it on the end table.

Andrew leaned down and picked her up into his arms causing excitement to run through her body. She put her arms around his neck and looked him in the eyes while he walked down the dark hallway to their room and placed her on the bed. Seeing him take his shirt off was one of the best parts of her day. He was a very fit and health conscious man which translated into well-defined pecks and the coveted 'six pack' that fitness freaks strived to achieve. She wasn't fat but she definitely didn't have the hard body that he had. Even after seven years of marriage, it was hard for her to understand why a man like him would be attracted to her.

He threw his shirt aside and gave her an evil grin as he grabbed the fabric of her yoga pants at her hips and pulled them off of her. If she didn't know what he was up to before, it was certainly clear now. He popped the snap on his jeans and practically hopped out of them and then climbed over her. He put his hand on the side of her face and looked deeply into her eyes before kissing her passionately on the lips. After they made love, they held each other closely. Sara lightly traced a scar on his bicep. She knew it was from a bullet wound that he got before they met but it still upset her. It was a physical reminder that he wasn't invincible. He must have intuitively known what she was thinking because he moved onto his side so he could look her in the eyes.

"Martinez agreed to go with us." He moved some stray hair out of her face.

Sara found it weird that he was bringing up Martinez at such a time but she went with it. "That's good. Between the two of you, I'm sure you can keep the peace." She scooted closer to him. "And there's the added bonus that he's your friend. You'll have someone to pal around with."

His voice was smooth and soft. "I just need you to know that if anything ever happens to me, you can count on him to be there for you and the kids."

She laughed. "So, you want me to marry Martinez if you die?"

"What?" Andrew raised an eyebrow and then grimaced hard. "God no!" He laughed and then thought for a moment. He tipped his head to the side. "But you could do worse. He's a good guy." He hugged her close to him. "I feel so much better just knowing that he's coming with us."

"What's his deal anyway?"

He rubbed his thumb back and forth on her upper arm. "What do you mean?"

"You know what I mean. He's never with anyone."

"That's not for me to say." He kissed her on the temple and closed his eyes before exhaling deeply. "He doesn't think he deserves happiness. He never has."

If that was true, she felt sorry for Martinez, but she couldn't help smiling as she watched him fall asleep. She loved to memorize every aspect of his face and the shape of his lips. They had been married for seven years and she loved him more and more every day. She didn't like thinking about life without him because it made her realize that she wasn't as strong as she liked to think. Before Andrew came along, she believed that she didn't need anyone to take care of her or to get through life. While it was true that she didn't need someone take care of her, she did need Andrew. So much that it actually scared her. As she watched his face her vision started to blur until she couldn't see him anymore. Her heart started to beat very fast as she realized she could no longer feel him next to her.

"No, please!"

She was moving in and out of consciousness and reality wasn't very much fun. She suddenly realized that her feet weren't touching the ground and that her neck hurt so intensely she could barely breathe. She opened her eyes slowly and hoped beyond all hope that she wasn't where she thought she was. But she was. She was in the custody of the bisector queen and she was being interrogated the only way the creature knew how. She was terrified but in the back of her mind she couldn't help feeling a little bit grateful for very vivid memory she just experienced. It was like she was given a very special gift. One more day with the man she loved. The queen didn't do it to be generous. That tendril that was in her neck ran right up into her brain and it was pulling out memories. Sara gripped the tendril as hard as she could and tried to pull it out but she was too weak. She became dizzy again and faded into another memory.

It was a warm day and many of the colonists were playing tag behind the rec center. Sara found herself just as immersed in the memory as she was with the first. Sara and Drew were hiding behind one of pseudo trees giggling. Andrew was looking for them but she knew her husband knew exactly where they were. They watched him creep around another tree and then pounce only to find no one there causing them both to laugh hysterically. They could see almost everyone from their vantage point. Junior was crouched behind a bush with small blue flowers on it. He smiled at her and gave her a thumbs up. That's when the screaming started. At first, Sara thought it was screams of glee at being caught but it quickly became apparent that it was pure terror.

She didn't know what was happening. All she knew was that people were running away from something. She held Drew close to her as she tried to figure out her next move. She wasn't going to run out into the open with her son at her side. She needed to protect him. Drew had a death grip on her arm and tried to pull her back the second she leaned around the tree. Her eyes went wide when she saw what was happening in front of her. There were large bug-like creatures crawling through the clearing. They were terrifying with elongated heads and horns that stuck out to the sides. When she heard the gunshots, she knew that Andrew and Martinez were riding to the rescue. When her eyes finally fell on Andrew she watched in horror as one of those things clipped his side with a lobster-like claw. She must have been twenty-five feet away but she still saw the blood and there was a lot of it. Her chest got tight and she could barely breathe. She needed to get to him.

Sara held onto Drew and crawled over to where Junior was crouched behind a bush. "Junior, take your brother somewhere safe!" She physically placed Drew's hand into Junior's. "Go!"

She watched them run in the opposite direction of the bugs while she ran to Andrew's side so fast that she didn't even remember the steps in between. She screamed as she knelt beside him and pressed her hands over his wound. His side had a huge open gash in it that she knew was beyond repair. She was in utter panic and on the verge of hyperventilating when she felt his hand on her forearm and she looked him in the face.

Andrew looked impossibly calm. "I love you, Sara. Never forget that." His eyes were getting heavier. "Make sure he knows it too."

Sara watched his eyes close and his entire body relax but she refused to let him go. She held her hands over his wound as his warm blood oozed through her fingers. She screamed. "No! Andrew! Somebody, please help me!"

83

Suddenly the point of view of the scene changed. Everything was slightly out of focus and it was a view of someone or something looking up from the ground. Sara could see herself, covered in her husband's blood, and screaming. But there was one detail of that day she never knew. Martinez was standing right behind her pointing his gun right at the person watching him. He apparently realized that the threat was over because he lowered his gun to his side and stared at his friend. He suddenly looked away and blinked a tear out of his eye before wiping his face with his hand. Martinez put his gun in its holster and knelt down behind her and tried to coax her away but she wouldn't move. She screamed and violently pulled away from him so that she could hold her husband and beg him to come back to her.

She couldn't take her eyes off of Martinez. He was obviously upset at his friend's death and he was left to deal with it on his own. It made her feel like a selfish monster.

Her consciousness floated back up to reality. This time she preferred reality over the memory. The queen was showing Sara what one of her children was seeing moments before it died. She could feel how intensely sad it made the creature which made her feel sorry for it. As she hung there in the bisector's grip, she was intensely aware that the queen felt she and her people had been wronged. In her mind, the queen believed that they had done nothing wrong before the humans attacked. She didn't speak to Sara in words but it was clear to her that the bisector queen knew that her people massively outnumbered the humans and could kill them all if they had wanted.

"Why don't you?" Sara croaked the words out.

The queen didn't really have to respond. It was obvious even to Sara. She didn't want to eliminate a race of intelligent beings. She wanted to form a truce.

Something moved behind the creature. It was dark but she knew it was a man. She looked at him and tried to focus on him but she was losing consciousness again. Did she know him? She wasn't sure. She tried to warn him by shaking her head but she could barely move.

She wasn't in pain anymore but she wasn't sure if that was a good thing or a bad thing. She was numb, physically and emotionally. In that moment, she wanted to sleep forever and never have to feel the pain of death again. In that moment, she just wanted it all to end.

The next time Sara opened her eyes she was looking at a man she didn't know... which was impossible. She literally knew everyone on the planet. At least she thought she did. She was laying on her back and looking up at him but she could only see him from the waist up. She thought she must be hallucinating because it seemed like she was in a coffin. The man looked like the classic cowboy with rugged good looks and hazel eyes that seemed to smile when he looked at her.

"Well hey there, Little Lady." He touched the tip of his hat. "My name's Captain Mason but my friends call me Britt." He put his hands on the sides of whatever it was she was laying in and asked, "what's yours?"

She blinked a few times and looked at the sky. 'What's my name?' She thought to herself for a moment. "Cake."

The man smiled broadly. "Cake?" He laughed. "That's cute."

She grimaced and tried to shake her head but she was very weak. 'No, that's not what I said. Did I?'

Something was wrong. She knew her name was Sara but she couldn't say it. She began to become increasingly aware of the fact that her neck hurt badly. She wanted to touch it but she couldn't move.

"I heard a man on your communicator call you Sara." Britt smiled at her again. "I tried to call them on it but it's broken." He disappeared for a moment and she heard a loud slam. He popped back up and looked around her. "Lucy? You there?"

Sara was confused. Her name wasn't Lucy so who was he talking to?

"Lucy?"

"Auxiliary power has been successfully initiated." Lucy paused for a moment. "This ship only has a few hours of power, Captain Mason."

He looked Sara in the eyes when he spoke. "It's good to hear your voice, Lucy. Will you please scan our beautiful guest and tell me if we can help her?"

"Our beautiful friend has lost nearly three pints of blood and will require a blood transfusion or she will die."

Britt grimaced. "Well, that sucks."

"There is more."

Sara could no longer understand the conversation. Her new friend, Britt, was speaking with someone she couldn't see but it didn't matter. She felt like she was floating away. She felt like she was dying. She tried to focus on Drew hoping that it would help her hang onto life but she was finding it hard to breathe.

She gasped for air as fear started to fill every cell in her body. "Please, I don't want to die. I'm scared." She closed her eyes and then lost consciousness.

Those would have been her last words if Britt didn't act fast. He pulled a medkit out from under the seat and opened it so quickly some of its contents flew out. He set it down on her legs and rifled through it until he found what he was looking for. He took out a device that looked like a piece of tubing about two feet long with a small pump in the center. He climbed into the ship and pushed up the sleeve of her jacket so that he could find a good vein. The captain leaned over her and inserted one end into her arm and one end into his. He turned on the pump and then watched his blood move down the tubing, through the pump, and then into her arm.

"I sure hope you and I don't regret this later, Little Lady."

Chapter Eight

The journey to hopefully locate and rescue Sara promised to be a complicated one. Starting with the fact that there was a canyon that needed to be crossed in order to get to her. The canyon was fourteen miles from the colony and was over forty-five feet wide at its narrowest point. This, of course, meant that a jeep and two motorcycles wouldn't be much good. The canyon was discovered shortly after they arrived when the colonists started exploring. That was before the bisector attack but the colonists still voted against building a bridge because it would change the ecosystem of the surrounding area. A bridge would allow any animal to easily cross to the other side and eventually lead them straight to the crops the colonists worked so hard to plant. Being that they were still new to the planet and that there were much more pressing issues, a bridge across the void was placed on the back burner.

It was two hours before sunrise and the only light to see by was from independent solar lanterns. They weren't very bright but they did the job. Mel sat outside the barn and watched as a team of men loaded a wagon with wood and the supplies they would need to build a bridge. It was actually quite fascinating to watch Felix's team build anything. They were very efficient and knew each other so well that it was almost as if they shared the same mind. She likened it to watching Amish people raise a barn in just a day. She heard the familiar sound of air blasting out of a snout. She smiled knowing that when she turned around, she'd see one of the crocks. It was the male crock named Clyde. She rubbed the animal on the nose causing it to close its eyes and make a humming sound. The crocks looked like crocodiles but had longer dog-like legs. The bones of this type of animal were found on Earth but no one could have imagined how playful and friendly the creatures would be.

Their colors varied between dark gray and brown and they stood as tall as a mule. They were very strong and could be very fierce depending on the situation. Mel loved the animals. Especially Bonnie and Clyde.

She helped Felix hook the harnesses to the crocks while the men climbed aboard another cart. Felix was a positive happy-go-lucky man that acted like everyone's grandpa. His short white hair was always covered by a United States Air Force ball cap that he never took off. He sat on the seat behind the crocks and grabbed the reigns. He looked at Mel and adjusted his cap.

"You comin' kiddo?" he asked her with his gravelly voice.

She shook her head. "That's okay, Gramps. We'll be right behind you."

She watched as the two wagons pulled away knowing full well that she and the rest of the team would be camped out at the canyon until the bridge is finished. In essence, there was literally no rush. But she was worried about Sara. Everyone throughout her life told her that she was incapable of loving anyone but she didn't think that was true. The chancellor was the only person who believed in her. If you researched Mel's condition, you would find tons of literature that would suggest that she couldn't feel love or guilt. You would also find sociopaths only maintained friends that they could manipulate to his or her advantage. But if you asked Mel, she would tell you that Sara was her friend and that she fights the urge to hurt her.

Mel never wanted to hurt people physically. It gave her a rush just to manipulate little things around her. All she had to do was watch people and listen then drop little bombs as she passed by. It was fun to watch the aftermath. But it was different with Sara. She was the only person she didn't want to mess with… but she couldn't help herself.

She grabbed her backpack and decided to go see if Tran needed help getting the vehicles ready. She zipped up her purple jacket and silently thanked the universe that the forecast promised a warm day. She found herself thinking about the reasons she volunteered for the moon mission. She had spent most of her life trying to prove her parents and everyone else wrong. She started by learning everything she possibly could about the characteristics her condition and then tried to do the opposite. She made herself follow the rules no matter how much she wanted to break them and she tried to do things for other people without expecting things in return. She graduated from high school and college at the same time at the age of sixteen. Her parents refused to let a sixteen-year-old stay at home and do nothing all day so they insisted that she go back to college. Her mother always liked plants so Mel thought going into Botany would bring them closer but nothing was further from the truth.

Thinking about the past was starting to depress her. On her way to see Tran she saw Dr. Bowman leave his suite and head for the mess hall which made a devious thought enter her head. She changed her course and headed straight toward the doctor's quarters and stopped in front of the door. Sneaking around was thrilling and exciting and it satisfied a need inside of her. She stood in the shadow just outside his door and looked around to see if anyone was around. When she felt satisfied that no one was watching her, she pulled open the door and crept inside. As expected, there was no one in his clinic. If anyone had seen her go inside, they would have assumed she was going to steal narcotics or something but that wasn't what she was after. Mel snuck into his private quarters and into his bedroom.

Zola was still in her bed sleeping. She was laying on her side facing away from Mel. Her dark hair was flipped up over the pillow and she had the blankets all the way up to her neck. She quickly kicked off her shoes and then pulled off her pants before gently lifting the blanket and climbing into the bed. She scooted forward until she was spooning Zola and nuzzled into her neck, kissing her lightly below her ear.

The half-asleep woman groaned and moved forward slightly. "No, Chad... I'm sleeping. Go get breakfast or something."

Mel didn't relent. She moved her hand around Zola's side to her belly and then into the front of her pajama pants. Zola simultaneously slapped Mel's hand away and turned around. Her shocked face relaxed a little when she realized who was rubbing up against her. Mel kissed her hard on the mouth and returned her hand to the warmth between Zola's legs. It wasn't the first time the two had sex and it probably wasn't going to be the last time. She had no idea how long Dr. Bowman would be gone but that was part of the excitement. Thinking about Zola's husband walking in on them brought her to the brink of orgasm without any external manipulation. Mel wanted him to come in. She often fantasized about being able to convince him to join in on the fun but she doubted he was the type.

Unfortunately, the doctor didn't walk in on them. Zola already knew about the search for Sara and begged Mel to find any reason to bow out and stay with her. With Chad out of the way they could be together without the fear of being caught. She was tempted to hurt Zola by telling her that she meant nothing to her except sex but she didn't. Instead, she kissed her good-bye and snuck out without being seen. If it excited her to sleep with the doctor's wife behind his back, it excited her even more to stand in front of him fresh from her bed. He was standing next to the jeep checking the supplies. She walked up to him and casually handed him her backpack.

"Can you throw this in for me?" It was amazing how much pleasure she took handing him her bag and looking him in the eye. She privately wondered if he could smell Zola on her as she watched him toss her pack in the jeep. "Thanks."

It was literally the best day of her life. For the next forty minutes, she sat next to Dr. Bowman as he drove the jeep. Junior sat behind her complaining about the lack of leg room and kept wondering out loud why Mel took the front seat when she was clearly the smallest. Tran and Martinez followed behind them on the motorcycles. She just loved the fact that she was sitting next to him and that he had no clue. She decided she had to break the silence.

"How do you think she got so far away?" She figured it was the most pertinent question of the hour. As far as Mel was concerned, there was no possible way that Sara could have traveled so far away without flying. Especially since there was a canyon in the way. She turned around and looked at Junior. "I'm a genius, Junior. I know you're keeping something from us."

That was when that little twit Junior rocked her world by telling her that there was a spaceship in orbit around Sarisart. So many questions peppered her mind. Starting with the location of Sara's comm. Why was she fifty-six miles away? Why was she still on the planet? It was all so fascinating and ridiculous all at once. Was Sara in danger at all? What were they going to find when they found her? She suddenly forgot all about the fact that she was turned on simply by her proximity to her lover's husband. She was more infatuated by the possibilities of everything they might find and what it might mean for Sara's paradox. The doctor shot Junior many of the questions that she wanted answered. Unfortunately, Junior didn't have any of them.

She was so focused on what she had learned that she didn't even notice when they stopped. It would still be an hour before the sun came up but light began to show in the sky. Mel watched Tran pull her motorcycle up next to the jeep and then get off. She had to admit that her knowledge of machines was impressive. The cycles were small with only four cylinders which ran on ethanol that was made exclusively out of the garbage the colony generated. Martinez pulled up next to her and she found herself a little miffed at him for not telling her about the ship. She got out of the jeep and stomped her way over to him but he made a beeline for the edge of the canyon. She crossed her arms across her chest as she followed him. They both looked over the side to the bottom. It looked deeper than it actually was. She was able to get across the canyon eight months prior by climbing down one side and up the other. She at least had the foresight to tie a rope to a tree on each side. This allowed her to use the rope to easily pull herself across when she returned. The rope was still there, pulled tight, across the canyon, making it easy for the builders to erect a temporary bridge. Unfortunately, it would also make it easier for the impatient sheriff who was hell-bent on finding Sara.

Martinez made it look easy. He hooked one leg over the rope and then masterfully pulled himself across to the other side in no time at all. Felix and his team were making impressive progress on the bridge but it still wouldn't be done for several more hours. He knew that he couldn't find Sara on his own but he could do the one thing that he was employed to do. Investigate. He looked around the ground hoping to find Sara's footprints. He wasn't an idiot. He knew there was no way that Sara traveled by foot and on her own. Whatever happened to her, she didn't leave on her own. Every time he thought about her, he got a bad feeling in the pit of his stomach. He was afraid he was never going to see her again and that he'd never get the chance to explain. He walked toward the tree line while he scanned the ground for any signs that a human traveled through the area. He knew he wouldn't find anything but he had to do something.

His comm chimed. "Uncle Martinez, did you find my mommy yet?" Drew's voice cut through the air like a hot knife through hard butter.

He smiled when he heard his voice. "Not yet, little man, but I will. I promise."

Martinez talked with the boy for a few minutes. The Anderson's were a very nice couple with a little girl that was around the same age but Drew didn't like her very much. He tried to reassure him that he wouldn't be staying with them very long but children had a tendency to be a little self-absorbed. He wanted Martinez to come back and get him so that he could help him find his mother.

"You know I can't do that." He laughed. "Your mom would kill me."

"Make sure you tell her that I love her." Drew's voice broke a little making it clear that he was crying but trying to hide it. "And make sure you bring her back with you."

"I will." Martinez felt like he was lying. "I won't come home without her."

He suddenly had visions of himself trying to explain to the boy why he came home without his mother. He literally had no idea what happened to her or if she was still alive but he had just promised to find her. He put his rucksack on the ground, opened the front pocket, and then pulled out his tablet. He poked at it a few times and then frowned. Desperation gripped his heart as he realized that she was much further away than she was before. He ran a hand through his hair as he tried to remain calm.

"Fuck." He pressed his comm. "Martinez to Sara… if you're there, say something."

His hands were tied. He couldn't go after her until the bridge was finished. The only thing he could do was grab a hammer and help. As he listened to the rhythm of the hammering, his mind floated back to the time he last saw his grandfather. He was born in Mexico back in the 1940's and became a naturalized citizen of the United States by joining the Army. After coming home from the Vietnam war, Angelo Martinez fell in love and married an American woman who already had a child, a daughter who he adopted. That single fact always slightly bothered Martinez. He was a fat white kid with black hair and light brown eyes with a decidedly Spanish name. But the only reason it bothered him was because he wished he was Spanish. He wished he was a direct descendant of Angelo's because he was a great man. He was also the only one on the planet who actually loved him.

Racheal loved her adopted father very much and decided to follow in his footsteps so she joined the Army straight out of high school. A little less than a year later, she gave birth to Martinez.

"Abu, I don't want you to die." Martinez leaned against his grandfather's hospital bed. He had dry tear tracks on his chubby cheeks.

Angelo took his oxygen mask off and smiled softly. "If I had my way, I'd stay with you forever."

Fresh tears fell out of Martinez' sad eyes as he briefly looked over his shoulder to the hallway. He lowered his voice. "Without you, I don't know what will happen to me."

Angelo put his hand on top of his grandson's. "Your mother loves you, Martinez. She'll take care of you."

"No, she won't, Abu." He was getting more and more upset, causing him to be louder. "She doesn't love me. I don't even think she likes me! Why, grandpa? Why?"

"You know why."

Martinez looked down because he was suddenly ashamed. "She didn't even give me a name."

His grandfather wheezed and labored to breathe. "Well, when you turn eighteen, you can choose your own name. And when that happens, it would be my honor if you would choose mine."

That day was one of the hardest days of his life. He had to say good-bye to his only father figure and the only person that made sure he had all the things he needed. He spent most of his childhood hating his mother and blaming her for the way she treated him. But as he got older, he understood that it wasn't her fault. She never loved him and never hid that fact. But who could love a product of rape? It happened while she was in boot camp and she wasn't even aware that she was pregnant until after she was assigned her first duty station. She couldn't bring herself to name him and wanted to give him away but his grandfather insisted that she keep him. He promised to help her but that help ended the day he died.

When Martinez reflected on his life, he knew that she tried her best. But he also knew that he paid for the sins of his father. If there was one thing that he knew, beyond the fact that his mother never loved him, it was that he looked like his father. His Abu should have let her get rid of him. It would have been better for everyone. She was only able to last a few more years. After that she went AWOL and he never saw her again. Which is how he ended up in the custody of the United States Army.

The Boy Scouts were a gaggle of orphaned children that supposedly had no other family to take care of them. Looking back now, he realized that was just a convenient story that the boys were given. Zeeman had been with the Scouts for a few years before Martinez joined them. He was like a brother that he never had. He protected Martinez from the other kids and took him under his wing. He was literally the only living person that Martinez considered family and he vowed to never betray him. Not even if he was commanded to do so.

Martinez suddenly leaned back on his heels and looked up at the hot sun. It was a warm day and he was beginning to break a sweat. He looked around him at the people working on the bridge and determined that it was probably good enough to get the motorcycles over. He was too impatient. He knew he couldn't take off without the medical supplies in the jeep. He stood up and balanced himself on one of the boards as he walked across to the vehicles. He took off his jacket and draped it over his bike as he got himself some water.

The doctor walked up behind him with his own water. He was sweating profusely. "So, there's something we need to talk about."

Martinez leaned on his bike. "Would this be about the spaceship in orbit... or Sara's baby?"

Chapter Nine

The small escape pod sat slightly crocked on the ground in a long trench that was created by the ship when it crashed. If someone happened along and looked inside, they would see two people lying face to face and sleeping. At least one of them was. After giving his new guest a blood transfusion, the temperature dropped so drastically that he had to lie down next to her and close the dome just to keep them both warm. It was awkward and incredibly uncomfortable because he didn't want to get too cozy with a person he didn't know. If the woman woke up and kicked him in the family jewels, he wouldn't be able to blame her. Sometime during the night, he had unconsciously wrapped his arms around her and pulled her close to him. He had nightmares about giant flying bugs that wanted to eat him so it was no surprise that he flinched when he felt something move against his chest. Her beautiful face was the first thing he saw when he opened his eyes. She was focused on running her finger over the embroidered words on his jacket. U.S.S. Newman.

"Hey, Little Lady." He moved some hair away from her face. "How you doin'?"

He watched her try to form the words with her mouth before speaking. She stuttered badly. "O k k kay."

The captain looked into her eyes and grinned. "Considering what you've been through, I think okay is really good."

Getting out of a pod with no power was harder than he thought it would be. Especially because there was an extra person inside. He felt his way around the armrest until he found the manual hand-crank for the glass dome. After that it didn't take him long to start a fire and get a kettle of coffee brewing. He glanced at the nose of his ship and eyed the dead creature that was evidently killed when they crashed. He felt like the thing was looking at him but he knew it wasn't. He adjusted his hat until it was comfortable and then went to check on Sara. He watched her as she sat in his pod almost as if she was in a trance or perhaps in shock. She touched the bandage on her neck and then looked down at the dried blood on her jacket. He frowned hard at her and then rummaged through his bag.

"I can take care of that for you." He held up a spray canister and shook it. "Gimme your jacket."

She looked at him like she was confused and then looked down at her jacket again. He helped her take it off. It appeared to be ruined by the stain. He laid it at the foot of the pod and then held the spray can over it.

"Watch this."

Sara eyed him for a moment and then watched him spray her jacket thoroughly. He quickly picked it up and showed it to her. The chemical that he sprayed on the jacket initially formed a gel coating which began to separate and slowly roll into individual beads that turned red as they seemed to drink in the stain. He held his finger up and then walked a few steps away from her to snap the jacket into the wind and then brought it back to her. When he showed it to her again the stain was gone. She furrowed her brow and then felt the jacket.

"It's dry, right?"

She nodded. He was excited to share the experience with her because he always got a kick out of it. He used to spill things on purpose just so he could watch the compound work. He helped her put the jacket back on when her comm started to speak.

"Martinez to Sara… if you're there, say something."

She pulled the communication device off her collar and looked at it. "Ass-hat."

Britt laughed. "Ass-hat, huh? I can't wait to meet him."

Sara fiddled with the comm for a few minutes and then sighed. "It's… b b bbroken."

She was so frustrated with her speech that she angrily rapped the side of her head with her knuckles. He held his hands up at her. "Hey! Hey, Little Lady." He gently took her by the wrist and guided her arm back down to her side. "It's gonna be okay." He pointed at her wrist where an odd-looking watch resided. "There are nano-bots inside your body trying to repair the damage that damn bug did to your brain. And this… this will keep them charged."

She suddenly took a deep breath and looked at the fire. "Cof… fee."

Britt nodded and headed over to the kettle and poured her a cup. "Do you remember my name?"

Sara carefully took the cup he held out for her. "Cake."

He chuckled. "Oh, so I'm Cake? That makes more sense." He nodded. "I have a few lewd comments and innuendos when you're feeling a little better. Like…" He held his hands out to his sides. "This is a piece of cake you can have and eat too."

She laughed as her face turned bright red.

"Sorry. Sometimes I can't seem to help myself around a pretty lady." He poured himself a cup of coffee. "My name's Britt. And I can tell," he held his cup up at her. "You and I are gonna be good friends."

Sara leaned toward him and placed her finger on the embroidery on his jacket again. He looked down at her finger and then back up into her eyes. She nodded slightly and then turned her finger toward herself. "N..New…man."

Captain Mason pressed his lips together as he squinted at her. It was a literal impossibility but the more he looked at her, the more he knew it was true. He turned his head away and then rolled his eyes toward her. "Captain Zeeman?"

Sara exaggerated a nod.

"The U.S.S. Newman was commissioned to find you." Britt was somewhere between shock and amazement. "I can't believe this. I've been searching for The Moon's Eye for years but I didn't think I'd find any of you alive."

Sara smiled and then her mood changed dramatically. Tears streamed down her face as she leaned over and touched his leg. "P..please take… us h..home."

She was begging him with her eyes. It made him feel terrible. He took her hand in his. "I'm sorry, Little Lady. We've been looking for a way home ever since we came through that damn wormhole." He leaned over and looked her in the eye. "But I'll do my best. You have my word."

Sara tried hard not to whimper but failed. Her voice broke. "I wanna go h..home."

Her face suddenly turned pale as she began a slow tilt backward. Britt dropped his coffee and lunged forward to catch her. He watched in fear as her eyes rolled into the back of her head and she started to shake violently. The seizure lasted less than thirty seconds but it was long enough to render her unconscious. He gently picked her up and carried her back over to his ship to lay her down and make her comfortable. She looked so peaceful even though she had vast amounts of turmoil going on in that pretty little head of hers. He couldn't help staring at her. The revelation that she was Sara Zeeman was unbelievable. Everyone on his ship knew who Sara Zeeman was. She was the Mother of Space Travel and should have died long ago. She was also the most hated person in history.

The captain reached into the pod and pulled out a tablet while he silently cursed the fact that he was on his own without Lucy. Before the pod lost power completely, he ordered her to upload her program to the Swagger. He punched the tablet a few times before holding it over her head. He eyed the viewscreen until a picture of Sara's brain appeared on the screen. He wasn't a doctor or a scientist but he knew enough to know that the little nanobot bastards that he injected her with caused the seizure. They all appeared to be grouped together in the same part of her brain. He could only surmise that being fully conscious while they tried to repair the damage wasn't a very good idea. You live, you learn. He poked the tablet a couple more times to check the rest of her vital signs. Other than being a little low on blood, she was doing okay.

He reached up and pressed a spot right behind his ear. "Commander Hayes, you there?"

"Aren't I always?" Her voice floated in his ear.

The captain gave her a brief rundown of what happened since he left but held back one minor detail. The fact that he not only met the famous Sara Zeeman, but that she was currently unconscious in his pod.

"Any word from the shuttle?"

Britt couldn't help thinking of Hayes' first day as his second in command. There were nearly five thousand people living on his ship and he felt like he knew all of them, at least a little bit. He basically watched her grow up. She was a scrawny child who was as black as space with one silver dead eye. With all the technology they possessed, they still couldn't fix a child's eye without the use of an electronic implant. But the girl's parents didn't believe she needed to be fixed so she never allowed herself to be altered.

"That's a negative," she answered, "but I have some coordinates for you."

He glanced back down at his tablet and watched a topographical map appear that marked his and the shuttles locations. He sighed and shook his head. Of course, the damn thing would be a two-day hike away.

"Thanks." He looked down at Sara and frowned. "Patch me through to Dr. Dixon and put us on private."

He spent the next few minutes talking to the doctor about Sara and the fact that he destroyed her entire life with a simple blood transfusion. When you're in life and death situations on a daily basis you learn to think on your feet and sometimes that means choosing the lesser evil. Giving Sara some of his blood was a bad idea from the start but it was the only way to save her.

"You need to find the shuttle and bring her back here before the incubation period is complete." The doctor's voice sounded grim. "It's different for everyone but if she goes past five days, you might as well dig a hole for her."

Getting together the things they needed to survive in the wild on their own was harder than he thought it would be. He knew that Sara would be fine, or at least seem that way, in a few hours but he wanted to get going. He suddenly realized that the logistics of carrying the supplies and an unconscious woman were going to be complicated. He stared at the backpack and the woman for a few moments as he tried to map it out in his head. Britt suddenly made a decision and marched over to his pack. When he found what he was looking for he pulled out the reflective blanket and then put the pack on. He fashioned a sling out of the blanket in order to make it easier to carry her in front of him. After about a mile his knee started to hurt. He apparently hit it harder than he thought during the crash. He needed to take his mind off of his knee so tried to focus on the nature around him. It was a marvel to him. There was an arboretum on board his ship but the trees dwarfed in comparison to the ones before him.

He suddenly stopped in mid-step as a giant elk-type animal walked out in front of him. It regarded him with minor interest and then casually walked away. Britt was in awe. He smiled to himself.

"Wow."

He found himself immersed in the fact that his feet were walking on a planet. His steps started to get slower and slower but not because his cargo was heavy but because his senses were on overload. The air smelled like a combination of damp dirt and fragrant flowers. He stopped and smelled deeply through his nose and found himself starting to tear up a little. The parklike setting in the arboretum aboard his ship was impressive but it was nothing like real thing. The sounds around him were silent and loud at the same time. A bird suddenly caught his attention so he looked up and squinted into the sun. The warmth on his face was enough for his body to believe he was falling in love.

The captain felt Sara slipping a little so he bobbed upward and pulled her up into place. He knew there was no way that he'd be able to carry her the whole way but he couldn't just sit around and wait for her people to find them. He shook his head when he thought about it. When the Moon's Eye blasted off the whole world watched at the edge of their seats. And when it disappeared without a trace no one knew what happened. When it was discovered that a wormhole was to blame it caused widespread panic. The messages the crew sent back were classified and not released to anyone except family for years. The prospect of a wormhole leading to another galaxy with a livable planet gave a lot of people hope for the future. Especially after the war. It didn't take long for the military to use Captain Zeeman's plans to colonize Mars. They were hoping to save lives but all they did was prolong the inevitable.

He wasn't a scientist but even he could figure out a few things based on some key details. Details, such as the fact that she looks exactly the same as she did as the day she left. Either Captain Zeeman fell into the fountain of youth or he and his crew traveled back in time to the tune of a few hundred years.

He was born on Mars one hundred years after the Moon's Eye disappeared. The only time he ever experienced fresh air was on Earth in one of the huge biodomes. There were several of them built around the world when it became apparent that the world was dying. That was around the time that the military and several private companies starting building massive spaceships. Everyone hoped the ships would eventually lead to the discovery of a planet like Earth. Britt eventually joined the United States Space Force. He passed all the physical fitness and health requirements, which was no accident. His parents had his DNA altered when he was a child so not only would he be physically fit but he'd live an exceptionally long life. Such things were illegal but he figured if no one ever found out, there would be no harm. No one ever did find out… until the plague.

It happened thirteen years after he was stationed on the U.S.S. Newman. One might think that the ship was named after the Mother of Space Travel but it wasn't. It was named after her father. General Charles Newman. When patient zero started to show signs of a hemorrhagic fever it created widespread panic all over the ship. The young man was quarantined immediately despite the fact that everyone wanted him jettisoned out of the nearest airlock. But when more and more people fell sick it caused pure chaos. Innocent people were killed if they showed any signs of being infected. Sometimes, all it took was an accusation. Britt was scared like everyone else was but since he was part of the enlisted crew, he had to help to keep the peace. Hundreds of people were quarantined to their quadrants for weeks while the scientists and doctors tried to come up with a cure.

Four hundred people had already died and it didn't seem like they were getting any closer to a cure when Britt became infected. He had never been so scared in his entire life. Dr. Dixon was a promising young physician who tried to learn everything related to medicine. Unfortunately, he was also a self-identified pedophile who leaned more toward little girls than little boys. The man could never hurt

107

anyone, let alone a child, but he insisted that someday his unholy desires would overpower him. He spent his time locked up in sickbay and was never allowed to go anywhere without an escort. And Britt was often his escort. He genuinely like the man and often argued that he wasn't a pedophile unless he actually acted on it. But doctor Dixon's fear always prevailed.

It was the doctor that noticed that Britt was sick in the first place. At first, it didn't seem like the same illness but several tests revealed the truth about both Britt and the virus inside him. He remembered the doctor's response. "There's no way you'll be able to keep your secret any longer but the good news is, I don't think people care anymore." He slapped Britt on the shoulder. "The bad news is, I'm gonna give you a bad case of super herpes."

That scared Britt a bit more than the fact that he contracted the plague. "Will this be done in the traditional sense or…"

The doctor explained that there were several different types of herpes viruses and that contracting them actually served a beneficial purpose. Of course, Britt's main concern was which virus he intended to give him. The doctor frowned. "There's about a dozen kids in sector twelve that have Sixth Disease, which is a form of herpes."

Dr. Dixon wasn't allowed to examine children but he often conferred with the pediatrician who did.

Apparently, Britt's altered DNA changed both the viruses in his body allowing the doctor to synthesize a cure for the crew. But for some reason, it didn't work on Britt. Instead, his body was forever at war with itself. Both the virus and the cure continuously fought for sole ownership of the body but neither side ever won. It wasn't ever an issue because, thanks to him, the entire crew was immune. It made him the hero of his own story and put him on the fast track to becoming the captain of the ship. Every time he looked back on his past, he was somehow able to convince himself that he actually deserved it. After all, he worked hard and was an advocate of the people. When the military ships were decommissioned and basically became home to thousands upon thousands of people, his shipmates elected him as captain. He found out rather quickly that even good captains have to make unpopular decisions or bad alliances. But all in all, he believed he was doing a good job.

The sun was high in the sky and it was getting hot. As he was walking through the trees, he swore he could hear water so he continued forward until he found the source of the noise. He could smell something fragrant in the air that reminded him of honeysuckle. The river was wide enough that it would be hard to cross. It was moving rather quickly and most likely got deeper in the middle. He set Sara down in the shade under a tree and then checked her vital signs. Her heartbeat was strong and steady which was a very good sign. Just as he moved her hair out of her face, her eyes opened and she made eye contact with him.

He smiled broadly. "Hey there, Little Lady. How ya feelin'?"

She rubbed her forehead. "Head hurts."

He helped her sit up and watched curiously as she reached into her jacket and pulled out a small tin box. She carefully opened it and took out an orange pill and put it in her mouth. He had to assume it was something for her headache so he dug into his bag for his water bottle and then held it out to her.

"Here. Drink some water." He handed it to her. "You're still low on blood. I don't want you to be dehydrated too."

The captain watched her drink the water for a moment before taking out his tablet and looking at his map. They were barely three miles closer to their destination. He rubbed the stubble on his chin while he silently chastised himself for helping her in the first place. No good deed goes unpunished. He looked down at her again. She was wiping water from her chin with her sleeve.

Sara looked up at him with a hint of fear in her eyes. "Where are you taking me?"

Chapter Ten

Sara's head hurt. If she was sitting on the doctor's exam table and she had to describe her pain, she'd have to liken it to someone sticking a hot poker stick through her left eye. The cowboy that saved her life was bringing her somewhere but she doubted it was back to her people. She could almost remember a conversation with the man in which she begged him to take her away from Sarisart but she couldn't remember his answer. He looked like a nice guy but she wasn't a naive teenager. But what were the chances that a serial killer would risk his life and overall wellbeing to save her? She decided to give him the benefit of the doubt. She squinted at him as if he was standing in the sun but they were in the shade. He was digging around in his backpack searching for something. His arm disappeared all the way to the bottom and then pulled out a sealed meal packet. The military's MREs or Meals Ready to Eat were okay if you were starving to death but she was never able to find one that she'd eat daily. She had a major headache and she felt like she was going to die but she'd be damned if she was going to eat that shit.

She got up but she was a little bit woozy so she had to concentrate on her footing. Of course, the cowboy followed closely behind her, insisting that she sit back down. He kept saying that she should rest but she wanted to move around. Sara looked around the unfamiliar terrain until she finally found what she was looking for. There was a very large seed pod at the base of an oak tree. It was curved like a large wooden ball with long stalks with fanlike cotton on top. They were just like the dandy lion poofs she used to have fun making wishes on as a child. She would blow on them as hard as she could and try like hell to get every last seed to fly away so she could make a wish. But these were much bigger. They were at least as tall as she was but they were

111

still very light. She chose one of the stalks and pulled hard on it until it popped out of the pod.

She turned to the man. "Knife?"

He raised his eyebrows at her briefly and then smirked before pulling one out of his back pocket and handing it to her. She used it to sharpen the stalk at the end and then handed it to him before pulling out another one. When she had two of them, she walked over to a large rock by the river and then asked him to turn it over. As soon as he lifted the rock, something crawled out and she stabbed it with the stalk. It was a trilobite the size of a dinner plate. Its many tiny legs flailed in the air as she held it out to him.

He grimaced hard and didn't want to take it. "What the hell am I supposed to do with that?"

Sara rubbed her temples. The orange that the doctor made for her wasn't really helping. She tried to smile at him and then tapped him on his chest. She made her voice lower and pretended to be a caveman. "Woman hunt, man cook."

He laughed. "Woman hunt, man cook. That's cute."

Sara watched him make a fire and then she showed him how to cook them. She picked up one of the stalks and pressed it through the meat of the creature and then held it in the fire. The smell of it cooking brought her back to the first time she ate it. After landing on Sarisart it became a requirement that every person in the colony learn survival skills. Trying to live off the land was harder than she thought it would be. Especially because she'd be required to kill, prepare, and eat her own food. She had no problems finding the animals but when it came to killing them, she didn't want to do it. Perhaps the worst part about it was the fact that it was still alive when placed on the fire. She didn't think it was right back then and she still didn't. Nothing should be cooked alive. Not a lobster, not a crab, and not a trilobite. But she was never sure if the animal was dead or not. It wasn't as if you could check its pulse.

Getting the cooked meat out of the animal was a synch. One just had to peel it out and eat it. It was by far the easiest meal a person could make and the tastiest too. She watched the man as he copied her and took his first bite.

He nodded in surprise. "Well I'll be darned." He eyed her closely for a moment. "Do you remember anything? You've been in and out of it for a while."

Sara pulled the tin out of her jacket again and placed another orange berry under her tongue. She nodded and then sighed. "I remember bits and pieces." She glanced at him. "There may or may not have been some cuddling the other night."

The man chuckled out of sheer shock. "That was out of pure necessity, I promise." He chewed some more of the meat. "You wouldn't want your savior to freeze the death, would you?" He suddenly grinned from ear to ear. "I ain't gonna lie, though. I kinda enjoyed it."

Sara smiled back at him and her face felt hot. "Remind me again… why do I think your name is Cake?"

When he laughed, she had to smile. It was so genuine that it was hard not to join him. His eyes seemed to twinkle for just a moment. "My name's Britt. But you can call me Cake if you want."

As soon as he said it, she remembered. His name was Britt Mason and he was the captain of a spaceship called the

Swagger. Her eyes focused in on the golden embroidery on his jacket again. It was all coming back to her. She was still trying to get used to the fact that this man came out of nowhere and saved her life. But he didn't just save her life. He walked into the pits of hell and carried her out in his arms. She watched him chew his food. She wanted to know everything about him and his ship. He peeled off and dug out every last piece of meat that he could find and then licked his fingers clean, which made her smile. He sucked on the tip of his thumb for a second before tossing the carcass into the fire.

"What were you doing before that bug-thingy tried to make a meal out of you?" The curiosity in his eyes was genuine.

Sara handed her half-eaten trilobite to him hoping that he would finish the rest. She wiped her hands on her pants and then suddenly realized she was wearing exactly the same clothes that she had on when she ran away from Martinez. She looked at her black leggings and wondered how cold it would get later that night. The orange that she took was starting to take effect and it was causing her thoughts to wander. She tried to stay on topic.

"They aren't bugs. They're warm-blooded intelligent beings that can somehow mimic a species DNA." She rubbed her lips because they were starting to feel numb. "Maybe even copy it, I don't know."

"Whatever the hell that means." He dug his finger under a line of meat and pulled it upward.

"And she wasn't trying to hurt me."

He laughed and then stopped himself. "What?"

He pointed to his neck and then to her. "The thing had part of its body inside yours. And not in a good way."

Thinking about the experience made her eyes sting and a tear trickled down her cheek. She wiped it away with her sleeve with a sniffle. "It was trying to communicate and that was the only way it knew how." That single sentenced spurred a conversation about judging a book by its cover. The bisectors were a scary looking species and the unevolved humans reacted badly. "I need to get a message to my people. Can your ship help me do that?"

He put down his food and then nodded. "Maybe. Contact with my ship has been very sporadic because of those damn solar storms." She watched him press the side of his face in front of his ear before calling his ship several times. Britt eyed her and then shook his head. "No dice. Sorry, Little Lady."

The damn solar storms were definitely a problem because they disrupted communications on a regular basis. Junior had a drone that he was trying to fix because it crashed when it didn't receive more commands from the controller. The satellite and most of the systems in the colony were built to withstand electromagnetic waves brought on by solar flares but there was one problem. When the satellite detected a solar storm, it went into protective mode. Unfortunately, being that Britt's comm was inside his head, she had to take his word for it. He showed her where his shuttle was on the map and it was still at least two days away. She knew that a group of her people led by Martinez would be looking for her but according to Britt, time was of the essence.

"So, your blood is going to make me sick?" She couldn't believe her luck.

He sighed sadly. "I'm immune but it is still active in my system. That's why I need to get you back to my ship."

There was no way in hell she was going to be able to walk forty miles. She wasn't feeling the effects of the virus the cowboy told her about but she was still very weak from her encounter with the bisector queen. If she was reading his map correctly, they would travel alongside the river for almost twenty of those miles, which was very good news. She helped put out the fire and headed back toward the giant seed pod. The first time her people came upon the pods she couldn't figure out how the seeds might fly. She wasn't a botanist but she was a scientist and by design, the seeds appeared to be designed to take flight but they were obviously too heavy. It wasn't long before she figured out how the seeds traveled. As they approached, a large bird with a wingspan of about six feet landed on a tree branch just above the pod. Sara gently grabbed Britt by the arm and pulled him behind the trunk of another tree and they watched the magnificent bird. It looked like a condor to her but its feathers were dark blue which would allow it to blend in perfectly with the pseudo trees.

The bird nipped at the tip of the seed stalk until it got a good grip of the cotton and then pulled at it until it broke free. They both watched as the bird flew away and when it was almost out of sight, the seed broke away from the stalk and fell to the ground. She grinned as her new friend watched the bird. "She's obviously going to use the fuzz to make a nest."

Sara began pulling the stalks out of the pod and laid them on the ground. The colonists used the stalks to make baskets and a number of other things but she had no use for them at the moment. Britt had no idea what she was doing but helped her remove the stalks anyway. After they pulled all of them out, the pod was nothing but a large mound with a bunch of empty holes where the seeds used to be. By the time they freed the pod from the ground and turned it over, the captain figured it out. He watched as Sara took half a dozen of the seed stalks and stabbed them into the sides at an angle so they would create shade and then they both stepped back to look at it.

"I'm guessing that you already know it will float." He looked at her briefly and then back at it before smiling broadly. "Looks like we'll be doing some more cuddling." He winked at her.

He wasn't wrong. The long ride down the river was going to be a little bit uncomfortable because the makeshift raft was very small. She used his tablet to figure out the speed of the current which was roughly five miles per hour, which meant they had to end their trip in five hours or else risk being miles off course. Being a little uncomfortable for a few hours was a lot better than trying to walk that distance. She picked out two long and thin branches that they could use to push the raft away from rocks while Britt pulled the pod raft to the water. No one from her colony had explored the area yet and she hoped beyond all hope that they wouldn't run into any surprises. But with her luck, they were bound to cross paths with the devil or one of his minions very soon.

The raft was slightly concave and reminded her of the top of an acorn if you turned it upside down. This meant that if they tried to sit at the sides with space between them, eventually they would end up squished together in the middle. Captain Mason, the cowboy that he was, couldn't bring himself to step into the water with his boots on so he took them off and shoved them into his pack. He seemed happy that he didn't have to walk but balked at the method of travel.

The blue of the water reflected in his eyes making them infinitely lighter. They showed the deep concern that he felt as he waded into the cold water and held the raft in place for her. "Would you think less of me if I told you that I don't know how to swim?"

She managed to climb in without getting wet at all. She sat so that she was facing him with her feet at his side. "Don't worry, the sea monsters will get you before you drown."

His eyes shot open and his voice was louder than he meant it to be. "Are there sea monsters?"

Sara laughed. "I have no idea."

The combination of floating down the river and the orange that she took made her drowsy and she ended up falling asleep for a few hours. When she opened her eyes again it was noticeably cooler and the sun was setting. She felt terrible for leaving him alone for the entire trip but she couldn't help herself. She was tired. In fact, virus or no virus, she was always tired. Sleeping, or being unconscious in general, was a miracle. The sun was just beginning its descent behind the horizon. She was laying her back looking up at the blue sky and thanking God that her head didn't hurt anymore when Britt's face leaned into her field of view. Somewhere along the line he had taken his cowboy hat off and placed it on his lap which allowed his beautiful red hair to blow in the wind.

His eyes seemed to smile before his lips did. "This might sound a little weird… but this has been the best day of my life." He looked away from her and took a deep breath. "Beautiful place you've got here."

She sat up and looked at the land as it passed. Colorful trees lined both sides of the river which was moving a bit faster than it was before. It was absolutely her favorite time of the day. It wasn't too hot, it wasn't too cold, and on a clear day, the sunsets managed to remind her that there had to be a God. The cowboy was talking to her but she wasn't listening. She was too busy trying to figure out where a slight humming noise was coming from. She could barely hear it over the water, but she could hear it, and it was bugging her. She pulled her comm off and put it up to her ear. It was definitely responsible for the noise. Every once in a while, she could hear part of a voice but she couldn't understand what was being said. She knew it was him again. Martinez. The mere thought of him made her feel sick to her stomach. Kissing him was an impulse that felt right at the time but considering the result, it was a bad idea. She kept blaming herself for making such a stupid mistake but at the same time she was incredibly pissed at him for how he reacted. It made her feel like a stupid teenager who put her heart on the line only to get it stomped on.

She tapped the comm against her hand a few times but the noise it was making didn't subside. That's when she remembered one key feature of the comms. Each comm was paired with another for easy comm to comm contact in case of emergency. Hers used to be paired with her husband's but after his death, it was paired with Junior's. If his unit was making the same annoying noise than perhaps, she could use it to her advantage. She pressed the transmit button repeatedly and then concentrated on her message. She repeated it over and over again unit her thumb got tired. There was no way of knowing how much time had passed but when she finally looked up at Britt he was still talking.

"I saw a dinosaur." His eyes showed the excitement of a child.

She smirked and started clicking the button again. "You didn't see a dinosaur."

He tilted his head and looked at her for a second. "Yes, I did!"

Sara tried to focus on clicking the button but the look on his face was distracting her. He was looking at her like a confused little puppy dog and she found it adorable. His whole body became animated as he described the beast to her. He said it had a body like an elephant only much larger with a long thin tail. It also had a long neck that could reach up into the tall trees. She had never seen the creature he was describing before. Her first trip to Sarisart was through a wormhole or vortex that was inside the atmosphere of the planet. It made her think of an article she read about a popular theory in the 1930's about how planets could be interconnected by way of wormholes. Like cells inside a body connected by veins. It was the way the author explained how plants and animals ended up on the planets in the first place.

"What color was it?" She paused for a moment to glance at him.

He put his arms up around his head and fanned his fingers out. "It had these blue and purple branch-like things that came out of the sides of its head and neck."

Sara frowned then nodded. "There's a very good reason most of the animals on this planet are blue or purple or both."

"Yeah? Why's that?"

She resumed her message. "Fucking sky piranha."

He furrowed his brow and frowned. "What's a piranha?"

Chapter Eleven

Martinez sat down on the ground in between Junior and Tran. They were forced to stop their journey when it got too dark for the solar cells on the jeep to charge. He was incredibly frustrated by the fact that they got a very late start. Something deep inside his gut told him Sara was in trouble but the universe was trying to make sure that he couldn't help her. The bridge took longer to build than they expected. He got so upset by the delay that he got on his bike and road it across two pieces of wood to the other side. It took all the self-control within him to stop himself from driving off without the rest of the party and looking for Sara on his own. He had no doubts that he would find her but if she needed medical help, he wouldn't be able to give it to her. They traveled for about six hours but it was slow going in a lot of places so they were only able to get thirty-two miles closer to her. He dug into his pack and took out the tracker interface and it revealed that Sara somehow put even more distance between them. Since the first time they tracked her location, she managed to travel an additional seventy miles. If he didn't know better, he'd think she was doing it on purpose. Martinez knew this meant that she had to be with someone. He didn't know if this 'someone' was a human or not but they were definitely responsible for her disappearance.

Tran handed him a package of jerky that Aggie made. The cook might have been a dirty old lady but she definitely knew how to make jerky. It was spiced just right and the perfect degree of chewy but he wasn't hungry. He watched the doctor as he chewed the jerky and noted the new bruising around his right eye. He didn't feel bad about punching him, not one little bit. He didn't like the way the doctor was playing god and he needed to be taught a lesson. He looked back down at his jerky. He reached inside to the bottom just to retrieve the smallest piece and then put it in his mouth. On any normal day he would have savored it for a minute or two before chewing it but it wasn't a normal day and he was a little stressed out. He chewed it into oblivion before swallowing it and then glanced at Junior.

"If we leave at first light, we might be able to catch up to her." He sealed his bag and shoved it back into his backpack.

Mel scoffed. "That's if she's even alive."

The sheriff looked down at his hands. "I think you're severely underestimating Sara." He picked at his fingernails. "I'm not supposed to tell anyone this, but I honestly don't give a shit anymore." He took a deep breath and sighed. "Zeeman and I, we were part of an elite special ops team."

Dr. Bowman raised his eyebrows for a moment and then frowned. "I have no problems believing that."

He tipped his head to the side briefly. "One of our missions... Our last mission as it turned out, was to escort General Newman's daughter back home. She didn't want to go... we basically kidnapped her and forced her onto a plane."

Mel's eyes were wide and she seemed to be listening carefully. "I didn't know that."

He got a far off look in his eyes as he smiled. "Back then, she was this hardheaded and stubborn woman who wouldn't take any shit from anyone. Not even my commanding officer, Strickland."

123

Tran shook her head. "Are you sure we're talking about the same woman?"

Martinez ignored her. "The plane crashed and we were in the wilderness for a number of days." He made eye contact with Tran briefly. "A couple dozen mercenaries and one woman... stranded. You do the horrible math." He rubbed his eyebrow. "Three of my team members beat her up and tried to rape her."

"I don't wanna hear this." Junior placed his hands over his ears and shook his head like a child.

Martinez waved his hand to dismiss him. "Not to mention the fact that Strickland was a psychopath. She kept getting in his face and defending herself which scared the living hell out of Zeeman." He smiled then laughed, obviously nostalgic. "They liked each other right away, you know?"

Tran poked a stick into the fire. "What happened?"

"Eventually we had to choose between Sara and Strickland. Guess who won." Martinez locked eyes with Mel. It was a simple look but it was intended to be small threat. "Believe it or not, she saved us all. If it wasn't for Sara, I wouldn't be here." He couldn't help smiling again. "I mean, we're out here trying to find her, but mark my words... she's going to be the one to save all of us."

He started to talk again but Junior shushed him. He shot him an ugly look. "Did you just shush me?"

Junior tipped his head to the side like he was trying to hear something. He threw up his hand at Martinez. "Shut up!"

That got everyone's attention. Everyone had the same surprised look on their face as Martinez. They all looked on in fear and waited for the sheriff to pound the life out of the kid but nothing happened. Everything was silent except the occasional chirp of a bird or bug. As he listened to the white noise, he realized why Junior wanted silence. Martinez let it go on for about a minute before speaking again. "Junior?"

Junior's mouth dropped open. "My comm is paired with Ma's. It's Morse Code." He turned his palm up and shrugged. "Truce with bisectors. Stand down."

"What the fuck?" Tran shook her head. "Are you sure you're getting that right?"

Junior looked insulted. "What do you take me for? Yes, I'm sure!"

Martinez chuckled and shook his head. "See? She's saving our asses."

He watched Junior as he attempted to send a message back but didn't get anything in return. His small team spent the twilight hours setting up a communication relay so that they could send messages back and forth to the colony without relying on the satellite. Martinez was the best climber and most likely the only one with enough muscle and stamina to make it to the top of one of the pseudo trees quickly. Junior took care of the technical aspect by loading the relay antenna onto the drone so that he could send it up to Martinez when he was ready. The sheriff had been to the top of one of the pseudo trees once before but it was on his first visit to Sarisart. The tree had served as a landing pad for the Unan but it also had several levels where the orchids grew and children played. It was all so magnificent and wonderful back then. He remembered being in utter awe of

125

the alien people only to find out much later that they were actually the descendants of the Moon's Eye colony. Martinez still had a lot of trouble trying to wrap his head around that fact. Apparently, when they blasted off in hopes of colonizing the moon in 2029, they got sucked into that wormhole and ended up traveling two thousand years into the past. He didn't spend too much time thinking about paradoxes because he simply didn't care. It wasn't as if he could do anything about it. If the past could be changed then after Andrew died all they needed to do was place a message inside the chancellor's desk where Andrin could find it centuries later. Of course, Sara tried that. If it had worked then Andrew would have avoided death. It meant that either the past couldn't be changed or that Andrin only told Sara certain facts and declined to inform her of others.

As he neared the top of the tree, he stopped to rest and have a look around. From his vantage point he could a few miles in each direction. He scanned the horizon for any signs of smoke from a fire but there was nothing. Martinez knew she was still too far away to catch up in one day but that didn't stop the feeling of urgency that was constantly pestering him. He broke through the top canopy and went to work setting up the relay. The relays were designed and planned months ago because it was obvious, they'd be necessary. Each relay needed a solar panel to provide it power. He carefully pulled the panel off the drone and fastened it to the canopy. As soon as he had the antennae in place, he hit his comm.

"This is Martinez with a colony-wide announcement." He waited for the familiar tone that would tell him that over seventy members activated their comms. "Chancellor Newman has secured a truce with the Bisectors. I'll say again, we have a truce with the Bisectors, effective immediately." He paused for a moment knowing that at least one person would object.

The comm crackled with white noise for a moment. "Martinez? This is Deputy Baxter. Did I hear you right? A truce? That's crazy!"

Martinez assured everyone that they did indeed h him right. Deputy Baxter wasn't the only one to object. After ten minutes of arguing back and forth he became positive that the entire colony would be decimated by the time they returned home. It was progressively getting dark and he needed to climb back down out of the tree soon or be stuck up there until morning. He addressed them all again. "Look, they massively outnumber us. A truce is a good thing. I don't care if one waltzes through the middle of town, do not engage."

Getting down from the tree was easier than getting up so he was back on the ground in no time. Everyone was sitting around the fire as Tran cooked two of the large rodents on a spicket. Junior and Chad had already made a small opening at the base of the pseudo-tree and cleared out some of the roots so that they could sleep in it for the night. He looked down at Mel as he passed and noticed that she was sketching a picture of a bird. He didn't like the woman but she definitely had talent. The bird she was drawing was so realistic it looked as if it could fly off the page and into the darkness. He sat down next to the doctor and looked him in the face. The black eye that he gave him was looking a little worse as time passed. Martinez knew it was part of the healing process but the more he was faced with it, the more it started to bother him. The doctor looked angry but it wasn't directed towards him.

He looked back and forth between them. "What the hell did I walk in on?"

Dr. Bowman ignored him completely. He leaned forward slightly and glared at her. "She doesn't love you. She could never love you." He threw a small twig into the fire. "No one could ever love you because you don't deserve to be loved!"

Martinez suddenly felt like he was punched in the gut. The words weren't aimed at him but he felt as if they were. He stuck a finger in the doctor's face. "Don't you ever say that to her again."

Chad's mouth dropped open. "She's sleeping with my wife!"

The sheriff's eyebrows shot up as he glanced at Mel. She didn't even look up from her drawing but her face glowed as she chuckled. She was obviously having fun. He turned back to the doctor and sighed as he placed a hand on his back for a moment. "Sorry, I didn't know that." He aimed his entire arm at Mel. "Carry on."

He left the two to argue. As long as they weren't killing each other, he didn't care. He crawled through the opening of the pseudo-tree and began stringing up his hammock. Those awful words kept haunting him. They stemmed from memories that he wished he could forget. Apparently, just hearing someone say them meant that he was doomed to have nightmares that night. He was that pudgy child again with that curly black hair that was so long it was always in his eyes. He was only eight years old but he was left alone daily and had to fend for himself. This meant that he had to make his own dinner most of the time, and most of the time, that was okay with him. He pulled the lid off a can of ravioli and stuck a fork inside it before grabbing a can of grape soda and pack of potato chips and taking it all into the living room. His best friend, other than his grandfather, was the television. He loved watching tv because the stories managed to take him away from his own life and make him happy, if only for a little while.

Martinez hated eating the cold ravioli but the microwave was broken and his mother blamed him for that fact so she refused to buy another one. But it was food and no one could say the boy wasn't well fed. He knew he was breaking several of his mother's rules but she wasn't home so he thought it didn't matter. Number one, he was eating in the living room. Number two, he was drinking in the living room. And number three, he was watching a show with vampires in it. Vampires preyed on victims. Even at the age of eight, he could see why she didn't like them. Unfortunately for him, that night, his mother came home early. He was so enthralled by the tv show that he didn't even notice when she came in until she slammed the door behind her. The noise scared him so bad that he spilled the grape soda on the floor. He jumped up out of his seat and picked it up quickly but it was too late. The damage had already been done. The beige carpet that was already quite dirty was now stained purple.

Martinez looked up at his mother in fear. He knew he was in trouble and it meant that he was going to endure a beating if he didn't act quickly. He was very familiar with the routine even when she didn't stick to her normal schedule. Normally she would come home drunk but he was usually barricaded in his room by then. She would often try to get in but he always leveraged a piece of wood against the door making it impossible. The next day she would never remember what she did and everything would repeat as normal. He watched her carefully for any sudden movements as his heart raced in his chest. That day marked the first day that he ever fought back which turned out to be a huge mistake. It was a mistake because she had vowed long ago that a man would never hurt her again and apparently, that included her son.

When she ran at him, he did the only thing he could think of... which was throw the half-filled can of grape soda at her. It hit her square in the chest and then fell to the floor. "You stupid fat fuck! Look what you did!" She screamed at him.

She pushed him up against the wall and kneed him in the stomach so hard it knocked the wind out of him. He gasped for air until he could squeeze out a plea. "Mama, please don't hurt me. I love you. Please!"

She slapped him across the face and growled at him. "Don't you ever say that to me again!" She repeatedly smacked his head a few more times, back and forth, with both hands. "No one will ever love you because you don't deserve to be loved!"

Martinez jolted awake covering his face with his arms. It made his hammock swing back and forth slightly which temporarily confused him. He looked around in a panic before realizing where he was. It was somewhat tragic. The retired mercenary had been through a lot in his life but the only post-traumatic stress he ever suffered was directly related to his mom and the hatred she had for him. She had said those words to him so often that he began to believe them. When he thought about his mother it made him very sad. He never knew what happened to her after she ran off but he hoped that she found peace. Raising him was her personal nightmare. He couldn't blame her for hating him. He had once told Sara that the only person he was interested in was himself. It was true at the time. He didn't want to invest his time and energy into a person who could use his affection as a method of torture. He knew that he was the only one who could give that power to a person so he denied himself for years.

"Something really bad must have happened to you," she said to him.

If she only knew. He was of sound mind and body but he was definitely a disabled broken man who couldn't function normally in society. Not because he was a trained killer but because he was punished for the sins of his father. Now he was about to have a child with the woman and it scared the living shit out of him.

Chapter Twelve

"You didn't see a dinosaur."

He laughed but part of him was insulted that she didn't believe him. He tilted his head and looked at her for a second. "Yes, I did!"

He watched her play with her comm for a few minutes. The sun was shining through her blonde hair making it look like golden strands of light. Her hair was messy and she had dark circles under her eyes but he couldn't take his eyes off of her. It was hard for him to reconcile his feelings because he spent a good portion of his life blaming her for the downfall of mankind. He couldn't help thinking about the first thing she said to him. She begged him to take her home. He told her that they had been trying to get home ever since they went through that damn wormhole, but that wasn't true. The truth was, there was no home to go to. Sure, there were probably people still living on Mars, Earth too, but not many. No, he had no intentions of going home. What he planned on doing was killing his white whale. The singularity that had haunted him for decades. Earth be damned, he intended to shut that damn door, and for good.

As he looked at her, he knew he was getting into dangerous territory because he started to think of the future and wondered if she would be in it. He noticed something large moving behind her so he looked downstream.

"Hey Sara." His voice was even but low as a smile played across his face. He waited for her to look at him before tipping his head up and looking past her. "Don't look now… but there isn't a dinosaur behind you."

Sara looked at him like he had four heads but eventually followed his gaze downstream. The giant creature was drinking from the river and they were on a direct collision course for its snout. She slowly backed herself toward Britt until she was practically in his lap. He suddenly felt her hand grab his and he marveled at the fact that she made him feel like a teenager with a crush. The massive mountain with eyes had branch-like appendages growing around its head and down its neck. Each one had blue and purple feathers that resembled leaves. Sara never finished what she was saying about the sky piranha but he suddenly realized the reason behind her comments about the colors. It was obviously camouflage and the realization terrified him. If the giant animal he saw before him needed camouflage against a foe from the sky, then what the hell were they going to do?

"It's a giraffe," she said softly.

"It's not a giraffe." He chuckled. "They may be extinct but I know what one looks like."

Its eye zeroed in on them as it suddenly raised his head and watched them as they passed by. Sara exhaled loudly. "Wow!" It was only a whisper but he could see her excitement when she looked at him. She smiled. "It's a Giraffatitan. It's a type of Brachiosaurus." She turned to watch it as they got further and further away. "My son's going to freak out when I tell him!"

Getting out of the boat proved to be harder than it was to get in. He had to get into the water and pull the pod and Sara to shore. Unfortunately, once the pod was close enough to touch ground, he tripped on a rock and fell face first in the water. Aside from the fact that he felt really stupid and embarrassed, it actually worked out in his favor. Sara hopped out of the pod and helped him up. She led him over to a large stone where he sat down while she got his things out of the boat. Britt looked down at himself. His clothes were completely soaked and it was getting colder by the minute.

She placed the pack next to him and asked him if had more clothes. He never intended to be on the planet overnight so he didn't pack any. She gave him a disappointed look before insisting they walk into the woods a little further. She said they needed to find a safe place to sleep for the night. Sara led him to one of the largest trees he'd ever seen and went to work carving a hole into the bark with his knife. In no time at all, she had a small hole cut into the tree large enough for a human being to crawl through. He watched her pull some roots out of the inside of the tree and build a fire. Britt found the woman utterly amazing. She apparently had no qualms at all about opening his pack and going through it. He may not have had any clothes but his pack did contain a thin reflective emergency blanket.

Sara handed him the blanket. "Here, take your clothes off."

He raised his eyebrows for a moment but decided to follow her orders. She watched him as he pulled his shirt off and wrung the water out of it. When he handed her the shirt, he noticed her looking at his chest. He put on his best act of irritation and eyed her. "What?"

She laughed. "You're super hairy."

He looked down and frowned before rubbing his hand back and forth over the hair on his chest. "Well… it's super soft though. Wanna feel?"

She laughed again and nodded before shaking her head. "Yeah… but… no."

"The carpet matches the drapes, by the way." He bounced his eyebrows at her.

She smacked him with his own wet shirt and when it hit his chest it made an incredibly loud noise. She laughed hard and then opened the shirt up before flattening it out against the tree. "Watch this."

Britt walked up behind her and looked over her shoulder. The tree seemed to be pulling the water right out of the shirt. She turned it over several times and pressed it up against the tree again. "It won't be one hundred percent dry but it'll be close. The fire can do the rest."

When darkness fell, he found himself looking up at the sky. He found it a little weird that they seemed more impressive from his current perspective. They were somehow brighter and more mysterious than they were from the bridge of his spaceship. He sat next to the fire wrapped up in the thermal blanket and feeling like a useless baked potato while Sara made him another meal. He watched her curiously while she skinned a deep red fruit with the knife when he suddenly remembered that she mentioned her son. It made him feel really bad about himself for flirting with her because as far as he knew, she was also a married woman. At least she was when she left Earth. He had seen pictures of the three of them. Andrew Zeeman was easily the best-looking guy Britt had ever seen. A fact that made him doubt he could ever sway her to his side. He watched her press some sticks through the fruit and held one in the fire. Apparently, the fruit can be eaten raw, but tastes better cooked. He figured he'd trust her judgment on that.

She was right. It tasted like warm cherries to him. It was delicious. He nodded at her. "Thank you for taking care of me."

"I kind of owed you." She knelt down next to his clothes. They were drying on some rocks next to the fire. She put her hand on his shirt to see if it still felt wet. She picked it up and tossed it to him. He caught it in his hand and immediately pulled it on. When his head popped through the hole and he got a look at her again, she seemed upset.

"I'm not an idiot, you know?" she said.

"Of course not." He was obviously confused. "Where's this coming from?"

She cocked her head to the side. "It took seventy thousand workers on three different round the clock shifts nearly a decade to complete my ship and we've only been here two years." She rubbed the end of her nose with her index finger. "And I would have known if other ships were being built."

Britt took a deep breath and held it for a moment as he tried to find the right words. Her eyes never left his face. He was suddenly aware of every move he made, however slight, as if she was trying to read him. He finished pulling on his jeans and then gave her the blanket. The light in his darkened blue eyes danced along with the fire. He was stuck for the moment. He had to tell her something. He stared at the ground before suddenly smiling. "There are several self-proclaimed wormhole-ologists aboard my ship, some of them actual scientists, who insisted that time travel through the wormhole was possible." He gestured toward her. "I never imagined that it could be true."

He watched her face closely when he told her what year he was from. Two hundred years is a long time. Long enough for a planet and its people to destroy themselves. She stopped looking at him about halfway through his story. Instead, she either stared into the fire or looked down at her hands. He wasn't trying to hurt her, but when he explained that most of the people left alive blamed the downfall of man on her, she cried. And he literally couldn't stand it. He folded his arms across his chest and looked out into the dark forest. It was very quiet except for the occasional chirp of a bug.

"Those wormhole-ologists thought that we could go back in time and change things." He looked back at her just in time to see her place something in her mouth. He had seen her take something before but he was becoming concerned. "What the hell was that?"

Sara looked up at him through red teary eyes. "It's just something the doctor gave me for anxiety." She shrugged slightly. "Sorta like a valium."

He didn't know what a valium was but he didn't like the fact that she just did something that he had no control over. He squinted at her. "Why do you have so much anxiety that you need to be medicated?"

She must have been cold because she rubbed her hands together. "What exactly were you going to do?"

He picked up his jacket. It was dry so he held it for her to put on. She grabbed the ends of her own jacket and pushed each arm through the holes and then pulled it around her. He fixed the shoulder for her and then looked her in the eye. "I don't know what you mean."

"How were they going to change the past?" She zipped up the jacket. It was a few sizes too big for her but at least she would be warmer.

Captain Mason knew that the woman was smart enough to figure it out. His butt started hurting from sitting on the hard boulder for too long so he slid himself off of it and down next to her. He tucked the blanket around her legs and then grabbed a stick that he used to play with the fire. One didn't really get the opportunity to play with fire aboard a starship. As a matter of fact, fire was a very very bad thing in that respect. He loved watching it dance about as it sent bright fire fairies toward the night sky.

"Before I met you, I would have ended you without thinking twice if I thought it would change things." He glanced at her and hoped that she would appreciate his honesty. "But the wormhole didn't bring us back far enough to make a difference."

Sara laughed as if he had said the funniest thing she had ever heard. It shocked and confused him and made him wonder what exactly was in those pills she kept taking. She covered her face for a moment and then wiped the tears from her cheeks. "If you only knew."

"If I only knew what?" He raised his eyebrows at her but she just stared blankly at him. "Hey, I was honest with you," he said.

"Were you?" She mimicked his look and sent it back to him. "Let's talk about why a starship captain would use an escape pod to come down to a planet to search for his shuttle. Why would he come himself instead of delegate that to someone else?"

She managed to insult him with the truth. His mouth dropped open for a moment. He wanted to demand that she give him his jacket back but he stopped himself. He nodded in frustration. She had a good point. "There are two very good reasons I came myself." He rubbed his palms back and forth on his pants. "But the most important one is... my grandson was one of the men on the shuttle and I aim to find him."

He could almost see the gears working in her head. She frowned. "How old is your grandson?" She suddenly reconsidered. "Wait... how old are you?"

Britt grinned broadly. "My grandson is twenty-five." He paused to see her reaction. She looked him over closely and shook her head. He continued. "And I'm ninety-two."

"Bullshit."

"Yeah, it's bullshit, alright." He agreed. "It's nothing sinister as you might think. Just a couple of misguided parents that wanted the best for their kid."

The captain gave her a very brief history of the events that occurred after the Moon's Eye colony disappeared. The Gene Wars spand only seven years but it had a lasting effect on the world. Genetic modification proved to be a miracle to millions of people who were unfortunate enough to be born wrong. It was used to cure Cystic Fibrosis and dozens of childhood conditions but it was also used to modify otherwise normal children. Normal children, such as Britt Mason and his unfortunate sister, Monica.

Even though genetically modifying children was illegal, rich people did it all the time. It created an unfair advantage and made it nearly impossible for the poor to get ahead.

Which is how back alley modifications started. The mods didn't take place in literal "back allies" but they might as well have. They were all performed by disgraced doctors or talented but young scientists looking to pay off their student loans and it wasn't as if you had your choice between the two.

His parents meant well. They just wanted the best for their children. They only wanted to level the playing ground. Britt got good looks and longevity and Monica got dead.

He cried the first time he held his own flesh and blood in his arms. He was serving as the first officer aboard the Newman and it was completely unexpected. He was on 'feeling overload' and couldn't stop the tears from falling. He was proud, happy, upset, and ashamed. Upset because he brought a child into a shitty existence and ashamed because he barely knew the mother. She was just one of the many women he slept with just for the fun of it. He was always very careful but this time, one of his little swimmers got through anyway. At first, he didn't believe the child was his but the DNA test proved the truth. The little human in his arms was so tiny that he was afraid he'd break it.

He actually intended to get to know the mother of his child but he never got the chance because she died shortly after giving birth. Her name was Brandi and she was a gorgeous girl who just turned twenty when he effectively ruined her life. That was the sum of the knowledge he knew of her before her funeral. But he vowed to learn everything he could about her from her family and friends so that he could tell Brandon about her when he was old enough to ask.

He didn't raise him on his own though. He was married to another woman when the child was born. She was a thirteen-year-old girl named Ellie and he only married her because her parents disowned her when she became an unwed mother. Things were hard aboard the ship. If there was no one to take care of Ellie and her baby they would both starve. Most of the people who knew him accepted the marriage for what it was, a sexless agreement. But there were some that thought they knew otherwise. Especially since Britt forced Ellie to have a procedure that would make it impossible to get pregnant again. That was part of the agreement. He wasn't going to keep taking care of babies that the child spit out. They agreed to put the boys first which seemed to be enough for them. At least for a while. Britt could bed whoever he wanted and Ellie was like the daughter that he never had.

"After Ellie turned twenty-five, she wanted a divorce." Britt accidentally broke the stick he was playing with so he threw the pieces into the fire.

Sara gave him a half grin. "Why? Let me guess… she fell in love with someone else and wanted to marry him?"

"Yes and no." He rubbed his eyes. He was getting tired. "I may have saw her as a daughter but she never saw me as a father. It got complicated. She tried to seduce me more than once. When she realized that it wasn't going to happen…" He shrugged. "We tried to be friends because of the boys but it was never the same." He took a sip of water from his canteen. "She died when she was only sixty-two." He stared into the fire. "Damn, I miss that girl."

Sara blinked slowly a few times. She was either tired too or the pill she took was starting to take effect. "The poor girl never had a chance."

"Hey, all I wanted to do was help her." He defended himself.

141

"No, that's not what I meant." She folded her arms across her chest. "She was a sexually active teenager who married a good-looking man like you. She probably thought she won the damn lottery." She tilted her head toward him. "She probably thought you'd eventually be a couple but you turned out to have morals." Her words made him smile. She obviously found him attractive and he liked that fact. She stood up slowly and waved to him to join her. "We have to go inside before the piranha come out."

Every time she mentioned the things, it worried him a little bit more. He stood up and followed her inside the tree. It was dark and creepy. There were flowers that seemed to glow in the dark all around and inside the tree. When he looked very closely at one, he saw a translucent spider. He didn't like spiders. There weren't very many species of bugs on the Swagger but spiders managed to survive and thrive.

Sara watched him curiously. "They won't hurt you as long as you leave them alone."

She used some of the dry roots to cover the hole they crawled through before she laid down on the ground. She pulled the reflective blanket over her before letting her head rest against her own arm. He found himself wondering what his next move was supposed to be. Was he supposed to lay down next to her but leave a foot between them? He only knew one thing… it was cold outside. He got down on his hands and knees and crawled up next to her and laid down. He scooted as close as he could to her and tucked the blanket over them both before pulling her close to him and making himself comfortable. He was somehow able to edge her head up underneath his arm and he held her close. She never once objected or pulled away from him so he figured it was okay. Sharing each other's body heat when it was cold was one thing but he wanted to do more. They had talked without really talking. He still didn't know about her family status or if she was free to be with someone. All he really knew was that he was right where he wanted to be. At least for the moment.

Chapter Thirteen

Dean Mason laid in his cot staring at the ceiling. He had been in the brig for a little over twenty-four hours and he was starting to feel claustrophobic. He was a redheaded lad with strong features who took after his grandfather in many ways except for one. He firmly believed that the Swagger should end its journey and land on the green planet below. He was put in the brig because he was caught trying to steal some fruit from the arboretum. Rations were strictly handed out according to rank or status aboard the ship. One would think that since Dean was a Mason, he would get a higher priority but he kept insisting that he was no better than anyone else. It was the topic of many arguments until grandpa Britt told him to prove it. He loved his grandfather very much but he wished that he'd see things his way. People weren't meant to live in space and he aimed to prove it.

He could feel her eyes looking at him but he ignored her. He was too busy trying to plot his next move. Dean knew that Britt would never keep him in the brig, but he was on the planet below looking for James. The sarcasm in his mind seemed to radiate out in all directions when he thought about his twin brother and his grandfather. They were working on something that they didn't want anyone to know about, including him. Whatever it was, it probably wasn't good.

He and his brother James were twenty-five years old and for a pair of twins, they couldn't be more different. When they were children they were like celebrities because twins had never been born on the ship before. It didn't hurt that the two of them took after their grandfather. Their hair was more brown than it was red but their resemblance to Britt was remarkable. Dean and James were inseparable brats

144

that loved to cause trouble. When they grew older, James started to take after his grandfather more and more. They always seemed to have their heads together, talking about the wormhole, and theorizing about time travel. It was all so ridiculous. He didn't care about the wormhole or time travel. All he cared about was Ava and giving her the life that she deserved. He wanted nothing more than to marry her and have dozens of children with her. But he wanted to do it in a place where they could be together without having to worry about the quality of air or if there was enough food to go around.

The two of them had known each other since they were old enough to talk. Dean couldn't quite pinpoint exactly when it was when he fell in love with her but he knew it must have been around the same time. There was never any other person for him. She, on the other hand, dated a few other men before realizing that she loved him too. Unfortunately, the Swagger had a strict policy on children. Perspective parents had to obtain permission to have a child and even if it was granted, the process took longer than normal. Pregnancies were all achieved by artificial insemination in order to choose the best outcome. It had been decades since a child with disabilities had been born. Dean knew that was a good thing but there was something to be said about throwing caution to the wind and just doing it the old-fashioned way.

He let his eyes roll to the side so that he could verify that she was still looking at him. Commander Hayes stared at him with her only working eye. Dean had known her all of his life but still found it hard to look her in the face for more than a few seconds. Someone once told him to focus on her nose instead but he found that just as hard. She was standing just outside the metal door looking at him through the window. He watched her sigh and then frown at him.

"I'm letting you out…" She lifted her hand which disappeared briefly. He knew she was hitting buttons on the keypad. She continued, "but I'm taking away all of your privileges. From now on, the only thing you have access to is your room and the canteen."

Dean swung his legs down and off the cot so that he sat up in one fluid movement. He pretended to be excited. "Oh my gosh! Thanks Auntie Hayes!"

"Don't call me that." She opened the door and then stood to the side. She folded her arms across her chest and watched him as he walked past her. "You may disagree with your grandfather but he's still the Captain of this ship."

He stopped in front of her and grinned so hard that his dimples made an appearance. "Thanks for the reminder."

He left her and the brig behind as he headed for his quarters. It wasn't his first day in the brig and he imagined it wouldn't be the last. He didn't like being stuck in the same clothes without being able to bathe so that's what he intended to do. His little piece of the Swagger was just that… little. When he thought about it in depth, he was certain that the cell he just vacated was bigger. That fact alone was one of the biggest reasons he wanted to leave the Swagger. As he walked through the door he was greeted with the familiar smell of damp and moldy dirt. He rolled his eyes and sighed. Living directly above the hydroponic bays was bound to give him a bad case of wet lung but he had no other options unless he and Ava got married. He wanted to marry her more than anything but not for something as silly as more room. No, he was going to give her the world… literally.

Dean pulled open the drawer that was just beneath his single sized bed and picked out some clean clothes. He officially only had one more outfit before he had to spend a day waiting in line to wash his clothes. It was easily his least favorite thing. He stripped down to his boxers and stepped in front of his sink and grabbed a towel. People in his class were only allowed one shower per week and it wasn't time for his yet so washing off in the sink would have to do. He wet the towel and went to work cleaning his most foul parts until he was satisfied he could be in public without grossing himself or somebody else out. He planned on meeting up with a few friends. It was Tuesday which meant he got to bust out his Dungeons & Dragons Holomat and get lost in fantasy land for a while. That, and discuss a little bit of mutiny.

The holomat was a fucking stroke of genius. He didn't know who invented the damn thing but he thanked God for him every time he used it. He placed the mat under his arm and headed for Oomie's quarters. As far as status, you couldn't get any higher than Oomie. That's why his grandfather married her. As far as Dean was concerned, there shouldn't be different classes aboard a starship but his grandfather always argued a valid point. If no one held a higher status than the other, what would people strive to be? A captain certainly wasn't equal to a deckhand. But the addition of Oomie's people changed things. The Swagger needed supplies that her people could provide, for a price. Not only did they want aboard the ship but they wanted to retain their hold on some of their supplies. This meant they had a controlling interest in who got what.

Oomie was a crass, dirty minded, little old lady who Britt married strictly for the power. Half the ship voted him captain on his own merit and the other half voted for him because of Oomie. Their relationship was one of convenience only. He got to be captain of the Swagger and she got to be the most powerful woman aboard the ship.

147

Dean's grandfather wasn't like a 'normal' grandfather. Even though the man was in his nineties, he looked barely forty. Instead of treating them like his grandkids he often told wildly inappropriate stories about his sexual conquests. He actually liked to brag about that fact that he's had two wives that he never slept with but that didn't stop him from sleeping with hundreds of women aboard the ship. More than a few of those women were Dean's age.

As he walked down the corridor he met up with his best friend, Alister. They were both the same age but Alister was much smaller and was very thin. Even so, he was tougher than he looked. The kid had a heart of gold and would give anyone the shirt off his back if he thought it would help them. Alister's hair was so long that he was often mistaken for a woman. Dean tried to convince him to get it cut several times but Alister insisted that his hair was the only thing that kept him alive. He often joked that he was like Samson. His hair gave him the strength to carry on. He greeted his friend the same way he always did.

He socked him in the arm. "Hey, Alice!"

"Oh, come on!" Alister's hand went to his arm as his mouth dropped open. "I told you not to call me that!"

Alice had a very important job aboard the ship. He was one of the best damn pilots the Swagger had and he singlehandedly saved it after being violently ejected from the wormhole. They made small talk as they walked down the corridor and that's when he saw her. Ava. It seemed like she was walking toward him in slow motion. His heart skipped a beat, or three, as he watched the light rhythmically reflect off of her green hair with each step. Her eyes lit up when she saw him and she smiled broadly. It was still hard for him to believe that she agreed to be his bride.

She lifted her hands and placed them on the sides of his face and gave him a gentle kiss on the lips before smacking him hard on the shoulder. She smirked at him.

"You got out of jail and I wasn't the first person you called?" She turned in one fluid movement and held his arm as they walked.

Dean chuckled. "I thought I'd surprise you!"

Ava rolled her eyes. "Oh, please! With a game of D and D at Oomie's?"

He smiled at her as she talked. She told him and Alister about her day which included getting her hair dyed green again. Ava was completely obsessed with the color because she loved plants. She was always wearing something green which complimented her hair. That day was no different. Her blouse matched her hair perfectly. He never thought about colors or cared about picking one as a favorite but if he had to choose, it would be green. He loved green because she loved green. A love by proxy.

They stopped in front of Oomie's door and he quietly prepared himself for what was to come. He looked at Alister who gave him an excited smile. One never knew what to expect when from Oomie. They stood frozen in their footsteps as they watched the door open to reveal the petite woman in an evening gown that revealed a little too much skin for Dean's comfort. The woman was an old lady when he was born which meant she was bordering on ancient at that very moment. Standing there in front of her, trying really hard not to look at the old woman's cleavage was perhaps the worst moment of his entire life. Her white hair had recently been curled and she had bright red lipstick on.

She eyed all of them, one at a time, and then moved to the side.

"Where's that handsome friend of yours?" She seemed to glide across the floor.

Dean's mind was still in freak-out mode from the old lady cleavage so at first, he didn't know what or who she was talking about. His mouth dropped open for a moment as he concentrated on her words. "You mean Reggie?"

"Who do you think?" She placed her hands on her hips. "Mama wants a sweet piece of caramel."

Dean's stomach lurched and threatened to rise as Alister chuckled somewhere in the background. Reggie wasn't exactly his friend but he was a much-needed associate. He had to admit that Oomie had good taste. If he 'played for the other team' he'd be into Reggie too. The man was a golden Adonis with blue eyes and chiseled good looks. He was also the only person Dean knew who could write a program that would allow them access to some key systems on the ship. He told Oomie that Reggie would be along shortly as he went to work on setting up the board. Dungeons and Dragons was one of the things he looked forward to every week. As much as he loved and cherished the old lady who apparently fancied young black men, he wished they had a more suitable place to play. Every week they'd meet at Oomie's to play and she would find a new and shocking way to make them uncomfortable. But it would only last an hour or so before she would retire for the night and leave them to their very important business.

When Reggie showed up, he surprised everyone in the room by kissing Oomie on the cheek and giving her a hug that lasted far too long for Dean's comfort. His eyes shot open as he made eye contact with Ava who shrugged and shook her head at him. He sat down at the table next to Reggie and slipped his glasses on. "Reggie, what the hell are you doing?"

"What? She's a woman, I'm a man. As long as it's wet, what do I care?" He picked up his tablet and started poking it.

Dean's face twisted in sheer disgust. "Goddamnit Reggie, if you ever say that to me again, I'm gonna kick your ass."

He laughed. "I know you'll try."

Dean wasn't stupid. He knew that Reggie had an ulterior motive of some kind but whatever it was, it wasn't clear yet. He just hoped that whatever his motive was… it was a good one. Alister put the twenty-sided die on the holomat and slid his glasses on. He was the best damn Dungeon Master a bunch of geeks could ask for. The kid was as creative as they come. Dean tried to convince him several times that he should turn some of their adventures into stories that everyone could download and read but poor Alice lacked his enthusiasm. He may have had a talent for storytelling but he didn't like attention. The overall goal of the night was to save a beautiful damsel in distress from being eaten alive by a dragon. Dean's character was a Druid who could draw power from nature. He looked down at the six-inch character that seemed to be alive. It was standing in front of him waiting for instruction. He found it a little bit strange that he actually had feelings for the little guy. After so many adventures together, he had a vested interest in him and only wanted good things for him. As he watched, a green-haired elven princess walked up to him and kissed him on the cheek which caused an instant smile to appear on his face. He looked at Ava out of the corner of his eye and she grinned as her cheeks turned pink. He had seen that look on her face before. It usually meant that she needed a little more attention from him and he intended to give it to her later on that night.

A knock at the door announced the arrival of their fifth player. Kaylee was a brilliant woman who was older than the rest of them, except Oomie. She was in her mid-thirties and seemed to have a thing for Alister who was completely oblivious to that fact. Ava made sure there was an empty seat next to Alister so that Kaylee would have to sit next to him. The two of them made brief eye contact until she visibly got nervous and turned away. She put on her glasses and picked up her tablet. "Let's get this show on the road!"

Oomie held out longer than usual. Two hours after they started playing, she walked up behind Reggie and put her liver-spotted hand on his shoulder. "It's time for me to go to bed."

As she walked away, she let her hand slip to his back and she gently let her fingers run across his it until she ran out of real-estate. Reggie turned and looked at her as she walked away. He winked at Dean. "I'm gonna go tuck her in."

Dean swallowed the vomit that managed to reach the back of his throat. "Good God," he turned and looked first to Alister and then to Ava. "I'll never be able to get that image out of my head."

He didn't want to picture them together but it was kind of hard not to when Oomie's voice penetrated the walls and into his ears. Thankfully, tucking in Oomie didn't take very long. Reggie came out and sat back down at the table as if nothing happened. "She won't bother us for the rest of the night."

Dean tried to hold back but he couldn't help himself. He pointed to Oomie's room. "What in the hell could possibly be worth that?"

"What do you care?" Reggie opened his arms out to the sides. "Do you want my help or not?"

He didn't just want Reggie's help. He needed it. He picked up his tablet and changed the holomat to a schematic of the ship. He couldn't help lowering his voice when he spoke even though he knew they were alone and that Oomie was sleeping. The plan was a fairly simple one. Dean and his friends wanted to land the Swagger on the planet below. The people of the Swagger had been living aboard the ship for the last seventy years because there was no other option. Earth was dead and Mars was overcrowded so the warships became home to thousands upon thousands of people. When the ship made the trip through the wormhole it rocketed through the solar system so fast that they missed the lush green planet on its first pass. Once they found the planet everyone assumed that they found their new home but Captain Mason had other ideas. He told the people that it would be irresponsible to land the Swagger on a planet they knew nothing about.

In truth, at first... Dean agreed. It would have been wholly irresponsible to land the ship without investigating first. But instead of using the shuttle to do just that, Dean found out that he sent James after Uranium. It seemed that the good captain had plans of his own.

"We need your grandad's ring." Reggie stuck out his index finger and placed it through a hologram at the rear of the ship. "Otherwise, this isn't gonna work."

Chapter Fourteen

Martinez stood next to what could only be described as the crash scene of a toy spaceship which apparently included the dead carcass of a bisector drone. The tiny ship sat in the long and deep wound that it made when it hit the ground. The unfortunate bisector must have been hit midflight and lay dead at the head of the ship. He eyed the charred wood of the now extinguished fireplace and noticed a piece of cloth with blood on it. He tried not to jump to conclusions but given the circumstances, it was very hard. He kneeled down next to the fireplace and took a close look at a shoeprint in the sand. It was definitely small enough to be Sara's but further investigation showed that only one set of footprints left the scene. The prints were bigger than the others and managed to tell him three things. Whoever made the prints was human, male, and wore cowboy boots. He looked sidelong at Junior who met his stare. With that one look they exchanged their mutual fear and dread. He looked down at his tablet which revealed that Sara, or at least her comm, was still twenty miles away.

"We should be able to catch up to them by nightfall," he said.

They were all silent but took their cue and headed back to the vehicles when a bisector suddenly stepped out in front of them. Before Martinez even realized it, his weapon was drawn and pointed at the beast. It was massive and towered above them. Its black body was almost reflective and its pinchers were large enough to snap any man in half. Both the creature and Martinez were frozen in some kind of weird science fiction standoff that neither one of them could break free of. It was strange to him. The creature obviously knew that he was holding a weapon that should be feared.

"Psst! Martinez!" Junior whisper shouted at him. "Truce!"

Martinez looked the thing in the face. It was impossible to read. It didn't have a human face or expressions. The round ant-like eyes on its head gave no hints as to what it was thinking. He hated the bisectors more than words could possibly express but he trusted Sara. Against every instinct he had, he lowered his gun. He let arm relax at his side and hoped like hell it wasn't the worst decision he's ever made. The creature slowly turned and walked toward the fallen bisector and stood at its side for a moment before bending over and picking it up. When Martinez realized what was happening it shook him to his core. The 'monster' that he saw in front of him was collecting its dead.

"Fascinating." Mel stepped forward and watched it closely. "I've never really gotten a good look at them before." She pointed at it. "Look, it has humanoid arms under the pincher arms."

The creature seemed to look at him again so Martinez nodded at it. "Sorry for your loss."

He felt weird saying it. He knew the creature couldn't possibly understand what he was saying but he hoped he understood the sentiment. He watched as Tran got on the other bike and made sure the others got in the jeep before starting his up and taking off. At least they were now able to assume that the spaceship in orbit around Sarisart contained humans. Otherwise they were aliens with cowboy footprints. When the thought occurred to him, he shunned it as stupid but the more he thought about it, the more he figured it was possible. After all, he just had an encounter with a giant bug-like lobster-like weird ass creature that apparently, they had a truce with.

If they were on a normal road trip, where an actual road existed, a twenty-mile trip would take less than thirty minutes. But it wasn't a normal road trip, nor were there actual roads. Martinez had to take the lead and carefully navigate the terrain head. They frequently had to stop and move downed trees or plan out an alternate route. It was a very frustrating journey that took so much longer than he expected. So, it shouldn't have surprised him that twelve miles into their trip for the day, the jeep got a flat tire. He took his jacket off and prepared to help Tran fix the damn thing. Not because he was being chivalrous but because he wanted it done quickly. But evidently, he only got in her way. He left her to her work and thought about ditching them again but he knew he couldn't leave his companions alone in the wilderness without protection.

Junior took that opportunity to send the drone out for a test flight. It hovered high above the trees and slowly did a 360-degree turn while Junior watched the handheld monitor. "I see smoke." He glanced over his shoulder to Martinez. "It's probably a campfire."

Martinez walked up to him and yanked the control out of his hand. "Let me see that."

Junior was right. It probably was a campfire. He was suddenly excited. Sara and her new friend stopped for lunch which was going to end up being a lucky blessing. He was mere minutes away from seeing for himself if she was alive or dead. He engaged the controls and flew it toward the smoke as the anticipation built up inside of him. He didn't even seem to notice that Junior was standing an inch away from him looking over his shoulder. As the terrain below went by, it all seemed to blend together, but they still managed to notice when the drone almost slammed into the thick neck of a dinosaur.

"Go back! Go back!" Junior screamed at him.

Martinez shook his head. "Not a chance."

He did think seeing a dinosaur was noteworthy but he wasn't willing to take any detours until he found Sara. When the drone got close to the smoke, he slowed it down. He knew from past experience that the drone was loud when it was running at top speed and he wanted to get a look at what was happening before anyone realized it was there. He lowered the drone down past the treetops and into the forest below where it got considerably darker. It took the video a few moments to adjust and when it did, he could see the campfire.

He felt Junior lean in closer to him and he pointed at the screen. "Is that her?"

Martinez was too focused on the screen to pay him any mind. He continued to lower the drone and inch it forward until he could get a better view.

"Martinez, wait." Junior did something to the screen so quickly that he didn't have time to protest. "Now look."

Junior had zoomed in on the two people sitting next to the campfire. His heart suddenly got warm as he was filled with relief. It was Sara and she was alive! And apparently, very happy. He watched as she belly laughed at something her companion said. She leaned close to a man wearing a cowboy hat. He couldn't quite see the man's face but he knew that he was smiling. She smacked the man on the arm causing Martinez to feel something he had never felt before. He didn't know the man in the cowboy hat but he suddenly wanted to punch him in the face. His heart raced in his chest.

He was grateful that she was alive but he couldn't help feeling like he had lost something.

"Can we talk to her?" Martinez glanced at Junior.

Junior was ecstatic and it showed all over his face. He nodded wildly and motioned for him to give him the controller. "Yeah."

Martinez handed it to him. "Tell her to stay put."

"Ma! Can you hear me?" They both watched as Sara seemed to make eye contact with them. She smiled broadly and touched her friend before pointing at the drone. She clearly said something but they couldn't hear her. Junior fiddled with his controller and then tried again. "Ma! Can you hear me now?"

That's when Martinez heard a familiar whistling sound coming through the trees and he was instantly filled with intense fear. But it wasn't coming from around them, it was coming out of the speakers of the handheld controller. They watched in horror as Sara and her friend looked frantically up at the sky. The video suddenly rocked before it went blank and dread filled his heart. They had found her alive but now she was surely dead.

Junior suddenly put his hand on Martinez' shoulder. "I still hear it!"

He turned around and screamed. "Piranha! Get in the jeep!"

Tran was actively turning a lug nut with the tire iron when she suddenly dropped it and climbed through the side door. Chad and Mel went in right afterward followed closely by Junior. Martinez dove toward the back of the jeep and dug into one of the rucksacks. He quickly pulled free a puff tent when he was hit in the arm by one of the piranhas. He grunted in pain as he looked down at his forearm. It was covered in blood. He stepped to the side and opened the tent quickly as another one flew past him so fast that it hit the back of the jeep with a sudden thud making Tran scream. The stunned creature fell to the ground and flapped wildly. The damn things were a disturbing cross between a bat and a crow. Their beaks were concave which they used to carve out a strip of meat from their prey as they flew at them at top speed. His lip curled up as he looked at the tiny creature before he stomped the life out of it.

"Martinez!" The doctor screamed. "What the fuck are you doing! Get in here!"

The whistling got louder and louder which meant more of them were coming. They hunted in groups and usually killed their pray due to their sheer numbers. The people of the Moon's Eye were protected within the confines of the colony because the lights conveniently emitted a frequency that the bastards didn't like. But out in the wilderness of Sarisart they didn't have the luxury of lights. His puff tent had been altered to look like the colorful leaves of the pseudo trees and acted as a great camouflage. He dove into it and zipped it up tight. Until that moment, he had never had the opportunity to test out the tent's effectiveness, so he prayed that it worked. That definitely wasn't the way he was supposed to die. He listened to the high-pitched whistles as his thoughts turned back to Sara and he again regretted the fact that he wasn't there to protect her. Before Zeeman died, he made him promise that if anything ever happened to him, he would take care of her. But he failed. And he continued to fail. He needed to find her and bring her home.

~ * ~

Captain Britt was wholeheartedly enjoying himself. There was a beautiful woman sitting next to him laughing at all his jokes and it was giving him a natural high. He looked into her eyes long enough to think it might be okay to kiss her but the happiness suddenly drained away from her face and she looked away. It made him focus on the bandage he placed over her neck wound. He leaned forward and gently moved her hair away from it so that he could see it better.

"Let me see?" He said softly.

She tipped her head to the side to give him a better view. He gently peeled up the end of the bandage until he could get a good grip and then slowly pulled it free. The wound was all but healed. He gently ran his thumb over the area before making eye contact with her again. This time, he was the one to look away because he thought he heard something. He looked around trying to find the source of the noise but he couldn't. When he looked back at Sara it was clear that she had heard it too.

"I'd know that sound anywhere." She turned to scan the woods too. "It's Junior's drone."

He watched her for a moment. "Well, then why can't we see it?" Even as he asked the question, he knew the answer. "Oh, that's pretty smart, I guess. You never know what you're walking into. You know what would be funny?" She let her eyes roll to the side as she looked at him and then waited for his answer. "If we were having sex when they found us."

Sara's eyes shot open almost as far as her mouth did. It apparently struck her as hysterical because she laughed so hard that her face turned red. He found it impossible to watch her without laughing too. She leaned in close to him and smacked him on the arm before finally calming down.

"Ma! Can you hear me?"

Both of them looked up just in time to see the drone hover slowly towards them. Sara smiled. "Hi Guys!"

A whistling sound started to penetrate the silence of the woods. Sara grabbed his hand so hard that it hurt him. "It's the sky piranha!"

"Ma! Can you hear me now?" The drone's speakers emitted Junior's voice again.

What happened next was as shocking as it was unexpected. Someone or something grabbed them and they weren't too nice about it. They were dragged into a dark place that smelled like damp dirt and feces. Sara screamed repeatedly and held onto him so tightly he could barely breathe. There was half a dozen of them, maybe more, and he didn't get a good look at any of them. After a moment he felt his feet leave the ground as they were carried upward into nothingness. He felt almost weightless as his legs dangled slightly as their unwilling journey progressed. Every time poor Sara made the slightest noise, they gave her a hard-insistent nudge, which only made it worse. He resolved that whatever was about to happen, he wasn't going to let them take her from him. He wrapped his arms around her tightly and held on for dear life. They were suddenly shoved to the ground where several of the animals laid on top of them. He could tell that the creatures were covered in hair because he could feel it up against one of his arms. Sara was whimpering and trying very hard not to make more noise but it wasn't working. Somewhere in the darkness

161

something growled so low that it seemed to reverberate through him and it scared the living shit out of him.

He needed her to stop so that they wouldn't hurt her. "Shush," he whispered softly.

"I'm so scared," she whimpered.

He felt another nudge against the arm that he had around her. He kissed her forehead lightly. "I know. But you need to be quiet."

One of them punched him in the back just hard enough to intimidate him. It worked. It was so dark that he couldn't see anything but he could still hear the whistling. Britt held her close to him and rubbed her back softly hoping it would help to keep her calm when her whole body suddenly relaxed. He knew that she was unconscious because he could still feel her soft breathing against his neck. He didn't know what the creatures wanted with them but he had the feeling that they wanted them alive. The one thing he did know was that the creatures were not the deadly and fearsome sky piranha that Sara was so worried about. He was actually a little jealous of her. She was unconscious and therefore no longer experiencing the terror of every slow minute that passed by. He kept rubbing her back softly but it wasn't to soothe her anymore, it was to soothe himself.

The darkness coupled with the fact that he eventually calmed down allowed him to temporarily checkout like Sara did. When he woke up, there was sunlight in his eyes. It took him a few minutes for his eyes to adjust but when they did, he was surprised and confused. They were alone inside one of the pseudo trees but this one was different. He seen pictures of nests when he was a kid and if he was a betting man, he'd bet it was a nest. It was made with the roots of the pseudo-tree and a lot of dirt but it was also made with great care. The bottom of the nest was mostly flat and covered with dirt. It was about the size of a small bedroom... if bedrooms were circular on the inside. He looked down at her. She was still unconscious and seemed to be sleeping peacefully.

Britt sat up slowly and turned his head toward the sunlight. It was streaming through a hole large enough to fit a person through. He nudged her shoulder gently. "Sara," he whispered, "Sara, wake up."

He shook her a little harder but she didn't budge. That's when he noticed something next to her shining in the sunlight. He leaned over her and grabbed it. It was the small tin that she kept her medicine in. He opened it and winced immediately. It was empty. He looked around for his pack but he must have lost it in the scuffle. He wanted his tablet so that he could take her pulse but he was forced to do it the old-fashioned way. He held his breath as he felt along the inside of her wrist until he felt a steady beat.

"Thank god," he said softly.

Chapter Fifteen

Junior's broken drone laid against a tree waiting for its master to come rescue it. It wouldn't be long now, after all, the jeep carrying him was speeding along at fifty-five miles an hour and closing in quickly. It had been two hours since the sudden and quite unexpected sky piranha attacked and everyone, even Martinez, was sure Sara was dead. The ugly predators from the sky usually only attacked at night and only when it's warm. So why was that day so different? Junior blamed himself. He watched the motorcycle in front of them swerve to avoid hitting a large rock so the jeep did the same. The sheriff was doing a great job of guiding them.

"It was the god damned drone!" He made a fist and brought it down hard on his thigh. "It was flying just above the treetops. It must have disturbed their sleep!"

Mel twisted the steering wheel again and swerved to avoid another obstacle in their way. "Will you quit the 'boo-hoo, I killed my mommy shit?' I'm trying to fuckin' drive here!"

Junior was overcome with the urge to backhand the bitch in the face but he resisted. He watched the two motorcyclists ahead of them swerve again as they approached a moving mountain. He leaned forward and placed his hand on the dashboard as he looked up. "Dinosaur!" He pointed as he screamed it again. "Look out for the dinosaur!" He was like an excited and scared little child that was being forced to do something dangerous. He watched, wide-eyed, while Martinez and Tran rode their motorcycles underneath the giraffatitian. "No! Are you crazy!"

Mel didn't alter the course at all. The jeep bounced and sped forward as she drove it right under the creature without it even noticing them. He immediately turned around to look out the back window. Chad looked at him with excitement that he could barely contain. He hooted loudly before shouting. "I can't believe that just happened!"

Junior was scared. He was scared for many reasons. First and foremost, he was scared that his mother was dead and that he'd never see her again. He suddenly found himself thinking back to the time when Sara eased his fear of the dark. She did it by using logic. She explained that there was a reason for everything, including the darkness. The darkness signals the human body to relax and prepare for sleep. And, of course conversely, sunlight signals the body to wake for the day. The problem with using logic on a six-year-old genius was that they typically know more than you think. Darkness was also the time that some animals and insects come out. Insects, such as cockroaches. He hated them. It didn't help that he had seen a video showing the extraction of one of the little bastards from someone's ear.

His own father found his fear annoying. He knew Travis O'Malley Sr. loved him but he wasn't equipped to be the kind of father that Junior needed. When Junior spelled out his fear for Sara, instead of treating him like he was a stupid little kid, she gave him a pair of ear muffs. It was just a stupid pair of ear muffs but it fixed the problem. He was able to sleep and his father didn't have to listen to him crying all night long. Sara may not have been his mother but she was the only person who acted like a mother should.

He looked out the windshield and watched the two motorcycles stopped next to one of the pseudo trees. Martinez quickly got off his bike and threw his helmet to the ground before making a beeline to the jeep. He looked the sheriff in the eye knowing exactly what he was after. He got out of the jeep and handed the locator to him.

165

He knew Martinez never liked him but the sheriff managed to gain some of his respect when Sara disappeared. He could see how much he cared about her because it was written all over his face. The man was desperate to find her and he couldn't blame him. She was easily the best person he had ever known. He had known Martinez for as long as he could remember and was raised to refer to him as Uncle Marty. He usually only saw him on holidays or special occasions and all he knew about the man was that he was Andrew's best friend. Over the last year, Martinez stepped in and helped out whenever he could. During that time, it became clear to Junior that the self-proclaimed ex-mercenary was in love with his mother. It left a bad taste in his mouth. Not because he thought Martinez was a bad guy. Not because he thought that he wasn't good enough for her. It was because he had to wonder exactly how long the man had been in love with his best friend's wife.

He watched Martinez follow the beacon on the tablet until he found the downed drone next to another tree. That's where they found Sara's comm and a backpack. They searched the surrounding area thoroughly but couldn't find any more signs of Sara or the mysterious man. Mel kneeled down next to the backpack to look inside and found a cowboy hat underneath it. She picked it up for a second and then dropped it on the ground next to her. If Junior didn't know any better, he would think that she was as upset as the rest of them.

He squinted and looked up at the sun through the trees. It would be dark in a few hours and it would be better for everyone if they found them before then. He watched Martinez cup his hands together over his mouth and prepare to belt out her name as loud as he could.

"SARA!" He listened carefully for a moment and then did it again. "SARA! WHERE ARE YOU?"

He walked over to his drone and examined it. Thankfully the damage wasn't too bad. He tipped it up on its side and looked it over carefully. One of the propellers was broken. He needed to fix the drone if they had any hope of finding his mother. He grabbed his toolbox from the jeep and quickly removed the drones broken wing. It was easy to fix and only took a few minutes. While he worked, he could hear Martinez calling out to Sara without any response. He picked up the drone's controller and hoped beyond all hope that when he hit the start button, it would fly. A still frame picture of Sara and her new friend was on the digital screen. He played it hoping that it would give him some clues. It was clear to him that Sara liked the man. They were sitting fairly close together and were laughing at something. Then the scene suddenly changed.

It was like watching a horror flick starring someone you knew and loved. Seeing the fear on her face was almost too much for him to handle and hearing her scream… was even worse. The video suddenly darkened and bounced around so badly that it was impossible to see what was going on but it definitely seemed like something attacked them. He tried to shake the thought he was having out of his head and started up the drone. Seeing it rise up off the ground made him happy. He walked behind it as it floated through the woods. Martinez yelled for her again.

"Sara!" The sheriff held a 3D printed shotgun across his chest. He was ever prepared for anything. Junior had no doubts that Martinez would find her. He called out to her again. "Sara! If you're out there, please say something!"

"Here!" A man's voice called out to them. "We're up here!"

167

It came from about twenty feet away and up high. Everyone hurried toward the pseudo-tree and stopped in front of it. It was massive and easily the largest he had ever seen. Everyone looked up expecting to see something, anything.

Martinez called out again. "Hello?"

A few stories up a man's head and upper body popped out of the trunk of the tree. "Hey! We're up here!" He waved his hand toward himself as if he was pulling them to him. "We need some help!"

"Well, this doesn't feel like a trap at all," Martinez said sarcastically.

Mel walked up to Junior and pointed at the drone. "I weigh a hundred and five pounds on a bad day. Can that thing carry me up there?"

He looked at the drone for a moment before answering. "Yeah, it can hold you long enough to get you up there."

She nodded and then walked up to Martinez and held out her hand. "Gimme your Glock."

He looked at her like she was crazy. He definitely didn't want to give it to her.

She snapped her fingers. "Come on, we don't have all day."

Martinez reached behind him and pulled the gun out of the back of his pants then gave it to her. "Do not kill anyone."

Mel took the gun and hid it in her jacket before positioning herself below the drone. Junior pointed at it. "Hold it here, and here." He looked her in the eye. "No sudden movements or it will crash. You must remain perfectly still, understand?"

She nodded. "I got it, mama's boy. Let's get on with it."

She put her hands up and grabbed the drone tightly while Junior prepared to overload the engines without killing her in the process. "Push off slowly."

Mel bent her knees a little and then pushed up fluidly with a small hop that seemed to carry her upward like she was a superhero taking flight. The propellers were taxed to the point that they whined and threatened to quit. They carried her up alongside of the tree until she reached the opening where she could see the man waiting. She looked down past her feet at the ground and estimated that she was around thirty feet off the ground. Just when the drone seemed like it would crap out, she let go and landed awkwardly on the canopy of leaves that surround the tree. One of her feet fell between the thick roots and as she pulled it back up, her shoe fell off. She watched it fall the thirty feet to the ground and then rolled her eyes at her own bad luck.

"Shit."

She wanted to take a moment to appreciate where she was and examine the rare yellow orchid that caught her eye but she was on a mission. She pulled the gun out of her jacket and pointed it at the dark opening in the tree. Mel didn't see any signs of the man or Sara so she cautiously approached it. The gun in her hand coupled with the fact that she was creeping toward possible danger made her feel like a badass. Her heart wildly thumped in her chest as she got closer. It amused her that she couldn't quite decide if she was scared or having fun but either way, she intended to save Sara. The clues so far had been few and far between but they did reveal the likelihood that there was only one foe so she liked her odds. She smiled inwardly because she knew that Martinez was on pins and needles waiting for an update. Well, he will just have to wait.

She stood next to the opening and pointed the gun inside as her eyes tried to focus on anything. It was impossible. The sun was shining at her back and the interior was dark so she couldn't see a thing.

"It's okay," a man's voice said, "you can come inside. I'm not gonna hurt anyone."

She lifted one leg through the opening and slowly stepped through. "Put your hands where I can see them!"

It took her eyes a minute to adjust to the darkness but eventually she was able to see the man standing against the far wall with his hands up. She pointed the gun at him while she assessed the situation. As far as men went, she supposed he was good looking. His hair was curly and about shoulder length. It was dark so she didn't know what color it was but she suspected it was red. That was when she noticed Sara laying on ground in the center of the tree. She eyed her closely. She wasn't moving.

"Don't move." She glanced at him and then knelt down next to Sara to feel her pulse.

"She's alive." His voice was low. "You a doctor?"

Her eyes rolled upward and looked him in the face. "No."

He grimaced. "Do you have one with you?"

When she stood up, she got a look at the room that they were in. There was a hole in the floor a few feet from where the man was standing. She pressed the button on the comm that was hanging from a string around her neck. "Martinez, there must be a way to climb up from inside the tree. Look for an opening."

She knew what would come next and she was right. His voice came out of the speakers of the comm. "Is Sara alright?"

A little voice inside her head told her to be gentle but "she's alive" was all she could manage.

Mel had no doubt that Martinez would move hell and high water to get to Sara which meant she didn't have much time alone with the stranger. "What happened?"

He said his name was Captain Mason and that it was his starship that was in orbit around the planet. If she hadn't already known about the spaceship, she may not have believed him, because it sounded unbelievable. But what he said next was even more ridiculous. He said that he plucked Sara out of the hands of the bisector queen, which was very odd indeed. Odd because she had no idea the bisectors even had a queen. She had to assume that was when Sara was able to negotiate a truce with the giant bugs but it was still weird. Unfortunately, Britt didn't have enough time to go into more detail because Martinez and the doctor climbed through the opening in the floor. She spent most of her life observing people and trying to figure out what made her different from them. She would watch them and try to predict what move they would make next and she got pretty good at it. Mel thought she had Martinez pegged. She thought she would be able to predict his next move and she fully expected him to climb through that hole and beat the

171

hell out of poor Britt while she watched with excitement. But he disappointed the shit out of her by going straight to Sara's side.

Mel watched him carefully. He showed no signs of anger at all. His eyes were wide with worry as he picked up her hand and held it. He didn't even look at the man or acknowledge him. "What happened?"

Britt gestured to Martinez. "Are you the doctor?"

Dr. Bowman glanced up at him as he picked Sara's hand up and pressed a medical USB up against her finger firmly. "No, I am." The doctor inserted the USB into his tablet and frowned as he read the results. "Her kidney function is very concerning and her red cell count is pretty low." He made eye contact with the stranger. "What happened?"

Britt looked uncomfortable. He looked away for a moment and then placed his hand inside his jacket pocket and pulled out a small tin. Mel noted the recognition on the doctor's face and then watched the man put the tin back in his pocket. Dr. Bowman looked back down at Sara. "Oh."

Martinez looked up but it was too late to see the exchange. "What?"

The doctor looked uncomfortable and then shrugged slightly. "Nothing, she's going to be okay."

While the doctor worked, the man explained how they got inside the tree. Mel found the story very intriguing. He said that even though he had been inside the bisector's nest and witnessed the queen's interrogation of Sara, the experience was nothing in comparison to what happened to them a few hours prior. He said that Sara was so scared that she passed out… which was obviously a lie based on the exchange she witnessed between the man and the doctor. The sky piranha were terrifying but they were very predictable. They usually hunted in groups at sunset. The birds could smell blood from a mile away. This meant that if they shed blood from an animal somewhere, they may smell it the next day and return. She suspected that whatever it was that abducted Sara and Britt knew that too.

Mel reasoned they must be primates of some kind. She had explored much of the surrounding area of the colony but she had never seen any signs of intelligent life until now. She put the gun back in her jacket and discovered the box of chalk she had in there. She always traveled with a box so that she could mark her path. She looked at it and thought for a moment while she watched Junior and Tran climb up through the hole.

"Ma?" Junior crawled over to Sara. "Ma? What's wrong with her?"

"Don't worry, she's going to be fine." Dr. Bowman stuck a capped syringe in his mouth while he prepared her arm for a shot. He bit down on the cap and then freed the needle from the cap before burying it in her arm and pressing the plunger. He spit the cap next to him and then activated the safety on the needle before letting it go. He rubbed her arm a little and watched her. "Give her a minute."

Mel turned to the interior of the tree and began to draw a bird with her chalk. She liked Sara but she found it irritating that everyone else did too. The woman was just as flawed as she was yet no one seemed to like her. She finished her bird and moved onto a sun and then a flower. It may have seemed like an odd time to doodle but Mel's intentions were pure. Sort of. If the inhabitants of the tree really were primates, the pictures were sure to confuse the shit out of them. But she hoped they would like them too.

Junior's voice came from behind her. "She's waking up."

Chapter Sixteen

She woke up terrified. It was almost as if someone had hit pause during her torment and now it was active again. Someone or something was touching her which made her remember the hairy creatures that grabbed her and her friend. She opened her eyes to a dark room but she was too afraid to think straight. She was laying on her back and felt very heavy as if she couldn't move but she knew someone was holding her hand. Her heart was beating so fast that she felt dizzy and was afraid that she may pass out again. She blinked a few times trying to clear her vision but it didn't seem to help. When someone touched her shoulder, she panicked. In her foggy mind she was being attacked so she fought back. She slapped at whoever it was and screamed.

They tried to hold her still. She knew who it was, yet she didn't. "Sara, it's me, Martinez!"

Those words didn't make the situation better for her. If anything, they made it worse. Before she passed out, she was experiencing the most terrifying moment of her life which made her do something stupid. She was at the mercy of some violent animals and she didn't know what was about to happen but she knew her only escape would be drug induced. There really wasn't much thought involved. It seemed logical, so she did it. Her eyes looked up at the center of the tree and she thought she saw something move.

"Cake!" Someone grabbed her and tried to hold her still. "Cake! I want cake!"

"Why the hell is she talking about cake?" Martinez looked around at everyone and only received shrugs in return. She tried to get up but he held her tight. "What the hell's going on?"

Sara was suddenly desperate. She kneed Martinez in the side so hard that he let her go. She got up and rushed over to Britt. He placed his arms on her shoulders and tried to calm her down. "It's okay, Little Lady. Your friends are here to help."

She put her hands on his chest and looked up at him. "We have to leave." She begged him. "Please, get me out of here, we have to leave!"

"Behold, our savior," Tran said sarcastically.

"Shut the fuck up!" Junior yelled at her.

Sara was beginning to recognize the people around her but when Junior yelled, it only managed to set her off more. "Please, Cake! Please! We need to leave!"

Martinez walked up to her slowly. "Sara, it's okay. We're here to bring you home."

She responded by leaning against Britt. She eyed Martinez sharply. "I'm not going anywhere with you."

He was definitely wounded but in her state of mind she couldn't feel badly for it. Mel closed her box of chalk and placed it carefully on the ground directly below her artwork. "She's right. We need to leave immediately."

"Why?" Tran asked.

"Because the original owners of this nest left them alone so that they would leave." She gestured to all of them. "But instead, more of the weird smelling humans came."

Britt rubbed Sara's back. "I agree. If we're still here when they return, it's not going to be good."

Mel smiled and then laughed. "They're way closer than you think."

She pointed upward which made everyone look too. Fear started to penetrate every cell in her body as she looked up and watched as the shadows above seemed to move. Sara gripped Britt's hand and pulled him toward the hole in the floor. Martinez quickly blocked their exit. "Wait," he put up his hands, "the climb wasn't that easy." He looked at Britt and then Sara. "Let me go first and we'll both help you."

He climbed down into the hole to the first cluster of roots and then held his hand out to her. At first, she was hesitant. She looked at Britt who nodded at her so they walked forward and he held one of her hands while Martinez prepared to help her down. Getting all the way down was slow and somewhat problematic. In several places, the next step down was farther away than the others. Of course, that would mean she had to let Martinez hold her in his arms while he carried her down. She hated to admit it but she liked being in his arms again and that mere fact made her angry. When they reached the ground, Martinez led them to the opening that would get them outside. There was a lot of roots that he had to move to the side and hold out of the way for her. She bent down and stepped outside as the sunlight threatened to blind her. Once she was outside, she was finally able to breathe. She walked forward away from the tree.

Sara wanted to be away from the monsters so she kept walking. When Martinez and the others met up outside the tree, the doctor convinced them to let him speak to her alone. He had to jog in order to catch up to her. "Sara, will you stop? Just stop for a minute." He grabbed her arm and turned her around. "Talk to me."

She pushed him away from her. "Why? Huh? Why would I do that?"

He pulled her tin out of his pocket. "I got this from your friend, Britt." He glanced back at the group. "Don't worry. He didn't say anything to any of them."

Sara laughed. "Like that matters. They all know."

"Why is this empty?" He held it so she could see it.

She looked down at the ground as a tear rolled down her face. "Did you bring more?"

"Sara."

"Look, lecture me about drug abuse later." She stepped closer to him and looked him in the eye. "Right now, I need more."

"I'm worried about you."

She rubbed her eye and nodded. "You should be."

The doctor put his hand on her shoulder. "Look, I know you've been having a hard time but there are people who care about you." He looked past her at the group behind her. He chuckled. "And most of them are right there."

Sara scrutinized his face closely. "Who gave you that black eye?"

He grimaced and absentmindedly ran his finger lightly under his eye. "Martinez."

"Why?"

Chad scratched at the back of his neck. "Because I deserved it." He needed to change the subject and it showed. "Drew is worried sick about you."

Sara turned around and looked at them and for the first time noticed that Junior was with them. "If Martinez and Junior are both here, who the hell is taking care of him?"

"Is that all you have to say? Sara, what the hell is wrong with you?"

She pointed at him. "You are!" She pointed at Martinez. "He is!" She pointed at Mel. "She is!" She pushed him. "Now, do you fucking have more orange or do I have to go find some for myself?"

"Jesus Christ, Sara." Chad stared at her in disbelief for so long it became uncomfortable.

She looked away for a moment and then back. Tears started to fall freely and she was having trouble keeping a straight face. "I was taking them as prescribed, I swear." She sniffed. "But I was so scared. You don't know what I've been through."

He looked back at the group again, specifically... at Britt. "Explain it to me then." He looked down at her and nodded. "And I'll give you more."

It wasn't something that she particularly wanted to do but it seemed like a fair trade considering the alternative. "Fine."

179

She folded her arms across her chest. "But I want to get away from here as soon as possible."

She looked back at the group and watched Martinez take Britt's gun from him. Anger filled her veins as she stomped toward them but the doctor got in her way and put his hand up. "This isn't something that you can get out of, Sara." He pointed at the group. "Me first, then that."

Sara knew that she would have to tell them what happened at some point but she didn't think it would be so difficult. She made eye contact with Britt and suddenly became fearful about the things that he might be telling them. He grinned and then winked at her. A gesture that didn't go unnoticed by Martinez. He turned his head and looked at her too. She could feel the doctor's eyes on her, waiting for her to speak. She swallowed hard. "I hate you."

She was true to her word. She explained everything in painstaking detail and was very clear on the points that she felt were 'doctor-patient confidentiality' but Dr. Bowman didn't agree. In his opinion, her current predicament was everyone's concern. The possibility of being infected with some kind of plague changed everything. At least she didn't have to worry about Martinez dragging her back to the colony by force. She sat in front of the doctor and let him examine her but she wasn't being a good patient. She didn't want any of them there, especially Junior. If she had the ability to tell them not to come after her, she would have. Now they were all in danger and it was very possible that her son Drew would grow up without them.

Chad placed her palm on his tablet and checked her vitals. "Your blood pressure is okay but your pulse is a little high." He glanced at Britt. "Are you sure we can trust this guy?"

She looked at Britt who was chatting with the machine expert. He seemed to be looking at Tran the exact same way that he looked at her. It must have been his natural talent. To look at someone like they were important and special. She watched Tran blush and wondered what he said to her.

"Sara?" The doctor was waiting for his answer.

She sighed. "I have no reason not to. He saved my life."

"And managed to doom you and everyone else at the same time." He reached into his bag and pulled out her pillbox and handed it to her. "Don't make me regret this."

Martinez joined them and made it a point to look over his shoulder at Britt before saying, "I don't trust him." When he turned back, his faced changed to concern. "How are you doing? Are you okay?"

He tried to touch her but she blocked him with her arm. "I'm fine," she said curtly.

He glanced at the doctor and then back to her. "Can we talk?"

Sara stared through him with her piercing blue eyes. "No."

He was taken off guard by her answer. "Sara, please."

"I said, no!" she growled.

Martinez looked at the doctor and then nodded before walking away. Chad looked at her sympathetically. "What's going on between you two?"

"None of your goddamned business." Sara said it through gritted teeth. She wanted one of her pills but she didn't want to take one in front of him. She began searching her mind for a feasible reason to step away and be alone. She only had two options. She relaxed her face and tipped her head to the side. "I don't suppose someone brought me some clothes? I've been in these for three days."

As it turned out, someone did think to bring her some clothes. It was the one person in the group that probably cared about her more than anyone else did. Junior. He packed her a bag with everything she would need... including feminine products. Thank god that it wasn't that time of the month but she still appreciated the thought. She put the bag on the ground and hugged him tight. "Thanks for comin' to get me, kid." She loved Junior like a son and she was very proud of him but she wished he stayed at home. Drew was going to need someone who cared about him as much as she did to raise him. But unfortunately, everyone he considered family was with her. "I love you."

"I love you too, ma." He rubbed her back as he hugged her.

She couldn't see his face but she knew he was crying. Sometimes she forgot that he was only a twelve-year-old boy who needed a mother. "It's gonna be okay, Junior." She cried too. "It's gonna be okay. I promise."

The sun was setting but it would still be an hour or so before it was dark. Mel had informed her that there was a hot spring about a hundred yards to the east so she headed that way. It was good to be alone but it was also incredibly terrifying. She was learning that Sarisart was a much scarier place than she thought it was. The sky piranha weren't likely to attack again that day because it was getting cold. She took out her pillbox and fished one out. She placed it under her tongue as she counted the others. The doctor had only given her eight berries. She grimaced hard and put the box back in her pocket. If she wanted or needed more pills she was at his mercy. When she gave the problem some thought, she wondered if the number of pills she had really mattered. She apparently only had about three more days to live, if that. That's when she knew for certain that she was addicted because she became anxious. Not because she may die in three days but because on that third day... she'd have no orange.

She could tell she was getting closer to the hot spring because she could feel the change in humidity and smell the water. There were a lot of boulders in her path that she either had to climb over or around until she could see the steam from the spring. When she was finally able to see it, she was surprised. Captain Britt was sitting in the water with his arms out to the sides as if he were sitting in a hot tub at a spa. He looked incredibly relaxed with his head laying back against a boulder with some moss on it and his eyes were closed. Her eyebrows went up a little when she saw his clothes and noted the fact that his boxers were folded nicely on his jeans. A small fire burned a few feet away making crackling sounds and sending sparks into the sky. It was something she planned to do once she arrived because it would be cold when she got out of the spring. His red hair was wet which made it look black and the hair on his chest was matted flat. She tried like hell to see lower but the water obstructed her view. She cleared her throat loudly. Britt opened his eyes and looked at her. She tried really hard to keep a straight face but she couldn't help smiling.

"Well hey there, Sunshine." He smiled back at her.

She put her bag down on the ground and started to take out the things she needed. "Martinez just let you walk away from camp?"

He chuckled. "That one is a bit intense, isn't he?"

She couldn't resist asking, "are you naked?"

"Uh yep, that I am." He laughed again. "How else do you take a bath?" He watched her for a moment as she pulled her hair back neatly on her head. He suddenly got serious. "I haven't been submerged in hot water since I was five years old."

"Wow." She stood up and slipped off her shoes. "For you, that's a really long time."

He looked at her funny. "Was that a joke about my age? Cause you're not exactly a spring chicken, ya know?"

She took off her jacket and hung it on a nearby branch of a tree. She smirked. "No one says that anymore, old man."

Sara had no intentions of bathing with the man naked. It wasn't proper. At least that was what the little voice inside her head kept saying. She put her thumbs inside her pants at her hips and prepared to pull them down and then paused to glance at him. Just looking at him was enough to make him look away so she continued to undress. Her underwear were a faded pink from being old and washed too much but they would be a sufficient barrier for wandering eyes. She pulled her shirt off and was privately glad that she switched from wearing traditional bras to sports bras years ago because they weren't sexy at all.

Britt frowned at her. "No fair." He nodded at her. "Be careful. The rocks are slippery."

She sat down at the edge and put her feet in first before easing herself into the hot water. Once she was in up to her waist, she bent her knees and let herself sink in up to her neck. "Oh my god, it feels so good." She groaned with pleasure.

Britt cleared his throat. "If you keep making noises like that it's going to be a bit uncomfortable for you when I have to get out."

She ignored him and hummed softly. She was in heaven. When she was on Earth, taking a hot bath was her favorite way to relax after a long hard day. She scooped some of the water up into her hands and brought it up to her face. "I think I'm going build a house right here just so I can do this every night."

He laughed. "I'm right there with ya, my friend." He gave her a devious grin and then a wink. "We can share a room."

They enjoyed the hot soak in silence while they listened to the birds happily tweeting in the trees before darkness fell. Sara watched the fire dance as she thought about what she was going to say to her son when she called him later. She needed to find the right words to say to him and make them good just in case it was the last time she'd ever speak to him. She felt responsible for Andrew's death because he followed her to Sarisart. But she had no control over the fact that she was abducted by giant bugs. Nor did she have control over how she was saved with tainted blood. She was going to leave her son without parents and she had no control over it. She stared at the fire as if she were hypnotized when she finally remembered that she was expecting a child. A child was going to be born that was half her and she was never going to meet it or hold it in her arms. She found herself wondering who the father was and what the child would look like. She always wanted a little girl.

Britt must have sensed her sadness and attempted to fill the silence. "Can I ask you a question?" She looked at him and waited so he continued. "When are we gonna do the nasty?"

Sara shook her head. "Britt! You need to stop saying stuff like that!"

He moved so that he was standing in front of her. "Why?" He put his hand on her neck and then ran his thumb along the side of her cheek. "I can see the 'want to' in your eyes, Little Lady."

He smiled so hard that his dimples made an appearance and then he turned around to get out of the spring. He wasn't bashful at all. She watched, wide-eyed, as his naked butt rose out of the water in front of her. As far as naked butts go, it was pretty nice. His legs were fairly muscular and just as hairy as his chest. She felt hot. She wasn't sure if it was because she was sitting in a hot tub or if she was turned on by his nakedness but... she felt hot.

"Woo! What do we have here?" Both Britt and Sara turned to find Mel standing there with a huge smile on her face. She opened her arms. "This... is... awesome." She turned around and left as fast as she came in.

Sara looked after her. "Shit."

Chapter Seventeen

Dr. Bowman was gathering more wood for the fire as he thought about Sara and the first time they met. He applied for the opportunity to be part of her crew and it had been months since he had heard anything at all so he believed he was out of the running. He was working as a general practitioner at a local hospital in Southern California even though his discipline was genetics. He only put in twenty-five hours a week at the hospital, the rest of his time was spent on genetic research and designer drugs. He believed that drugs should be designed for the individual, not the masses. Most people were aware that drugs had side effects that only affected certain people but what they didn't know was why. Not everyone was created equal. Some people have mutations that make it difficult or impossible for their bodies to process medicines properly. Instead, it builds up in their system to toxic levels and makes them sick, or worse, kills them.

He was a reading file of a young woman whose genetic profile was something of an anomaly. Normal human beings have twenty-three pairs of chromosomes and having more or less was usually a very bad thing. His new patient was the very definition of a mutant. She had twenty-seven complete pairs of chromosomes which was as amazing as it was bullshit. He was instantly convinced that someone was trying to pull one over on him. But the puzzle was still irresistible. Extra chromosomes usually resulted in severe mental retardation but this person was a normal functioning human being. Perhaps the most interesting part of the file was the fact that she was able to have a child. The mystery occupied his brain for several weeks before their first meeting. He needed to know how and why this came about. Was this individual born this way or was genetic modification involved? And if so, did the modification come before or after the birth of her child?

The four extra pairs of chromosomes were not simply duplication but something he had never seen before. He literally became obsessed with finding out more. He wanted to meet the person responsible for such an amazing feat. S. Newman was the only thing he had to go on. It was also a military file with a lot of redacted information. He needed some of her blood so that he could study it further which meant he had to contact the person who sent him the file. Shortly afterward, he was abducted by men in black who wouldn't answer any direct questions. It was literally the scariest day of his life.

When he thought about it now, the fear he felt that day was nothing compared to the kind he felt later. Since landing on Sarisart there were several 'scariest days' that he could think of that contained maximum levels of terror... all of which he didn't want to repeat. He sighed as he picked up another stick. He still wouldn't change a thing. He loved Sarisart. There was no way he'd ever leave the planet permanently. Not even to go back to Earth.

When he finally met Sara, he was struck dumb and couldn't string an intelligent sentence together. It was like meeting a movie star that you've thought about every night for the last several years. He knew everything about her and her Moon's Eye Colony project. That's why he wanted to be a part of it. Back then, she couldn't say or do anything that would make him think any less of her. Her opinion meant something to him. He respected her more than anyone on the planet. He frowned and shook his head. He wished he knew how to help her. Every time he thought she was making progress something would happen and she'd have a setback. In his own misguided way, he believed that a new baby in her life would be good for her. He had made a serious mistake and he regretted it. But it wasn't as if he could take it back. She already hated him for what he had done so he definitely wasn't looking forward to telling her who the father of her child was.

He took a step into the clearing of their camp and was immediately greeted with a knife flying at his head. It stuck blade first into the tree a few inches away from his face. His heart jumped into his throat as he turned to look at it and then trace it back to its source. Martinez walked toward him making serious eye contact with him before grabbing the knife and pulling out of the trunk.

"You okay, Martinez?" Chad put the sticks down on the ground.

He walked a few paces from the tree and then turned around. He pointed the blade at the tree for a moment before letting it fly. It struck and stuck into the tree in the exact spot that it had before. He looked at the doctor. "I don't understand what the hell's happening."

"What do you mean?"

"She's only known him for a few days and now they seem inseparable." Martinez walked to the tree to retrieve his blade.

Chad smiled. If he wasn't sure how the sheriff felt about Sara before, he was now. "Traumatic events often bonds people together." He stacked the sticks into a little teepee and prepared to light them. "Sometimes it more intimate than sex."

Martinez pointed the knife at him. "You do realize I'm holding a knife, right?"

The doctor suddenly remembered Sara's behavior toward Martinez. "What did you do to her?"

He threw the knife again. "Forget I said anything."

Dr. Bowman took his lighter out of his pocket and lit some of the dry leaves he placed in the fire pit and watched it spread. "Fine by me."

Martinez sat on a big rock next to the fire and looked at the doctor. "What are you going to do?"

"About what?" He rubbed his hands together and held them close to the fire to warm them.

The sheriff looked around the camp and lowered his voice. "Your wife."

"Oh." Chad picked up a stick and poked the fire with it. "Nothing."

"Nothing?"

"Does that surprise you?" He placed a larger piece of wood on the fire to build it up higher. "Marriage is hard. You don't just give up on someone when they make a mistake. I love my wife and I know she loves me. Mel... is of no consequence." He poked at the fire again. "Besides, it's not as if there's enough women to go around." He laughed.

Martinez smirked and nodded slightly. "That may change soon."

Chad thought about that for a moment. None of them knew what Captain Britt's intentions were but the sheriff was right. The introduction of his crew opened up a lot more possibilities for the colonists. From what Sara told him, Britt's ship had thousands of people aboard. Apparently, he planned to bring her to his ship for treatment before she succumbed to the virus that was currently trying to kill her. But he had to wonder if that was even possible. Sara wasn't a normal. For all he knew, her genetic abnormalities might give her the ability to fight the virus on her own. He didn't think it was a good idea to let Britt take her aboard his ship but they also couldn't risk bringing her back to the colony. He was her doctor, which meant he had to do what was best for both her, and the colony. Which meant he intended to go with Sara to his ship.

Mel suddenly walked into the clearing and stood in front of Martinez until he looked up at her. The doctor had never seen her look happier. She opened her arms and said, "Hey Murder, you'll never guess what Suicide is doing!"

Chad's mouth dropped open as he looked from Mel to Martinez and then back. "Whatever you're up to, let's not, okay?"

She smiled wildly and shouted, "Cake! She's having some Cake!" She could barely contain herself. She busted out laughing so hard she bent over and held her stomach. "Oh my god! I'm gonna die!"

The doctor watched Martinez and wondered if he was going to live up to Mel's pet name for him when the man suddenly got to his feet and stomped away. Witnessing his angry departure only made her laugh harder. Chad shook his head in disgust. He was a doctor so he understood the fact that she was technically mentally disabled but there was no

191

excuse for her behavior. He walked up to her and said the worst thing he think of. "Your mother should have aborted you."

It was literally the worst thing he had ever said to anyone in his entire life but it didn't seem to faze her. If anything, it made her happier. He looked in the direction that Martinez fled and wondered if he should go after him but decided against it.

It wasn't long before Junior appeared carrying several rodents that he had caught for them to eat. They went to work preparing dinner for everyone when suddenly they heard a god-awful yell followed by the sound of something falling, rolling, and hitting other things. Everyone turned to look in the direction of the commotion and the doctor got to his feet when Tran appeared waving her hands at them.

"Martinez has got issues." She was wide-eyed and nodded with the 'believe me' look on her face. "You don't want to go that way."

The doctor sat back down. "What a fun day."

It was almost dark when Sara and her friend came back into the camp. She looked a lot better than she did just an hour prior. She was dressed in some stone washed jeans and burgundy t-shirt and her hair looked neat and combed. Her cheeks actually had some color in them and she looked good. It certainly seemed like she may have had sex because she also looked a little guilty. And of course, as if on cue, another one of Martinez' half-growls half-yells scared everyone in the camp.

Sara looked at Junior. "What the hell was that?"

Junior pointed toward the noise. "Martinez."

Sara looked passed them all into the woods. She walked up to her godson and held out her hand. "Can I borrow your flashlight?"

Without even saying a word, he handed it to her. Despite the fact that Tran warned her not to, Sara set off to find Martinez. It was dark and she was a little afraid of being alone but she had to find him. She heard him groan loudly as something rolled and fell down what she assumed was a hillside. She assumed wrong. Even though she had a flashlight she nearly stepped off the side of a cliff. She stood at the edge and looked both ways before turning just in time to witness him hurl a boulder the size of a basketball off the side of the cliff. It hit several rocks below and rolled down the side of the cliff until she couldn't hear it anymore. She carefully made her way over to him and stood a few feet behind him. She was afraid that if she said anything that she might scare him and he was standing dangerously close to the edge of the cliff.

The last time they were alone together he hurt her feelings and humiliated her and she was still mad. But mad or not, she needed to see if she could help him through whatever it was he was going through. He was out of breath from the physical exertion it took to hurl rocks that must have weighed twenty or thirty pounds off the cliff. He let another one go and looked at her. "I don't do relationships for a goddamned reason." He looked out into the darkness and then to the bottom of the cliff. "Seriously, Sara, why don't you just kill me now and get it over with?"

Sara's eyes started to sting with tears. She was frozen in place and her mind was having trouble staying on one topic.

She puckered her lips together briefly and then smiled. "That's a really weird way to tell me you like me."

"Sara, what do you want from me?" Martinez was exasperated.

Her mouth dropped open as she actively tried to stop herself from losing control. She took a deep breath and then let it out slowly before shrugging. "Friendship? Love?" She looked at the ground. "You're a good guy, Martinez. You are. You're a kind, caring, and loyal person. You're amazing with Drew... I'm sorry if I messed things up."

He gestured to her with his hand. "You see what you just did there? Listing some of the things you like about me? I'm never going to do that." His voice got progressively louder. "I'm never going to share my feelings or say those three little words, because I can't. I'm never going to tell you that I love the way your eyes change color depending on what you're wearing or that they get way brighter when you're pissed!" His hand went above his head for a second and then he let it fall to his side.

Sara had a tear that was making its way down her cheek as she was trying to process everything he said when she suddenly burst into laughter.

"Why are you laughing at me? I'm being serious!" Martinez looked hurt at first but couldn't help smiling.

"Was that a direct observation about my eyes or did you just pull that example out of your ass?" She chuckled a little more and then wiped her eye. "We don't have to go from zero to sixty. We can go slow." She hugged herself and looked down at the ground. "It's probably a good idea that we didn't make love the other night."

"Why?"

She rubbed the back of her neck and kept looking away. "Because I would have went home and cried for several hours." She tried to laugh it off but it didn't work. "I kinda feel like I'm betraying him."

Martinez nodded. "Trust me, I'm familiar with the feeling."

"You don't have to share your feelings with me." She touched the side of his face. "You don't have to talk about your childhood or your time with the Boy Scouts." She grinned softly and then touched his chest above his heart with her index finger. "I like you the way you are at this moment. You don't have to be more for me. Okay?" She cleared her throat and looked away briefly. "I'm glad that you were Andrew's friend and I'm glad you came here with us." She swallowed hard. "I don't know what I would do without you. You're part of my family. Regardless of what does or does not happen between us. I'm always gonna need you. Do you understand me?"

She noticed his eyes start to tear up so she hugged him. At first, it was a decidedly one-way hug but eventually she felt his arms around her. "There is one thing I'd like to know though."

"What's that?"

She listened to his heartbeat for a moment before answering. "Your name."

When he didn't answer her, she stepped back and looked at him. He was looking up at the sky with his mouth agape. He whispered, "Sara, look."

There were glowing orbs floating in the sky. They all had a barely discernable yellow color that got progressively lighter toward the center until it looked like a small sun. There were hundreds of them and she couldn't quite tell if they were plants or animals but they were beautiful. One floated within a few feet of them so she held out her hand and it grew brighter where she touched it. They were so delicate they could have been woven by a spider.

Sara squinted at it. "I think it's a seed. You must have disturbed them when you threw the rocks."

"Whatever they are, they're the coolest thing I've ever seen." He reached out and waved his hand back and forth beneath it and watched it float higher into the sky.

She looked him in the face while he watched the seeds. The light they gave off reflected in his brown eyes making them look lighter. He looked down at her with a smile and then moved the hair away from her eyes. She watched as tears formed in his eyes and he quickly looked away as he tried to get control of himself.

Sara suddenly didn't know what to do or how to react. "Should I leave you alone?"

"No." He pressed his hands together and then smiled. "This is hard for me. Just bear with me, okay?"

"Okay."

"My mom never gave me a name." Martinez couldn't seem to look at her. "But my grandfather did."

She was instantly curious about the reasons why a woman wouldn't give her own child a name but he didn't want to ask. Sara took his hand and gave him a reassuring smile. "Okay."

"It's Angelo." He cleared his throat again. "But you can call me, Ange."

It made her so happy that he shared something so personal with her. She smiled broadly. "What about Angie?" She stepped closer to him. "Can I call you Angie?"

He chuckled. "You can. But if anyone else does they'll get beat up. And it'll be all your fault."

"What if I called you Angel?"

He put his arms around her. "That'd be okay too."

He leaned in closely and they looked into each other's eyes. Her heart raced and thumped in her chest as she grabbed some of the fabric of his coat into her hands.

"Okay."

It was strange to her. She wasn't used to Martinez looking so happy and seeing him that way made her happy too. His face was so close to hers that she could feel his body heat. She wanted him to kiss her but at the same time she was terrified of the prospect. It was too bad that she didn't remember anything after that.

Martinez grabbed her before she slipped out of his arms. "Sara?" Her eyes were closed and her breathing was shallow. He shook her gently. "Sara!" Seeing her unconscious scared him. He knew he needed to get her to the doctor and he needed to do it fast. He scooped her up in his arms and quickly set out for camp. "Doc!"

Chapter Eighteen

Dr. Dixon sat at his desk playing holographic chess with Lucy. He was staring at the board and hadn't made a move in over fifteen minutes. It was his idea to play in the first place but he found that he wasn't in the mood anymore. His sickbay served both as a medical clinic and his quarters and was easily the cleanest place on the ship. There were several sickbays located around the ship but his was the largest and had the most bells and whistles. His eyes rolled to his desk at the picture of his daughter and granddaughter. They both looked so much alike they could have been twins if only they were the same age. He loved them both very much but the only contact he usually had with them was over video chat. For special occasions he would request an escort but for the most part, he never left the clinic. His eyes focused on his own reflection in the glass of the picture and he frowned. His hair was dark gray and his face had deep wrinkles. It was because he was old. He had literally given his whole life to the USS Newman. He could have been a different man. He could have been a good husband and a good father. All he needed to do was agree to have his unnatural desires eradicated by way of brain surgery. It seemed like a decision any normal person would make except for only one thing. There was a sixty percent likelihood that he would never be able to practice medicine again.

Dr. Dixon had the utmost confidence in the other doctors aboard the Newman but when he thought about what might have happened during the plague without him… he wondered if anyone would have survived. He was the one that figured out that Captain Mason was special and he was the one to synthesize the cure. Without him, all would have been lost. He thought about getting the surgery many times but he couldn't bring himself to do it. He wanted to be different but he also didn't. He knew that every normal person hated something about themselves and would love to be able to change it. But how many of them would cut it out of them knowing that it may change them more than they intended. He once read an article about an opera singer who had brain surgery to stop her hands from twitching. The surgery was a complete success. Her hands didn't shake and her fine motor skills improved one hundred percent. But the woman never sang in the opera again. Perhaps the most interesting part of her story was the fact that the woman could still sing just as beautifully as she had before, she just didn't want to. Singing no longer brought her the same joy as it had before.

But now his life was nearing its end. If he had the surgery now, he could live out the rest of his life as a normal grandfather who wanted to spend time with his family. All things considered; he was a good person who deserved to be happy.

The doctor pointed his finger at his queen knowing that all he needed to do was say his move out loud. "Queen to rook."

"Check." Lucy disembodied voice immediately countered. "There is no way you can protect your king. I win, Dr. Dixon."

The doctor knew she was going to win. Not only was his mind distracted but he was playing against an artificial intelligence. His mind drifted back to the day he met Britt. He was a young recruit that had to report to sickbay for some booster shots. The crewman was very charismatic and funny so he was easy to like. When the doctor asked him how old he was he didn't hesitate to answer. He said he was twenty-five and Dixon never questioned it. Admittedly, that was due to the fact that Britt was a smooth-talking personable guy who made the doctor feel special, he wanted to be his friend. After all, they were the same age. Or so he believed. When the doctor found out that Britt was nearly twice his age, he felt deeply betrayed but he understood why he lied.

"Dean Mason is at the door, Dr. Dixon." Lucy's voice was soft and smooth, just the way he designed it. "Shall I let him in?"

Lucy's continuous evolution always amazed him. Not only was she able to hold a thoughtful conversation… but she was also able to break the rules. He blamed Britt for that fact. "That depends. What is the proper protocol?"

"The proper protocol for entering this sickbay is to obtain permission from security."

"Unless?" The doctor couldn't help treating her like a child.

"Unless it is a verifiable emergency." Lucy's voice was matter-of-fact.

"Very good, Lucy." Dr. Dixon nodded. "And is it an emergency?"

"No, it is not. Shall I explain the proper procedure to him?"

Her answer made him laugh. He shrugged while he shook his head. "It's okay, Lucy." He glanced at the sliding doors at the entrance. "You can let him in, just this once."

"Okay." It may have been his imagination but he could have sworn he heard confusion in her voice. "I will let him in, just this once."

Dean sauntered into the clinic like he owned the place. The lad was the very definition of swagger and one of a kind… even though he had a twin brother. The captain's grandkids may have looked alike but they were completely different. Aside from the fact that they chose to have different hairstyles, they had very different personalities. Britt once regaled the doctor with a story about how the twins tried to trick him by switching places. They were only twelve years old which should have aided them in their plan but it didn't. Because even as youngsters they were too different to pull off the switcheroo effectively. Dean had plans with his friends to go see a rock band performing in the arboretum but he had been grounded for cursing at his mother. His brother James felt sorry for him because he knew how much Dean wanted to hang out with Ava. They soon hatched a plan that ended with them getting caught because James wasn't scowling enough. In the end, they both got their butts blistered and spent a week on kitchen duty washing dishes. But Dean was happy. He got to see his favorite band and kissed a girl for the first time. To him, it seemed like a fair trade.

Dr. Dixon looked at the lovable brat in front of him and crossed his arms over his chest as he leaned against his desk. They stared each other in the eyes for a minute. The last time they were in the same room together they got into a pretty serious argument. The doctor rubbed the end of his nose and waited. He knew if he remained silent, eventually, Dean would tell him why he was there. He didn't have to wait long.

Dean squinted at him for a moment and then sighed. "If you're trying to drive me slowly insane, you're doing a good job."

The old doctor knew exactly what he was talking about. He grinned slightly. "I told you that I wouldn't say anything and I didn't."

Dean waved his hands to the sides. "I get that you're loyal. I love him too." He stood next to a window that featured a great view of the green planet below. He gestured to the window. "Do you even know what he's planning? Because I do."

The doctor shook his head. "I don't care what he's got planned. I won't help you."

Dean was obviously frustrated but the doctor remained firm. He wouldn't betray his friend. Not even if it was the right thing to do. Dean looked out the window again and frowned. "Are we getting closer to it or is it getting closer to us?"

Dr. Dixon walked over to the window to see what the lad meant. Sure enough, it did appear that the Swagger was getting closer to the planet. As he stood there in front of the viewport trying to figure out what was going on, he used the heel of his left foot to rub up against his right ankle. The ankle bracelet that would alert security if he left his quarters was chaffing his skin again. He was beginning to believe he was developing an allergy to the metal housing on the alarm. He shared a quick look with Dean before returning his eyes back to the planet.

A tone pulse sounded twice and then a female voice filled the room. "Commander Hayes to Dr. Dixon."

He quickly responded. "Yeah, Faye. What's up?"

"Captain Mason has been trying to hail us so I'm moving the Swagger closer to the planet to improve our chances of picking him up." She paused for a moment. "He said he needs to talk to you. I'll be patching him through momentarily."

As soon as the comm blipped out he looked at Dean. "You need to leave."

~ * ~

Dean locked eyes with the doctor. He considered defying or challenging him but he couldn't see how that would do any good. His eyes wandered back to the beautiful planet below. When he noticed that the Swagger was getting closer to it, his first thought was that someone figured out how to execute their plan and land the ship. He couldn't bring himself to leave. He wanted to know if his brother was okay. Everyone always believed that he and James had a special connection. They believed ridiculous notions that one could feel the others pain and so on and so forth. But that wasn't further from the truth. He had no premonitions or intuitions or bad feelings that he was in trouble. There was nothing.

He slowly turned away from the window and watched the doctor as he walked toward the large digital screen over one of the beds. He had his back turned away from Dean so he took advantage. People needed permission to enter Dr. Dixon's sickbay, but they didn't need it to leave. Everyone had their theories as to why the man spent the last thirty years on house arrest but that's all they were. Theories. People thought perhaps he had committed murder or perhaps took advantage of unconscious women. Dean couldn't imagine the doctor doing any of the things he has heard so he tried to keep an open mind. He walked to the exit and scanned his hand to open the door and waited. Most of the doors aboard the ship slid open fairly fluidly but the one in Dixon's sickbay always made a noise. He let the door slide open and then closed knowing that the doctor would think he left. He crept slowly along the wall until he could safely peer around the corner without being seen.

"Yo, Doc! Can you hear me?" His granddad's voice filled the air. "Hello?"

He was very glad to hear his voice because it meant that he was alive and hopefully, okay. His grandfather repeatedly insisted that he and his brother just call him Britt. He respected his request, at first... but as he got older and realized it bothered him, he started using a variety of different terms ranging from grandpappy to granddaddy. None of which were ever received well but he can no longer help himself. Now it was almost as if it was an expected running gag. He listened to Britt and the doctor ask each other if they could be heard several times before they were able to have a proper conversation.

Dean listened carefully hoping he'd hear any news of his brother. The two of them disagreed on a lot of things but that didn't mean he didn't love him. He peeked one eye around the corner and watched as a video appeared on the digital screen above the bed. The image of an unconscious woman appeared on the screen and he instantly recognized her, which caused him to gasp. He saw the doctor's back stiffen as he realized he wasn't alone. He was afraid the doctor would turn around and give away his position but somehow, he resisted the impulse. He examined the stats on the screen after Britt uploaded medical scans of her entire body.

"She's been unconscious for a few hours." Britt's voice crackled and the transmission blanked out at times but he could still be understood. "Is there anything we can do?"

"Exhaustion is one of the symptoms. Maybe she's just sleeping." The doctor rubbed his chin. "I need you to take a blood sample and upload the results. Her cell count will tell me what I need to know."

A man's voice that he didn't recognize protested. "Hey! No one said you could take her blood!"

"Dr. Bowman relax! What the hell is wrong with you?" It was another man he didn't know.

He wasn't sure why there was an argument over Sara Zeeman's blood but he knew her very existence was impossible. Or so he thought. The mere fact that she was alive meant that some of his brother's cockamamie theories about the wormhole were true. Her existence meant that the Swagger traveled back in time at least two hundred years. It meant that his grandfather wasn't crazy at all but his plan still was. He couldn't let his grandfather exact his revenge or all would be lost. The screen jiggled a little and then stabilized on her face. There was no mistaking it. It was her. Dean spent the better part of his school years learning about the Mother of Space Travel and he considered himself an expert on her. He idolized her for many reasons but most especially because she designed the Moon's Eye from stem to stern almost exclusively by herself. It was a brilliant design that was copied and improved upon for many years until humans took to space permanently.

There were at least five other ships like the Swagger and all of them were listed as status unknown. He thought about those ships many times and wondered how their crew evolved. Did they transition from military to civilian like the Swagger? What became of them? Did they travel through the wormhole too? Were they lost forever? All Dean knew for sure was that the people of the Swagger found their forever home and he meant to give it them. He listened to people he didn't know argue over Sara's blood and whether or not his people should be able to analyze it without her permission. It went on for a minute or two until Captain Mason had enough of it.

"Look, Dr. Bowman, the whole reason y'all are still out here is because we need to get her to my ship. What do you think is going to happen once we get there? Now, if you're not going to help, then get the hell outta my way."

Dean was very familiar with the sound of irritation in his grandfather's voice. When he was younger, that irritation was accompanied by a hard smack in the butt. He moved into the room without fear because he knew the doctor had no intention of revealing his presence. A person didn't need to be in the medical profession to know that the results before him were very bad.

That was when both the doctors on the case cursed in unison. "Jesus Christ."

The doctor on the planet below was the first to voice the problem. "She needs to be bled."

Dean couldn't imagine a situation where a person would need such a procedure. He watched Dr. Dixon rub his chin as he examined the results further. "Obviously, when you give her more blood, it should come from anyone except Captain Mason." He paused for a moment. "Captain Mason? We need some privacy." He knew the doctor was waiting for the all-clear before he spoke again. Unfortunately, Dean also knew that he'd only be able to hear one side of the conversation because of the subcutaneous personal comms. The doctor pressed the skin below his ear and then spoke again. "I don't know what that woman is, but she's not human. Be careful."

Everything he saw and heard while he was in that room left him in a state of disbelief. The old doctor suddenly turned around and looked Dean in the eyes. "I thought I told you to leave!"

Dean pointed at the monitor above the bed. It still showed the image of the woman he idolized his entire life. "That woman is Sara Zeeman!"

Dr. Dixon shook his head. "That's not possible."

Dean pointed again. This time with more conviction. "I'm telling you, that's her!" He looked out the window at the planet below. "You know what this means, don't you? We can't let him destroy that wormhole. It'll ruin everything."

Dixon put his hand up to silence Dean as his eyes rolled to the side. He was obviously listening to his comm and then he responded. "She's not infected anymore, Captain Mason. Her body somehow destroyed the blood you gave her." He listened again. "Well, if you want her aboard the ship... you're going to have to lie to her."

Chapter Nineteen

Sara was laying on a sleeping bag with Martinez kneeling next to her and holding her hand. He looked desperate and wide-eyed as he watched Dr. Bowman place an IV in her arm. Black blood flowed slowly through the tubing to the end until it started to drip freely into a small canister. The doctor did some mental calculations in his head. He glanced over his shoulder at Tran. She was a tall woman and could likely donate two pints of blood without even noticing the loss. He had everyone's blood type committed to memory and he knew for a fact that she and Sara shared the same type, but he still had to make sure. He picked up his tablet and poked at it until he got the information he wanted. Tran and Martinez were the best choices. He moved to the opposite side of where Martinez was and went to work setting up his field transfer kit. He knew it was risky, but he didn't want to start transfusing her until he drained at least two pints of the bad blood. He placed the IV needle into Martinez' arm and inserted the catheter and then went to work on hers.

Even with everything that was going on, the doctor was acutely aware of Junior and the fact that he was pacing back and forth behind them. He also noted the fact that Sara's savior, Captain Mason, was nowhere in sight. Even though he was concentrating on something important; his mind couldn't help thinking about what he had just seen on the captain's tablet. The doctor's own device was capable of remarkable things but his paled in comparison. They weren't even in the same league. The technology was far beyond anything he had ever seen. He glanced around at his surroundings one more time. Mel was sitting a few feet away from them pretending not to be upset about what was going on. He lowered his voice.

"Where'd he go?" His eyes flicked up to Martinez' and they shared a look.

The sheriff was barely able to concentrate on anything except Sara, but he shook his head. "I don't know." His eyes never left Sara as the doctor checked to see how much blood was in Sara's container. He released the valve that would allow Martinez' blood to flow through the tubing and into Sara's waiting veins but there was a problem. "Doctor," Martinez softly, "I don't think she's breathing."

"What?" Junior's voice came from behind them. He dove down on the ground and crawled over to her side. "Ma? Ma!"

"Her heart's not beating." Dr. Bowman positioned himself above her and placed one hand over the other on her sternum and began chest compressions. "Junior, get ready to give her breaths." He counted out the compressions until he got to thirty. "Now."

He waited for Junior to give a successful breath and then resumed the chest compressions. After a few minutes he was sweating profusely and bordering on muscle exhaustion, but he knew he needed to keep going. Each time he forced his hands down on her chest, he was pumping new blood into her body, so he just kept going. He felt someone brush up against his side. It was Mel.

"Get ready to switch, Doc." She placed one hand over the other and held them in the air, preparing herself for the switch.

Every adult in the colony was trained and proficient in cardiopulmonary resuscitation. It was a necessary evil and has proven useful many times already. Junior gave Sara another rescue breath while the doctor and Mel switched places and they continued until everyone, except Martinez, had a turn. After ten minutes had gone by, Dr. Bowman was ready to call it. He told everyone to stop while he felt for her pulse again. They all waited in silence and watched her chest for signs that she was breathing. She wasn't.

The doctor sat back on his heels and tried to catch his breath. "I'm sorry."

"No." Junior had tears running down his face. He sniffed hard and stared down at her. "This isn't happening."

Martinez acted like he didn't know what was going on. "What are we doing? Let's go. Keep going!"

When he saw no one moving to help, he placed his hands on her chest and started compressions. At first, the doctor was concerned that the transfer tubing would come loose from either of their arms but considering the circumstances, he didn't think it mattered. Sara was dead and Martinez needed to feel like he did everything he could to save her. His refusal to give up just made it worse for everyone else. Tran and Junior cried while Mel quietly moved away. He thought he might have seen the fire reflecting off the remnants of a tear on her face but dismissed it as a hallucination brought on by emotional stress. When Martinez hit the count of thirty, he tipped Sara's head back, pressed his lips against hers, and blew air into her lungs.

The doctor watched the sheriff's face and knew he was about to lose control. "Martinez, you need to stop."

"No," he said between counting, "you need to help me."

Junior moved back into position. "I'll help."

Tran suddenly put her hand on Martinez' shoulder. "I think I just saw her head move. Stop."

Everyone was still. They watched her. The doctor couldn't help mentally noting how intensely quiet it was. It was like the universe was holding its breath along with them. That's when the doctor noticed Britt standing just out of sight in the shadow of a tree. His hands were jammed in his pockets as his sad eyes met his stare. Cowboy or no, it was obvious the man had feelings for her. Chad thought that Tran's declaration of movement was just wishful thinking, but he leaned forward to check her pulse anyway. Before he could even touch her, she took a deep breath.

"Oh my god! She's breathing!" Tran laughed joyfully.

Junior covered his face and just cried freely. His voice was muffled but the doctor heard him say "thank you, God" over and over again.

Sara's eyes opened as she took quick labored breathes. There was fear in her eyes. "I can't breathe."

"Junior, go get the oxygen tank out of the jeep!" The doctor pointed to the jeep. "And be quick about it!"

She looked between Chad and Martinez. "I'm scared."

"You're going to be okay." Martinez whispered to her and smoothed her hair back. He leaned down and kissed her on the forehead. "I promise."

~ * ~

Sara felt like she was drifting on the ocean. Birds chirped somewhere in the distance and there was a light breeze that seemed to gently caress her face and move her hair to the side. It seemed like she was stuck between the dream state and reality, but she was working hard to resolve that. She felt someone's warm hand on top of hers and for a moment, during her time between, she thought it was her husband's and it made her happy. It made her heart beat a little faster which made her journey back to consciousness a little bit quicker. In that moment, she squeezed his hand. It was only a moment, but it passed quickly, moving her into sadness as she remembered his death.

When Sara finally opened her eyes, it was Martinez that she saw. His face was about a foot away from hers and he appeared to be sleeping. It took her a few seconds to realize that they were lying side by side facing each other on the ground. She was wrapped pretty snugly in a sleeping bag with her hand sticking out the side so that he could hold it. She didn't know exactly when it happened, but she liked the man. If she allowed herself to think about it a little too deeply, she might think that she was trying to self-sabotage herself. After all, Angelo Martinez was a bit screwed up. But then again, so was she.

She squeezed his hand again and he opened his eyes. She watched his eyes adjust to the low light of the morning until they focused in on her. They laid there silently looking into each other's eyes for a few moments before she whispered to him. "I'm sorry."

Angelo's eyebrows crinkled in confusion. "For what?"

Sara searched her thoughts for the right words. "Leaving you to grieve alone." She felt tears rising up within her, but she pushed them away. "We both lost him. We all did. But I was too self-centered to acknowledge anyone else's pain but my own."

He looked at their hands and watched her thumb as it moved back and forth over his. He scooted closer to her so that they were only inches apart before lovingly moving some hair out of her face and smoothing it behind her ear. When he settled back down, he took her hand in his and brought it to his chest and held it there. "You know, a couple of days before he died, we were fishing together and just shooting the shit," he smiled softly as his eyes seemed to focus on the past. "He had just told me this story about Drew." He laughed. "He said that he ran into the living room completely naked... when you guys had company and pointed to his penis as he jumped up and down and said," he paused for dramatic effect but she beat him to it.

"Look, ma! Boingy boingy!" She smiled and laughed. Her eyes shot to the side as if she suddenly became aware that there were other people around and that they were sleeping. She snickered softly. "Oops."

Angelo stifled a laugh too. "He was so proud of Drew." His eyes suddenly filled with sadness. "He loved you both so much." He looked away. "I was jealous of his happiness and I told him as much."

"What did he say?" She knew Andrew, so she felt she knew the answer.

"He said that I could be happy too but I just didn't know how." He tipped onto his back and looked up at the sky. "And he tried to convince me that I'd be a good dad someday."

"Jesus Christ!" Mel's angry voice interrupted the peace. "If I have to listen to any more of this, I'm going to kill myself! Some people are trying to sleep!"

Angelo made eye contact with Sara again. She rolled her eyes and ignored Mel's outburst. "You will."

He didn't laugh. He didn't even smile. If anything, he looked scared. The doctor appeared above her causing a shadow to darken her view. He knelt down beside her and asked her how she felt before taking her pulse with his hand. She had apparently been unconscious for the last twenty hours and he seemed very concerned about her. She sat up slowly but it still made her dizzy. Talking about children made her remember something she had forgotten. She thought about Izzy and wondered how she was doing. Even though she didn't plan on having a new baby in her life she didn't want anything to happen to it and wondered if it was okay. She looked at the doctor as he placed her hand on his tablet and read her vital signs. The bruising on his face was beginning to fade away but it was still there. She glanced at Martinez for a moment. He was watching what the doctor was doing and patiently waiting for a report.

"Hey, doc?" She squinted up at him.

"Yeah?"

She looked around the camp to see if anyone was listening. "Did you have a chance to speak with the baby's father?"

Dr. Bowman's head didn't move but his eyes rolled toward Angelo and then back to her. She slowly turned her head to look at Martinez too. The tension was unmistakable. The doctor nodded. "Why don't we talk about that when we get back to the colony, okay?"

"Why did Martinez give you that black eye?" Her eyes grew wider and then she focused in on him. "Is it you?" She held her breath.

214

The doctor smiled. "As much as I'd like that, I wasn't one of your matches."

Sara's head snapped back to Martinez and as soon as their eyes met, he looked away. He practically jumped to his feet and walked away without looking back. She was dumbfounded. "Each time that I think I'm getting closer to him, something happens and we're right back to square one." She shook her head as she felt the heat of her anger rising up. She gritted her teeth. "I really hate you."

Chad tipped his head and grimaced. "So, you've said... several times."

She looked down at her arm as he removed the IV and tubing from it. The only thing she could remember about the night before was being with Martinez and hoping that he'd kiss her. As she watched him remove the IV, she noticed a large black and blue hematoma about the size of a quarter. She looked up at him as he placed a bandage over it. "What happened?"

He glanced over his shoulder at Britt and then lowered his voice. "We need to talk in private." The doctor took her by the elbow and helped her up. Sara felt a little lightheaded and almost fell but he caught her. Martinez stood up instantly and took two steps toward her but Chad put his hand up to stop him. "Don't worry, I've got her."

Martinez sought her agreement with his eyes. She nodded at him so he sat back down. Chad made it known to everyone in earshot that he was taking her to the hot spring to wash up. The morning was warmer than normal and as they got closer and closer to the spring, it became more humid. It made her remember when she was a young girl visiting her grandmother in Louisiana. As much as she loved the woman, she didn't believe in air conditioning. Sara spent the days trying to stay cool by sitting in front of a fan but it didn't work. The nights were worse because she couldn't get comfortable enough to sleep. She must have stepped on a rock or pebble because her ankle tipped sideways causing her to fall against the doctor. He put his arm around her to stabilize her as they walked.

The hot spring looked so much more impressive in the daylight. The water was so clear the rust-colored rocks at the bottom could be seen. Steam rose off the surface and then slowly dissipated into the air. The doctor helped her sit down on a large rock next to the water and then took a towel out of his bag. He knelt down and dipped the towel into the hot water and then rung it out until he was satisfied and then brought it to her. Sara took it and dabbed it on her face. He watched her for a moment before turning around to seek out a place to sit.

"Your sudden and severe medical issues brought a few things to light." Chad sat down on a tree trunk that had long since fallen and put his elbows on his knees.

Sara had an idea of what he might mean but she didn't want to have certain conversations unless she was forced to. "What things?"

"Well, for starters, even though your new friend speaks English he seems to have technology that far exceeds ours." He weaved his fingers together and pressed his lips flat for a moment. "That tablet he has showed us a view of what was happening in your blood on a cellular level." He shook his head. "There is no way Earth's technology has advanced to that point in only two years."

He waited for her to say something, but she didn't. She just stared at him blankly. Her heart was beating so fast that she felt dizzy. She was scared that he had figured it all out. She looked down at her hands and then started picking at her fingernails. Instead of addressing his current concerns, she decided to shift his focus. "What did the tablet show you? Am I going to die?"

Chad suddenly gave her a half grin and shook his head in disbelief. "There's literally no reason why you should be alive right now." He waved his hand from one side of him to the other. "None."

She became more insistent. "What happened?"

He was silent for a moment. It made her wonder what he was thinking about. Was he trying to be just as strategic as she was? He took a deep breath. "You wanted me to join the mission because of your unique physiology. You said it was because you were afraid it would cause you problems in the future."

And there it was. The doctor was putting two and two together and coming up with twenty questions. She threw her hands up and then slapped them down on her knees. "Chad! What is wrong with me? Am I going to die? And why does my goddamned chest hurt?" She placed her hand on her sternum. "Will you please just tell me what is going on?"

His eyes widened. "Fine. For lack of better words? Your blood killed his. All of it. And bodies aren't equipped to get rid of large amounts of blood like that." Dr. Bowman explained in detail what they had to do in order to save her and it horrified her. He said that they had no other choice but to drain some of her blood out and then give her another blood transfusion. His voice got an octave or two lower. "We had to give you CPR for almost ten minutes. I was ready to call it but Martinez and Junior wouldn't let me give up." He shook his head. "I wasn't sure who I should be more concerned about. You... or Martinez." He got more and more frustrated as he spoke. "And, while we're on the subject, I didn't mean to screw up your budding relationship by forcing you two into parenthood. Martinez wasn't just on your compatibility list, he was the goddamned list. There was no one else on this planet that could have fathered a child with you." He turned his palm up and then bounced it slightly. "And about four months back there was a containment issue. I lost almost all of your eggs. I had to fertilize the surviving ones or risk losing them. And guess what happened?" He didn't wait for her to ask. "They all died except one."

She squinted at him and shook her head. "So, you decided to implant it in a teenager who hates me?"

Chad looked surprised. "Yes, I did! I did because I didn't want it to die too." His mouth dropped open almost as if he was shocked by her audacity. "I didn't expect it to live. I didn't. So, I chose not to tell you until she entered the second trimester."

He took his tablet out and called something up on the screen before handing it to her. It took her breath away. The tablet featured a computer-generated image of a beautiful little girl around the age of three on it. She had shoulder length black hair and striking blue eyes. Sara's eyes began to sting with tears. "It's a girl?"

"Yes."

A tear trickled down her cheek and then dropped off her chin to her shirt. She held the tablet out for him to take. "Don't let him name her Sara."

"Are we going to talk about this, or not?" He stood up and looked around as if he was afraid of being heard. "I don't trust that guy."

Sara rubbed her eyes. "Look, I know that things don't really seem to add up but, to tell you the truth, I haven't really had much time to talk to him." She frowned hard. "I've been unconscious most of the time."

The doctor nodded. "Yeah, well... we need to be careful. Something's off about all of this." He yanked his comm off his collar and then gave it to her. "You need to call your son before anything else happens."

Sara took it and held it in her hands. Something about what he said and how he said it upset her. The harder she tried not to cry, the more the tears fell. The doctor stood next to her and rubbed the back of his neck awkwardly before deciding to give her a hug. She felt so childish. Crying seemed like part of her daily routine and she was tired of it. She put her head on his shoulder and let the tears flow as she vowed to herself and god above that she wouldn't cry anymore. She knew it wasn't something that she could pull off forever but she wanted to put the past behind her and move forward. Whether that would be alone or with someone else didn't matter. She wanted to get back to the strong independent person she used to be.

Dr. Bowman rubbed her back before letting her go and then looked her in the eyes. "I'll leave you alone for a few minutes."

She watched him walk back towards camp as she held the comm in her hand wondering what she was supposed to say to Drew. It was hard. She had to force herself to press the button on the comm and make the call. Her heart pounded in her chest as she made contact with the woman who was taking care of him. Mrs. Anderson was delighted to hear from Sara and gushed over her son's wonderful behavior. When she heard his little voice, she felt like the love in her heart could physically travel the distance between them and touch him. He was so glad to hear from her but he was only interested in one thing.

"When ya comin' home, mom?"

She didn't know what to tell him. Given her current state of health she wasn't one hundred percent sure she'd ever see him again. But… she couldn't say that to him, could she? She didn't want to lie to him so she told him the one true thing she knew.

"I'm not sure, Drew. But as long as I'm alive there is nothing that could stop me from getting back to you. You just gotta be patient, kiddo. I love you."

Talking to him gave her renewed strength and conviction. No matter what, she needed to get back home to him. She took a deep breath and tipped her head up to the sun for a moment. It shined brightly through her eyelids causing her discomfort but the heat felt good on her skin. She looked back down and opened her eyes. She watched the steam from the hot spring dance above the water and then dissipate into the air before getting up. Her legs were still a little shaky but she actually felt a little better. She kneeled down at the edge of the spring and scooped some of the water into her hands and gently washed her face. Getting back up from the ground proved to be more complicated then she thought it would be. The world started to spin and she felt dizzy but someone caught her.

"Ma? You okay?"

It was Junior. He helped her up and then held her close so that she wouldn't fall. When she looked at him closely, she noticed that his eyes were red and puffy. Her godson may have looked like a fully grown adult but she knew better. Poor Junior, barely twelve-years-old, had a front row seat to her near-death experience and he was doing everything he could to hide his feelings. Sara smiled up at him and then smoothed some of his hair behind his ear. "Are you?"

Those words were all it took for him to lose all composure. Tears fell freely from his eyes. "Ma..." He shook his head at her.

"I know." She hugged him tight and let him cry. "I know."

Chapter Twenty

Britt stood at the edge of a wide canyon with a huge frown on his face. There was a dense forest on the other side with a looming dark mountain in the distance. He looked down. He didn't know how far it was but he figured five or six stories was a good guess. The center of his ship featured an atrium where exactly twenty-five trees grew. All of the them were hybridized which grew an interesting array of fruit. It was a wonderful little parklike area where birds chirped and bees buzzed. His favorite place on the ship was his balcony. It overlooked the fruit trees below and allowed him to feel like he was actually outside. If he was a betting man, he'd wager that the bottom of the canyon was about as far down as it was from his balcony to the floor of the atrium. Six stories was a very long way to fall. The canyon was very colorful with some red and orange rocks. A deep blue river raged at the bottom and was very likely how the canyon was sculpted in the first place. Very beautiful indeed. But it was huge problem.

He looked down at his tablet at the topographical map that was displayed on it. If they couldn't find a way to cross it, they would have to travel thirty miles to get around it. He sighed and frowned again. His shuttle, and hopefully his grandson, was only five miles from where he was standing. The captain was incredibly frustrated by the fact that he could be there in minutes if it wasn't for the damn obstacle in front of him. He wanted the uranium he sent his grandson after and he wanted to get back to the Swagger as soon as possible. He put his tablet in his pack and then took his cowboy hat off before smoothing his hair back and replacing it. He didn't hear her or see her when she walked up but somehow, Sara appeared next to him. Maybe it was his imagination but she looked better than she had in days. He watched her look out over the canyon while the wind gently waved her hair back and forth at the sides of her head. Something flew by in his peripheral view so he turned back to the canyon. It was the drone.

"Junior says that he found your shuttle but there's no signs of anyone around it. At least, not right now." She looked up at him. "We need to talk."

Britt grinned at her so hard his dimples made an appearance. "Is this where you tell me that you're into Ass-hat even though you're wildly attracted to me?"

Sara blinked a few times and then stared down at her feet for a moment. "I'm not going to deny that there's an attraction but there's a difference between attraction and…"

"Love?" He challenged her. "So, you love him then?"

She breathed in quickly and shrugged. "It's complicated."

He smirked at her. He knew he was making her uncomfortable and he was enjoying every minute of it. "What's so complicated about it? You either love him or you don't."

She folded her arms across her chest. "I love my husband."

That momentarily stunned him. He completely forgot about Andrew Zeeman. "Oh? Where is he? Shouldn't he be here too?"

As soon as he asked the question, he regretted it. He watched her struggle with her emotions for a moment before making eye contact with him. "He's dead. He died over a year ago." She suddenly flipped her palms up at him. "This is not why I wanted to talk to you!"

Britt felt about two inches tall. He should have been able to put two and two together and figure out that if her husband was alive, he would have led the search party to find her. Instead, it was ass-hat. He watched the Mother of Space Travel try to blink away the shiny tears that glistened in her eyes and wished he could fix everything that was wrong in her life.

"I'm sorry," he said softly, "I didn't know."

Sara stuck a hand into her inside pocket and brought out her little pillbox causing Britt to involuntarily grimace. He turned his head and pretended not to notice as she placed one of the berries under her tongue. He wanted to confront her about it. He wanted to yell at her and ask her if she was stupid, but he didn't. Instead he moved closer to her and touched her forearm. "I didn't know your husband but I know that he'd want you to move on. He'd want you to be happy."

She shrunk away from him and jammed her hands into her pockets. "He was the love of my life." She shrugged. "I guess I'm just scared."

"Of what?"

She laughed. "What if no one ever measures up? Or worse... what if someone does? Then what? Does it somehow mean it was all meant to be? I mean FUCK THAT!" She suddenly shoved him which caused him to take a step backward. The look of shock on his face turned hers to guilt. She said it again but softer. "Fuck that." She tipped her head to the side. "I don't even know who I am anymore."

Britt stepped closer to her. "You're Captain Sara Zeeman. You're a strong, brave woman who's been dealt a bad hand, but you will get through it."

He had to resist the urge to kiss her. In his younger days he may have used her vulnerability to his advantage but he wasn't that stupid, selfish kid anymore. He was attracted to her but he also respected her. That single realization stunned him a little. He was putting a woman's wellbeing above his own. That wasn't like him at all. Perhaps being ninety-two-years old meant that he was all grown up. She rubbed her eyes and blinked a few times. He felt bad for her so he hugged her and then rubbed her back.

"I promise you, Little Lady, you'll get through this."

The fact that she smelled like vanilla made it so much harder for him to behave. He closed his eyes and held her as the warm breeze blew a few strands of her hair up into his face and tickled his nose. Moments such as that were causing him to wonder if he was doing the right thing. When he took his ship through the wormhole, no one was sure what they would find on the other side but everyone was hopeful for a better future. But once they exited the anomaly, the ship was traveling so fast that it overshot the solar system so far that the sensors almost missed it. Humans could build spaceships and travel through space but unfortunately those ships weren't capable of lightspeed which meant getting back to the green planet took them far longer than desired. There was actually a good possibility that the Swagger arrived before the Moon's Eye.

The captain had spent many nights drinking and shooting the shit with his grandson James. Many of the discussions were about the wormhole and the possibility of time travel. It actually seemed silly to Britt but he loved his grandson and he loved science-fiction so he was glad to do it. But the Swagger was a very old ship and the trip through the wormhole wasn't exactly a smooth one. It caused damage to many of the systems and if wasn't for Swagger's dedicated crew, they'd all be dead. Britt hated that damn wormhole for more reasons than one but the biggest one was the fact that no one knew it was there until it was too late. If the people of Earth had known that there was salvation just beyond the event horizon, millions of people could have been saved. If time travel was actually possible, would it not be his duty to restore a timeline in which billions of souls would be saved? Those were just some of the discussion the two of them had but he never imagined that the possibility of time travel was true. But now he was holding proof of it in his arms.

As it turned out, Sara wanted to talk to him about time travel and wanted him to keep his mouth shut about it. It actually spurred the first argument between them. The captain pointed out that it would soon be obvious to everyone that the technology he possessed was far beyond their own.

Sara looked desperate. She shook her head. "I know you're right but there is no reason we need talk about it unless we have to."

Something didn't add up. He squinted at her. "What are you hiding?"

Her mouth dropped open. "What? Nothing! Why would you ask that?"

"You're obviously lying." Britt frowned as he turned away from her. "But, no worries, Sunshine. I got your back."

He led the way back to their camp. He didn't know what the plan was for getting across the canyon but he wanted to get on with it. If something happened to his grandson, he'd never be able to forgive himself. The aforementioned ass-hat was securing the motorcycles to the jeep and looked at them as they walked into camp. It made him feel like he had done something wrong. He decided to shake things up a little so he gave Martinez a nod and a smug grin before looking over his shoulder at Sara. He had hoped it would drive a wedge between them and make him suspect something went on. The sheriff glanced in Sara's direction briefly and then went right back to work. Either the man had unwavering devotion for his woman or he just didn't care. Tran offered him some beef jerky and gave him some coffee. Britt loved coffee. He always joked that if he had it his way, he'd be on a caffeine drip twenty-four seven. The beef jerky made him want to cry. Real meat from a real animal wasn't possible on the swagger. All the 'meat' was grown in a lab and even though it tasted 'like' meat... it definitely wasn't. But the taste only disturbed the older generation who knew the difference. His time with Sara and her people was making him question everything.

Their plan, as it were, was to zipline across the canyon on a wire. He wasn't afraid of heights until you asked him to step off the side of a cliff holding a fucking wire. After Martinez pulled a tarp over the jeep and the motorcycles, all of them found themselves standing at the edge of the canyon looking across.

Britt felt like he was putting on a brave front but he couldn't stand still. He fidgeted or rocked back and forth while he watched Junior and Tran secure the wire to a tree. None of it seemed safe but he knew when the time came, he would man up and do it. He watched as Junior ran a few calculations and then programmed the drone to carry the wire across to the other side. The kid seemed to like exposition and was more than happy to explain how the drone would secure the line on the other side. Apparently, the drone was equipped with two drills that was supposed to be used to obtain samples. Junior planned to utilize those drills to anchor the drone to one of the trees on the other side. As he listened to the kid talk, he found himself distracted by Tran as she dug into one of the packs. If he was going to do something so foolhardy, he was going to do it well informed. She was easily the tallest Asian woman he had ever seen. He found it both strange, and alluring. She had her hair pulled back into a messy ponytail which made him focus on the many piercing she had in her left ear. He watched her pull two harnesses out and place them on the ground before reaching back into the bag. Her search produced something elongated and shiny. The space cowboy was no stranger to things of mechanical nature. He could tell by looking at it that it had a handbrake on it which lead him to an educated guess. He wasn't wrong.

Tran pointed at the mechanism and explained how it worked. "This is the trolley for the line. Normally, it's just a wheel that uses gravity to move the rider across to the other side." She motioned over her shoulder at the canyon behind her. "But this little baby is motorized and can ferry the rider across even on an incline."

She stood on her tip-toes and snapped the trolley on the line and then showed Britt the harness. It all seemed simple enough but it still made him nervous. As the day progressed, he expected it to get hotter but it was noticeably cooler than the last couple of days. The sky was overcast and it looked like it might rain. The thought of it excited him. The last time he saw rain was nearly four decades ago on Earth. He suddenly got the feeling that someone was watching him so he turned around. It was Martinez. He was staring at him so intensely that he had the humorous and fleeting thought that the man was trying to shoot lasers out of his eyes. He wondered was going through the sheriff's head. Did he want to kill Britt because he obviously has a thing for his woman and sees him as a threat? Or perhaps he was experiencing legitimate fears about the captain and what his appearance has in store for them. Something behind Martinez caught his eye so he tipped to the side to see. Everyone seemed to be doing their own thing and didn't seem to notice that Sara was quickly putting on a harness.

Junior was completely focused on the drone's controller. "The drone has established a good hold in a tree on the other side."

Martinez starred at Britt for a few moments until he turned away and addressed everyone. "I'll head over first to secure the line on the other side."

Captain Mason pointed passed him. "Um…"

He looked at the machinist. "Tran, you should go last just in case something happens to the trolley."

Britt's eyebrows shot up as he watched Sara clip herself to the trolley and step off the cliff. Britt pointed again. "Look!"

Martinez turned around in just enough time to see Sara glide across the canyon. "Damn it! What's she doing?" He held his hand out to Tran. "Give me the other Trolley."

She shook her head at him. "It's jammed. You'll have to wait until she sends back the first one."

"It gets worse." Junior pointed over the canyon and into the distance.

Lightning flashed. It was still miles away and everyone seemed overly concerned about a little rain. Martinez put on his pack and secured it before putting on a pair of utility gloves.

Junior took charge. "When I was searching for the captain's shuttle, I discovered a cave at the base of the mountain. I'm programming the drone to fly straight to it so all you have to do is secure the line and disengage it. After that, all you have to do is follow it."

Britt watched and listened to them both but he wasn't sure what was about to happen until Martinez grabbed the line. In mere moments the man had his legs hooked around the wire and was pulling himself across the canyon at impressive speed.

"Well I'll be damned." Britt smiled. "Who'da thunk it? The sheriff's a bonafide superhero."

"You should see him with his shirt off." Tran quickly packed her things. "I totally wanna fuck him."

He folded his arms across his chest as he watched Martinez. "I can see why."

"Come on, we have to get back to camp." Junior grabbed his backpack too. He made eye contact with him. "Let's go."

Britt let everyone else go ahead of him and brought up the rear. He watched the doctor in front of him and kept a step behind him until the brush got thicker. He pretended to have difficulty navigating the path until he was lagging so far behind, he felt confident he was alone. As the minutes passed it became darker and darker and he could hear thunder in the distance. Apparently, the storm was going to be a little worse than a light enjoyable rain. He pressed the comm under his ear and contacted his grandson. He briefly re-established contact with James the night before and if the incoming storm worried his new friends, then it worried him too. He ordered his team to take cover until the danger was over. He looked around for a moment to make sure he was truly alone before making his other desires known.

"I just want her. Be careful of him. He's dangerous." He paused for a moment noting the severity of his words. "Do whatever you have to do."

Chapter Twenty-One

Martinez pulled himself across the wire as quickly as he could. It was a pretty cool day and getting colder but that didn't stop the sweat from dripping off his brow. He was angry. He was angry at Sara for being so selfish, careless, and stupid. Being mad at her was a new thing for him and he found it extremely difficult to reconcile. He had never been mad at her before. The last few days had been completely insane. She was apparently kidnapped by the bisector queen and then rescued by a cowboy from space. It sounded like the plotline to a high budget blockbuster movie. He could smell moisture in the air and hear thunder crack in the distance. As he neared the other side of the gorge, his anger melted into a combination of worry and fear.

The wind started to pick up and blew his black hair into his face making it hard for him to see. The storms on Sarisart were dangerous and unpredictable. They often produced ice shards large enough to kill anyone they hit. A fact they learned the hard way only a month after landing. There was no warning at all. No obvious warnings of impending doom. Nothing. The colonists were still busy trying to set up perpetual survival. Perpetual Survival was one of those impossible things that every scientist hoped to achieve. A self-contained colony with enough crops and supplies to last indefinitely. They didn't waste any time. From day one they started planning and planting fields. It was hard work and very stressful but such was the nature of the beast.

It happened out of nowhere. It was an hour or so before sunset and the colonists were having a picnic. That was before the cafeteria was completely set up and before the rec center was even a thought in the designer's mind. It was a peaceful setting. A tranquil day. And then it was utter chaos. A large ice dagger from above struck a promising young botanist in the shoulder. Unfortunately, Martinez had an up close and personal view of it because he was standing less than six feet away from her at the time. He sprang into action immediately and tried to stop the blood but it was no use. Her shoulder had been all but severed and stopping the blood with his bare hands was impossible.

It didn't take long for them to set up barometers to help predict the weather better. Not all storms were deadly and it was important to know what to expect. But Martinez and his small team of rescuers didn't have the ability to measure what kind of storm was coming. All they had was a healthy fear of all storms, which was why it was so important to get to Sara before it arrived.

He pulled himself into the tree that the drone was anchored in and lowered himself onto a large branch. He took a moment to catch his breath before accessing the drones casing in order to free the cable. His heart still thumped wildly in his chest from the massive physical exertion but that didn't stop him from taking a moment to scan the ground below.

"Sara!" He called out for her as he worked. "Sara!"

"Angie?" He saw her walking toward the tree carrying her harness.

Martinez pulled the wire around the trunk of the tree and tightly screwed the clamp shut. Knowing she was safe caused a wave of relief to wash over him. He made sure he sent the trolley back before jumping down. There was a humming sound behind him so he looked up. The drone's drills were retracting so it could disengage from the tree. His anger returned. "Sara, why the hell did you do that?"

"Because I'm freaking out!" Her arms flared to the sides and then bounced dramatically. "We haven't had a chance to talk about what's going on!"

The drone floated over his head and into the forest toward the mountain. He grabbed her arm and turned her around. "That'll have to wait. There's a storm coming!"

They jogged behind the drone for almost a half mile when an ice shard struck the ground next to them. The impact caused dirt and bits of rock to explode in every direction. Sara screamed and instinctively grabbed Martinez' arm. He could plainly see that she was struggling and hoped that the cave wasn't too much farther away. It seemed to get darker with each footfall. Huge raindrops started to fall like water balloons from the sky.

"I'm not going to be able to keep up!" Sara was breathing heavily and her face was bright red.

He put one arm around her and then scooped up her legs with the other. He ran with her in his arms as she held him tightly. "It's not much farther!" He assured her.

The drone suddenly dipped under a branch and then slowed down. He watched as it entered the darkness in front of him but he kept up his pace. The cave wasn't very big but it would definitely protect them for a little while. He held her against him while he tried to catch his breath. He was afraid to put her down just in case they had to run again. If he knew anything about surviving in the wilderness, he knew that caves were usually occupied. He scanned it from end to end, half expecting a creature they had never seen before, to pop out and eviscerate them. He felt her hand slip from his neck to his chest where she tapped him.

234

"It's okay. Put me down."

He glanced down at her. Her eyes were wide and her pupils were getting bigger as she looked around in fear. She definitely wasn't 'okay' but was thinking about him and the fact that he was about to collapse. He set her down on a large rock and then crouched down to look her in the face. He smoothed back the hair on both sides of her head. "Are you okay? Were you hit?"

She gently grabbed his hands and took them away from her face. "I'm fine, Angie." She pointed at his leg. "But you're not."

She called him Angie again. When she first proposed it, he thought that he wouldn't like it because it was a girl's name, but he was wrong. He liked it. He liked it a lot. He didn't know he had been injured until she pointed it out. He looked down at his leg and saw a thin ice shard protruding from his thigh. He grabbed ahold of it and pulled it out. The son-of-a-bitch wasn't very big but it hurt like a bastard. Liberating the shard caused the wound bleed freely. He quickly fetched a small towel out of his backpack and held pressure to it.

Sara stood up. "Take your pants off and sit down." She knelt down next to his pack and rummaged through it until she found what she was looking for. She took out a small first-aid kit and then looked up at him. "I said take your pants off."

"I'm fine."

"Did I ask you if you were fine?" She stared up at him. "What? Are you shy? Going commando or something? Get over it."

He knew the woman kneeling in front of him and he knew her well. Which meant he wasn't going to win. His belt jingled a little as he released it and then undid the snap on his pants as he slipped off his shoes. "This isn't how I imagined this would go."

He had a black pair of form-fitting boxer briefs on underneath his pants. When he looked down at his leg, he didn't expect to see so much blood. Sara immediately pressed the towel up against the wound and told him to sit down. She cleaned the wound with antiseptic which made him hiss in pain. She glanced up at him briefly.

"I'm sorry you got hurt saving me." She pressed down a specially designed bandage and then pulled the sides closed. When she was satisfied that the wound was sufficiently closed, she pressed down the sides. "I'm glad you're here." She rubbed the end of her nose and then sniffed. "I mean, if you were never born, I'd hate to think about where I might be." She smiled weakly. "I'd probably be dead if it wasn't for you." She shrugged. "And I'm not just talking about today."

Her words affected him more than he expected. He was filled with so much joy that he actually laughed. He put his hand on the side of her face and looked into her eyes for a moment before kissing her gently on the lips. Her lips were soft and warm and he didn't want to stop. He looked into her eyes again. They twinkled slightly in the outside light as thunder cracked overhead. She smiled at him before launching herself at him, mashing her lips against his, and kissing him passionately. It wasn't how he imagined any of it happening. He certainly didn't think the first time they would make love it would be in a dirty and dank cave while a storm raged outside. There was a thick moss that grew at the bottom of the cave that served nicely as a makeshift bed.

Feeling her against him made his heart pound wildly as he kissed her and fumbled with the snap of her jeans. It had been years since he had made love to anyone but it was clear that he didn't forget how.

It was as passionate as it was natural. She kissed his neck softly as she embraced him with both her arms and her legs while he thought about nothing except that moment. The first time they were in that position, his mind kept pestering him and telling him that he was making a mistake. He was afraid that if they made love their relationship would change. Sara was very important to him and he didn't want to lose her. But it was different this time. He couldn't think of anything else except her and his need to be with her.

After they made love, they laid on the moss-covered floor of the cave as they held each other and tried to catch their breath. He had never felt so equally good and bad at the same time in his whole life. His only consolation was that he knew that she was feeling the exact same way. It would be hard for them to get past the fact that the only reason they were together was because someone they loved died. How do you deal with something like that?

She told him about Britt and the fact that he and his people were from the future. She laid her head against his chest and played with some of the hair that grew there. "You know that old question; if a tree falls in the woods and there is no one to hear it, does it make a sound?"

He rubbed her shoulder gently. "Yeah, why?"

"If you travel back in time and there's nothing to clue you in on that fact, did you actually go back in time?" She rubbed her eye briefly and then sniffed. He knew she was wiping away tears but he opted to pretend not to notice. She took a deep breath and then let it go. "If we weren't here, they would have never known." She sat up and pulled on her pants. "Maybe time travel and paradoxes don't exist when you do it in a different galaxy than where you started."

He was a little concerned. "Sara? You alright?"

She fixed her shirt and then suddenly climbed on top of him before leaning down to kiss him. The tip of her nose was cold against his. "Yeah, you?"

His heart thumped hard against his chest. Her warm body on top of his felt too good. He put his arms around her and kissed her passionately before replying. "Yeah."

As he got dressed, he watched her carefully roll her harness up and place it in a small mesh bag beneath the drone. The rest of their party would need it to get across the canyon. Martinez contacted Junior as soon as the storm subsided enough to venture out. He could hear birds singing joyfully all around him, which was a very good sign. If they were out and about playing, it meant the danger was over. When they left the cave, they discovered that it rained a great deal. The ground was covered with debris and mud which was bound to make their travels cumbersome. The bright sun peeked through the clouds hurting his eyes as he tried to get his bearings. He watched as Sara pressed a button on the drone and a small display popped up showing Junior's face.

"Hey kiddo," she said, "I'm glad to see you're alright. How is everyone else?"

Everyone was fine. Their new friend, Captain Britt, was a little shell-shocked but other than that everyone was okay. Martinez didn't like him. Not one little bit. If it wasn't for the fact that he saved Sara's life, he would have left him in the wilderness to survive on his own. Sara admitted that she genuinely liked the guy and believed him to be a good person. But she also believed he was keeping something from her. As they followed the drone back to the canyon, he thought about what she said. Britt knew that he traveled back in time because it was obvious. But he believed that he and his crew only travelled back two hundred years, not two thousand. It was a fact that she purposely kept from the captain.

He thought he heard a twig breaking behind him so he looked over his shoulder. He didn't see anything but experience had taught him to be on high alert. If there was one thing that their little impromptu trip had taught him, it was that they didn't know Sarisart as well as they thought they did. He checked his Glock and took another look around. He had fallen back a few steps behind her and found himself staring at her hand. Not because there was anything wrong with it but because he wanted to hold it. His mother showed him no affection at all. Holding hands wasn't exactly something you did with a kid you hated. But if he wanted to be happy, he needed to learn from his past relationships and try to get beyond his upbringing.

Sara turned around and grinned at him. "Are you staring at my butt?"

Martinez laughed. "So, what if I am?"

She laughed and then grabbed his hand and held it while they walked. He squeezed it and then leaned in close. He whispered, "we're being followed. When I say run, run."

Most people would think developing the ability to detect when you're being stalked is alarming. Because if one develops an ability like that, it means they've spent an abnormal amount of time being in danger. He knew there were at least three of them in different locations. It was a classic ambush. He knew they had to be Captain Mason's men because no one else would be out there. That realization also meant that their new friend wasn't their friend at all. They were all approaching from the rear but two of them were coming from opposite sides. This only left one way for them to go. They were being corralled.

He looked at Sara. If he told her to run too early, it would tip off the enemy that they knew about them. He had to maintain the control as long as possible. He could tell that she was scared. He carefully assessed his surroundings and determined a good hiding spot.

He squeezed her hand again and then pointed at it. "Run!"

As soon as she started running, he saw someone dressed in a black jumpsuit running after her. He had to make a decision and make it fast. The smartest thing to do would have been to turn around and disable the two coming after him but… Sara was in danger. His emotions got the best of him as he ran at top speed for her pursuer. The sheriff watched helplessly as the man in black caught up to her, grabbed her by the hair, and then pushed her to the ground.

"SARA!" He yelled.

Someone grabbed him from behind. He instantly went into mercenary mode. He grabbed his attacker by his arm and yanked him forward while simultaneously sweeping his knee. After the man was on the ground, he grabbed him by the head and turned it until he heard that familiar crack. He had hoped that going to Sarisart meant that he wouldn't have to kill anyone ever again but that obviously wasn't true. He dropped the body in the mud and turned just in time to receive a foot to his face. He caught his attacker's foot as it was on the way down and twisted it until he was on the ground. That was the first time he got a good look at him. He was just a kid to Martinez but that wasn't going to stop him from ending him.

The kid was on his feet again in a flash. Martinez reached behind him, grabbed his Glock, and prepared to fire.

"Stop!" A man screamed at Martinez so he hesitated. The man that attacked Sara had her by the hair and was walking her back to them. He held a knife at her throat. "I will kill her."

Martinez locked eyes with Sara. Her eyes were full of fear but she shook her head. He couldn't help looking at the blade of the knife at her neck. He had no idea who the man in front of him was but he seemed to be a much younger version of Captain Mason. His hair was military high and tight and he wore black clothes like the others. He also had a scar above his right eye. The bright red and bloody scratches on the man's knife hand made him happy. They were an obvious gift generously given to him by his captive.

Sara whispered, "Angie."

He looked at the kid next to him. He was pointing a military issued Glock at him. He leaned in timidly and took the sheriff's gun. Martinez was already planning his next move.

The Britt look-alike holding Sara gestured toward the man on the ground. "Check on Archie."

The kid knelt down and held two fingers to the fallen man's neck. "He's dead." He stood back up. "The captain did say he was dangerous."

241

Martinez suddenly kicked Sara in the side which sent both her and her captor backward. He hoped it would give her enough of a distraction to allow her to get away while he grappled with the other man. He punched the man in the stomach hoping to knock the wind out of him while he tried to pull his gun out of his hand. That's when he felt the burn of a bullet tearing through the skin of his shoulder and bursting through the other side.

He heard Sara scream and cry and it broke his heart. "Angie! No! ANGIE!"

Chapter Twenty-Two

It was impossible for her to think straight. Sara was being pulled along by ropes that were tied at her wrists. She tried to concentrate on her steps as she stared at the back of the man who shot Martinez. Her mind kept picturing his lifeless body on the ground. She was in denial. She refused to believe he was dead and held onto the hope that she would see him again. Captain Mason had betrayed her and he was going to pay for that fact. The other man was directly behind her walking so closely that he stepped on the back of her heel. She jolted forward and tried to catch herself before falling but it didn't work. She ended up face first in the mud. The man grabbed her by the arm and yanked her to her feet. Her clothes were completely caked in mud and her hair was matted to her face. She wanted to kill them all. Twelve years ago, she would have fought back and probably would have won but back then it was only her. But now, she had people who depended on her and it made her too careful.

It wasn't long before she was shoved to the floor of their shuttle. If you asked her what the shuttle looked like on the outside, she wouldn't have been able to tell you. She was too immersed in her thoughts to even care. Her captors were talking to each other but she couldn't focus on them or what they were saying.

Somebody shoved her hard. "I'm talking to you!" Sara looked up at him. His green eyes stood out brightly against his red face. He must have been angry at her for some reason but she didn't know why. He got down on her level and yelled in her face. "Can you fix it or not?!"

Sara blinked a few times and cowered. She knew she was losing it but tried to hold it together long enough to figure out what was happening. When she tried to speak, nothing came out, so she cleared her throat. "What?"

The red-faced man pointed at an open access panel. "The ship! Can you fix it!" He practically spat when he yelled. "You are the Mother of Space Travel, aren't you?"

The fact that he called her the Mother of Space Travel wasn't lost on her. It meant that Britt had been in contact with them. She focused in on the access panel for a moment and suddenly realized that they were stranded. As wonderful as the human race was, people were stupid. They would buy a vehicle, year after year, and drive it every day without ever knowing a thing about it. Apparently, two hundred years didn't change that fact. She shook her head as a smug smile crawled slowly across her face.

Sara looked him in the eye. "Fuck you."

His eyebrows shot up before he backhanded her hard across the face. Getting smacked like that brought back some very bad memories about a very bad man. She instinctively buried her head against her knees and covered it with her tied hands.

"Tommy! What the fuck?" James plopped himself down in a chair. "Lay off, will ya?"

"We have to fix the ship and get back somehow!" He was insistent. Tommy grabbed her arm away from her face. "I know you know how to fix it, bitch!"

Britt suddenly stormed in and slammed Tommy up against the wall before punching him in the gut. He put a finger in Tommy's face. "If you ever touch her again, I'll kill you. You understand me? I'll kill you!" He immediately knelt next to Sara and placed his hand on her shoulder. "Are you okay?" He noticed the ropes on her wrists. "What the hell is this?"

Britt took his knife out and cut the ropes. Tommy's face turned redder as his anger built up inside of him. "Her boyfriend killed Archie!"

Sara slapped Britt across the face as hard as she could and then stared hate at him. "They shot Martinez!"

Britt looked hurt and then turned to his grandson. "Is that true? Is he alive?"

James shrugged as if the answer didn't really matter that much. "How the hell would I know? We left him where he fell."

"I told you that he was dangerous but I didn't expect you to kill him!" The captain looked at James as if he were a disappointment.

Sara growled at him. "I hate you."

"That hurts, Little Lady." Britt frowned. "It really does." He pointed to the access panel. "Now hows about you fix my ship before the rest of your friends figure out where I disappeared to and we have to kill them too."

And there it was. The threat that was guaranteed to get her to help them. There was no way she was going to let Britt kill Junior and the others. They kept calling her the Mother of Space Travel but Junior was responsible for the propulsion technology that they still used. As his guardian, she was with him every step of the way and helped him when she could. Sara considered herself a very honest woman so she had no problems giving credit where credit was due. Unfortunately, considering Junior's origins, she had to protect him. She crawled over to the access panel and looked inside. She knew if anyone was going to tell her what was wrong with the shuttle, it would be the shuttle itself. After all, she came from a time where cars told their owners when it needed an oil change. She scrolled through the computer and read the last maintenance report.

She turned to Britt. "If I do this, will you let me go?"

He winced and shook his head. "No, I'm sorry, Sara. You're too important to me. I need you."

"For what?" Sara was genuinely curious. What could he possibly need with her?

James chuckled. "We found out that the wormhole is omnipotent and that it sends people where they need to be."

"If that were true, it'd just send me right back here." She glared at James.

The shuttle had a problem with a power coupling which meant it wasn't getting any power to a key system. She pushed her hair back behind her ear and leaned through the small door into the engine as far as she could. She wiggled every cord she could find until she found the culprit. The first thing you always do when troubleshooting a power issue was check all the connections. Britt's men had been trapped on the planet for several days just because the maintenance crew failed to press a cord in all the way.

Sara didn't want to help them but she also didn't want anyone else to get hurt. She suddenly felt dizzy and sick to her stomach so she backed out slowly. Sweat began to drip off her brow and she started to shake. She couldn't remember how she ended up on the floor but she suddenly became aware of how cold it was against her cheek. Britt had his hand on her back and was saying her name but he seemed so far away. His soft voice echoed like he was sitting in a tin can as he repeatedly tried to bring her back. It was a strange feeling. She couldn't move or do anything but she was completely conscious and aware of her surroundings. She didn't know what was happening but she was afraid she was going to die. She also became acutely aware that her fear was making her heart beat out of control.

She felt like she was walking through a tunnel. It was dark except for a dim light but she could hear voices that she couldn't quite make out. She moved closer to them hoping that it would bring her closer to salvation. As her consciousness floated toward them, her surroundings got a little brighter allowing her to see better. She was in a cave of some kind. The walls were made of clay or mud with cylindric holes dug into them. In her state of mind, it almost seemed like she was in a mausoleum and the holes were filled with the bodies of the departed. But it soon became clear what they actually were. She was in a bisector nursery and those holes contained their growing young. Each one was filled with an amber colored jelly that served to protect and feed the young ones as they matured. She tried to look inside one, but she was distracted by the need to find the voices and the way out.

Sara heard them again so she moved toward them. It was Britt's grandson and his crew. They were all dressed in dark jumpsuits with work boots and gloves. There were three of them. She recognized James and Tommy but not the third. The unknown man looked to be around twenty or so but closely resembled Tommy. It made her wonder if they were related. She watched as they placed charges along the floor of the cave and became alarmed. She didn't know why they were in the nursery but it was clear that they meant to destroy it. Sara couldn't allow that to happen.

She confronted James. "What the hell do you think you're doing?"

James just ignored her and kept working. He set the detonator for five minutes and then picked up a gun and his backpack. The weapon was an automatic rifle of some kind that she had never seen before. She tried again.

"Are you crazy?" She stepped in front of him. "You can't do this!"

Not only did he ignore her again but he walked right through her. That's when it became clear to her that what she was seeing what had already happened and she knew exactly who was showing it to her. The Bisector Queen. She shook her head as sadness overtook her mind. Britt had told her that his grandson's mission was to find more uranium. Apparently, he and his crew weren't above killing innocent creatures to get it. It ashamed her.

She tried to follow James as he left the cavern but she couldn't. She was a captive witness to the horrible events that were about to occur. It didn't feel like a full five minutes had gone by when the cave exploded around her. If she thought her first conversation with the queen was terrifying, it paled in comparison to this one. Not only did she watch as the cavern caved in around her, but she heard the high-pitched screams of the bisector young as they were injured or dying. Her heart ached for them and she wanted to help but she knew it was too late.

She could feel the queen's anger grow above her sorrow. She knew what this trespass meant for her people but she hoped she would get the chance to defend them. Her consciousness suddenly sped away until her eyes could detect light behind her lids and she again felt the coolness of the floor. Someone had turned her onto her back. Britt was still talking to her.

"Come on, Little Lady, open those beautiful blues for me."

The man confused the shit out of her. He seemed like a nice guy who cared about her yet he had no problems kidnapping her. That thought made her cringe. Wasn't that what Andrew had done to her the first time they met? The light hurt her eyes and her head was pounding. Britt was leaning over her looking worried and somewhat scared.

"Sara?" He smoothed her hair back. "You okay? What happened? You get zapped or something?"

She slowly sat up and then rubbed her face. Britt was still looking at her like a worried man about to lose his true love. She looked from him to Tommy and then to James. She shook her head in disdain. "You fuckers just signed a death warrant for my people."

Britt flashed a look at James. "What are you talking about?"

Sara moved to her knees and then put her hands on the ground before standing slowly. "They blew up a bunch of bisector babies and now the queen thinks we broke our truce."

That captain's eyes went wide as his mouth dropped open. "What?" He looked at his grandson. "Is that true?"

James crinkled his brow and grimaced hard. He pointed outside the shuttle but looked at Sara. "What? You mean those gross little bastards in the cave walls?" He shrugged. He pointed to the metal crates stacked along the wall. "So fuckin what? Who cares about bugs? We needed the Uranium."

Sara looked out the open door of the shuttle. It was a hatchback that opened up toward the sky so that loading and unloading it would be easy. "She's here and she's gonna kill us all."

Tommy's voice erupted behind her. "How does she know this shit?"

Britt stood next to her and scanned the tree line. "Shut up, Tommy."

Sara took his hand in hers and held it. "I need to talk to her." She begged the captain with her eyes. "Please."

He nodded sadly and whispered. "Go."

As she stepped out of the shuttle, she heard James. "Gramps, what the hell are you doing? You're letting her go?"

She ignored the stupid brat and kept going. Her main concern was pleading her case to the queen. The sun was setting behind the trees as she stepped out into the clearing. Sara couldn't see her but she knew exactly where to go. She walked to the tree line and waited for the queen to come out. Her heart was pounding in her chest. The Bisector Queen was scary and formidable and made her feel like a frightened little girl. She Moreover, she felt responsible for the loss of her nursery even though she had nothing to do with it. Perhaps it was because humankind was still stupid enough to believe that there was no intelligent life in the universe other than their own. They were despicable and deserved her wrath. Herself included.

She cowered and wrung her hands together as the queen walked out of the shadows. She was just as big as she ever was but somehow managed to evolve since the last time she had seen her. Both her pinchers and her arms had small spikes or stingers on them. It made her wonder if the queen intended to use them on her. Britt and his crew watched from the shuttle but she could hear movement from the woods behind the queen. She was finding it hard to stay in place because all she wanted to do was run and hide. Before that day, she could count the number of times she felt sheer terror on one hand and they were all tied to Sarisart. The first time was when the plane she was on got sucked through a wormhole and crash landed on another planet. The second time was sitting in the command chair of the Moon's Eye and blasting off. The third was her first meeting with the bisectors where she watched her husband die and the fourth was her intimate conversation with the queen. All of those events paled in comparison to the terror she felt at that moment.

She clasped her hands together under her chin almost as if she was praying and looked up at the queen's massive ant-like head. That's when something caught the corner of her eye. James stepped out of the back of the shuttle with his gun and started firing at the queen. When you are facing death, everything seems to slow down. It's a defense mechanism of the mind that is supposed to give you enough time to plan your next move, and possibly save your life. As she turned back to the queen, she saw him.

Martinez jumped in front of the bisector and held his hand up at James. "No! Stop!"

A few of the bullets hit the queen but they only ricocheted off of her as if she were bulletproof. It must have been another advancement she added in order to protect herself from them. Unfortunately, Martinez wasn't so lucky. He was hit in the abdomen and fell to the ground at Sara's feet as the queen prepared to do some firing of her own. She held up one of her arms and pointed it at James and let a flurry of those stingers loose. She watched in horror as Britt kicked his grandson in the side causing them both to fall to the ground as the stingers flew past them and hit Tommy squarely in the chest. Everything was happening so fast. The doctor stepped out of the woods and knelt next to Martinez while the bisector queen aimed one of her stingers at him.

Sara held both her hands up at her. "STOP! STOP! PLEASE!" The queen's attention was suddenly on her. "Please, I know you can understand me." Her bottom lip trembled. "They weren't my people! We didn't break our truce." She felt like she couldn't breathe. She looked down at Martinez. There was so much blood. She kneeled down and held his hand. "Angie," she cried his name.

His eyes were sad and it seemed like he wanted to say something but he lost consciousness. She looked at the doctor who sadly shook his head at her. "He isn't going to make it without surgery."

She stood back up as tears streamed out of her eyes. The queen seemed to be looking down at him. 'Was he trying to protect you, or me?'

Sara was finding it hard to speak. She swallowed hard. "He was trying to protect you. He knew about the truce and didn't want anyone to jeopardize it."

'This trespass will not go unpunished.'

She tried to remain composed as she noticed Junior and the others behind the doctor. She looked up at the queen again. "Please, let us go. I promise you, you'll get your justice."

The Queen did let them go. But only with the promise to kill all of her people if she didn't return in three days' time. Junior and the doctor picked up Martinez and walked behind Sara as they headed toward the shuttle. Britt was frantically trying to rouse Tommy but it wasn't working which left James holding a gun on them. She bravely walked in front of her people until she was standing in front of him. She stared hate into his eyes. He was the reason Angie was bleeding to death behind her. Her eyes flicked over to Britt and then back.

She knew how the captain felt about her and she decided to use it to her advantage. "Cake, can I get your attention for a minute, please?"

Sara knew what was going to happen but she was glad to see it just the same. When Britt looked up and noticed that James was pointing a gun in her face, he launched toward them, pulled the gun from his hands, and then smacked him upside the head. "What the hell's wrong with you! Aren't you the one that said we needed her?"

She stepped aside so that he could see Martinez. "You need me, I need you... to fix him." She blinked new and heavy tears out of her eyes. "Please," she whispered, "I'll do anything."

Britt looked past her at Martinez and the rest of her group. He sighed and then nodded. "You know I can't refuse you, Sunshine." He pointed behind him. "Fire her up, and let's go."

Chapter Twenty-Three

Dean watched the shuttle arrive on the monitors and knew it was time to put their plan into action. He had to find Ava as soon as possible so that she could do her magic. He hurried down the corridor wishing his boots were made of pillows. He hated the way they clanked against the metal grating that covered the floors. They were a necessary evil on a spaceship. The access panels allowed them to easily get to and fix components between the floors. Components like water lines, air channels, or electricity. It made him think of the dark year. Fifteen people in sector ten died of affixation because of a short in the air filtration system. Not only was the short very hard to locate but the only people who knew the system like the back of their hands had died long ago. The line had to be traced from the source to the break which took nearly eight months. Which meant everyone in sector ten had to double up with other people. Some had to live in the bulkheads while others lived in the hangers. By the sixth month the residents were ready to kill or be killed. As a matter of fact, one man shot himself out an airlock because he wanted space. Well… he sure got it.

He pressed the skin just beneath his right ear and called Reggie. "It's do or die, man."

"Hope it's not do and die. I'll get him," Reggie responded.

Dean wished that things didn't have to get dirty but he was left without any options. He picked up the pace. Ava was right where he expected her to be. She was in her quarters. She shared it with her aunt and her uncle because her parents died when she was young. She was in her room laying on her bed watching an old tv show that was filmed on Earth over two hundred years ago. He used to spend time watching those shows too but at a certain point, you run out

255

of things to watch. Ava was always fond of pointing out that was when you started over. It wasn't as if they made new live-action shows. There were a few people on the ship who thrived at making animated movies. Some of them were quite realistic. It was why he was so hell-bent on landing the Swagger instead of remaining in space forever. One of the animated shows he watched took place on a green planet that depicted treehouses and sunsets. The children laughed and played out in the open and didn't have a care in the world. That's what he wanted for the children he planned on having with Ava.

Dean was by no means stupid. He knew that living on the planet below wouldn't be all sunshine and rainbows, but it had to be better than spending his whole life aboard the Swagger. Landing the ship on that planet would give all of them a whole new set of problems, but it was the right thing to do. Ava deserved to spend the rest of her days in a beautiful place with fresh air and infinite possibilities. He stood in her doorway for a few moments watching her.

She smiled as soon as she saw him. She had obviously darkened her green hair and it looked good. She jumped up and hugged him tight before kissing him softly on the mouth. He liked feeling her in his arms. Dean looked down at her and smiled. "Today's the day."

Ava smiled broadly. "Really?" She frowned as she touched his hair and let it pass through her fingers as she brought it down to his shoulder. "I'm gonna miss it."

"You've got the stuff?" He slipped his hand around to her butt and gave it a squeeze.

She instantly pulled his hand away but gave him a seductive smile. "Of course."

The game was on. Dean knew that it wouldn't be hard for Reggie to get James to visit Oomie. The old lady was having issues with her health due to her advanced age and guilt always worked on his brother. Of course, if he didn't come willingly, he would need to be nabbed. The walk to Oomie's reaffirmed the need for the people of the Swagger to be on a planet with lots of sunlight. It was faster to cut through the poor sector. Dean was always taught not to judge people. Each class always thought they were better than the lower one. But Dean knew the plight of the poor sector first hand. The other classes complain that the children are a bunch of unruly thugs. This was because those children had no one watching them while their parents were working. The children were basically left alone. If one of them had a bad idea, the other egged him on until he did it. At least the children were required to have sensitivity training in school. They knew right from wrong but the problem was getting them to feel the difference.

They passed a few children ranging from around six to ten years who were playing in the corridors. They were kicking around a ball made of foil and causing a ruckus. Dean knew that it wouldn't be long before someone came out and yelled at them so he just let them play. The children had to play in the corridors because their quarters weren't big enough to do much of anything. There were several small parks around the ship where the kids could potentially play but they were all regulated and children under the age of twelve had to have an adult with them. Ava smiled and played with them as they passed. He loved to watch her with the children. Her eyes would always light up and her mood would change for the better. She loved kids and it showed. He stood at the end of the hall and waited for her as she launched the foil ball back to them.

He smiled at her as she walked up to him. "You're gonna be a great mom."

She hugged him and then smacked him on the ass. "I think we should get right on that once we land," she whispered.

Her slightest mention of the possibility of sex made the front of his pants slightly tighter. She definitely knew how to motivate him. She hooked her arm through his and happily walked next to him. It made him feel good when she did that. It was as if she wanted everyone to know that she was his. When they made it to Oomie's they found that Reggie was already there, looking very grim. He explained that the landing crew had some casualties.

Dr. Dixon's sickbay was directly above the main hanger for a reason. It had a dedicated elevator so that patients wouldn't have to travel very far to get the immediate help they needed. According to Reggie's sources, not only were the Burton brothers killed, but they were bringing aboard people that were found on the planet below. Dean knew who at least one of those passengers might be. He looked at both of his friends and took a deep breath.

"Look, guys… there's something I need to tell you."

He had known them for a long time and hoped that he could trust them. He filled them in on what he witnessed while he was hiding in the sickbay and both of them were shocked. The fact that time travel was actually a possibility was astounding. Reggie had the most to say about it. He spouted theories about how time travel was only possible when it didn't affect the timeline of that particular galaxy or universe. But it was what he said next that scared the shit out of him.

Reggie leaned back in his chair. "This new revelation is much worse than you think it is. I've studied quantum mechanics and physics and I've talked to more of those wormhole quacks than I'd like to admit and…" He shook his head. "If he detonates a nuke in that wormhole like he wants to, it'll likely reset the timeline."

Dean's mouth dropped open as he gave Reggie a dumb look. "I don't understand what you mean."

Reggie smiled. "That's not surprising, man." He looked at the ceiling for a moment. "Think of it like this, the wormhole exists throughout time and space. This means if you go through it, where you end up is a crapshoot."

Ava picked up one of the chairs and put it behind Dean who took the hint and sat down. She reached into her pack and pulled out a brush. "That still doesn't explain why blowing up the wormhole would reset time."

Reggie blinked a few times and took a moment to think. He chopped both of his hands forward. "Think about it. If you erase the wormhole then the Mother of Space Travel never goes through it. Instead, she colonizes the Moon as planned." He leaned back again and shrugged. "If she were still around, she could have found a way around nuclear propulsion. There would have been no wars. Earth would still be Earth. This ship would have never been commissioned." He gestured to his friends. "And we would have never been born."

Dean starred at Reggie with blank eyes. "In other words, granddad will get what he wanted in the first place. To save the world."

Reggie nodded. "Yeah, by erasing all of us."

Ava pulled out a pair of clippers and turned them on. Dean nervously placed his hands on his knees. "It has to look exactly like his."

"Relax, baby, I'm a professional." She gave him a quick peck on the cheek. "I have a picture of him right here."

She pointed to the table next to him where a tablet featured a picture of James. If he was going to get close enough to Grandpa Britt, he was going to need to look and act like his twin. The new developments meant that they would need to act fast. He loved his grandfather but he was obviously friggin nuts. Dean didn't know where Britt got the idea that the wormhole could transport people through time but the captain had been planning something behind closed doors for years. He didn't find out until recently what he was up to and why. He had absolutely no doubt that his brother came to the same conclusion that Reggie did and it was a huge problem. It meant that both his brother and his grandfather were willing to sacrifice themselves and all the people on the ship in order to 'reset' time and possibly save billions of people.

Billions of people. He had to admit that he would willingly sacrifice himself for the sake of billions of people too. But there was no guarantee that his plan would even work. In Dean's humble opinion, Captain Mason should be focusing on the needs of his people, not that damn wormhole. He took the tablet off the table and fixed it so that he could see his own face. Ava was doing a good job. His hair looked just like his brother's. The only crucial thing that he needed now was a scar above his right eye.

Grampa Britt told James that the scar was a rite of passage, somehow putting a positive spin on the fact that Dean beat the shit out of him for wearing his shirt without asking. It was over a decade ago, and they were just kids, but the shame he felt still carried the same weight. It was a stupid thing to do and he felt really bad about it. Having a twin brother wasn't as fun as it seemed. At a certain point, all Dean wanted to do was be different. His 'black sheep' status started when he refused to get his haircut even though his father threatened to beat him if he didn't. He was sick of being called James by mistake that he tried to distance himself from him as much as possible. He wanted to be different and have his own life but James didn't understand. That's when he decided to take one of Dean's shirts and wear it around the ship. People who were close to Dean knew that it was his favorite shirt so they assumed it was him. And so did Ava. She ran up to him and pecked him on the lips before realizing her mistake. Dean saw red. He did. If folks hadn't pulled him off James, there was a strong possibility he would have killed him.

Ava tipped his head back and kissed him on the forehead before holding a small piece of clear thin plastic in his view. He didn't know exactly how she made the fake scar but he was grateful that he had such a talented girlfriend. He couldn't help staring into her eyes while she was affixing it because he literally had nowhere else to look. It was one of those silent moments where they both knew what the other was thinking. That goddamned scar had come back to haunt them. He spent his adult years trying not to look like James and now a fucking scar, a scar he put on him, could be his undoing.

Of course, despite the fact that he apologized at least a hundred times, their relationship was never the same after that. They hung out with different people and tried to steer clear of each other. The only times they would find themselves in the same room together was usually some kind of family function or a special occasion. The twins only had one friend in common and he was currently sitting across from Dean trying to figure out the best way to lure James into their trap. He was entirely too focused on his laptop computer.

"Looks like the doc called O negs to the infirmary." Reggie's voice suddenly pierced through the silence.

"James?" Dean felt dread building up within him and churning in his stomach. "Gramps?"

Reggie shook his head. "Naw, man, I hacked into the feed. It's some guy I've never seen." He turned the computer to face Dean. "See?"

The computer screen featured a view of Dr. Dixon's sickbay. The video was full color and high definition and showed the doctor tending to a man in one of his beds. A small blonde woman in clothes caked with mud was standing next to the bed holding his hand.

He scooted his chair over to Reggie but Ava protested. "Babe, I wasn't done yet!"

Dean leaned in close and looked at the video. He pointed at the woman. "That… is Captain Sara Zeeman."

Reggie rubbed his face. "This is some pretty fucked up shit."

Dean looked up at Ava and then nodded at his friend. "Yeah, it is."

Reggie gave his friend a serious look. "Our friend on the bed has two bullet wounds." He tipped his head down but kept his eyes on his friend. "That means somebody shot him."

"I know what it means, Reggie."

"I'm just pointing out that they want this bad enough to kill people." He watched the laptop. "How hard are we willing to play?"

Reggie definitely had a valid point. How far was he willing to go? Was he willing to kill his brother or his grandfather? He suddenly had visions of hand to hand combat with his granddad and he didn't like it, not one little bit. If he had his way, everything would end with everyone still intact.

He also wondered exactly what would happen to him and his friends once they landed the ship. He may be the captain's grandson but he would also be a mutineer, which is punishable by death in any time. He pressed his palms together and looked at his friend.

"It'd be one thing if everyone on this ship was aware of his plan and willing to sacrifice themselves right along with him," he stood up and put his arm around Ava, "but no one deserves to be erased. Someone needs to fight for them."

Reggie pointed at the laptop. "Look."

James appeared on the video. He found it very weird that he was wearing a standard utility jumpsuit from the ship. He knew that his brother wouldn't be caught dead in such an outfit. He watched as he stepped up to Sara and grabbed her by the upper arm. She obviously didn't want to leave the man in the bed but she reluctantly let go of his hand. What did they want with The Mother? It didn't make any sense to him. His plans to destroy the wormhole shouldn't change either way because of her. Her presence would just verify what they suspected all along. He wished he knew what was going on but at least they knew where his brother was.

Dean smiled. "This actually got a little bit easier."

Chapter Twenty-Four

It felt good to be back aboard his ship. He just wished that he didn't have to betray his new friends in order to do it. Captain Britt looked around the sickbay's waiting room. Everyone except the doctor and Sara were sitting on the two sofas. He was impatient. He wanted to get Sara alone so that he could talk to her. Perhaps the word 'interrogate' was more appropriate because he intended to get to the truth. He looked around the medical bay and grimaced inwardly when he saw the armed guards at the door. They were both wearing dark blue military uniforms that featured an American Flag and The USS Newman imprinted on them. He hated the fact that they were armed but it was necessary. He felt someone watching him so he turned his head. It was Tran. As soon as he made eye contact, she quickly looked away. After the storm, it was fairly easy to convince her to let him zipline across the canyon first. He didn't tell her that he didn't intend to send the trolley back so they could use it too. Of course, he had no doubt that she would find a way to fix the one that was broken. Their mere presence on his ship was proof of her impressive skills. He looked sidelong at James who was leaning against the wall with his arms across his chest. The kid was seriously trying his patience. Britt was willing to do what had to be done but not if involved murder.

He turned his head to look into Dixon's trauma room and took another hit to his heart. Martinez nearly died because his grandson shot him. Not once, but twice. He watched Sara dote over him as the doctor placed a surgodisc over his wound and then pressed the button. The surgery disc would extract the bullet and then inject Martinez with nanobots. The bots would spend the next several days pretending to be part of him while he healed. Dr. Bowman hung another bag of blood on the IV pole and then checked his patient's vital signs the old-fashioned way. It made Britt smile because all the information the doctor needed was on the display above the bed. When he really thought about it, he couldn't blame the doctor for not trusting them. In theory, the digital display could be altered to reflect whatever they wanted him to see.

He felt like he was being patient. They had already been aboard the ship for several hours and he wanted to get things moving. His eyes wandered to one of the exam rooms where a sheet covered Tommy's body. It had several stingers, or whatever the hell those things were, in its chest and the doctor wanted to examine them as soon as possible. Britt shook his head. It seemed like such a senseless death but realistically, if he accomplished what he wanted, none of it would matter.

He listened carefully while the Dr. Dixon assured Sara that Martinez would be fine and then moved into the doorway.

"Sara, we need to talk." The captain tried to be gentle but he was afraid of how it sounded.

She shook her head. "No, I need to stay with Angie."

Dr. Bowman smiled at her. "Okay, I gotta ask, why do you keep calling him Angie?"

She rubbed her eye and sniffed without ever looking away from Martinez. "His name is Angelo."

Britt glanced over his shoulder at his grandson. It was all too easy to make him the bad guy. James instantly took the hint by walking into the room and grabbing her upper arm. She tried to pull it away but he held it firm.

Dr. Bowman protested. "Hey! What the hell do you think you're doing? Let her go!"

Britt had to intervene before things escalated. "Sara," she made eye contact with him, "you promised."

The way she looked at him made him feel like he was worse than a criminal. It made him feel like the worst human who ever lived. She reluctantly let go of Angelo's hand and let James lead her out of the room.

Dr. Dixon followed them out. "Where do you think you're taking my patient?"

"Actually, she's my patient." Dr. Bowman stepped forward. "And I'd like to know too."

Britt got hot. "Doctor, this is my ship…"

"Captain," Dr. Dixon cut him off, "I need to examine her. Or have you forgotten that fact?"

He was taken back for a moment. He tipped his head and eyed the doctor. A day ago, Dr. Dixon claimed that Sara was out of danger and to get her aboard his ship, he may have to lie. Now he was insisting that he needed to examine her. The man was a good friend who he trusted, which meant circumstances may have changed. "I'm sure your examination can wait a few minutes, can't it?"

"Take a look at her." Dr. Dixon pointed at Sara. He met the captain's stare. "Just take a good look at her."

He looked at her but he didn't know what the doctor was getting at until he stopped and really looked at her. Sara had dried mud in her hair and on her face. The mud was white and crusty which made it very easy to see the tracks that her tears left behind. It was strange, but her eyes no longer looked blue and instead were dark. Her clothes and shoes were covered in mud too. She didn't just look bad, she looked broken, and he was the one responsible for it. She stared at the floor without blinking, almost as if she was in a trance.

Britt gently put his hand on her shoulder. "Sara? Are you okay?"

She didn't answer. Instead, her head slowly turned to Martinez. He could tell it was killing her to leave his side.

"Whatever you want with her," the old doctor began, "I'm sure it can wait until she gets cleaned up." He pointed to the floor. "Besides, she's getting mud all over my sickbay."

"Fine." Britt looked at his grandson. "I guess we could use a little sprucing up too."

"What?" James yelled, "why are you letting him tell you what to do?"

He glared at James. "Since when is it okay for you to second guess me?" He got within inches of him and looked him in the eye. "This can wait an hour."

James tried his damnedest to stare down his patriarch but eventually relented. He turned slowly and headed for the door. "Fine. But when I come back, she better have some answers for us."

Dr. Dixon touched Sara's elbow and then pointed down a hallway. "This way, my dear." As he led her down the corridor, he called behind him, "we'll need you to override the time limit on the shower. I'm sure she'll need more than three minutes."

Britt knew he was right. Three minutes to shower was atrocious but it was necessary. He had to restrict water usage to a minimum due to shortages. It unfortunately meant that there were a lot of stinky people in close quarters. The mandate restricted shower frequency to once a week for three minutes unless there was an exception. An exception usually meant that something unexpected or terrible happened. He followed them into the clinic's bathroom. It was white as white could be with pristine walls and clean tiles. It was so bright it hurt his eyes.

Dr. Dixon pulled open a large shiny aluminum cabinet and took out a sealed pack with clothing in it. "These should fit you until we can get you something more suitable."

"I can have her clothes laundered." Britt offered but neither of them acknowledged that he said something.

Sara took the pack and stared blankly at it. The clothes he gave her were nothing more than a standard pair of surgical scrubs with some hospital booties for her feet. She placed the pack on the stool next to the shower and then slipped her muddy shoes off. Dr. Dixon pointed at her wrist where the nanocharger was fastened. "Here, let me take that off for you. Those bastards are long dead anyway."

The captain walked up to the control panel for the shower and held his ring up to the scanner. "I can only give you ten minutes." He glanced at her briefly. "When you're ready just hit this button. Sorry, it's not hot. Just warm."

He nodded at the doctor and they both left the bathroom. He caught the image of her peeling off a mud-encrusted sock and dropping it on the floor before he slid the door shut. "She hates me."

The doctor practically snarled at Britt. "With good reason!" His friend was mad at him and it showed. He pulled him into his quarters to confront him. "What the hell is going on?"

It didn't matter to the doctor that Britt wasn't the one that shot the man in his sickbay, all that mattered was that he was responsible. There definitely was a marked shift in the way she looked at the captain and it made him feel incredibly bad about himself. Although his friend wanted an explanation, he declined to give him one. He tried to be as polite as possible and excused himself before he said or did something stupid. He walked back out to the clinic's waiting room where he told his men to guard the door.

"Make sure no one leaves."

As he walked away, he thought about the command he gave them. He wanted to qualify it and tell them to be non-violent with any confrontations but he couldn't look weak in front of his men. His ship suddenly groaned. The poor old gal was experiencing growing pains. In truth, it was built to last but supplies were hard to come by. They had to reclaim metal from seldom-used areas to make new parts for her more than once. If they were still near Earth, they could salvage whatever they needed from derelict ships or from the planet itself but food was a whole other monster. Before they found the green planet the inhabitants called Sarisart, he and his grandsons spent many nights talking about the wormhole. Dean was fascinated by the fact that a hole in space could bring people from one place to another in the blink of an eye. It might have been a rough ride but the ship and everyone aboard got through in one piece.

Dean was obsessed with Sara Zeeman, not only because she was The Mother of Space Travel, but because she and her people were the first to travel through the wormhole. The ship was christened a military ship and therefore had a huge cache of classified files. All of the Star Class ships possessed a complete hard drive of military files just in case something happened to Earth. Britt had made the distinct mistake of unlocking the files with his clearance and giving the lad access. If he had denied his request, things would have been a lot easier. Most of the kid's research turned up information that everyone already knew. But that was before he got his hands on some heavily redacted medical files. That's when everything changed. Once he shared the information with Britt and James, they had a mystery that all three of them could bond over.

Both of his grandsons were very smart but each of them excelled in different ways. James was the more scientific one. The kid had probably watched every episode of an old Earth show called Dr. Whozit or something of the sort. He loved talking about the adventures the doctor had and liked to speculate about many things related to it. Needless to say, James could think outside of the box. Way outside of it. So, when Dean showed them General Newman's redacted medical files, James drew conclusions that only he could see.

The files weren't your average run-of-the-mill medical files in which one could find out that the man had adult-onset diabetes. When the general turned seventy-two years old it became evident that he was suffering from dementia. People with secrets and dementia couldn't be placed in any old nursing home. No, General Newman was placed in a very special retirement home for high ranking military officials where he could be monitored around the clock by military personnel. Apparently, at a certain point, it became evident

271

to his babysitters that the general had secrets that even they didn't know. They began to record the odd things that he said and place them in his digital files. Britt watched all of the recordings just like his grandsons did. They really were remarkable. And terrifying. The recordings were the reason why they risked flying through the wormhole in the first place.

He stopped in front of the elevator that would take him to the top of the ship where his quarters were. When the elevators opened a black woman and her young daughter stepped out. They were both dressed in gray drab clothing and looked dirty. Their mere presence made him instinctively hold his breath as he passed. The woman looked at him as if he was about to yell at her. It made him cringe inwardly. He knew it was because his own men treated the lower class like animals. He didn't like it, nor did he condone it, but he failed to stop it. She put her arm around the child and pulled her close.

"Good morning, Captain," she said.

He tried to smile at her but it probably looked as awkward as he felt. He nodded and tipped his hat at them. "Good morning."

He had been off the ship long enough to forget what time it was. When they left the planet below it was getting dark and it would soon be time to sleep. The ride in the elevator seemed to take longer than usual, leaving him with his own thoughts. He had spent his entire life loving women without actually loving any of them. When he wanted company, it was never very hard to find. He had been with more women than he could count and he never felt sorry for it. But for some reason, riding in that elevator up to his room, he felt lonely. He kept thinking of Sara and the way she looked at him. He betrayed her and it was weighing on him.

When he arrived at his quarters, he stood looking at the sliding metal door for a moment. He sighed and shook his head before holding his ring up in front of the scanner. The door made the familiar squeak that it always made as he walked inside. It was his home but it didn't feel right. Somehow, it was bigger and more empty. He took a deep breath and looked from one end of his quarters to the other. It was spacious but very bland and ordinary. It consisted of exactly two rooms. His bedroom and living room were basically the same room which featured a kitchenette, and of course, his bathroom was separate. His place was always spotless. Not because he was a neat freak, but because someone cleaned it every day. He walked into the kitchenette and opened the refrigerator. He grabbed a bottle of water and gulped it down as if he hadn't had anything to drink in days.

"Welcome home, Captain Mason." Lucy's voice suddenly broke the silence scaring the shit out of him.

He wiped his mouth with the back of his arm. "Hey, Lucy, how's it hanging?"

There was a long pause. The last time he asked her that question, she asked him to clarify and he spent nearly twenty minutes explaining that it was just a way of asking how someone is doing. He took his cowboy hat off and placed it on a hook next to the door. As he took his jacket off, he got a good whiff of himself. He smelled like a mixture of dirt and sweat.

"I won't be able to tell you 'how it's hanging' until you take your pants off," She sounded matter-of-fact but added a cute little laugh at the end.

Britt's eyebrows shot up as his eyes rolled to the side. He was both shocked and a little weirded out. "Wow, Lucy, that was almost funny." He pointed at the bathroom. "I'm going to go take a shower but I don't want you in there looking at my junk, okay?"

"Yes, Captain."

He headed for the bathroom.

"Captain?"

He stopped outside the door. "Yes, Lucy?"

"I missed you."

He smiled. "I missed you too, Lucy girl, I missed you too."

Before he could take another step, she spoke again. "Captain?"

Britt exhaled loudly and rubbed his face. "Yes, Lucy?"

"Can I come in if I promise not to look at your junk?"

His mouth dropped open. "No, you can't." He knew he sounded rude and wondered if she noticed it too. "Look, Lucy, I just need some time to myself, okay?"

"Yes, Captain."

When he finally got into the bathroom, he found himself wondering if Lucy was watching him. She could be anywhere and he wouldn't know it. But the doctor had it right. He wanted to clean up. He had been wearing the same clothes for almost four days and he was ready to throw all of them away. Especially his unspeakables. He dropped everything to the floor as he made his way to the shower.

Even the shower made him feel guilty. He was the captain so he had the luxury of bathing in hot water and with no time limit. He may have felt guilty about it, but not enough to take a lukewarm shower or get out before he was completely satisfied. He let hot water pour over the top of his head as he closed his eyes. He thought about his endgame and wondered if he'd actually be able to go through with it. He had nearly five thousand souls aboard his ship, but that was nothing compared to the billions he could save. If he was fighting a war, five thousand people lost in the name of a nation was an acceptable loss. But these were his people. It was his ship. And it was his family.

He ran his hands through his hair and let the water flow down the front of his body. "What the fuck am I doing?" he whispered to himself.

Chapter Twenty-Five

Sara paced back and forth in the bathroom actively concentrating on breathing. She put on the clothes that the old doctor gave her, which turned out to be green surgical scrubs, and didn't include underwear. She felt like she was going to have a panic attack. Somehow, she had to return to Sarisart within three days with James Mason or else all her people will die. That little bastard was responsible for killing the bisector young and for shooting Angie. She needed to find out what they wanted from her and escape as soon as possible. Her heart was pounding in her chest and she was literally incapable of staying still. She looked at her mud-caked clothing on the floor and then suddenly dove for her jacket. She frantically searched through the pockets until she finally found it. Her pillbox. She opened it and stared the contents. There were only five berries left. It made her feel like someone had gripped her heart in their hand and started squeezing it. She wanted to take one more than anything but she needed to have a clear mind. She needed to remain in control. She slipped the pillbox inside her pocket and then nervously rubbed her hands together. Someone knocked on the door.

"Sara, it's Dr. Bowman," there was a pause, "are you okay?"

She walked over to the door and pressed the button to open it. When the door slid open, he stood looking at her as if he were seeing her for the first time. He grinned slightly and tipped his head to the side. "So… these people are from the future, huh?"

She shook her head back and forth and whispered. "I don't know what's happening."

Chad turned his palms up for a moment and then let his hands fall to his sides. "A couple of days ago we set out to find you and bring you home. Now, we're in a spaceship from two hundred years in the future."

He put his hand on her shoulder and she tipped her head forward until it was resting against his chest. "I just want to go home."

"I know, I know." He rubbed her back. "Come on. We need to get you checked out."

He gently nudged her toward the door. On a normal day, in a normal situation, she would have elbowed him in the ribs. "I still hate you."

"As you should."

Home. She didn't just want to go home. She wanted to go back to Earth. But the goddamned wormhole was the only way to get there and it wasn't likely to bring you where you wanted to go. The ship she was in may have been from the future but it wasn't capable of lightspeed. And even if it was, they probably didn't know which way home was. When she walked back into the clinic, her first instinct was to check on Angelo. She looked into his room expecting to see him resting but he was wide awake and made eye contact with her as she passed. Chad showed her into another examination room where Dr. Dixon was already waiting. Sara found herself a little scared. She laid down on the bed like they wanted her to and looked up at the ceiling as she prepared herself for the bad news she expected to receive. She watched Dr. Bowman out of the corner of her eye as he looked at the digital display above her head. As she waited for answers her mind began to wonder. She wanted to see her son Drew and his sweet little face. If she had known that the last time she saw him… might be the last time she saw him, she would have hugged him a little bit longer. She couldn't bear the thought that he might meet his end being terrorized by the bisectors and his mother won't be anywhere in sight. She needed to get back to the planet. She needed to protect her son. If she had to grab him and run away, that's what she would do. She would do anything for Drew. Anything. Including turn herself into the bisector queen and hope beyond hope that she would take her as payment.

Dr. Dixon's face appeared above her. His old tired eyes showed genuine concern for her but she barely noticed when he drew her blood. She was too busy worrying about her son and what might happen to him. She half listened as the doctors talked.

"I can't believe technology has advanced this far in only two hundred years." Dr. Bowman said as he grabbed her wrist to take her pulse. He pointed at the screen. "Is this accurate?"

The old man moved to see what the doctor was pointing at. "Yes. Her telomeres are exceptionally long."

Dr. Bowman furrowed his brow at her. "Damn."

Sara rolled her eyes. "What now?"

He looked back up at the display and shook his head. "Nothing. Everything's fine. You're gonna be fine."

"What the hell is a telomere?" Angelo's voice came from the door.

Sara immediately sat up with a look of shock on her face. He was standing in the doorway with no shirt on. The surgodisc was attached to his stomach just to the left of his bellybutton. The center glowed slightly and seemed to be moving. A white bandage was wrapped snugly around his right arm just beneath his shoulder. Her mouth dropped open. "What the hell are you doing out of bed?"

"It's okay, he's fine," Dr. Dixon waved his hand at her as if she was being overprotective.

Martinez smiled and then looked down at the disc. He touched it lightly. "It kinda makes me feel like Iron Man."

Sara jumped down from the bed and walked up to him. She stopped within inches of him and looked him the eyes. Watching him get shot was very traumatic for her and she wasn't handling it well. Her bottom lip trembled as the tears shined in her eyes. She really liked Martinez and really wanted to be with him but she couldn't bury another man that she loved. He moved her hair behind her ear and then let his hand rest at the back of her neck. She suddenly felt like she couldn't breathe. She had to get out of there. She turned on her heel and ran down the hall toward the doctor's quarters. The only thing she wanted to do at the moment was come up with a plan. She either needed to get off the ship and get back to her son or she needed to convince Britt to evacuate her people. She stuck her hand in her pocket again and let it enclose around her pillbox. It somehow made her feel better just to hold it in her hand.

A commotion came from the clinic behind her. She could hear her friends yelling at someone in protest. Her first instinct was to go see if she could help. Just as she turned around, James grabbed her and pushed her all the way into the doctor's quarters. It was very small with nothing but a sofa and coffee table in the living room. It faced the wall which had a large monitor on it that served as his entertainment. Once they were inside, James shoved her forward which almost made her trip. He suddenly put both his hands up at her.

"Wait!" His eyes were wide and he waved his hands back and forth. He lowered his voice. "I'm not James. We need to talk and we don't have much time!"

Dr. Dixon rushed down the hallway and grabbed James. "Hey! You can't just burst into my clinic and just go wherever you want!"

"It's me, doc! It's Dean!"

Sara looked at the man closely. He definitely looked like the man who attacked her and shot Martinez. The doctor squinted at him and then reached up and tried to touch his eyebrow but the man slapped his hand away. It was that move that revealed the truth to Sara because she got a good look at his forearm. She grabbed it and pulled it closer to her so she could inspect it. She clearly remembered digging her fingernails into his flesh and pulling back as hard as she could.

She looked at the doctor. "This isn't James." She pushed his arm downward and away from her. "I scratched him pretty badly when he was holding a knife to my neck."

Their mouths dropped open and wanted her to confirm what she said in unison, "James held a knife to your throat?"

Sara tipped her head back to the ceiling and pointed to a small cut on her neck. Dean told her his story but all she could think about the berries in her pocket and how much she wanted one. She tried to focus on what he was saying but it was getting harder and harder as the minutes ticked by. When he said that he intended to thwart his grandfather's plans and land the Swagger on Sarisart, she forced herself to concentrate. Landing the ship would make it easier for her to get James to the queen.

"I need the captain's ring, it's the key to everything." Dean looked over his shoulder. "He's going to be here any minute."

"He's going to know it's you" The doctor grabbed Dean's hand and wrapped a bandage around it. "You're not as big of a jerk as your brother."

Sara rubbed the back of her neck. "I'll get the key."

Dean spoke to Dr. Dixon first. "No, he won't. Shut up." He turned to Sara. "How?"

Sara saw Britt walking toward them. "I'll get it. Just be ready."

As Britt walked down the hall, he pointed behind him. "The guards tell me that you ordered them to lock our friends up?"

Sara could smell him before he fully entered the room. He was wearing a cologne that she had never smelled before. It was a little strong but didn't overpower. Ever the cowboy, he was wearing jeans, a button up navy blue shirt, and his hat. He made eye contact with her immediately and then gave her a nod before turning to Dean.

"James? I expect an answer." He pushed his finger into Dean's chest. "I told you not to question her without me."

Sara took that as her cue. She tried her best to look afraid and stepped in close to Britt. She grabbed his elbow and cowered behind him. Her calculated manipulation worked. He instinctively put his arm around her.

"Keep him away from me!" She stared into Dean's eyes silently telling him to play along.

Dean's face was suddenly full of anger. "Fine! See if you can get some answers out of her!"

"I don't think so!" Britt threw the anger back at him. "You're the one who convinced me that billions of lives are more important than the ones aboard this ship." He glanced at Sara. "Now, are we blowing up a goddamned wormhole? Or are we asking aliens to bring us back to Earth?"

Her breath was taken away as if the air was sucked out of the room. Her heart pounded in her chest as she looked from one of them to the other. The room seemed to get a few degrees hotter and she began to sweat. Her eyes widened as she waited for Dean to speak. She was no longer pretending to be afraid; her fear was real. She let go of Britt and backed away with her mouth hanging open. There were only three people alive who knew how her first trip to Sarisart ended. Her mind started connecting the dots. Britt and James were still oblivious to the fact that the Swagger traveled nearly two thousand years back in time, not two hundred. They had to believe that it was the year 2031 and that they still had time to prevent the downfall of mankind. It was definitely a cause she could get behind but there was no way to get back to the Earth she left behind. At least not without chancing the wormhole several times until they landed in a time where they could make a difference.

The faux James eyed Britt for a minute and then moved to the console next to the monitor on the wall. She watched him as he hit a few keys and then a video appeared on the screen behind him. It was paused on a man sitting at a table. He was very old with white hair and bald on top. At first, she didn't recognize him but it soon became evident that it was her father. A myriad of emotions hit her all at once. Her father obviously lived to a ripe old age and she hoped his life was a happy one. She swallowed hard and inched her way over to the couch until she could sit down. She wondered if begging them to not show the video was an option. She didn't want to see it because she didn't want to add to her mental distress. As much as she wanted to see her father again, she knew what they were about to show her wouldn't be good. Her dad had that soft familiar smile on his face he always had when he was telling stories about her mother. He had his favorite Airforce jacket on. She always thought it matched his eyes perfectly. Other than the fact that he was very old, he looked healthy. He appeared to be in a high-end hotel with a beautiful painting of an orchid on the wall behind him. Her eyes were eventually drawn to the corner of the screen where the date was.

March 13, 2062

Her father was sixty years old when they left Earth. The man she was looking at was ninety-three years old. His eyebrows were white just like his hair and almost just as long and bushy. Tears stung her eyes and threatened to fall but she fought them off. She glanced at Britt who was already looking at her. He had the look of a guilty man on his face but his eyes seemed sympathetic.

She tried to appeal to his good side. "Do we have to do this?"

The captain looked at his grandson and nodded. She watched as the video played and tried to be strong.

"You know my Sara is on another planet?" General Newman was speaking to someone who couldn't be seen.

"Yes, Sir, everyone does." It was a woman's voice.

"She'll be back soon." Her father nodded. "That nice alien man promised." He furrowed his brow. "What was his name?" He pointed at the unseen woman. "Andrin! That's it."

"And who was he, General?"

He grimaced at the woman. "I just told you! The nice Unan from that planet she's on!"

"Okay, it's okay. I didn't mean to upset you."

The woman spoke to him as if he were a child. Sara couldn't see the bitch, but she hated her. She watched as the general wrung his hands together. "I miss her." He chuckled softly. "Sara's a very brave girl. I'm so proud of her."

She wished that she could step through space and time and give him a hug.

Dean stopped the video and then glared at her. Either the brat was doing a good job pretending to be James or there wasn't very much of a difference between them. He walked in front of the monitor and clasped his hands together. He raised his voice. "Where are your Unan friends and can they take us to Earth?"

Sara rubbed her hands together and then glanced at Britt. She didn't know what to say or how to proceed so she just remained silent.

Britt sat down on the coffee table in front of her. "Sara, the simple fact that you and I are in the same room proves that time travel is real." He looked down at the floor. "James believes that the wormhole somehow exists in all places at all times." He looked at her out of the corner of his eye and then back to the floor. It was if he was ashamed to look at her. "He thinks that if we destroy the wormhole, it will reset time."

Sara laughed. "You can't be serious."

Thoughts flew through her mind. Thoughts about time travel and the paradox. She wasn't sure if she should reveal bits and pieces or just give in and tell them everything. If they were right, blowing up the wormhole wouldn't just reset time, it would ensure that the Unan never existed. If there were no Unan, there would be no Andrin. He was the one who told her father about her and Sarisart. It was the reason her father tried like hell to prevent it from happening by making her fly home where she'd be safe. Little did he know that was the very thing that set everything in motion. If they blew up the wormhole, it would change her entire life. She would never meet Andrew and she would never have a son by him. Travis O'Malley wouldn't be cloned and Junior wouldn't have been able to make the propulsion drive for the Moon's Eye.

It suddenly dawned on her that Britt and his grandson were willing to sacrifice everyone aboard the ship in order to restore Earth and prevent its destruction.

"Blowing up the wormhole won't save Earth." Sara looked the captain in the eye. "The only thing you'll accomplish is the elimination of all mankind. Don't you get it? We're it."

She tried to explain that other people were working on the same kind of propulsion engine that she helped Junior develop. Sooner or later, someone would have cracked it and the fate of the world would have been the same.

"I don't buy it." James stepped to the side of them. "She's lying."

Britt looked up at his grandson. "Have some respect." He turned back to her. "Sara, when we first met, you begged me to bring you back home." He put his hand on hers. "You'll be with your husband again, Sweetness. Isn't that what you want?"

She looked down at his hand. There was his ring, practically staring back at her. She suddenly realized that he would never be swayed and that age-old saying entered her mind. If you can't beat them, join them. She placed her hand on his and looked him in the eye. "You're not looking for my permission, you're just looking for my approval." She took a deep breath and then let it out. "When are you going to do it?"

He got up. "The nuke will be ready in a few hours." He looked at Dean. "I guess we'll see if your plan works."

The captain walked down the hall toward the clinic leaving Sara alone with Dean. He played James well. He smiled smugly at Sara. "I guess we will."

She looked down the hall after Britt and then whispered to Dean, "make sure my people know the plan," before running after him.

"What plan?" He whisper-shouted after her. He looked at Dr. Dixon. "I don't know the plan!"

Chapter Twenty-Six

Junior was worried about Sara. One of the men with Captain Mason came back into the clinic and locked them all up before he could get to her. He stood at the door and looked through the window but he couldn't see anything. The guards had separated them. The men were locked in one room and the women were locked in another. The doctor insisted that Martinez lay back down and rest but he definitely didn't seem to be resting. He adjusted the bed so that he was reclined and he kept glancing toward the hallway where Sara disappeared. It was painfully obvious to him that the sheriff was going to be a close and permanent fixture in their lives from then on. At least he was able to get a little information. The second they arrived on the ship, Dr. Bowman was firing off questions, and Junior took note of every answer.

Junior already surmised that the ship was from the future of an alternate universe. Believing in time travel was ludicrous and impossible, however, travel to a different universe that was the same, only different, was. There was never any danger of messing with timelines or paradoxes. Junior was a hundred percent sure that there was a universe out there somewhere in which Sara and the Boy Scouts never made it back to Earth because the Unan never existed. Conversely, there was probably another one in which they did make it home but never completed the Moon's Eye and decided scrap the project altogether.

The little disc that Dr. Dixon placed over Martinez' bullet wound was truly remarkable. It removed the bullet and was repairing the damage it made by using nanobots. Just that little piece of technology would tip off even the dumbest person that perhaps they weren't from the same Earth. Two hundred years was apparently long enough for people to figure out space travel and destroy the world. He had known for some time that his mother wanted to go back to home and now he wondered if that actually might be possible. It might not be the Earth they left... but maybe it would be close enough. He looked over his shoulder at Martinez.

"What do you think they want with her?" He leaned to the side a little to see down the hall better.

Martinez was busy trying to maneuver his wounded arm through a shirt the doctor had given him but he wasn't doing it very well. "I don't know." He grimaced as he pulled it over his mid-section. "But she told me they blame her for the downfall of man."

Chad's mouth fell open. "What? Why?"

Martinez shook his head as if he didn't quite understand either. "It was something about the propulsion engine that she helped Junior develop."

Junior loved his godmother very much but she took more credit for the engines than she deserved. She always said that it was to protect him by drawing attention away from him. He had no reason to doubt what she said, after all, he was a clone who aged at twice the normal speed as a regular human. She said that if anyone ever found out about him, they would take him away from her and they'd never see each other again. His ma did help him though. He finished much faster than he would have otherwise. He was more analytical but she always seemed to think outside the box. She was always there when he got stuck. She'd make him a sandwich and help him talk it out. What else do mothers do?

"Ma regrets coming here." Junior looked sidelong at

Martinez and then shrugged. "Maybe these people can take her home."

Martinez' eyes rolled to the side as if he was wondering whether he should voice what he was thinking out loud. "She wanted to talk to me alone. That's why she ziplined across the canyon first. She knew I'd follow her." He sat up at the edge of the bed. "Apparently, once they found out time travel was possible, they figured if they went back in time far enough, they could save the world just by changing one thing. Her."

Junior's eyes shot open. "Are you saying they're gonna kill her?"

Martinez looked at him as if he was genuinely stupid. Junior had been so distracted by that thought that someone wanted to kill Sara that he missed the part where killing her at that point in time wouldn't change a thing. If the Swagger had been able to get back to an Earth prior to liftoff and kill that universe's Sara Zeeman, then it would definitely affect the future of that universe. Except for one little thing. Several teams around the world were working on the same technology. And Junior was continuously leaking information to three of them. He looked down the hall again.

Being on a ship from the "future" was a dream come true for a person like him. A huge part of him wanted to explore the ship and reverse engineer a few dozen things. Too bad he was currently a prisoner who was too worried about his mommy to think straight.

Everyone's attention turned to the hall again when the heavy clop of Britt's cowboy boots echoed toward them. He stopped in front of the room that the women were in and hit the keypad to unlock it and then repeated the process on Junior's room. "I'm sorry my grandson locked you folks up. You're free to roam about but you still have to stay in here for the time being." He continued on to the exit. "So, make yourselves comfortable."

"Where's ma?" Junior demanded.

Ask and you shall receive. Sara rushed down the hall with James close at her heels. She appeared to be desperate.

"Britt! Wait!" He turned around just before he reached the door. She looked him in the eye as she walked up to him and stood within inches of him. "Where are you going?"

"I have a bomb to check on, Sweetness."

"You said it wouldn't be ready for a few hours." She touched his bicep. "I thought we could spend some time together."

Junior wretched inwardly and glanced at Martinez. The man's eyes were full of betrayal or confusion or perhaps both. He turned back to the horrid train wreck before him hoping that he heard her wrong.

"Captain." James used a commanding voice to get his attention but didn't work.

Britt visibly sized her up and then smirked. "Define 'spend some time together' for me."

Sara lowered her voice but Junior could still hear her. "I want some Cake."

The captain slipped his hand around her waist to her back.

"You want some Cake?" he repeated.

She pointed her finger toward her face and made an invisible circle with it. "Yeah, all over my face."

"Britt! You can't be falling for this." James motioned to Sara. "It's obviously a stall tactic."

Junior watched Sara's face turn deep red as she kept her focus on the captain. He knew she had something up her sleeve but the whole thing was making him physically ill. Britt said something so low to her that he doubted anyone could hear it and then started to lead her out of the clinic.

James ran after them. "Captain!"

Britt turned around and then sighed before rolling his eyes. He took two steps to the side and pressed a button on the console on the wall. "Captain Mason to Commander Hayes."

"This is Commander Hayes." A female's voice seemed to come from all around them.

Britt winked at Sara. "I'm going to be spending a few hours with a lovely young lady."

Junior knew the captain had a communication device implanted under his ear. The fact that he didn't use it meant that he wanted them all to hear the conversation. Her voice filled the air again. "Since when do you need my permission to spend time with a woman?"

"Well, Commander, as you know, I'm an old man." Britt couldn't seem to take his eyes off of Sara. They both genuinely seemed infatuated with each other. "And things are gonna get freaky. So, if I have a heart attack and die as a result, my last wish is for you to carry out my last order and blow up that goddamned wormhole."

"Understood, Sir."

Britt finally looked at James. "Satisfied?"

James nodded. "Yes, Sir."

"Good boy." He took Sara's elbow. "Give us two hours and then to come get me."

Junior couldn't believe it. His godmother made it painfully obvious to everyone that she wanted to bed the captain and then disappeared with him. Every child eventually figures out that their parents like to do things behind closed doors. He clearly remembered one specific occasion when he was only five where he walked in on Sara and Papa Zee. It caused him a lot of distress and sleepless nights because, at the time, he couldn't understand what he was seeing. Over the next few years he came to the understanding that humans were nothing but animals with slightly higher brain function. When animals need something, they go after it. The main question currently occupying his mind was whether or not his mother was answering the call of the wild or if something more nefarious was going on.

Mel slid into the room where Martinez was still sitting on the exam bed. He was blankly staring off into space. She stepped into his view with the biggest smile on her face. "Hey, Murder... Are we gonna have to put you on a suicide watch now?"

Martinez suddenly breathed in swiftly and then jumped down from his bed. Junior watched as the sheriff stepped up to Mel until there was only inches between them and then looked her in the eye.

"Which is more dangerous, Mel? A genius sociopath without a conscience or a professional killer you affectionately call Murder?" He dared her with his eyes. "Call me Murder one more time."

Junior expected Mel to do what she always did, which was smile or laugh as if threats didn't bother her, but that's not what happened. The next few moments were uncomfortable for everyone as they watched the two have a staring match until Mel eventually backed down. A glint of fear showed in her eyes before she folded her arms and turned away. Junior had no idea that she was a sociopath. He, like everyone else, just accepted the fact that she wasn't exactly user-friendly. Before they left Earth, he had a friend who was very similar only he never intentionally caused problems. Oscar was a misunderstood autistic kid who could out-math anyone on the planet. Junior found him very annoying at first because he didn't understand him. It was Sara who explained that Oscar wasn't mentally disabled at all because his brain functioned normally. She said if anything, poor Oscar was socially disabled. The kid would talk about Pokémon nonstop for hours even if no one was interested... or listening. Junior always assumed that Mel was the same way. A high-functioning autistic person who didn't understand social situations. He watched her fold her arms over her chest and lean against the wall like a child who was just denied a slice of birthday cake.

That was when everyone seemed to collectively realize that James was still in the room. Junior's head immediately swung back to Martinez who was clenching his jaw and his fists together. James' eyes flicked toward the guards at the door and then back to Martinez. It was an obvious message to the sheriff that he shouldn't try anything.

James glanced at the guards again. "We need to talk."

The ship's doctor walked into the clinic shaking his head. He suddenly flipped his hands up toward the ceiling and went on a rant. "I don't know what you've gotten me into, Dean." He shook his head back and forth dramatically. "Whether we or not we blow up the wormhole or land the ship, it's all gonna end the same. We're all gonna die."

Junior's mind instantly started to calculate all the ways blowing up the wormhole could end in everyone's death. He always believed a very unpopular theory about the relationship wormholes had with the universe. If you thought of the universe or universes as one giant animal, then wormholes would be the veins that brought important nutrients to and from them. It stands to reason that removing or closing off one of those veins might make the giant animal upon which they live very ill. Would it simply just chew off its own leg and continue on with its new normal, or would it kill the animal and everyone who resides within it? He raised his brows at the possibility that the universe would just repair itself by growing a new one when something suddenly hit him.

"Wait, who's Dean?" He looked from the doctor to James and then back again.

"Start talkin' kid," Martinez began, "because I'm sure I can kill you before those guards even realize what happened."

Apparently, Dean was masquerading as his twin brother James who was currently hogtied and gagged somewhere safe. He immediately and simultaneously brought relief and

295

torment to everyone's mind by informing them of Sara's true intent. Junior found himself overly concerned with how Martinez was taking the news. It was strange, given the fact that he really didn't care for him. Perhaps the man was growing on him. He definitely cared about Sara more than he cared about himself.

The theory about the wormhole existing throughout time in a single universe was an interesting one. If they were correct, blowing up the wormhole would reset the timeline but not to where they thought it would, and Sara most definitely came to that conclusion too. They were about to erase the lives of tens of thousands of people who were born and lived in their timeline in order to bring billions of people back from the dead. It was a noteworthy endeavor. Too bad that it wouldn't work.

"Think of the universe as a pearl necklace connected by a thread. In the beginning, the pearls were exactly the same, but over time, their stories changed. If a person were to leave one universe by way of wormhole, they would be arriving in a similar but different universe. When you guys flew through that wormhole, it wasn't the same one we went through, it was a different one entirely." Junior tried to explain his thought process to the mundane and stupid amongst him but the only one who was able to grasp it was Mel.

"That's an interesting theory, Junior, but it doesn't really change the objective, does it?" Surprisingly, she wasn't being rude, just matter-of-factly. "Sara has to get the key and give it to Dean so he can land this ship or we're all toast."

She was right. If Captain Mason was allowed to execute his plan it would cause irreparable damage to the universe, or the fabric of time, whichever theory was correct. After Dean made his departure, he watched Martinez pace back and forth in front of him. Everyone was in danger. Everyone aboard the ship and everyone on the planet below were in danger and none of them knew it. But Junior knew the sheriff didn't care about any of them, all he cared about was Sara and what she was doing at that very moment.

Junior suddenly smiled up at him. "Remember what you said a few days ago?"

Martinez suddenly stopped pacing and rubbed his face. The look of annoyance on his face made him think twice about reminding him but it was too late to back out. "You told us that ma was going to be the one that saves us, not the other way around."

The sheriff suddenly laughed and nodded his head. "Yeah, I did, didn't I?"

The reminder seemed to put his mind at ease but only for a few minutes. Whatever was going to happen in the next few hours was guaranteed to change everyone's lives forever. The question was, would it be for the better?

Tran crossed the room and plopped down on the couch. She couldn't seem to stay still. She crossed and then uncrossed her legs and then leaned her head against the back of the couch. She stared up at the ceiling and then shook her head at whatever thought that was running through it. The only thing he knew about the woman was that she was Asian and that she was very beautiful. He sat down next to her.

"Are you doing okay?" Junior watched her eyes move back and forth as if she was reading something written on the ceiling that only she could see.

297

She shrugged. "I'm pretty sure I hate Sara."

Chapter Twenty-Seven

Sara was nervous as hell but she hoped it didn't show. She let Britt lead her through the ship to his quarters as she tried to memorize landmarks so that she could find her way back on her own. She knew she had to be convincing and that soon she would have to put up or shut up. He held her arm just above her elbow making her feel more like a prisoner being led to a cell instead of his bedroom. She decided that she was going to change that. As soon as they stepped into the elevator and the doors closed, she pushed him up against the wall and kissed him. She didn't know what she was doing, or how he'd react, but she needed him to be focused on her. His reaction was a rather passionate one. Their kiss progressed into a deeper more sexual one where their hands did some exploring to regions usually reserved for private rooms and not elevators. When she heard the tone that alerted them that they had arrived, she broke away from him and looked him in the eyes. That's when she knew she was in a lot of trouble. Not because she thought that Britt might hurt her but because he was a desirable man and an incredible kisser.

"Come on, Sunshine." He grabbed her hand and guided her out of the elevator and down the hall.

His room was a little smaller than she thought it would be but considering that it was the captain's quarters aboard a military ship, it was probably standard. It was a bedroom, living room, and kitchen in one with a stand-alone bathroom. Sara was prepared to take the lead again and pull him toward the bed but the captain had something else in mind. He walked over to his kitchenette and pulled open the cabinet. She watched as he took out two glasses and then a bottle of wine before turning around and bringing them back to the table. He poured some wine in both glasses but gave himself considerably more than he gave her. Britt sat down and then gulped down the wine in just a few swallows and poured himself some more.

"So, what's the plan, Sara?" He sipped his wine but held her gaze.

He was on to her and it scared her. She picked up her glass and took a sip while she tried to think of an appropriate or clever response. "I'm not sure what you mean."

"Well, if it's to make me fall for you and think we have a future together so that I don't go through with my plans, it won't work." He held his drink up to her briefly and then drank some more.

Sara smiled. "No?"

The captain stared at his drink for a moment. "You just spent several hours holding Martinez' hand and now you're spending the last few you have left with me." He shrugged. "Makes perfect sense, right?"

She put her drink down on the table and walked over to him as she looked him right in the eye. "Like I said, you blow up that wormhole and none of this ever happened." She gently took his drink out of his hand and put it on the table. "Besides, have you forgotten my pet name for him?"

"You mean Ass-hat?" Britt laughed. "Yeah, how'd did he earn that designation anyway?"

Sara stepped over him and then slowly sat down on his lap. She put her arms around his neck. "He humiliated me by throwing me out of his bed and his house after I asked him to make love to me." She scooted her body up close and

SARISART 2

then brought her lips within an inch of his. She could feel his body heat on her face and it was exciting her. She looked him in the eye again and then whispered. "Are you going to do that too?"

His eyes widened a little. "No. Not by a long shot."

She kissed him gently on the lips as his arms enclosed around her. Her heart was beating so hard in her chest that she was sure he could hear it. He pulled her hips forward sending fear and excitement shooting through her body. She didn't expect him to be so passionate and she didn't expect to like it. She rolled her hips forward making his excitement for her more evident.

"Take your shirt off," she whispered.

"Take yours off first," he grinned at her.

She gave him a sly smile before lifting her shirt up over her head and revealing her naked breasts. She suddenly felt very self-conscious about herself as she felt his hand on her naked back. With each passing minute she became more and more afraid that getting his ring might mean she'd actually have to have sex with him. It didn't help that she also really really wanted to. But thoughts of Angelo kept popping into her head and she didn't want to hurt him. She also couldn't help thinking of Drew and the fact that she needed to make sure he was safe and had a happy, healthy, long life. In order for that to happen, she needed to get that key, and she was prepared to do anything to get it. She unbuttoned the top button of his shirt before he took the hint and pulled it off himself. That was the moment she needed. The moment that his eyes would be temporarily off of her and completely covered by his shirt. She reached up quickly and stuck her tongue between her fingers to retrieve the two orange berries she hid there. As soon as his head was free, she popped the berries against the roof of her mouth with her tongue and then kissed him as deeply as she could. As her tongue danced around with his, she hoped that he absorbed more of the orange than she did.

Over the last few months she had built up a tolerance for her drug of choice, but even so, two berries were usually enough to knock her out. The addition of the drug to the mix made it even harder to resist him. As they kissed, he grabbed her under the ass and picked her up to put her on the bed. When he climbed on top of her and kissed her again, she realized that she made a calculated mistake. His warm skin felt good against hers. Too good. His hand explored downward until he slipped it inside her scrub pants. He soon proved he knew his way around a woman when his hand found its mark and started to gently massage it. She moaned softly as she kissed his neck next to his ear.

She began to feel like she was floating and every time she opened her eyes, she struggled to see straight. She knew if she was feeling the effects of the orange than he probably was too. She just needed to hang on a little while longer. The hair on his chin tickled her neck a little as he kissed her it and then slowly made his way down her chest to her navel. Excitement filled every part of her as she felt his hands grip the elastic of her pants and pull them down to just above her pubic bone. She breathed hard as she felt him kiss her gently and then suddenly collapsed on the lower half of her body. She found herself both relieved and colossally disappointed.

Sara was tired. The doctor had given her the orange to help her sleep and it was certainly doing its job. She rubbed her face and eyes as she tried to clear her mind but it wasn't working. Britt's head was laying on her stomach and his torso was heavy against her legs but she felt so warm and comfortable that she didn't want to move. She closed her eyes... but only for a second.

She was floating again. Dreaming. Angie was holding her in his strong arms and she felt safe and warm. And happy. It was a feeling that she didn't think she'd have again without Andrew. They were back on Sarisart watching Drew and Junior laugh and play catch together. It was the perfect day, not too hot, not too cold... except for one tiny thing. There was an annoying tone that kept going off and she couldn't find the source.

When she opened her eyes again, she didn't know where she was. The lower half of her body felt very heavy and she couldn't feel her left foot. A soft tone repeated twice and then the silence returned to reveal the sounds of someone snoring below her. She was groggy and couldn't see straight and struggled to move.

The tone returned. What the hell was it?

Sara struggled to prop herself up on her elbows and look down at herself. Seeing Britt passed out on the lower half of her body managed to remind her of her goal. The double tone rang out again causing her to glance at the door. Someone was obviously out there and they were being very persistent. When she struggled and kicked her way out from beneath the captain he turned over onto his back. His mouth gaped open to the sky making his snoring infinitely louder. Once she was free, she dug her hand into her pants pocket and retrieved her pillbox. She quickly opened it and emptied the last two berries out into her hand and then leaned over him. She was seeing double and it was impossible to focus so she had to touch his face for guidance. Once she knew where his mouth was, she pressed the berries against teeth and then dropped the skins inside.

Another double tone rang out. Each time it happened it sent more adrenaline pumping through her body. She slid herself off the side of the bed and immediately fell to the floor. Britt had been laying on her body for so long that her left foot was completely asleep. She crawled toward the door and looked at it as if she were a child trying to figure out a puzzle. Everything was blurry and she couldn't understand how to open it. The door toned again. It was starting to annoy her. She looked up at it again.

"Who's there?" It was worth a try.

"It's James. Open the door."

Was it James? Or was it Dean? Her left foot began to feel like pins and needles were being jammed into it as the blood pumped back into it. She carefully got to her feet and leaned against the metal door. "I don't know how."

"You need the key." Came the answer. "You need to get the ring."

Sara turned back to the bed where Britt was still out cold and snoring. She limped over to him and felt around for his right hand until she found the ring. She yanked it off his hand and limped back to the door, feeling around until she found the keypad, she held the ring to it and the door slid open. Sara came face to face with Dean whose expression went from concern to absolute shock.

"Holy shit!" He got an eyeful of Sara's naked chest and then looked into the room and saw Britt unconscious on the bed. He grabbed her and quickly stepped into the room bringing her with him. "Give me the ring." Dean took it out of her hand before she could give it to him and used it to close the door. He quickly walked over to the bed and checked on his grandfather. "Is he alive?"

Sara was leaning against the door struggling to remain standing. He glanced at her and then grabbed the first shirt he could get his hands on and helped her put it on. It was the blue button-down shirt that Britt had been wearing before their encounter. Her legs were shaking as he helped her button the shirt when they suddenly gave out and he caught her.

"You have the key. Just leave me." She just wanted to go back to sleep. "He won't hurt me."

Dean put his arm around her and walked her out of the captain's quarters and into the hall. "Yeah, but your friend Martinez made it clear that he'd kill me if I came back without you."

That definitely sounded like Martinez. She struggled to put one foot in front of the other as she pulled her shirt down. It was definitely two sizes too big for her and smelled like the captain but she was only concerned about one thing. "Does this shirt cover my giant boner?"

Dean laughed. "When this is over I wanna try some of that shit."

Once he got her on the elevator, he leaned her up against the wall and then reached inside his jacket. When his hand appeared again, he had a bright red object that looked like a pen. He smiled and then opened his arms. "Come give me a hug."

In her stupor, she was more than happy to oblige. She raised her arms and put them around his neck and held him tight while he took the opportunity to expose her butt cheek and inject something into it with the pen. He quickly fixed her pants and then put the pen back into his pocket. "You'll start feeling better soon."

Sara closed her eyes and leaned against him hoping that whatever he gave her would start working and fast. She couldn't be sure but it seemed like they were in the elevator longer than they should have been. When it finally stopped, he gently pulled her hands away from his neck and politely gave them back to her. In her condition, her feelings were magnified, and she felt bad about herself for many reasons. On a normal day she would have no problems betraying Captain Mason because that was what he did to her, but at that moment, she felt like the worst person alive. She also felt bad about Dean. Unbeknownst to him, he was helping to ensure his brother's eventual death at the hands of the bisector queen.

He put his arm around her and led her down a long dark corridor. With each step, there was a little more clarity and long dark corridors with someone you didn't know very well didn't seem like a good idea. She glanced over at Dean and realized that he could just as easily be James. "Where are you taking me?"

"The aft bridge," he said as he half helped, half pulled her along. "We have to hurry." He pressed underneath his ear. "Reggie, we just cleared checkpoint one."

Heavy fireproof doors slid into place behind them and slammed shut with a loud clang. Her heart raced as she fought to keep up with him. Her mind was still a little bit foggy but she did remember his plan. He wanted to land the ship but she wasn't sure about his motivation. She didn't really care at the time because the end result would help her to achieve a certain goal. Dean announced another checkpoint to Reggie and another blast door clanged shut behind them. Her brain constantly began to pester her as if there was something she was forgetting. She suddenly became overly aware of the navy-blue shirt she was wearing as she was being hustled down the hall. The only thing she could remember about the last few hours was the fact that she promised to get Britt's ring. Her face swung over to Dean.

"Did we get the ring?" She looked at his hand hoping to see it.

He furrowed his brow at her and waved his hand at her. The ring was on his index finger. "Yeah, you got it. Don't you remember?"

Sara tried to remember but only received flashes of memory that seemed out of order and didn't make any sense. Another sound of a blast door sliding shut behind them as voices echoed down the hall in front of them. Somewhere in the mix of those voices, she swore she could hear Martinez. She looked down at the shirt she was wearing again and became worried. She couldn't remember what she did or did not do with Captain Mason but the fact that she was wearing his shirt spoke volumes. They were quickly closing in on light that was spilling out into the corridor from what she could only assume was the aft bridge. Both Dean and Sara were about to achieve their goals but at what cost?

Walking through the door was one of the hardest things she'd ever had to do. Angelo must have been nervously staring at the door because his eyes were already on her when she walked through. It was hard to imagine a time when she felt more ashamed of herself. Dean didn't wait for niceties, he walked her over to the sheriff and practically shoved her into his arms before walking up to a scanner next to a heavy metal door. Martinez reflexively put his arm around her and held her close to him. She purposely looked away, to anywhere, except him. Junior and two other men were waiting next to the door Dean was standing at. They all watched as he used the captain's ring to open it and they quickly went inside. The room was small and circular with several consoles along the wall with attached chairs.

Sara walked out of Angelo's arms and made a beeline for Junior. She loved Junior and legitimately wanted to check on him but her main goal was to avoid the sheriff and his questioning eyes. Junior grinned at her. "We're about to land another spaceship, ma!"

One of Dean's men was a ridiculously good-looking black man with blue eyes. She watched him sit down at one of the consoles and insert a thumb drive into it. Dean sat down next to him. "Reggie, as soon as you have control, I need you to eject the core. We ain't bringing that shit to the planet."

Reggie looked at him out of the corner of his eye and chuckled. "Yes, Sir."

Dean suddenly reached up and peeled the fake scar off his eyebrow before addressing the other man. He was small and very thin with long hair. "Alice, as soon as we're past the point of no return, disable the ships artificial gravity and reroute the power to the secondary propulsion units."

The man's fingers danced across the console. "Call me Alice one more time and I quit."

Martinez walked up behind her and lightly touched her back but she flinched away. He let go of her and stepped out in front of her causing her to instinctively look away. He gently turned her face back toward him and looked her in the eyes. She didn't know how it was possible, but she didn't see hate there. His thumb ran back and forth across her chin.

"You okay?" He asked.

"No." She looked down. "Are you?"

"Hey, look at me." He tipped her head back up. "You did what you had to do. I'm not mad." He looked down at her shirt. "But you kinda ruined blue for me." He pointed at it. "I mean, you're not allowed to wear it anymore."

She smiled softly. "Okay."

He kissed her gently on the lips and then leaned his forehead against hers. "I mean ever."

She fell into his arms and hugged him tight. Blue was her favorite color but if that was her punishment for what she had done, she was willing to accept it. "Okay."

Chapter Twenty-Eight

Dean tried to project confidence but he was terrified. He literally had the lives of everyone aboard the ship in his hands. But even fear couldn't stop him from doing what had to be done. He looked down at his console and watched the world below rotate. He didn't know what to think of his new friends after what he had seen. The Mother of Space Travel successfully seduced his grandfather and took his ring. It was as disturbing as it was remarkable. Captain Mason was promiscuous and a giant slut but he wasn't gullible. There was no possible way anyone else in the universe could have done such a thing. That could only mean one thing... his grandfather actually liked her. It made him feel sorry for him. His own insecurities have often pestered him about Ava because sometimes he wondered if, perhaps, she was just manipulating him into doing what she wanted. He eventually came to the conclusion that it didn't matter. Regardless of whether or not she was only with him because of his connections, landing the ship was in everyone's best interest, not just his. If she left him after they landed, he would have to deal with that later.

He may not have known what to think of Captain Zeeman, but her genius godson was a different story. Junior had a remarkable mind. Not only did he write a program to divert all available resources to the alternative propulsion drives but he also did it on the fly. They had to decide where to land the Swagger on their own even though Junior insisted that Captain Zeeman should be consulted first. There simply just wasn't enough time.

"The gravitational pull of the planet will be so great that we won't be able to pull out very soon." Reggie looked up at the monitor.

"Are we talking about the planet or Oomie?" Alister's eye rolled to his friend briefly.

Dean rolled his eyes. "Alice, you're fuckin' sick."

"Commander Hayes undoubtedly knows where we are and what we're doing by now." Reggie looked behind him at Captain Zeeman. "But she won't be able to stop us. No one will."

"How are we going to get out of here alive after we land?" Sara asked from behind him.

He looked over his shoulder at her. Martinez was holding her in his arms as they watched the screen. The Mother of Space Travel helped him and everyone else on the ship but he couldn't help being angry at her for what she did to Britt. He took a moment to think about his answer before he responded. "Hopefully, by then, Captain Mason will have recovered from whatever you did to him and he'll let us out of here."

"You really think he's just going to let us out?" She countered.

The ships alarms started blaring. Reggie looked at Dean. "You better do it, now."

"Yes, I do. He knows when he's been beat." He returned his attention to his console and pressed a button. Dean nodded. Reggie was right. He needed to make the announcement. "This is Dean Mason coming at you from the aft bridge and I'm about to land this bitch! So, if you haven't already, buckle up cuz it's gonna be a bumpy ride!"

"Wow, what a dick," Martinez said.

Sara squeezed his arm. "Angie."

Reggie laughed. "See that, Alice? That's a man who doesn't mind people calling him by a woman's name." He smiled hard. "*That's* a man."

Dean knew exactly what his shipmates were doing at that moment because the crew often ran drills in case of such an emergency. He remembered the first drill he took part in because it made a lasting impression. He and his classmates were led to believe it was a genuine emergency and that they were in danger of losing their lives. He was only seven years old and very afraid. The adults led them out of the classroom and into the nearest corridor where they secured themselves to the walls with built-in pulldown seats with straps. He remembered being so worried about his father because he worked in the engineering section. Back then, he and Alister were just kids, which made it acceptable for them to comfort each other by holding hands. He was so afraid that he threw up and had to spend the rest of the day stinking of it.

The ship suddenly lurched forward and there was an immediate thump from behind him. He glanced over his shoulder again only to see Martinez helping Sara up off the floor. "Did you not hear me when I said buckle up?" He pointed to the seats. "As weird as it might sound, I'm pretty sure grandpa Britt would have my head if anything happened to you."

He knew that lurch they felt was the Swagger hitting the atmosphere of the planet below. The ship was built entirely in space wasn't meant to fly in oxygen-rich environments. Alister was one of the ship's best pilots and clocked in more hours on the bridge than anyone else on the ship. The kid was literally the only person alive who know how to land the ship because he had done it on Mars several times. He looked over at his friend while adrenaline was being pumped into his veins and hoped beyond all hope that they didn't make a serious mistake. The ship shook violently and Dean began to feel sick.

"You good, Alice?"

Alister's fingers danced across the console at lightning speed. "I don't think now is the time to irritate me, do you?"

On the other side of the ship and six floors up, Commander Hayes was on the main bridge and she was furious. The bridge was one of the most spacious places on the ship. The entire end of one of the outer walls was one giant viewscreen that showed the Swagger entering the atmosphere of the planet below. It was designed to appear as though the crew was looking directly out into space as if it were mere glass. The commander had been afraid many times in her life but nothing compared to that moment. The Swagger was going down and there was nothing she could do about it. She tried to call Captain Mason several times but he never answered. The fact that the ship was in the process of landing coupled with the missing captain didn't bode well for anyone. She wondered if he was even alive. Just before the ship started moving on its own, she received word that the captain's missile was ready to fire. But the further away from the wormhole that they got, the less likely it would hit its target. She leaned over her console and put in the coordinates before hitting the button. She watched the monitor as the little ball of light raced toward the wormhole and she prayed. The ship lurched forward again causing her to lose her footing and fall to the ground. She looked up just in time to see the bright blast of white light that filled the entire video screen. She smiled broadly knowing that Captain Mason would be proud of her. For just one moment she felt weightless as she realized that the artificial gravity was taken offline. There was nothing more that she could do except sit in the dark and think about how much she wanted to choke the life out of the captain's grandson.

She couldn't do anything about Dean Mason at the moment so she resolved to find the captain. The last communication from him had been about two hours ago when he told her he'd be spending some time with a woman. This meant that he had to be in his quarters... which meant he was within her reach. The captain's quarters and the bridge were on the same deck as a matter of convenience. The lights blinked out and the viewscreens went dark as the dim emergency lights came on. She made her way off the bridge and down the hall knowing that the thrusters would be engaged very soon, and when that happened, she'd be plastered to the floor. She seemed to be flying down the corridor when she arrived at his door. She pressed the chime several times and banged on the door.

"Captain! Are you in there?" She yelled at the top of her lungs as people passed her in the hall. She didn't waste any time. She pressed her thumb against the scanner. "Emergency override Hayes 39260 Alpha."

The door slid open and she ran inside. Just as her eyes fell on Captain Mason, the thrusters kicked in and she was pulled to the floor. She pushed with all her might to get back to her knees and crawled to his bed.

"Captain!" She screamed.

Almost as soon as she reached his bed, the G-forces of the thruster blast subsided as if God himself answered her prayers. She climbed over him and felt for a pulse and an intense relief swept over her. She shook him.

"Britt, goddamn it!" She slapped his face hard.

His eyes opened slowly as he seemed to focus in on her. He put his hand to his head. "What's going on?"

Back in the aft bridge, Dean was getting more scared and excited by the minute. He looked over at Junior who reflected the same level of excitement before his expression turned to concern.

"We're coming in too fast!" Junior swiped at the screen in front of him. "We need to engage the thrusters!"

"How about letting me fly this baby!" Alister put his hand against the console and pushed it upward. "Engaging thrusters now!"

It was so violent that it felt like they hit an actual object as the sudden opposing pressure made him feel incredibly heavy. The pull was so hard he had to fight to stop his head from hitting the console. Captain Zeeman grunted behind him. She was still recovering from a drug overdose and was probably very weak. Fear started to grip his heart when it became hard for him to breathe. The ship was shaking so badly that he could actually hear it begging him for help. The poor old girl wouldn't be able to take much more of the abuse.

"Alice!" He had to scream it through his gritted teeth because he couldn't open his mouth.

Suddenly the pressure he felt completely subsided and Alister yelled back at him. "I have to fire the thrusters in ten-second increments."

While Alister starting counting down to the next blast, Dean took a moment to check on Martinez and Captain Zeeman. Sara's chin was leaning against her chest and he couldn't see her eyes. The dark-haired brute behind him was leaning forward as far as he could to check her pulse. There wasn't enough time to reposition her.

"Three, two, brace yourselves!"

Dean was having a problem dealing with the pressure too. He silently counted down to the next time he could breathe. When the pressure subsided again, Alister informed them that they would need to do it three more times. The simple fact that The Mother of Space Travel was currently unconscious from the G-force meant that there were probably going to be many deaths throughout the ship simply because he thought he was doing the right thing. The displays began to show the ground below. The terrain was rushing by so fast he could barely see it before the thrusters engaged again.

"One more to go! And it's going to be a long one!"

Dean forced his head into a position where he could watch the landing. He briefly saw the Moon's Eye as the Swagger slowed and the land got closer and closer. His vision began to blur as he realized he was no longer breathing. He prayed that Alister was doing better than he was because he was pretty sure he was going to pass out. He found himself fixated on the purple and blue trees that he could see mixed into all the green. He could feel his heart pounding in his head as blood dripped out of his nose. He narrowed his eyes hoping it'll help him see better as a clearing appeared on the viewscreen. He had been waiting for that moment for years and couldn't wait to share it with Ava. He wanted her to be there in the aft bridge with him but she wanted to make sure the kids in the poor sector were safe. Just when he thought he couldn't bear the G-force any longer, the ship touched ground with the loud strained sound of fatigued metal.

As the ship settled it started to lean. A loud double tone played over the speakers and Commander Hayes' voice was heard. "Citizens of the Swagger, as you're aware, the ship was taken over by mutineers and we have landed on the planet we have been orbiting for the last few days. If there are any medical emergencies, please attend to them accordingly. Otherwise, please stay put while the stabilizers initialize. Once the ship is level and the power is restored, everyone will be able to move around freely."

Dean looked at his pals. Alister was rubbing his face and Reggie was passed out on the console in front of him. Junior unbelted himself and immediately went over to Sara. "Ma?" He gently picked up her head to look at her while Martinez joined him. "She's got a good strong heartbeat." He left her in the sheriff's hands and walked over to Dean. "Just before we entered the stratosphere the ship fired a missile toward the wormhole."

Dean's mouth dropped open. "What?" He looked at Alister. "Is that true?"

"Wipe your face, man." Alister looked down at the console again. "Unfortunately, it is."

Dean and Junior shared mutual doom and then he turned to the pilot. "Well, don't keep us in suspense. Did it destroy the wormhole or not?"

Alister unbuckled himself and then stepped over to his unconscious friend. "Reggie?" He rubbed Reggie's back and then looked at Dean. "We won't be able to get that answer from down here. We'll have to schedule a field trip with the shuttle." He shrugged. "Assuming we're not executed. We need to get out of here."

"I thought you said we were going to hold up in here until Captain Mason came for us." Martinez gave him an angry stare.

Dean met his stare. "I know what I said."

Captain Zeeman was beginning to wake up when he walked past her and knelt down on the floor. Alister followed him. He pulled open a hatch in the floor and then handed the door to him. Sara walked up behind him and looked down the hatch.

She looked angry. "If there was another way to get in, why did you need the ring?"

There was a very good reason. The hatch led down into the underbelly of the ship and directly to an airlock to space. It was specifically designed for people in the aft bridge to use in case of an emergency landing. He pointed to the wall where eight spacesuits waited for potential users while he explained there was only one way into the room from inside the ship. As they made their way down the metal ladder, he couldn't help wondering how Ava faired but he knew contacting her now would be ill-advised. It was better if she looked innocent. The fact that he was about to set foot on a real living planet started to sink in when he realized it was warmer than it should have been. Unused parts of the ship weren't typically heated unless there was equipment in the area that required it. Reggie held the torch behind him as he led the way to the manual airlock. None of them had ever been in that part of the ship so it was new to all of them. It was completely devoid of color except for the occasional sign written in red all capital letters.

When they finally found the hatch, he was ready to explode. His heart pounded and his breath quickened as he grabbed the turn wheel that would eventually let them outside. He took a moment to drink it all in. They won. They landed the ship. No matter what happened to him, from that point on, the citizens of the Swagger had a planet to live on. He turned around and looked at Martinez.

"Sheriff, can to help me with this?" He stepped to the side a little so that Martinez could get a good grip on the wheel.

At first, it wouldn't budge, but they kept trying. Eventually, Dean had to step aside and let Reggie and Martinez give it a try. As Dean watched he couldn't help holding his breath, and when the wheel started to move, he gave a sigh of relief. He and Alister looked at each other as if they were excited children about to open the greatest Christmas gift ever given.

"Can you believe this?" He slapped his friend on the shoulder and then pulled him into a hug. "We did it!"

The door opened with whine that hurt his teeth. His nose was immediately met with unfamiliar but pleasant smells. He sniffed the air purposefully and tried to imagine how beautiful the plant giving off that wonderful aroma might be. Sara walked past him and put her hand on Martinez' shoulder.

"She's here."

The sheriff looked down at her. "Who?"

That was Dean's thought too. Who.

Chapter Twenty-Nine

Britt was still very groggy but he was at least able to follow Commander Hayes down the corridor followed by a dozen heavily armed men. One of the medics gave him a shot of something that was traditionally used to help bring patients out of sedation. He felt intensely stupid and ashamed of himself because he had underestimated The Mother of Space Travel. He knew she was up to something but couldn't see how she could possibly succeed with whatever it was. Little did he know that she was devious enough to drug him. He also didn't know when or how Dean managed to secure an alliance with her. Injury reports were coming in from all over the ship but, thankfully, no deaths had occurred. It's amazing how quickly he was forced to go from a plan, which included no future, to a future with absolutely no plan.

"I want confirmation on that wormhole as soon as possible." He led them into the elevator that would take them down to the hanger bay.

Commander Hayes nodded. "Yes, Sir."

He frowned as he walked. He knew damn well the wormhole was still fuckin' there. He knew it. He knew it because he was still there. He was still alive and kicking and stringing thoughts together. The hanger would give them the easiest exit because it was designed to lower a ramp onto the surface of Mars to get supplies. He had a feeling that once they opened it that it might never be closed again. He watched impatiently as it slowly lowered and the sunlight from outside began to assault his eyes. They walked on to the ramp before it was actually done moving. The captain and his people were taken completely off guard by what they saw when they reached the ground. His ship was comparable to the size of a US Navy aircraft carrier but that evidently wasn't too big for the bisectors to surround with impressive numbers. The closest ones were at least twenty yards away from them but still close enough to scare the shit out of Britt. There were big ones, small ones, some that looked like a different species entirely, and one queen... whom he had met before. He turned his head and followed the line of giant bugs all the way down until he saw her.

Sara stood about thirty feet away with Martinez. He couldn't help being angry and feeling used, especially since she was clearly wearing his shirt. As he glared at them, he realized he recognized a few of the people in her party as his own. Commander Hayes was certain that his 'newest plaything' helped Dean steal the ring but it was James that he saw in front of him. Or so he thought.

"What the hell's going on?" Came a voice from behind him as if on cue.

Britt turned around and saw James as reality slammed him in the head. The boy had a black eye, a fat lip, and a colossally dumb look on his face. He shook his head and half rolled his eyes as he turned back to Dean. He knew the kid wanted a planet to live on but he apparently underestimated how much. Army of bisectors be damned; he was going to confront them. He stomped toward them as if the horde didn't exist and stopped in front of Dean.

Britt stuck a finger in his face. "How could you betray me like this?" He turned to Sara. "And what about you?"

Her mouth dropped open. "Me? You were going to erase me!"

"I wasn't going to erase you, Sara." He was obviously exasperated. "I was going to reset you and the whole goddamned timeline. There's a difference."

Martinez stepped in front of him and put a hand to Britt's chest. "Step back, now."

"What about me, Gramps? Huh? What about all of us?" Dean was visibly hurt.

"You can't erase a soul after it's been given, son." Britt looked at his grandson sympathetically. He suddenly waved his hand. "None of that matters now. What's going on here?"

Sara glared at James. "The bisector queen demands retribution for the loss of her nursery." She eyed Britt. "She said she'd kill everyone in my colony if I didn't bring her the one responsible."

Britt looked over his shoulder at James and Commander Hayes. He didn't need for Sara to clarify, he knew exactly what she meant, and he wasn't about to let the bisectors have his grandson. He looked Sara in the eye. "Well then, I'm the one responsible."

Her mouth dropped open. "What? No!"

"He was following my orders." Britt held her gaze. "I'm the one that sent him down here for the uranium."

Sara was upset and it showed. Tears glowed in her eyes and he couldn't help being happy the prospect of losing him was hurting her. The bisector queen was easily picked out by her size. He looked at her for a moment and thought about all his options. He and his people could go back into the

Swagger and lock themselves in until they starve to death or they could start a war in which most, if not all, his people would die. Or, he could sacrifice himself so that his people could live on. Now that the Swagger was grounded, everyone's lives were about to change dramatically. He could either ensure a good start for them or doom them. He always tried to do the right thing and that day would be no different.

"Tell the queen that I need time to put my affairs in order." Britt nodded at her. "Please."

Dean couldn't believe his ears. "Grandpa Britt, you can't do this!"

Sara wiped tears from her face as she turned around and looked at her godson. "Junior, go home, please. I need you to look after Drew."

"Ma…" He looked as if he suddenly realized she expected him to do it without question. He looked at the horde in fear.

"It's okay, Junior. They won't hurt you." Sara nodded at him. "I love you."

As Junior stepped toward a row of the bisectors, they started to move out of the way. Sara watched him until it seemed like he was clear and then took a deep breath. Britt suddenly understood the position he was putting her in. She was the only person who could communicate with the Bisector Queen which meant she either had to help him or serve him up as an appetizer. She made eye contact with Martinez as she walked past him and then stood before Britt. She was obviously angry. Her face was red and her jaw was clenched shut as her eyes narrowed at him.

"I'm not going to argue a stay of execution for you or anyone else." She glanced at James briefly. "If you need time, ask her yourself."

Britt had to crane his head up to look her in the face. He never got a good look at the creatures when he first encountered them because he was too busy running for his life. She had horns that pointed away on each side of her head and ant-like eyes. Her thin body reminded him of the time he accidentally saw Oomie naked. He suddenly shuttered at the thought as he felt the hairs on the back of his neck stand at attention. The captain wasn't trying to pull a fast one on anyone. He fully intended to turn himself in after he had the chance make sure his people would be okay. He scratched at the back of his neck as he tried to come up with the right words.

"Uh, listen…" He suddenly realized he didn't know what to call the queen. "Your Highness? As you know, being the leader of your people isn't easy." He gestured to her horde and then motioned to his ship. "My people have lived aboard this ship for decades. They don't know how to live on this planet of yours." He grinned. "I mean, there are dinosaurs and something called 'sky piranha' that are apparently terrifying but I really haven't seen them yet." He chuckled as he looked at Sara. She wasn't laughing in any sense of the word… not even a smile. Britt looked back up at the queen. "I just want a little time to make sure my people are okay before turning myself in, is all."

He held his breath as he waited for her answer. Sara was standing in front of the Queen and appeared to be having an intense staring contest with her. He fully believed she was going to kill him right in front of his grandsons, and if that was the case, he hoped his death would be quick. Even in his considerable fear he noticed more people joining them.

324

Ava ran past him and into Dean's arms. He watched them hugging and it brought a hint of a smile to his face. He didn't appreciate the betrayal but he still loved Dean and he was happy he had someone to spend his life with. Especially since it was obvious the current timeline was going to continue. The rest of Sara's party must have been with Ava because the three of them walked by slowly eyeing everyone and wondering what was going on. Britt found himself becoming a little angry and frustrated. His heart was beating so hard that he briefly believed the queen wouldn't get a chance to kill him because he'd die of a heart attack.

It genuinely took him by surprise when the bisectors started to move away. Most of them headed north of the ship by foot but some of them took flight. His mouth dropped open in shock as he turned to Sara. "What's going on?"

She seemed to be a little confused as she held her hand out toward Martinez. He put his arm around her to steady her and held her hand. When her eyes finally met his, he saw contempt in them and it surprised him how much it hurt. "You have your time. I hope you use it wisely."

Britt nodded and then looked over his shoulder at his men. He couldn't help noting how relieved they all looked. Commander Hayes, on the other hand, looked angry. "What do you want to do with Dean?"

Martinez loudly cleared his throat. "At this time, I'd like to extend an offer of sanctuary to Dean Mason and his friends."

Dean was surprised. He suddenly smiled and looked at his buddies. They all nodded in agreement. "Offer accepted."

Britt stared at his grandson in disbelief. "You don't have to be scared of me, son. You pissed me off something fierce but I still love ya. Nothing'll ever change that."

"It's not you who scares me." Dean eyed his brother briefly before giving Britt a nod. He held his ring up briefly before handing it to the captain. "We'll see each other soon."

Britt's men disbursed from behind him and started to walk back to the ship. He watched as Sara walked away aided by the good sheriff and followed closely by his own grandson. He imagined he'd be using much of the time he was awarded thinking about all the mistakes he had made and wondering if he had just earning his place in hell. He looked down at his boots in shame as Sara passed him.

"I imagine you'd like to go home and spend some time with your family for a few days but eventually we're gonna have to meet to discuss the future of our people." He finally tipped his head up as he waited for her answer but she didn't respond.

Mel brought up the rear. She smiled broadly as she walked by. "It's best to book an appointment. Does a year from next Friday sound good?"

The next hour was spent arguing with James and Commander Hayes in his war room. It was nothing more than a conference room with a large monitor. He mostly used it for watching old movies and tv shows. James was convinced that his grandfather had some grand plan and that buying himself some time was all part of it. Not only was the kid impulsive and full of himself but he was also apparently okay with Britt taking his punishment. He openly protested several times but never once took responsibility for his actions. He loved both of his grandsons but if twins had a good one and a bad one, then James was obviously the bad one. Or perhaps he was just misunderstood. Still, he couldn't let the boy be executed by the bisector queen when he could do something to prevent it.

When Oomie and the other section heads arrived, they didn't look very happy. There were twelve of them, including Oomie, and each claimed to have the best interest of their people at heart but most of them only cared about what their status could give them. Landing on the planet was sure to change that. Britt laid out the facts as plainly as he could. The Swagger was permanently grounded on a planet that was going to be their home forever. None of his people had any experience building things out of wood because there wasn't any wood to be had aboard a starship. None of his people had ever hunted for their own food, let alone killed, skinned, and deboned it. Obviously, there were some great benefits the people of the Swagger could bring to the table, but it was clear they were at the mercy of the Moon's Eye for the time being.

James seemed to get angrier by the minute. "You can't be serious! We outnumber her people five to one!"

Britt slammed his fist down on the table at the exact moment he said his grandson's name. "James!" His anger and the noise his fist made on the table caused everyone to look at him. He gritted his teeth. "I love you but you are not making this easy for me!" He rubbed his eyes. He was sorely overdue for some sleep. "While it's true that our people outnumber hers, we won't be able to survive without them." He stood up and leaned on the table. "Obviously, Captain Zeeman will have a seat at this table. She'll have an equal voice, just like all of you."

No one seemed to like the fact that The Mother of Space Travel would be allowed to make decisions about their future but most of the leaders agreed it was a necessary evil. He looked at Oomie and held the old woman's gaze for a moment. He knew that if she voted with him that the others would follow. She folded her fingers together in front of her and smacked her lips together before speaking. Everyone at the table was looking at her and waiting for her decision.

Oomie cleared her voice. "Look, there's obviously a lot I'm missing here because you people keep on talking about The Mother of Space Travel as if she's a real live person but… the bottom line is, we're on a green planet with breathable air and drinkable water. Isn't this what we've always wanted?" She looked at everyone, one by one. "Well isn't it?"

Everyone either nodded or verbally agreed.

"Well then, I agree with my husband." She looked at Britt. "Captain Zeeman will have a seat at this table and be given equal vote." She raised her hand. "All in favor?"

Britt watched as nine of the twelve raised their hands. Their decision lifted some of the weight he had sitting on his heart. He knew that their next meeting would include Captain Zeeman and Sheriff Martinez so that they could hammer out a temporary agreement and make some much-needed new laws. It wasn't something you could possibly do in an afternoon.

After a few days had passed he began to realize that Sara was avoiding him. He couldn't really blame her. He had spent those days thinking about how stupid he had been. He wanted to reset the timeline so that he could save billions of people but who was he to decide who deserved to live and who didn't? He was convinced that it was the right thing to do but he was clearly misguided. Besides, he didn't decide things, the wormhole did.

The next meeting took place in the colony's recreation center where Sara spent the entire time looking anywhere except at him. Their people seemed to be getting along just fine but he knew there would eventually be trouble but, thankfully, he wouldn't be around to fix it. Britt watched her as she talked with a teenaged girl. The kid was evidently pregnant with Sara's child. It shocked him when he found out what the colonists were doing but who was he to judge? He watched as they both laughed and then Sara hugged her. He didn't know what they were saying but it certainly seemed like they were making up after a fight. As Sara stepped away from her, she looked at him as if she had known someone was looking at her. He smiled and tipped his hat but she didn't return the sentiment. She turned away from him and made a beeline for Martinez. That's when he realized that she didn't intend to speak to him ever again. He was obligated to turn himself into the bisector queen in just a few days and the woman he had feelings for was avoiding him like the plague. He decided to head back to the ship and finish packing up his things.

Knowing when you're going to die had its benefits. He was able to personally give cherished belongings to the people he knew would appreciate them. He held his cowboy hat in his hand and knew it was meant for Dean. He tossed it on the bed when the door chimed and he walked over to open it. He wasn't expecting to see Sara but there she stood. She looked incredibly upset and stood there wringing her hands for a moment. At first, it looked like she was going to bolt away but she didn't. She threw her hands up at him and then shrugged.

"It's not what you think." She stepped through the doorway and it slid shut.

He leaned against his table and folded his arms. "What's not what I think?"

"I just…" Sara's eyes started to shine with tears as she took a deep breath and let it out slowly. "I just can't do this." She shook her head. "I can't act like everything's fine. I can't look at you without thinking about what she might do to you." She couldn't hold it in anymore. She held her hand to her chest as if her heart hurt and she cried. "I just can't do this! I can't!"

Britt couldn't stand seeing her that way. He took her into his arms and let her cry against him. He had thought that she was avoiding him because of what happened between them but he was wrong. "Yes, you can, Sunshine." He rubbed her back. "You have to. You're the only one who can."

Chapter Thirty

Sara woke up feeling warm and comfortable. She was still getting used to sharing a bed with someone again. She felt like she was being spooned by a man made of fire. Most of the time, she didn't mind because it helped her sleep. But on rare occasions she felt trapped and claustrophobic. And on those rare occasions, she usually had somewhere else to be. She ran her hand down his forearm slowly until her hand was over his and held it for a moment before pulling his arm off of her so that she could make her escape. She inched her way forward slowly, trying not to wake him, and just when she thought she was free... his arm enclosed around her and pulled her close to him. He nuzzled in close to her ear and hummed before whispering softly.

"Where do you think you're going?"

Sara smiled as she allowed him to tip her towards him. Angelo's dark eyes twinkled in the low light coming from the window. She put her hand on his scruffy face and kissed him. Her voice was soft. "I'm supposed to go see Dr. Bowman this morning."

He kissed her neck close to her ear. "Do you want me to come with you?"

He maneuvered himself on top of her and then inched her legs apart with his. It wasn't hard for her to figure out what he had in mind. She put her hands on his chest and tried to halt his advancement but it didn't work. "Angie," she whispered. "Stop, I have to go."

He grabbed her leg just underneath her butt and pulled up to give himself some leverage. The man was definitely good at turning her on. Feeling his excitement for her was hard for her to resist. She did need to go, but she was fairly certain that the world wouldn't end if she was an hour late for her appointment. Life on Sarisart was dangerous which meant that everyone's life expectancy was shorter than it would be on Earth. In other words, life was short, and at that very moment, she was living it. She didn't know what the future would hold for her and Martinez but she wanted to enjoy it. She was falling in love with him and it was hard to comes to terms with that fact. It scared her and excited her but she refused to run away from it.

An hour later they were both dressed and ready for the day. When she walked out into his living room she looked around and shook her head. It was so empty. For the last two weeks they had been all but inseparable. He either slept at her place or she slept at his. She knew at some point he would be forced to give up his cabin out of necessity. It didn't make sense for him to live in it alone.

Martinez walked her to the door. "Are you sure you don't want me to go with you?"

Sara kissed him and then gave him a hug. "No, it's okay. I'll see you later."

She hopped down the steps to the motorcycle that was parked outside. The Swagger was only a few miles away but she didn't feel like walking. During her ride, she couldn't help thinking about how drastically her life had changed in just two weeks. The one big thing that always bothered her about the paradox was the fact that one hundred and twenty people couldn't possibly start a sustainable civilization by themselves. She was so scared of creating a new race of people simply because there wasn't enough genetic diversity that she insisted on bringing one hundred embryos with them. Unfortunately, most of them were lost when the containment unit lost power and no one noticed until it was too late. The addition of the Swagger's people fixed that problem entirely. Andrin had told her that she was singlehandedly responsible for colonizing Sarisart. She frowned to herself and at her own stupidity. She believed Andrin wholeheartedly. She thought the human civilization rested squarely on her shoulders, when in reality, it relied heavily on several key individuals. And if you took one little piece of that puzzle away… it would all fall apart. The only reason the Swagger took that trip through the wormhole was because of the video files Dean Mason found of General Newman.

When the Swagger landed and Sara was finally able to go home, the first thing she did was spend time with Drew. She had only been gone for a few days but it seemed like he had grown. It took her almost two days to remember the role her father played in the paradox which prompted her to immediately request digital copies of her father's videos. The videos were very depressing and made her feel incredibly guilty for leaving him behind. Sara fought back tears when she thought about the day she begged him to go with them but he refused. He told her that a useless old man shouldn't take up space on the Moon's Eye. If she had known he would be spending his twilight years alone in a special retirement facility designed especially for top-secret individuals like her father, she would have never gone without him. Not only did she have to learn how to deal with her new reality, she also had to accept the mental burden of knowing her father's end. She needed to find a way to deal with the things that weighed on her without using orange.

When she arrived at the Swagger, she drove the motorcycle up the ramp and into the hanger bay before pulling it to a stop. The clinic was just above the hanger so she was there in no time at all. She found it strange that she seemed to be in the same position that she was in just fourteen days ago. She was in a clinic, waiting for Dr. Bowman, and agitated about her future. She was the one who was late so she had no right to be mad about the fact that she had to wait. Dr. Dixon was apparently retiring and grooming Dr. Bowman to be his replacement. The clinic aboard the Swagger was definitely a huge upgrade to the one they were used to using. Her feet dangled off the side of the examination table just as they did before. It wasn't long before she sighed loudly and decided to lay down.

When she opened her eyes again, she didn't know how much time had passed. Chad leaned his head into her view and smiled broadly. "Hey, sleepy head." He walked out of her view for a moment and then returned. "You've been sleeping for an hour."

"What?" She sat up. "Why didn't you wake me up?"

The doctor squinted at her. "You're kidding, right?" He laughed as he clicked on a monitor above her head. "Besides, you probably needed the sleep." The monitor he turned on featured a scan of her brain. He pointed to a cluster of black that looked more like a paint splatter than part of her brain. "I'm pretty sure this is why you can communicate with the bisector queen."

Sara already assumed the bisector queen had somehow left part of her body inside her brain. The queen shared visions that her children had witnessed, which meant that they were somehow connected. The queen and Sara were connected somehow. Most of the time she felt fine, but every now and then she felt a presence. She was convinced that the queen was spying on her but she wasn't certain about whether or not she saw it that way. The monarch was used to keeping tabs on her people and communicating with them telepathically, and apparently, she was now one of them.

"Has it gotten any worse since the first time you scanned me?" She rubbed her face.

Chad shook his head. "No, it looks exactly the same."

She suddenly gave him a funny look. Something had been on her mind and she wanted an answer. "How did you know?"

The doctor crinkled his brow and shook his head. "About what?"

"How did you know that Dean would need the antidote for the orange?" She tipped her head to the side. "You couldn't have known what I was up to."

He suddenly looked uncomfortable. "Honestly, Sara... you're right. I didn't know what you were up to. I gave it to him because there was no doubt in my mind that he'd need it."

Sara's pressed her lips together. "Ouch."

Ouch indeed. His words hurt her because it was clear that he had no faith in her. He fully expected her to overdose again... and she didn't disappoint. It was weird that such a bad thing ended up working out in her favor.

He sat down in his chair and picked up a tablet. "Speaking of the orange..." He looked right into her eyes. "I don't detect any in your system. When's the last time you took some?"

Sara held his gaze. "I haven't had any since this ship landed."

His eyebrows shot up. "Really? That's great. How have you been managing your symptoms?"

"With sex."

The doctor chuckled. "Has our relationship progressed to the point where we talk about that now?"

Sara rubbed her palms on the top of her legs. She was nervous. Their relationship, as it were, wasn't close enough to talk about sex, regardless of the fact that he was her doctor. "I missed my period."

He nodded in recognition. "That's because you're two weeks pregnant." He paused. "I didn't think today would be a good day to tell you, considering the circumstances."

She shook her head slightly and blinked tears out of her eyes. He had just confirmed what she considered the worst-case scenario. If she was two weeks pregnant than she couldn't be sure who the father of her child was. She couldn't remember whether or not she slept with Captain Mason but she had convinced herself that it didn't matter. She couldn't remember so it was almost as if it didn't actually happen. But now that there was a life growing inside of her, it mattered. It mattered a lot. Martinez seemed to be a very understanding person, but how much would he understand it if she was pregnant with another man's baby?

Dr. Bowman put a hand on her shoulder. "Are you okay?"

Sara was having one of the worst moments of her life. So, obviously that meant Mel needed to be there. When she walked in, Sara expected her to say something incredibly cruel but she didn't. Sara couldn't put a finger on it, but she didn't look right. There was something different about her eyes. When she saw Sara, she suddenly looked very concerned. She rushed up to her and grabbed her hand.

"Oh my gosh, Sara! Are you okay? Why are you crying? Is it because of me? It is because of me, isn't it?" Mel held one of Sara's hands with both of hers. "I'm so sorry for everything. There's really no excuse! I'm a horrible person!"

Chad put his hands on Mel's shoulders and gently pulled her away from Sara. He injected something into her shoulder and then walked her to the next room. "It's okay, Mel. It's okay."

"Melody! I told you to call me Melody! Not Mel! Mel was the mean me!" She cried.

"Okay, okay, Melody. Why don't you lie down for a little while, okay?" He led her to the next exam room and returned almost as quickly.

Sara's mouth dropped open. "What the holy fuck?" She gestured toward the exam room that Mel was in and tried to keep her voice down. "What the hell did you do to her?"

"It wasn't me, it was Dr. Dixon." Chad waved his hands to the sides as he shook his head. "He said that he could fix her."

Apparently, two hundred years into the future, being a sociopath was easily fixed but was usually done in childhood. Mel may have been an asshole but she seemed to be managing. Now, she just seemed crazy. The doctor

337

explained that it would take her a while to come to terms with her new feelings. When Sara thought about it, she figured it would be a hard thing to go through. Mel had been living her life either oblivious to the fact that she was hurting people, or knowing and not caring. Now she was faced with the memories of what she had done and feeling the shame and guilt. It was probably enough to make anyone go mad.

Sara wished she had been consulted before Mel went through with such a thing. Most people who knew and loved someone with a disability would swear up and down that they wouldn't change that person because there was nothing wrong with them. But if you asked the individual, it would be hard to find one that didn't want to fix it. Mel was certainly flawed but she was managing. The way Sara saw it, the person she knew as Mel was dead.

She stared off into space for a moment. "Fuck." She turned her head to Chad. "I'm gonna go now."

"You going to be okay?"

She nodded and assured him that she would but she felt the rug had been pulled out from underneath her. Prior to their first kiss, she had never been afraid to talk to Martinez about anything. Now being afraid of him and what he might think of her seemed like a daily thing. She needed to see him right away. No matter what, she always wanted to be honest with him. She took the elevator down to the hanger knowing that she didn't have much time. If she left the Swagger to go talk to Angelo, she'd just have to turn around and go back in just an hour so she had to hurry.

The hanger was impressive. She had been in it several times but it seemed like she noticed something new each time.

There were several shuttles inside it even though she was told only one of them actually worked. That was probably why both Tran and Junior were inside one of them pulling it apart. They were working alongside several other people that Sara assumed were engineers from the Swagger. One of the first unified goals that the tribunal set forth was to fix as many of the shuttles as possible so that the Sarisart could be explored on a much larger scale. Now that the Swagger was grounded, parts of it could be harvested to repair or build other things.

When Junior noticed Sara walking to the motorcycle, he approached her with a smile. She didn't really have the time to talk to him, nor did she want to. She considered pretending like she didn't see him and leaving but she didn't want to upset him. For the last week and a half, Junior pestered her with long talks about alternate dimensions and pearl necklaces. He had become good friends with Dean Mason who gave him unlimited access to the historical files in the Swagger's database. It was his aim to prove that the Swagger wasn't from the same timeline but so far, he hasn't found anything. The kid was adamant about the fact that even if he didn't find anything to prove his theory, it didn't mean it wasn't true. A parallel world could have differences that were so subtle that no would be able to pick up on them.

"Junior, if you're going to tell me that you found proof, save it. I don't want to hear it." Sara got on the motorcycle and prepared to start it.

"But ma, you could find a world where Papa Zee is still alive." He had a towel in his hand that he nervously twisted back and forth.

Sara put her hands on the handlebars and sighed sadly. How could she make him see? "First off all, Junior, any Andrew Zeeman I might find wouldn't be ours. He'd be different."

"I didn't mean to upset you." Junior asked just before she flipped the switch on the bike. "What's the second of all?"

"What?"

Junior wrung his towel in his hands again. "You said first of all… what's the second?"

"I'm with Angie now. I have to move forward, not backward." When she looked up, he didn't seem to be paying attention. Instead, he was looking past her at something. "Junior?"

She swung her head to the side to see what he was looking at. Of course, it was Martinez. Her eyes rolled slowly back to Junior only to see him walking back toward the shuttle. Her goal was to find Angie but now that he was standing right in front of her, she wanted to crawl under the nearest shuttle. It was obvious that he heard what she said because he had the smallest hint of a smile on his face. With each step toward him she felt more and more like her whole world was about to end. The hanger was noisy and echoed with sounds of metal on metal and people yelling at each other so she grabbed his hand and pulled him down the ramp. She could tell that he was a bit confused but he let her lead him away as she became more and more nervous.

Sara stopped near one of the massive feet of the ship so that they would be in the shade. She could hear her heart beating in her ears and she began to sweat. Martinez was either very good at reading people or just very good at reading her because his face suddenly showed concern.

"Sara, what's wrong?"

She couldn't seem to stand still and struggled to look him in the face. "You're going to hate me."

Angie touched her shoulder. "That's not possible. Just rip the band-aid off quick, what's going on?"

She put her hands together as if she were praying. Tears began to trickle down her face. She had to work hard to control her breathing. She swallowed hard and looked him in the face. "I'm two weeks pregnant."

His expression didn't change at all. He let his hand slip down her arm to her elbow where he grabbed it and pulled her toward him. "We never really talked about it because it didn't seem important." He held her close to comfort her. "Did you sleep with him?"

Sara frowned hard as fresh tears left her eyes. She shook her head slightly. "I'm not sure. I honestly don't remember."

The sheriff suddenly smiled. "I guess we'll know if it comes out with a full head of red hair." He chuckled.

"That's not funny." She looked away but smiled slightly. The fact that he was joking about it managed to give her some relief. She found herself staring at his gold badge for a moment before looking up at him. "Would you be able to raise his child without hating it?"

Angelo's dark eyes turned serious. "Sara, my mom never gave me a name because I'm the product of rape."

Sara was in utter shock. She felt so bad for him that all she wanted to do was hold him. "I'm sorry."

"I could never treat any child badly because of something it had no control over." He reached up and wiped a tear from her cheek with his thumb. "Like it or not, you're stuck with me." He looked down at her stomach. "And so is whoever you got in there."

Sara felt a wave of relief wash over her as she hugged him tight. She smiled up at him through her tears. "You know, we have two children on the way and we can't say 'I love you' to each other, but I feel it."

She pulled on his shirt which caused him to lean in until their lips met and she kissed him. His eyes shined a little as he smiled. "I feel it too."

They held hands as they walked back into the hanger and Angelo explained that he was only there to ensure that Captain Mason remained true to his word. People of all ages started to fill the hanger as it became crowded and difficult to navigate. They all wanted a chance to say good-bye to the man who had commanded the Swagger for decades. She walked with him to the only working shuttle and put a hand against his chest.

"Is it okay if I go get him alone?" Sara hoped that he would agree, but realistically, he knew if he refused the result wouldn't be good. "I need to speak with him."

She could tell that he didn't want to let her go but he nodded his head anyway. She quickly kissed him on the lips and then pushed her way through the crowd until she got to the elevator. She needed to talk to Britt for obvious reasons but her pregnancy and who the potential father was wasn't her main focus. She needed a favor that only he could grant.

Chapter Thirty-One

Britt closed a box he just finished packing when the door chime sounded. He sighed and half rolled his eyes. He thought he had made it clear to Commander Hayes that he didn't want to be disturbed. He rolled his eyes up to the ceiling briefly.

"Lucy, who's at the door?"

"It's the bitch." Her voice was decidedly sour for an artificial personality.

Britt's mouth dropped open. "Lucy! Where in the hell?" Sudden realization hit him. "Have you been talking to Commander Hayes?" He swept his hand to the side. "Never mind, open the door." Nothing happened. "Lucy." He gave in and walked over to the door to open it himself. "Remind me to wash your mouth out with soap before I go."

He expected to see Sara outside his door at some point that day but he didn't expect that she'd be his escort, especially considering how much the prospect of giving him to the bisectors upset her. Her eyes were a little red and puffy which made it clear that she had already been crying. He had made a lot of mistakes in his life but betraying her was the one he regretted the most. He stepped aside so that she could enter and then closed the door. After they exchanged niceties, she remained relatively quiet. It was obvious that something was bothering her. Something beyond the fact that he was going to meet his eventual doom later that day.

Britt walked over to his kitchenette and grabbed a bottle of wine with two glasses. Just like he had done before, he poured wine into both glasses but gave himself considerably more. He placed hers on the table in front of her and then

343

held the bottle up. "It's my last bottle of Rosé and I don't want to let it to go to waste." He suddenly squinted and then tipped his head to the side. "Actually, I just don't want anyone else to have it." He watched her look at the wine for a moment and then glance at the bed. He looked over his shoulder at it too. "You know, one can go without the other. You can't waste Rosé."

Sara rubbed her palms against her sides as her eyes flicked over to the bed again. She put her hand on her glass and rubbed her thumb along the rim. "I was hoping that you'd do me a favor but I'm not sure how you'll feel about it."

She told him a story that featured an airplane, a wormhole, and a bunch of mercenaries. It was amazing, and he would have thought it was unbelievable if he hadn't experienced time travel for himself. It was only then that he began to understand the depths of her betrayal. She played him, she kept information from him, and she seduced him. All in the name of protecting her people. And yet, he still understood. At what point in their little adventure was she supposed to point out that he and his people actually traveled two thousand years into the past? Britt put her in an awful position. She either had to confess her secrets or play her own game and she aimed to win. When she began to explain the paradox to him, his brain started to hurt. He found it very difficult to wrap his brain around the fact that everything they did was all part of it. Even the thing that she was about to ask him for.

"I want you to delete every video and every file that has to do with me or my father. All of it." She was dead serious but he didn't understand it. She sat down across from him and then placed a finger on the rim of her glass and began to trace it lightly. "One of the aliens, Andrin, he wanted me to leave him messages and information in a specific place for him to find but something suddenly dawned on me, today."

Britt found every bit of it confusing but he couldn't think of a better person to spend the last few hours of his life with. "What?"

Sara rubbed her eyes and then moved the hair out of her face. She shrugged. "If he didn't find anything in that secret drawer inside my desk… that means I deliberately refused to do it."

He picked up his glass and drank the last bit of wine and then crossed the room to his desk. He used his ring to open his terminal and then started typing. He assured her that the only copy made of her father's files was the one he gave to her. "Just to access these files you need a senior command code." He showed her the details of the file. It contained the names of the people who have accessed it and the number of times it had been copied. Just as he said, it had only been copied once. "Now, if one of my grandsons decides to write in a journal about the things they found…"

"Thank you," she said as her eyes turned toward the bed one more time.

He watched her curiously. "Is it speaking to you or something?"

She gave him a confused look. "What?"

"The bed. You keep looking at it." He laughed. "Is it talking to you?" He returned to his bottle of wine. "You know, you don't have to be ashamed of anything we did that night. I'm not." He emptied the remainder of the bottle into his glass. "I just wish I could remember it."

She suddenly looked at the ground and shook her head. "You mean you can't remember either?"

"What does it matter now anyway?" He sipped his drink and grinned. "The parts I can remember were real nice."

Sara looked at the ground and couldn't seem to stand still. "I just thought that maybe you'd remember if we did or not." She suddenly covered her face for a moment and then blew air out of her mouth quickly. "I'm pregnant, Britt."

He chuckled. "Well, hell, Sunshine, if that's what you're worried about, it ain't mine. I got my boys clipped decades ago after Brandon was born."

He saw the relief wash over her and he had to admit, it kind of hurt a little. She must have picked up on that fact because her expression changed. "Britt," she began but he cut her off.

"Don't. It's okay, Sara." He waved his hand to the side. "Really."

He only had himself to blame for his foolishness. He had known she had feelings for the sheriff before they even set foot on the Swagger. He knew it, and yet he still let himself be drawn in by her. But he wasn't angry. Not anymore. He walked over to the bed to retrieve his cowboy hat. After he put it on, he looked down at his ring for a few moments before pulling it off. It was purely symbolic because he was quite certain that Commander Hayes would shut down the rings access before the day was over, but having the ring would show his people how much he trusted her. Undoubtedly, the sheriff wouldn't like his woman wearing another man's ring, but he'd have to get over it.

He smiled broadly and again thought about that fact that he had placed symbolic rings on the fingers of two other women that he never loved. Now he was about to give his ring to Sara and he was damn certain that it meant more to him than it meant to her. He placed it on her index finger but it was still a little too big for her. "You need to wear it. Especially for the big important stuff. Trust me, my people will notice."

She frowned as she looked up at him and tears started to form in her eyes. She nodded. "Okay." She suddenly grimaced and then grabbed her head as if she were in pain. He stepped close to her and grabbed her before she fell forward.

"Are you okay?"

"It's the Queen." Sara rubbed her temple. "It's time."

The two weeks that the Bisector Queen had generously given him was up. Now it was time to face the music. Walking through the crowd of people that had gathered to say good-bye was harder than he thought it would be. He had watched a great number of them grow up, have kids, and then grandkids. He had never seen so many teary-eyed people in his entire life. He hugged them, shook their hands, and kissed a few cheeks before making it to the shuttle. Although he had already introduced Sara to the entire ship through many ship-wide announcements, he did it again as they passed several key people.

The people gathered around the shuttle were sure to be the hardest. His son Brandon and his family were there along with the twins. Seeing their faces made an intense sadness build up inside of him. Sara left his side and headed toward Martinez who was waiting by the shuttle. There had been a time when he and his son looked so much alike that they could have been brothers. But as time went by, Brandon started to look older than him. His son stood before him with gray hair and tears in his eyes, begging him not to go through with it. Britt felt for the kid but it made him realize something important. There was no way he would be able to watch his own son, or his grandsons, die of old age. His special genetic alterations would make him live far beyond all of them. It made him oddly grateful for the fact his life would soon come to an end. When it became time to say good-bye to Dean, the boy was angry.

"James should be the one to die, not you!" Dean tried to be strong but tears were streaming down his face. "Grandpa, please don't do this."

James pushed his way up to Britt and his brother. "He's right, Captain. It should be me."

He put a hand at the back of each of their necks and pulled their foreheads to his. "I'm really proud of you boys. Promise me you'll bury the hatchet between you and take care of each other."

He was proud of the boys. Not only did Dean fight against his own grandfather to do what he believed was right but James finally owned up for what he had done. But that didn't mean he'd let the boy die in his place. He hugged them all one last time before taking off his cowboy hat and placing it on Dean's head.

"Take care of this for me, kid," he said before turning toward the shuttle. Sara was standing there nervously playing with the ring on her finger and pacing back and forth while the Sheriff watched her. 'It wouldn't be long now,' he thought.

There were only four people in the shuttle. Sara had to accompany him because she was the only one that could communicate with the bisector queen. Martinez insisted on going because he didn't trust Captain Mason and then there was the pilot. He was just a kid that Britt barely knew but they needed someone to fly the ship and he was it. The trip only took about a minute and a half but it was the longest minute and a half he had ever experienced. Mostly because it was as awkward as it was scary. He couldn't stop thinking about his impending doom and hoped that his death would be fast.

~ * ~

Sara had a lot of trouble coming to terms with the fact that she was about to hand a human being over to the bisectors. James Mason may have been the person responsible for blowing up the nursery but she knew she'd have difficulty handing him over too. A feeling of panic was starting to build up inside of her. She wished that she had more time to hammer out a deal with the queen but the reality was, she had been more than reasonable. If the rolls had been reversed, humans would have tried to annihilate every single one of them. If an alligator makes a meal of a baby, people get out their guns and kill as many of them as they can. The queen had every right to hate humans because of what they had done. Yet, instead of killing them all, she demanded one.

Britt sat across from her clenching his jaw so tight she could actually see the tension. The shuttle landed with the bisector mound looming in front of them. She couldn't help it. The bisectors still terrified her. As soon as they landed, Britt stood up and left the shuttle without being asked. Being 'gung ho' about it was probably better than spending an hour trying to coax him out. She followed him out and up the hill while Martinez stayed behind and watched them from the shuttle.

Sara felt the queen's presence before she arrived. She stood next to Captain Mason resisting the urge to hold his hand because she knew Angie would be watching. She touched his upper arm causing him to look at her. She needed to say one last thing to him. "Thanks for saving my life."

His only response was a furrowed brow as if he didn't understand. She continued.

"I'm not just talking about what happened in that mountain." She glanced at it and then back to him. "When you found me, I was barely hanging on. You made me fight for my life." She looked over her shoulder at Angie. "Right here on Sarisart. And I have to thank you for that."

"That's funny. You're thanking me for everything and I'm sorry for it." He frowned at her and then touched her face. "Everything except for pulling you out of there."

The queen landed six feet away from them along with two of her guards. Her body language was impossible to read. There was no way to know if she was angry, sad, or indifferent. All Sara had to go on was the feelings that were being projected to her. Her heart started beating fast as fear gripped at her very being. She had to actively stop herself from moving in front of Britt in a misguided attempt to protect him.

"You care about this one?"

"Yes." Sara held Britt's arm at his elbow. "What are you going to do with him?"

"That is not your concern."

Captain Mason turned to her. "It's okay, Sara. She has to answer to her people just like you have to answer to yours." He leaned down and kissed her on the cheek. "Good-bye, Little Lady."

Sara blinked tears out of her eyes. She could barely speak. "Good-bye, Cake."

Britt had just enough time to smile before the queen grabbed him with her humanoid hands and flew away. The exit was so fast that Sara had no time to protest. As she watched the queen fly through one of the openings of the mountain, she got the distinct feeling that she was no longer welcome and should vacate the premises immediately. Her legs felt weak and threatened to give out beneath her when she felt Angie's arms around her. She was so distraught that she didn't even remember how she got back to the colony or into her own bed. It was hard for her to believe that she would never see Britt again or that she participated in such an event. Angie held her as she cried and stroked her hair until she fell asleep.

She woke up a few hours later with the kind of sinus headache that one only gets after several hours of crying. She sat at the edge of the bed she once shared with her husband and watched Martinez sleep. She was emotionally drained but she was grateful that he stayed with her. She eventually found herself in her office, staring at a hand carved wooden box. The box had been a gift from Andrew on their eleventh anniversary. Andrew made it specifically to hold a framed wedding photo of the two them. It was a sweet and thoughtful gift that somehow found its way into a paradox that continued to haunt her. This was because it was the same box that Andrin told her he found in a secret compartment hidden in her office. The same box that he asked her to leave important information in for him to find.

She opened it and removed three handwritten letters. The first was written shortly after arriving on Sarisart and gave a brief summary of the events that led up to the landing, the second was written one year after they had landed detailing the hardships they had faced, and the third was written after Andrew's death. She stared at them as she recalled the conversation she had with Andrin. He told her that the only things he found in the box were the photo and a thumb drive that contained the farewell recordings the colonists had made to their family members.

She didn't know whether or not Junior's theory about multiverses was true or not, and she didn't care. All she knew was that she wasn't going to be an active participant in the paradox. From that point on, she was determined to live her life without ever thinking about it again. It was one thing if it happened organically but it was quite another to try to influence it. She had to believe that everything happened for a reason.

She picked up the letters and ripped them up into pieces so tiny that even Junior would have difficulty piecing them back together again and then placed them in the garbage. She took out a blank piece of paper and picked up a pen and wrote:

Andrin, you're a dick.

It was such a silly thing but it made her laugh. She seriously considered folding it up and placing it in the box but only for a few moments. She suddenly mashed the paper into a ball and threw it in the trash too. Moments later she was crawling into her bed slowly, trying very hard not to wake

Angelo up. She cuddled in close to him and laid her head against his chest and listened to his heartbeat.

He suddenly pulled her closer to him and then rubbed her arm. "You okay?" he asked.

"Yeah," she said softly. "You?"

"Yeah." He kissed her on the forehead. "I love you, Sara."

Epilogue

Twenty-four years is a long time. For some, it's a lifetime. To Britt, it was torture. The queen didn't kill him like everyone believed. No, the insect queen jammed one of her tendrils into his brain and placed the same type of biological communication device inside his head that Sara had in hers. And then after that, the vindictive monarch placed him in a form of stasis. On the outside, it doesn't seem so bad, does it? Spending twenty-four years in stasis can't actually be torture, can it?

It can when you're watching the woman you love... love someone else.

Yes, twenty-four years is a very long time.

The End

C. J. Boyle

Please consider reading some of my other work!

Adventures Inside the Moon
The Kirk Rogers Series; Book One - Strangers suddenly find themselves inside the moon and tasked with fixing an alien device before the entire solar system is destroyed. Rated PG13 for Language and Sexual Situations
https://www.amazon.com/dp/B071WFBBG4

The Adventures of Kirk Rogers
The Kirk Rogers Series; Book Two – The continuing series finds Kirk and his friends stranded on an alien planet and tasked with rescuing a woman in stasis before a prince kills her and takes the crown. Rated PG13 for Language and Sexual Situations
https://www.amazon.com/dp/B078VK3976

The Adventures of Kirk Rogers and The Illuminati
The Kirk Rogers Series; Book Three - Captain Rogers and his band of heroes must save Robyn from the Illuminati and prevent them from getting a foothold in Atlantis. Rated PG13 for Language and Sexual Situations
https://www.amazon.com/dp/B07LG8B3FQ

The Link Between Us - After a mummified cavewoman was found deep in the permafrost of Siberia, an ancient virus was released that soon evolved half of mankind into vicious monsters that fed on anything that moved. When her son turned into a Link, it caused Kera to lose all hope but that didn't stop people from looking to her for direction and leadership. Taking refuge in a prison, she became The Warden. She found it very hard to adjust to the new normal and went on many dangerous missions hoping that she'd eventually be killed. As time went by and more was learned about the Links, Kera finally realized that losing her son didn't mean her life was over. Rated R for Adult Content/Violence/Sexual Situations.

354

https://www.amazon.com/dp/B01MS2H17S

Sarisart - When Sara Newman woke up in the morning that day, she had no plans to be kidnapped by a bunch of mercenaries, or being transported to another planet via wormhole...but that's what happened. Being the only woman amongst a dozen men, Sara finds herself drawn to one while trying to keep the others away. With very little hope of getting home, they must learn to get along and survive in a harsh environment. Rated R for Adult Content/Violence/Sexual Situations.
https://www.amazon.com/dp/B01DOXY442

Melody's Penny - When Ian Murphy quit his job at the FBI to take care of his niece fulltime, he certainly didn't have any desire to meet someone new or fall in love. After his online gal pal disappears without a trace he is compelled to find her. (PG13)
https://www.amazon.com/dp/B01BIRZAO4

Hollywood Games - After breaking up with a girlfriend who was only using him, the last thing on Orlando Baldwin's mind is finding new love. After all, being a bigtime movie star isn't easy. His life takes an unexpected turn when he gets trapped in an elevator with a newbie screenwriter, Sara Jenkins. When they get caught in a compromising position their agents advise them to pretend to be in a relationship. They reluctantly do it to further their careers but things – of course – get complicated. PG13
https://www.amazon.com/dp/B01BIRZATE

46298036R00206